PENGUIN BOOKS

FORTY STORIES

John Updike was born in 1932 in Shillington, Pennsylvania. He attended the public schools of that town, Harvard College and the Ruskin School of Drawing and Fine Art at Oxford, where he spent a year on a Knox Fellowship. From 1955 to 1957 he was a member of the staff of the *New Yorker*, to which he has contributed short stories, essays and poems. His novels include *The Poorhouse Fair*, *Rabbit, Run*, *The Centaur*, *Rabbit Redux*, *Bech: A Book*, *Couples*, *A Month of Sundays*, *Marry Me*, *The Coup*, *Rabbit is Rich*, winner of the 1982 Pulitzer Prize for Fiction. *Bech is Back*, *The Witches of Eastwick*, now a major feature film, and *Roger's Version*. He has also published several volumes of short stories – *The Same Door*, *Pigeon Feathers*, *The Music School*, *Museums and Women*, *Your Lover Just Called* (published in America as *Too Far To Go*), *Problems* and *Trust Me*; a children's book – *The Magic Flute*; books of poetry including *Hoping for a Hoopoe*, *Telephone Poles*, *Tossing and Turning* and the Penguin selection of his poetry entitled *Seventy Poems*; plus three collections of essays and criticism – *Picked-up Pieces*, *Hugging the Shore* and *Assorted Prose*. Many of John Updike's books are published in Penguin.

JOHN UPDIKE

FORTY STORIES

PENGUIN BOOKS

PENGUIN BOOKS

Published by the Penguin Group
27 Wrights Lane, London W8 5TZ, England
Viking Penguin Inc., 40 West 23rd Street, New York, New York 10010, USA
Penguin Books Australia Ltd, Ringwood, Victoria, Australia
Penguin Books Canada Ltd, 2801 John Street, Markham, Ontario, Canada L3R 1B4
Penguin Books (NZ) Ltd, 182–190 Wairau Road, Auckland 10, New Zealand

Penguin Books Ltd, Registered Offices: Harmondsworth, Middlesex, England

This collection first published by Penguin Books 1987
Reprinted 1988

Typeset, printed and bound in Great Britain by
Hazell Watson & Viney Limited
Member of BPCC plc
Aylesbury Bucks
Typeset in Linotron 202 Plantin

Contents

Foreword   7

Olinger Stories

You'll Never Know, Dear, How Much I Love You   11
The Alligators   15
Pigeon Feathers   21
Friends from Philadelphia   42
Flight   49
A Sense of Shelter   64
The Happiest I've Been   75
The Persistence of Desire   89
The Blessed Man of Boston, My Grandmother's
   Thimble, and Fanning Island   98
Packed Dirt, Churchgoing, a Dying Cat,
   a Traded Car   110
In Football Season   130

Out in the World

Ace in the Hole   137
The Christian Roommates   145
Still Life   168
Dentistry and Doubt   181
A Madman   187
Who Made Yellow Roses Yellow?   198
Toward Evening   210
Sunday Teasing   215
Incest   222
A Gift from the City   234
The Stare   252
The Orphaned Swimming Pool   258

Contents

The Witnesses 262
The Day of the Dying Rabbit 267
The Family Meadow 277
At a Bar in Charlotte Amalie 281
Under the Microscope 292
During the Jurassic 296

Tarbox Tales

The Indian 305
The Hillies 310
A & P 315
Lifeguard 321
The Deacon 326
The Carol Sing 332
The Music School 336
Leaves 341
Four Sides of One Story 344
I Will Not Let Thee Go, Except Thou Bless Me 353
The Corner 360

Acknowledgements 367

Foreword

This selection, made especially for Penguin Books, contains forty stories chosen from my first four short-story collections: *The Same Door* (1959), *Pigeon Feathers* (1962), *The Music School* (1966) and *Museums and Women* (1972). Ten were taken from each volume, with some thought to variety of scene and style as well as intrinsic merit. None of the stories concerning Richard and Joan Maple, available in the Penguin collection entitled *Your Lover Just Called*, is included, nor any involving Henry Bech, whose adventures are bound into the two volumes *Bech: A Book* and *Bech Is Back*. The first section here, called *Olinger Stories*, was made in 1964 for Vintage Books, with an introduction that explained, 'I have let the inconsistencies stand in these stories. Each started from scratch. Grand Avenue here is the Alton Pike there. In "Pigeon Feathers" the grandfather is dead, in "Flight" the grandmother' and that concluded, 'If of my stories I had to pick a few to represent me, they would be, I suppose, for reasons only partially personal, these.' The two other sections have been contrived as a way of giving *Forty Stories* a certain shape, which dimly echoes the shape of my life. The oldest story is 'Ace in the Hole,' written in college in 1953; the most recent, I believe, is 'The Carol Sing.' Social contexts change; it is perhaps useful to know that 'The Hillies' was written in 1969, and 'A Gift from the City' in 1957. To amuse the English reader, all three stories based upon impressions gathered in my year as an art student in Oxford (1954–55) have been included. In general, the years in which these stories were composed were ones in which my main business was writing short fiction; whatever wit or passion I had, these stories had first call upon it, and I am pleased to have had this chance to consider them anew, and to make this distillation.

J.U.

Olinger Stories

You'll Never Know, Dear,
How Much I Love You

Carnival! In the vacant lot beyond the old ice plant! Trucks have been unloading all afternoon; the Whirlo-Gig has been unfolded like a giant umbrella, they assembled the baby Ferris wheel with an Erector Set. Twice the trucks got stuck in the mud. Straw has been strewn everywhere. They put up a stage and strung lights. Now, now, gather your pennies; supper is over and an hour of light is left in the long summer day. See, Sammy Hunnenhauser is running; Gloria Gring and her gang have been there all afternoon, they never go home, oh hurry, let me go; how awful it is to have parents that are poor, and slow, and sad!

Fifty cents. The most Ben could beg. A nickel for every year of his life. It feels like plenty. Over the roof of crazy Mrs Moffert's house, the Ferris wheel tints the air with pink, and the rim of this pink mixes in excitement with the great notched rim of the coin sweating in his hand. This house, then this house, and past the ice plant, and he will be there. Already the rest of the world is there, he is the last, hurrying, hurrying, the balloon is about to take off, the Ferris wheel is lifting; only he will be left behind, on empty darkening streets.

Then there, what to buy? There are not so many people here. Grown-ups carrying babies mosey glassily on the straw walks. All the booth people, not really gipsies, stare at him, and beckon weakly. It hurts him to ignore the man with the three old softballs, and the old cripple at the merry-go-round, and the fat lady with her plaster Marys, and the skeleton suspended behind a fountain of popcorn. He feels his walking past them as pain. He wishes there were more people here; he feels a fool. All of this machinery assembled to extract from him his pathetic fifty cents. He watches at a distance a thickset man in earnestly rolled-up shirtsleeves twirl a great tinselled wheel with a rubber tongue that patters slower and slower on a circle of nails until it stops between two, and the number there wins. Only a sailor and two boys in yellow silk high-school athletic jackets play. None win. The thick tattooed arm below the rolled-up shirtsleeve carefully sweeps their nickels from a long board divided and numbered as if for hopscotch. The high-school boys, with sideburns and spotty whiskers on their bright pink jaws, put down nickels again leadenly, and this time the man spinning the wheel shouts when it stops, seems more joyful than they, and reaches into his deep apron pocket and pours before them, without counting, a perfect little slipping stack of nickels. Their gums showing as if at a dirty joke, the two boys turn – the shimmer on their backs darts and shifts in cool *z*'s – and walk away, while the man is shouting, 'Hey, uh winneh. Hey, uh winneh, evvybody wins.' His table is bare, and as his mouth continues to form the loud words his eyes lock Ben into a stare of heartbreaking brown blankness that seems to elucidate with paralysing clarity Ben's state; his dungarees, his fifty cents, his ten years, his position in space, and above the particulars the immense tinted pity, the waste, of being at one little place instead of everywhere, at any time. Then the man looks away, and twirls the wheel for his own amusement.

The fifty-cent piece feels huge to Ben's fingers, a wide oppressive rigidity that must be broken, shattered into twinkling fragments, to merge in the tinsel and splinters of strewn straw. He buys, at the first stand he strikes, a cone of cotton candy, and receives, with the furry pink pasty uncoiling thing, a quarter, a dime, and a nickel: three coins, tripling his wealth.

Now people multiply, crowd in from the houses of the town, that stand beyond the lot on all sides in black forbidding silhouettes like the teeth of a saw. The lights go on; the faces of the houses flee. There is nothing in the lot but light, and at its core, on the stage, three girls wearing white cowboy hats and white spangled skirts and white boots appear, and a man also in white and bearing a white guitar strung with gold. The legs around Ben crush him towards the stage; the smell of mud mingles with the bright sight there. One of the girls coughs into the microphone and twists its neck, so a sharp whine pierces from the loudspeakers and cuts a great crescent through the crowd, leaving silence as harvest. The girls sing, toetapping gingerly: 'The other *night*, dear, as I lay *sleep*ing, I dreamt I *held* you in my *arms*.' The spangles on their swishing skirts spring prickles like tears in Ben's eyes. The three voices sob, catch, twang, distend his heart like a rubber band at the highest pitch of their plaint. '– I was mis*taken*, and I *hung* my *head*, a-and *cried*.' And then the unbearable rising sugar of the chorus that makes his scalp so tight he fears his head will burst from sweet fullness.

The girls go on to sing other songs, less good, and then they give way to a thin old man in suspenders and huge pants he keeps snapping and looking down and whooping into. He tells horrible jokes that make the nice fat ladies standing around Ben – nice fat factory and dustmop women that made him feel protected – shake with laughter. He fears their quaking, feels threatened from beneath, as if there is a treacherous stratum under this mud and straw. He wanders away, to let the words of 'You Are My Sunshine' revolve in his head. 'Please don't *take* my *sunshine away*.' Only the money in his pocket weights him; get rid of it, and he will sail away like a dandelion seed.

He goes to the booth where the wheel is turning, and puts his nickel on the board in a square marked 7, and loses it.

He puts the dime there and it too is taken away.

Squeezed, almost hidden, between the crusty trousered haunches of two adults, he puts down his quarter, as they do, on the inner edge, to be changed. The tattooed man comes along picking up the quarters and pouring, with his wonderfully automatic fingers, the little slipping stacks of five nickels; Ben holds his breath, and to his horror feels his low face catch in the corner of the man's absent-minded eyes. The thick solemn body snags in its smooth progress, and Ben's five nickels are raggedly spaced. Between the second and third there is a gap. A blush cakes Ben's cheeks; his grey-knuckled fingers, as they push out a nickel, are trembling sideways at each other. But the man goes back, and spins the wheel, and Ben loses three nickels one after another. The twittering wheel is a moon-faced god; but Ben feels humanity clouding the space between them, that should be unobstructed. When the tattooed arm – a blue fish, an anchor, the queer word PEACE – comes to sweep in his nickels, he feels the stippled skin breathing thought, and lowers his head against the expected fall of words. Nothing is said, the man moves on, returns to the wheel; but Ben feels puzzled pressure radiating from him, and the pointed eyes of a man in a suit with chalk stripes who has come to stand at the far side of the stand intersect this expanding circle, and Ben, hurrying to pour his money down a narrowing crack, puts down his last two nickels, still on 7.

The rubber tongue leaps into pattering and as the wheel whirls the tattooed man leans backwards to hear the one in chalk stripes talk; his tongue patterns silently but a tiny motion of his polished hand, simultaneous with a sideways stab of his eyes, is towards Ben.

The rubber tongue slows, flops, stops at 7 – no, 8. He lost, and can leave. The floor of his stomach lifts queerly. 'Hey kid.' The man with stencilled arms comes over. Ben feels that no matter how fast he would run, those arms would stretch and snare him.

'Huh?'

'How old are you, kid?'

'Ten.'

'Whatsamatta with ya, ya daddy rich?'

A titter moves stiffly through the immense adult heads all around. Ben understands the familiar role, that he has undergone a hundred times with teachers and older boys, of being a comic prop. He understands everything, and wants to explain that he knows his eyes are moist and his cheeks red but that it's because of joy, freedom, not because of losing. But this would be too many words; even the one-word answer 'No' sticks to the roof of his mouth and comes loose with a faint tearing noise.

'Here.' With his exciting expert touch, the man flicks Ben's two coins back across the painted number. Then he digs into his pocket. He comes up with the usual little stack of five, drops four, but holds the fifth delicately between the tops of two fingers and a thumb, hesitates so that Ben can reread PEACE in blue above his wrist, and then flips the fifth nickel up into his palm and thence down with a plunge into his dirty sagging apron pouch.

'Now move away from the board, kid, move away. Don't come back.'

Ben fumbles the coins into his hands and pushes away, his eyes screwed to the sharp edge of painted wood, and shoulders blindly backwards through the legs. Yet all the time, in the midst of the heat and water welling up from springs all over his body, he is figuring, and calculates he's been gypped. Forty: he had the quarter and dime and nickel and they gave him back only six nickels: thirty. The injustice, they pretend he's too little to lose and then keep a dime; the waste. The lost dime seems a tiny hole through which everything in existence is draining. As he moves away, his wet knees jarring, trying to hide forever from every sailor and fat woman and high-schooler who witnessed his disgrace, the six nickels make a knobbed weight bumping his thigh through his pocket. The spangles, the splinters of straw and strings of light, the sawtooth peaks of houses showing behind the scattered white heads scented sweetly with mud, are hung like the needles of a Christmas tree with the transparent, tinted globes confusing his eyelashes.

Thus the world, like a bitter coquette, spurns our attempts to give ourselves to her wholly.

The Alligators

Joan Edison came to their half of the fifth grade from Maryland in March. She had a thin face with something of a grown-up's tired expression and long black eyelashes like a doll's. Everybody hated her. That month Miss Fritz was reading to them during home-room about a girl, Emmy, who was badly spoiled and always telling her parents lies about her twin sister Annie; nobody could believe, it was too amazing, how exactly when they were despising Emmy most Joan should come into the school with her show-off clothes and her hair left hanging down the back of her fuzzy sweater instead of being cut or braided and her having the crust to actually argue with teachers. 'Well I'm sorry,' she told Miss Fritz, not even rising from her seat, 'but I *don't* see what the point is of homework. In Baltimore we never had any, and the *little* kids there knew what's in these books.'

Charlie, who in a way enjoyed homework, was ready to join in the angry moan of the others. Little hurt lines had leaped up between Miss Fritz's eyebrows and he felt sorry for her, remembering how when that September John Eberly had half on purpose spilled purple Sho-Card paint on the newly sand-papered floor she had hidden her face in her arms on the desk and cried. She was afraid of the school board. 'You're not in Baltimore now, Joan,' Miss Fritz said. 'You are in Olinger, Pennsylvania.'

The children, Charlie among them, laughed, and Joan, blushing a soft brown colour and raising her voice excitedly against the current of hatred, got in deeper by trying to explain, 'Like there, instead of just *reading* about plants in a book we'd one day all bring in a flower we'd *picked* and cut it open and look at it in a *microscope*.' Because of her saying this, shadows, of broad leaves and wild slashed foreign flowers, darkened and complicated the idea they had of her.

Miss Fritz puckered her orange lips into fine wrinkles, then smiled. 'In the upper levels you will be allowed to do that in this school. All things come in time, Joan, to patient little girls.' When Joan started to argue *this*, Miss Fritz lifted one finger and said with the extra weight adults always have, held back in reserve, 'No. No more, young lady, or you'll be in

15

serious trouble with me.' It gave the class courage to see that Miss Fritz didn't like her either.

After that, Joan couldn't open her mouth in class without there being a great groan. Outdoors on the macadam playground, at recess or fire drill or waiting in the morning for the buzzer, hardly anybody talked to her except to say 'Stuck-up' or 'Emmy' or 'Whore, whore, from Balti-more'. Boys were always yanking open the bow at the back of her fancy dresses and flipping little spitballs into the curls of her hanging hair. Once John Eberly even cut a section of her hair off with a yellow plastic scissors stolen from art class. This was the one time Charlie saw Joan cry actual tears. He was as bad as the others: worse, because what the others did because they felt like it, he did out of a plan, to make himself more popular. In the first and second grade he had been liked pretty well, but somewhere since then he had been dropped. There was a gang, boys and girls both, that met Saturdays – you heard them talk about it on Mondays – in Stuart Morrison's garage, and took hikes and played touch football together, and in winter sledded on Hill Street, and in spring bicycled all over Olinger and did together what else, he couldn't imagine. Charlie had known the chief members since before kindergarten. But after school there seemed nothing for him to do but go home promptly and do his homework and fiddle with his Central American stamps and go to horror movies alone, and on weekends nothing but beat monotonously at marbles or Monopoly or chess Darryl Johns or Marvin Auerbach, who he wouldn't have both-ered at all with if they hadn't lived right in the neighbourhood, they being at least a year younger and not bright for their age, either. Charlie thought the gang might notice him and take him in if he backed up their policies without being asked.

In Science, which 5A had in Miss Brobst's room across the hall, he sat one seat ahead of Joan and annoyed her all he could, in spite of a feeling that, both being disliked, they had something to share. One fact he discov-ered was, she wasn't that bright. Her marks on quizzes were always lower than his. He told her, 'Cutting up all those flowers didn't do you much good. Or maybe in Baltimore they taught you everything so long ago you've forgotten it in your old age.'

Charlie drew; on his tablet where she could easily see over his shoulder he once in a while drew a picture titled 'Joan the Dope': the profile of a girl with a lean nose and sad mince-mouth, the lashes of her lowered eye as black as the pencil could make them and the hair falling, in ridiculous hooks, row after row, down through the sea-blue cross-lines clear off the bottom edge of the tablet.

March turned into spring. One of the signals was, on the high-school grounds, before the cinder track was weeded and when the softball field was still four inches of mud, Happy Lasker came with the elaborate aeroplane model he had wasted the winter making. It had the American star on the wingtips and a pilot painted inside the cockpit and a miniature motor that burned real gas. The buzzing, off and on all Saturday morning, collected smaller kids from Second Street down to Lynoak. Then it was always the same: Happy shoved the plane into the air, where it climbed and made a razzing noise a minute, then nose-dived and crashed and usually burned in the grass or mud. Happy's father was rich.

In the weeks since she had come, Joan's clothes had slowly grown simpler, to go with the other girls', and one day she came to school with most of her hair cut off, and the rest brushed flat around her head and brought into a little tail behind. The laughter at her was more than she had ever heard. 'Ooh. Baldy-paldy!' some idiot girl had exclaimed when Joan came into the cloakroom, and the stupid words went sliding around class all morning. 'Baldy-paldy from Baltimore. Why is old Baldy-paldy red in the face?' John Eberly kept making the motion of a scissors with his fingers and its juicy ticking sound with his tongue. Miss Fritz rapped her knuckles on the window-sill until she was rubbing the ache with the other hand, and finally she sent two boys to Mr Lengel's office, delighting Charlie an enormous secret amount.

His own reaction to the haircut had been quiet, to want to draw her, changed. He had kept the other drawings folded in his desk, and one of his instincts was towards complete sets of things, Bat Man comics and A's and Costa Rican stamps. Halfway across the room from him, Joan held very still, afraid, it seemed, to move even a hand, her face a shamed pink. The haircut had brought out her forehead and exposed her neck and made her chin pointier and her eyes larger. Charlie felt thankful once again for having been born a boy, and having no sharp shocks, like losing your curls or starting to bleed, to make growing painful. How much girls suffer had been one of the first thoughts he had ever had. His caricature of her was wonderful, the work of a genius. He showed it to Stuart Morrison behind him; it was too good for him to appreciate, his dull egg eyes just flickered over it. Charlie traced it on to another piece of tablet paper, making her head completely bald. This drawing Stuart grabbed and it was passed clear around the room.

That night he had the dream. He must have dreamed it while lying there asleep in the morning light, for it was fresh in his head when he woke. They had been in a jungle. Joan, dressed in a torn sarong, was swimming in a clear river among alligators. Somehow, as if from a tree, he was looking down, and there was a calmness in the way the slim girl and the green alligators moved, in and out, perfectly visible under the window-skin of the water. Joan's face sometimes showed the horror she was undergoing and sometimes looked numb. Her hair trailed behind and fanned when her face came towards the surface. He shouted silently with grief. Then he had rescued her; without a sense of having dipped his arms in water, he was carrying her in two arms, himself in a bathing suit, and his feet firmly fixed to the knobby back of an alligator which skimmed upstream, through the shadows of high trees and white flowers and hanging vines, like a surfboard in a movie short. They seemed to be heading towards a wooden bridge arching over the stream. He wondered how he would duck it, and the river and the jungle gave way to his bed and his room, but through the change persisted, like a pedalled note on a piano, the sweetness and pride he had felt in saving and carrying the girl.

He loved Joan Edison. The morning was rainy, and under the umbrella his mother made him take this new knowledge, repeated again and again to himself, gathered like a bell of smoke. Love had no taste, but sharpened his sense of smell so that his oilcloth coat, his rubber boots, the red-tipped bushes hanging over the low walls holding back lawns all along Grand Street, even the dirt and moss in the cracks of the pavement each gave off clear odours. He would have laughed, if a wooden weight had not been placed high in his chest, near where his throat joined. He could not imagine himself laughing soon. It seemed he had reached one of those situations his Sunday-school teacher, poor Miss West with her little moustache, had been trying to prepare him for. He prayed, *Give me Joan*. With the wet weather a solemn flatness had fallen over everything; an orange bus turning at the Bend and four birds on a telephone wire seemed to have the same importance. Yet he felt firmer and lighter and felt things as edges he must whip around and channels he must rush down. If he carried her off, did rescue her from the others' cruelty, he would have defied the gang and made a new one, his own. Just Joan and he at first, then others escaping from meanness and dumbness, until his gang was stronger and Stuart Morrison's garage was empty every Saturday. Charlie would be a king, with his own touch-football game. Everybody would come and plead with him for mercy.

His first step was to tell all those in the cloakroom he loved Joan Edison now. They cared less than he had expected, considering how she was hated. He had more or less expected to have to fight with his fists. Hardly anybody gathered to hear the dream he had pictured himself telling everybody. Anyway, that morning it would go around the class that he said he loved her, and though this was what he wanted, to in a way open a space between him and Joan, it felt funny nevertheless, and he stuttered when Miss Fritz had him go to the blackboard to explain something.

At lunch, he deliberately hid in the variety store until he saw her walk by. The homely girl with her he knew turned off at the next street. He waited a minute and then came out and began running to overtake Joan in the block between the street where the other girl turned down and the street where he turned up. It had stopped raining, and his rolled-up umbrella felt like a commando's bayonet. Coming up behind her, he said, 'Bang. Bang.'

She turned, and under her gaze, knowing she knew he loved her, his face heated and he stared down. 'Why, Charlie,' her voice said with her Maryland slowness, 'what are you doing on this side of the street?' Carl the town cop stood in front of the elementary school to get them on the side of Grand Street where they belonged. Now Charlie would have to cross the avenue again, by himself, at the dangerous five-spoked intersection.

'Nothing,' he said, and used up the one sentence he had prepared ahead: 'I like your hair the new way.'

'Thank you,' she said, and stopped. In Baltimore she must have had manner lessons. Her eyes looked at his, and his vision jumped back from the rims of her lower lids as if from a brink. Yet in the space she occupied there was a great fullness that lent him height, as if he were standing by a window giving on the first morning after a snow.

'But then I didn't mind it the old way either.'

'Yes?'

A peculiar reply. Another peculiar thing was the tan beneath her skin; he had noticed before, though not so closely, how when she coloured it came up a gentle dull brown more than red. Also she wore something perfumed.

He asked, 'How do you like Olinger?'

'Oh, I think it's nice.'

'Nice? I guess. I guess maybe. Nice Olinger. I wouldn't know because I've never been anywhere else.'

She luckily took this as a joke and laughed. Rather than risk saying something unfunny, he began to balance the umbrella by its point on one finger and, when this went well, walked backwards, shifting the balanced umbrella, its hook black against the patchy blue sky, from one palm to the other, back and forth. At the corner where they parted he got carried away and in imitating a suave gent leaning on a cane bent the handle hopelessly. Her amazement was worth twice the price of his mother's probable crossness.

He planned to walk her again, and farther, after school. All through lunch he kept calculating. His father and he would repaint his bike. At the next haircut he could have his hair parted on the other side to get away from his cowlick. He would change himself totally; everyone would wonder what had happened to him. He would learn to swim, and take her to the dam.

In the afternoon the momentum of the dream wore off somewhat. Now that he kept his eyes always on her, he noticed, with a qualm of his stomach, that in passing in the afternoon from Miss Brobst's to Miss Fritz's room, Joan was not alone, but chattered with others. In class, too, she whispered. So it was with more shame – such shame that he didn't believe he could ever face even his parents again – than surprise that from behind the dark pane of the variety store he saw her walk by in the company of the gang, she and Stuart Morrison throwing back their teeth and screaming and he imitating something and poor moronic John Eberly tagging behind like a thick tail. Charlie watched them walk out of sight behind a tall hedge; relief was as yet a tiny fraction of his reversed world. It came to him that what he had taken for cruelty had been love, that far from hating her everybody had loved her from the beginning, and that even the stupidest knew it weeks before he did. That she was the queen of the class and might as well not exist, for all the good he would get out of it.

Pigeon Feathers

When they moved to Firetown, things were upset, displaced, rearranged. A red cane-back sofa that had been the chief piece in the living-room at Olinger was here banished, too big for the narrow country parlour, to the barn, and shrouded under a tarpaulin. Never again would David lie on its length all afternoon eating raisins and reading mystery novels and science fiction and P. G. Wodehouse. The blue wing chair that had stood for years in the ghostly, immaculate guest bedroom, gazing through the windows curtained with dotted swiss towards the telephone wires and horsechestnut trees and opposite houses, was here established importantly in front of the smutty little fireplace that supplied, in those first cold April days, their only heat. As a child, David had been afraid of the guest bedroom – it was there that he, lying sick with the measles, had seen a black rod the size of a yardstick jog along at a slight slant beside the edge of the bed and vanish when he screamed – and it was disquieting to have one of the elements of his haunted atmosphere basking by the fire, in the centre of the family, growing sooty with use. The books that at home had gathered dust in the case beside the piano were here hastily stacked, all out of order, in the shelves that the carpenters had built along one wall below the deep-silled windows. David, at fourteen, had been more moved than a mover; like the furniture, he had to find a new place, and on the Saturday of the second week he tried to work off some of his disorientation by arranging the books.

It was a collection obscurely depressing to him, mostly books his mother had acquired when she was young: college anthologies of Greek plays and Romantic poetry, Will Durant's *Story of Philosophy*, a soft-leather set of Shakespeare with string bookmarks sewed to the binding, *Green Mansions* boxed and illustrated with woodcuts, *I, the Tiger*, by Manuel Komroff, novels by names like Galsworthy and Ellen Glasgow and Irwin S. Cobb and Sinclair Lewis and 'Elizabeth'. The odour of faded taste made him feel the ominous gap between himself and his parents, the insulting gulf of time that existed before he was born. Suddenly he was tempted to dip into this time. From the heaps of books piled around him on the worn old floorboards, he picked up Volume II of a four-volume set of *The Outline of History* by H.G. Wells. Once David had read *The Time Machine* in an anthology; this gave him a small grip on the author. The book's red binding had faded to orange-pink on the spine. When he lifted the cover, there was a sweetish, attic-like smell, and his mother's maiden name written in unfamiliar handwriting on the flyleaf – an upright, bold, yet careful signature, bearing a faint relation to the quick scrunched backslant that flowed with marvellous consistency across her shopping lists and budget accounts and Christmas cards to college friends from this same, vaguely menacing long ago.

He leafed through, pausing at drawings, done in an old-fashioned stippled style, of bas-reliefs, masks, Romans without pupils in their eyes, articles of ancient costume, fragments of pottery found in unearthed homes. He knew it would be interesting in a magazine, mingled with ads and cartoons, but in this undiluted form history was somehow sour. The print was determinedly legible, and smug, like a lesson book. As he bent over the pages, yellow at the edges, they seemed rectangles of dusty glass through which he looked down into unreal and irrelevant worlds. He could see things sluggishly move, and an unpleasant fullness came into his throat. His mother and grandmother fussed in the kitchen; the puppy, which they had just acquired, for 'protection in the country', was cowering, with a sporadic panicked scrabble of claws, under the dining-table that in their old home had been reserved for special days but that here was used for every meal.

Then, before he could halt his eyes, David slipped into Wells's account of Jesus. He had been an obscure political agitator, a kind of hobo, in a minor colony of the Roman Empire. By an accident impossible to reconstruct, he (the small *h* horrified David) survived his own crucifixion and presumably died a few weeks later. A religion was founded on the freakish incident. The credulous imagination of the times retrospectively assigned miracles and supernatural pretensions to Jesus; a myth grew, and then a church whose theology at most points was in direct contradiction of the simple, rather communistic teachings of the Galilean.

It was as if a stone that for weeks and even years had been gathering weight in the web of David's nerves snapped them and plunged through the page and a hundred layers of paper underneath. These fantastic falsehoods – plainly untrue; churches stood everywhere, the entire nation was founded 'under God' – did not at first frighten him; it was the fact that they had been permitted to exist in an actual human brain. This was the initial impact – that at a definite spot in time and space a brain black with the denial of Christ's divinity had been suffered to exist; that the universe had not spit out this ball of tar but allowed it to continue in its blasphemy, to grow old, win honours, wear a hat, write books that, if true, collapsed everything into a jumble of horror. The world outside the deep-silled windows – a rutted lawn, a white-washed barn, a walnut tree frothy with fresh green – seemed a haven from which he was forever sealed off. Hot washrags seemed pressed against his cheeks.

He read the account again. He tried to supply out of his ignorance objections that would defeat the complacent march of these black words, and found none. Survivals and misunderstandings more far-fatched were reported daily in the papers. But none of them caused churches to be built in every town. He tried to work backwards through the churches, from their brave high fronts through their shabby, ill-attended interiors back into the events at Jerusalem, and felt himself surrounded by shifting grey shadows, centuries of history, where he knew nothing. The threat dissolved in his hands. Had Christ ever come to him, David Kern, and said, 'Here. Feel the wound in My side'? No; but prayers had been answered. What prayers? He had prayed that Rudy Mohn, whom he had purposely tripped so he cracked his head on their radiator, not die, and he had not died. But for all the blood, it was just a cut; Rudy came back the same day, wearing a bandage and repeating the same teasing words. He could never have died. Again, David had prayed for two separate war-effort posters he had sent away for to arrive tomorrow, and though they did not, they did arrive, some days later, together, popping through the clacking letter slot like a rebuke from God's mouth: *I answer your prayers in My way, in My time.* After that, he had made his prayers less definite, less susceptible of being twisted into a scolding. But what a tiny, ridiculous coincidence that was, after all, to throw into battle against H. G. Wells's engines of knowledge! Indeed, it proved the enemy's point: Hope bases vast premises on foolish accidents, and reads a word where in fact only a scribble exists.

His father came home. Though Saturday was a free day for him, he had been working. He taught school in Olinger and spent all his days performing, with a curious air of panic, needless errands. Also, a city boy by birth, he was frightened of the farm and seized any excuse to get away. The farm had been David's mother's birthplace; it had been her idea to buy it back. With an ingenuity and persistence unparalleled in her life, she had gained that end, and moved them all here – her son, her husband, her mother. Granmom, in her prime, had worked these fields alongside her husband, but now she dabbled around the kitchen futilely, her hands waggling with Parkinson's disease. She was always in the way. Strange, out in the country, amid eighty acres, they were crowded together. His father expressed his feelings of discomfort by conducting with Mother an endless argument about organic farming. All through dusk, all through supper, it rattled on.

'Elsie, I *know*, I know from my education, the earth is nothing but chemicals. It's the only damn thing I got out of four years of college, so don't tell me it's not true.'

'George, if you'd just walk out on the farm you'd know it's not true. The land has a *soul*.'

'Soil, has, no, soul,' he said, enunciating stiffly, as if to a very stupid class. To David he said, 'You can't argue with a femme. Your mother's a real femme. That's why I married her, and now I'm suffering for it.'

'*This* soil has no soul,' she said, 'because it's been killed with superphosphate. It's been burned bare by Boyer's tenant farmers.' Boyer was the rich man they had bought the farm from. 'It used to have a soul, didn't it, Mother? When you and Pop farmed it?'

'Ach, yes; I guess.' Granmom was trying to bring a forkful of food to her mouth with her less severely afflicted hand. In her anxiety she brought the other hand up from her lap. The crippled fingers, dull red in the orange light of the kerosene lamp in the centre of the table, were welded by paralysis into one knobbed hook.

'Only human indi-vidu-als have souls,' his father went on, in the same mincing, lifeless voice. 'Because the Bible tells us so.' Done eating, he crossed his legs and dug into his ear with a match miserably; to get at the thing inside his head he tucked in his chin, and his voice came out low-pitched at David. 'When God made your mother, He made a real femme.'

'George, don't you read the papers? Don't you know that between the chemical fertilizers and the bug sprays we'll all be dead in ten years? Heart attacks are killing every man in the country over forty-five.'

He sighed wearily; the yellow skin of his eyelids wrinkled as he hurt himself with the match. 'There's no connexion,' he stated, spacing his words with pained patience, 'between the heart – and chemical fertilizers. It's alcohol that's doing it. Alcohol and milk. There is too much – cholesterol – in the tissues of the American heart. Don't tell me about chemistry, Elsie; I majored in the damn stuff for four years.'

'Yes and I majored in Greek and I'm not a penny wiser. Mother, put your waggler *away*!' The old woman started, and the food dropped from her fork. For some reason, the sight of her bad hand at the table cruelly irritated her daughter. Granmom's eyes, worn bits of crazed crystal embedded in watery milk, widened behind her cockeyed spectacles. Circles of silver as fine as thread they clung to the red notches they had carved over the years into her little white beak. In the orange flicker of the kerosene lamp her dazed misery seemed infernal. David's mother began, without noise, to cry. His father did not seem to have eyes at all; just jaundiced sockets of wrinkled skin. The steam of food clouded the scene. It was horrible but the horror was particular and familiar, and distracted David from the formless dread that worked, sick and sore, within him, like a too large wound trying to heal.

He had to go to the bathroom, and took a flashlight down through the wet grass to the outhouse. For once, his fear of spiders there felt trivial. He set the flashlight, burning, beside him, and an insect alighted on its lens, a tiny insect, a mosquito or flea, made so fine that the weak light projected its X-ray on to the wall boards: the faint rim of its wings, the blurred strokes, magnified, of its long hinged legs, the dark cone at the heart of its anatomy. The tremor must be its heart beating. Without warning, David was visited by an exact vision of death: a long hole in the ground, no wider than your body, down which you are drawn while the white faces above recede. You try to reach them but your arms are pinned. Shovels pour dirt into your face. There you will be forever, in an upright position, blind and silent, and in time no one will remember you, and you will never be called. As strata of rock shift, your fingers elongate, and your teeth are distended sideways in a great underground grimace indistinguishable from a strip of chalk. And the earth rumbles on, and the sun expires, and unaltering darkness reigns where once there were stars.

Sweat broke out on his back. His mind seemed to rebound off a solidness. Such extinction was not another threat, a graver sort of danger, a kind of pain; it was qualitatively different. It was not even a conception that could be voluntarily pictured; it entered him from outside. His protesting nerves swarmed on its surface like lichen on a meteor. The skin of his chest was soaked with the effort of rejection. At the same time that the fear was dense and internal, it was dense and all around him; a tide of clay had swept up to the stars; space was crushed into a mass. When he stood up, automatically hunching his shoulders to keep his head away from the spider webs, it was with a numb sense of being cramped between two vast and rigid volumes. That he had even this small freedom to move surprised him. In the narrow shelter of that rank shack adjusting his pants, he felt – his first spark of comfort – too small to be crushed.

But in the open, as the beam of the flashlight skidded with frightened quickness across the remote surfaces of the barn and the grape arbour and the giant pine that stood by the path to the woods, the terror descended. He raced up through the clinging grass pursued, not by one of the wild animals the woods might hold or by one of the goblins his superstitious grandmother had communicated to his childhood, but by spectres out of science fiction, where gigantic cinder moons fill half the turquoise sky. As David ran, a grey planet rolled inches behind his neck. If he looked back, he would be buried. And in the momentum of his terror, hideous possibilities – the dilation of the sun, the triumph of the insects, the crabs on the shore in *The Time Machine* – wheeled out of the vacuum of make-believe and added their weight to his impending oblivion.

He wrenched the door open; the lamps within the house flared. The wicks burning here and there seemed to mirror one another. His mother was washing the dishes in a little pan of heated pump-water; Granmom fluttered near her elbow apprehensively. In the living-room – the down-stairs of the little square house was two long rooms – his father sat in front of the black fireplace restlessly folding and unfolding a newspaper as he sustained his half of the argument. 'Nitrogen, phosphorus, potash: there are the three replaceable constituents of the soil. One crop of corn carries away hundreds of pounds of' – he dropped the paper into his lap and ticked them off on three fingers – 'nitrogen, phosphorus, potash.'

'Boyer didn't grow corn.'

'*Any* crop, Elsie. The human animal –'

'You're killing the *earth*worms, George!'

'The human animal, after thousands and *thou*sands of years, learned methods whereby the chemical balance of the soil may be maintained. Don't carry me back to the Dark Ages.'

'When we moved to Olinger the ground in the garden was like slate. Just one summer of my cousin's chicken dung and the earthworms came back.'

'I'm sure the Dark Ages were a fine place to the poor devils born in them, but I don't want to go there. They give me the creeps.' Daddy stared into the cold pit of the fireplace and clung to the rolled newspaper in his lap as if it alone were keeping him from slipping backwards and down, down.

Mother came into the doorway brandishing a fistful of wet forks. 'And thanks to your DDT there soon won't be a bee left in the country. When I was a girl here you could eat a peach without washing it.'

'It's primitive, Elsie. It's Dark Ages stuff.'

'Oh, what do *you* know about the Dark Ages?'

'I know I don't want to go back to them.'

David took from the shelf, where he had placed it this afternoon, the great unabridged *Webster's Dictionary* that his grandfather had owned. He turned the big thin pages, floppy as cloth, to the entry he wanted, and read

> **soul** . . . 1. An entity conceived as the essence, substance, animating principle, or actuating cause of life, or of the individual life, esp. of life manifested in psychical activities; the vehicle of individual existence, separate in nature from the body and usually held to be separable in existence.

The definition went on, into Greek and Egyptian conceptions, but David stopped short on the treacherous edge of antiquity. He needed to read no farther. The careful overlapping words shingled a temporary shelter for him. 'Usually held to be separable in existence' – what could be fairer, more judicious, surer?

His father was saying, 'The modern farmer can't go around sweeping up after his cows. The poor devil has thousands and *thou*sands of acres on his hands. Your modern farmer uses a scientifically-arrived-at mixture, like five-ten-five, or six-twelve-six, or *three*-twelve-six, and spreads it on with this wonderful modern machinery which of course we can't afford. Your modern farmer can't *afford* medieval methods.'

Mother was quiet in the kitchen; her silence radiated anger.

'No now Elsie; don't play the femme with me. Let's discuss this calmly like two rational twentieth-century people. Your organic farming nuts aren't attacking five-ten-five; they're attacking the chemical fertilizer crooks. The monster firms.'

A cup clinked in the kitchen. Mother's anger touched David's face; his cheeks burned guiltily. Just by being in the living-room he was associated with his father. She appeared in the doorway with red hands and tears in her eyes, and said to the two of them, 'I knew you didn't want to come here but I didn't know you'd torment me like this. You talked Pop into his grave and now you'll kill me. Go ahead, George, more power to you; at least I'll be buried in good ground.' She tried to turn and met an obstacle and screamed, 'Mother, stop hanging on my *back*! Why don't you go to *bed*?'

'Let's all go to bed,' David's father said, rising from the blue wing chair and slapping his thigh with a newspaper. 'This reminds me of death.' It was a phrase of his that David had heard so often he never considered its sense.

Upstairs, he seemed to be lifted above his fears. The sheets on his bed were clean. Granmom had ironed them with a pair of flatirons saved from the Olinger attic; she plucked them hot off the stove alternately, with a wooden handle called a goose. It was a wonder, to see how she managed. In the next room, his parents grunted peaceably; they seemed to take their quarrels less seriously than he did. They made comfortable scratching noises as they carried a little lamp back and forth. Their door was open a crack, so he saw the light shift and swing. Surely there would be, in the last five minutes, in the last second, a crack of light, showing the door from the dark room to another, full of light. Thinking of it this way too vividly evoked his own dying, in a specific bed in a specific room, specific walls mottled with wallpaper, the dry whistle of his breathing, the murmuring doctors, the nervous relatives going in and out, but for him no way out but down, down through the grass, into the earth, the hole. *Never touch a doorknob again.* A whisper, and his parents' light was blown out. David prayed to be reassured. Though the experiment frightened him, he lifted his hands high into the darkness above his face and begged Christ to touch them. Not hard or long: the faintest, quickest grip would be final for a lifetime. His hands waited in the air, itself a substance, which seemed to move through his fingers; or was it the pressure of his pulse? He returned his hands to beneath the covers uncertain if they had been touched or not. For would not Christ's touch *be* infinitely gentle?

Through all the eddies of its aftermath, David clung to this thought about his revelation of extinction: that there, in the outhouse, he had struck a solidness qualitatively different, a rock of horror firm enough to support any height of construction. All he needed was a little help; a word, a gesture, a nod of certainty, and he would be sealed in, safe. The assurance from the dictionary had melted in the night. Today was Sunday, a hot fair day. Across a mile of clear air the church bells called, *Celebrate, celebrate*. Only Daddy went. He put on a coat over his rolled-up shirt-sleeves and got into the little old black Plymouth parked by the barn and went off, with the same pained hurried grimness of all his actions. His churning wheels, as he shifted too hastily into second, raised plumes of red dust on the dirt road. Mother walked to the far field, to see what bushes needed cutting. David, though he usually preferred to stay in the house, went with her. The puppy followed at a distance, whining as it picked its way through the stubble but floundering off timidly if one of them went back to pick it up and carry it. When they reached the crest of the far field, his mother asked, 'David, what's troubling you?'

'Nothing. Why?'

She looked at him sharply. The greening woods cross-hatched the space beyond her half-grey hair. Then she showed him her profile, and gestured towards the house, which they had left a half-mile behind them. 'See how it sits in the land? They don't know how to build with the land any more. Pop always said the foundations were set with the compass. We must try to get a compass and see. It's supposed to face due south; but south feels a little more *that* way to me.' From the side, as she said these things, she seemed handsome and young. The smooth sweep of her hair over her ear seemed white with a purity and calm that made her feel foreign to him. He had never regarded his parents as consolers of his troubles; from the beginning they had seemed to have more troubles than he. Their confusion had flattered him into an illusion of strength; so now on this high clear ridge he jealously guarded the menace all around them, blowing like a breeze on his fingertips, the possibility of all this wide scenery sinking into darkness. The strange fact that though she came to look at the brush she carried no clippers, for she had a fixed prejudice against working on Sundays, was the only consolation he allowed her to offer.

As they walked back, the puppy whimpering after them, the rising dust behind a distant line of trees announced that Daddy was speeding home from church. When they reached the house he was there. He had brought back the Sunday paper and the vehement remark, 'Dobson's too intelligent for these farmers. They just sit there with their mouths open and don't hear a thing the poor devil's saying.'

'What makes you think farmers are unintelligent? This country was made by farmers. George Washington was a farmer.'

'They are, Elsie. They are unintelligent. George Washington's dead. In this day and age only the misfits stay on the farm. The lame, the halt, the blind. The morons with one arm. Human garbage. They remind me of death, sitting there with their mouths open.'

'My *father* was a farmer.'

'He was a frustrated man, Elsie. He never knew what hit him. The poor devil meant so well, and he never knew which end was up. Your mother'll bear me out. Isn't that right, Mom? Pop never knew what hit him?'

'Ach, I guess not,' the old woman quavered, and the ambiguity for the moment silenced both sides.

David hid in the funny papers and sports section until one-thirty. At two, the catechetical class met at the Firetown church. He had transferred from the catechetical class of the Lutheran church in Olinger, a humiliating come-down. In Olinger they met on Wednesday nights, spiffy and spruce, in the atmosphere of a dance. Afterwards, blessed by the

29

brick-faced minister from whose lips the words 'Christ' fell like a burning stone, the more daring of them went with their Bibles to a luncheonette and smoked. Here in Firetown, the girls were dull white cows and the boys narrow-faced brown goats in old men's suits, herded on Sunday afternoon into a threadbare church basement that smelled of stale hay. Because his father had taken the car on one of his endless errands to Olinger, David walked, grateful for the open air and the silence. The catechetical class embarrassed him, but today he placed hope in it, as the source of the nod, the gesture that was all he needed.

Reverend Dobson was a delicate young man with great dark eyes and small white shapely hands that flickered like protesting doves when he preached; he seemed a bit misplaced in the Lutheran ministry. This was his first call. It was a split parish; he served another rural church twelve miles away. His iridescent green Ford, new six months ago, was spattered to the windows with red mud and rattled from bouncing on the rude back roads, where he frequently got lost, to the malicious satisfaction of many. But David's mother liked him, and, more pertinent to his success, the Haiers, the sleek family of feed merchants and innkeepers and tractor salesmen who dominated the Firetown church, liked him. David liked him, and felt liked in turn; sometimes in class, after some special stupidity, Dobson directed towards him out of those wide black eyes a mild look of disbelief, a look that, though flattering, was also delicately disquieting.

Catechetical instruction consisted of reading aloud from a work booklet answers to problems prepared during the week, problems like, 'I am the ____, the ____, and the ____, saith the Lord.' Then there was a question period in which no one ever asked any questions. Today's theme was the last third of the Apostles' Creed. When the time came for questions, David blushed and asked, 'About the Resurrection of the Body – are we conscious between the time when we die and the Day of Judgement?'

Dobson blinked, and his fine little mouth pursed, suggesting that David was making difficult things more difficult. The faces of the other students went blank, as if an indiscretion had been committed.

'No, I suppose not,' Reverend Dobson said.

'Well, where is our soul, then, in this gap?'

The sense grew, in the class, of a naughtiness occurring. Dobson's shy eyes watered, as if he were straining to keep up the formality of attention, and one of the girls, the fattest, simpered towards her twin, who was a little less fat. Their chairs were arranged in a rough circle. The current running around the circle panicked David. Did everybody know something he didn't know?

'I suppose you could say our souls are asleep,' Dobson said.

'And then they wake up, and there is the earth like it always is, and all the people who have ever lived? Where will Heaven be?'

Anita Haier giggled. Dobson gazed at David intently, but with an awkward, puzzled flicker of forgiveness, as if there existed a secret between them that David was violating. But David knew of no secret. All he wanted was to hear Dobson repeat the words he said every Sunday morning. This he would not do. As if these words were unworthy of the conversational voice.

'David, you might think of Heaven this way: as the way the goodness Abraham Lincoln did lives after him.'

'But is Lincoln conscious of it living on?' He blushed no longer with embarrassment but in anger; he had walked here in good faith and was being made a fool.

'Is he conscious now? I would have to say no; but I don't think it matters.' His voice had a coward's firmness; he was hostile now.

'You don't.'

'Not in the eyes of God, no.' The unction, the stunning impudence, of this reply sprang tears of outrage in David's eyes. He bowed them to his book, where short words like Duty, Love, Obey, Rite were stacked in the form of a cross.

'Were there any other questions, David?' Dobson asked with renewed gentleness. The others were rustling, collecting their books.

'No.' He made his voice firm, though he could not bring up his eyes.

'Did I answer your question fully enough?'

'Yes.'

In the minister's silence the shame that should have been his crept over David: the burden and fever of being a fraud were placed upon *him*, who was innocent, and it seemed, he knew, a confession of this guilt that on the way out he was unable to face Dobson's stirred gaze, though he felt it probing the side of his head.

Anita Haier's father gave him a ride down the highway as far as the dirt road. David said he wanted to walk the rest, and figured that his offer was accepted because Mr Haier did not want to dirty his bright blue Buick with dust. This was all right; everything was all right, as long as it was clear. His indignation at being betrayed, at seeing Christianity betrayed, had hardened him. The straight dirt road reflected his hardness. Pink stones thrust up through its packed surface. The April sun beat down from the centre of the afternoon half of the sky; already it had some of summer's heat. Already the fringes of weeds at the edges of the road were bedraggled with dust. From the reviving grass and scruff of the fields he walked between, insects were sending up a monotonous, automatic chant. In the distance a tiny figure in his father's coat was walking along the edge of the woods. His mother. He wondered what joy she found in such walks; to him the brown stretches of slowly rising and falling land expressed only a huge exhaustion.

Flushed with fresh air and happiness, she returned from her walk earlier than he had expected, and surprised him at his grandfather's Bible. It was a stumpy black book, the boards worn thin where the old man's fingers had held them; the spine hung by one weak hinge of fabric. David had been looking for the passage where Jesus says to the one thief on the cross, 'Today shalt thou be with me in paradise.' He had never tried reading the Bible for himself before. What was so embarrassing about being caught at it, was that he detested the apparatus of piety. Fusty churches, creaking hymns, ugly Sunday-school teachers and their stupid leaflets – he hated everything about them but the promise they held out, a promise that in the most perverse way, as if the homeliest crone in the kingdom were given the Prince's hand, made every good and real thing, ball games and jokes and pert-breasted girls, possible. He couldn't explain this to his mother. There was no time. Her solicitude was upon him.

'David, what are you doing?'

'Nothing.'

'What are you doing at Grandpop's Bible?'

'Trying to read it. This is supposed to be a Christian country, isn't it?'

She sat down on the green sofa, which used to be in the sun parlour at Olinger, under the fancy mirror. A little smile still lingered on her face from the walk. 'David, I wish you'd talk to me.'

'What about?'

'About whatever it is that's troubling you. Your father and I have both noticed it.'

'I asked Reverend Dobson about Heaven and he said it was like Abraham Lincoln's goodness living after him.'

He waited for the shock to strike her. 'Yes?' she said, expecting more. 'That's all.'

'And why didn't you like it?'

'Well; don't you see? It amounts to saying there isn't any Heaven at all.'

'I don't see that it amounts to that. What do you want Heaven to be?'

'Well, I don't know. I want it to be *something*. I thought he'd tell me what it was. I thought that was his job.' He was becoming angry, sensing her surprise at him. She had assumed that Heaven had faded from his head years ago. She had imagined that he had already entered, in the secrecy of silence, the conspiracy that he now knew to be all around him.

'David,' she asked gently, 'don't you ever want to rest?'

'No. Not forever.'

'David, you're so young. When you get older, you'll feel different.'

'Grandpa didn't. Look how tattered this book is.'

'I never understood your grandfather.'

'Well, I don't understand ministers who say it's like Lincoln's goodness going on and on. Suppose you're not Lincoln?'

'I think Reverend Dobson made a mistake. You must try to forgive him.'

'It's not a *question* of his making a mistake! It's a question of dying and never moving or seeing or hearing anything ever again.'

'But' – in exasperation – 'darling, it's so *greedy* of you to want more. When God has given us this wonderful April day, and given us this farm, and you have your whole life ahead of you –'

'You think, then, that there is God?'

'Of course I do' – with deep relief, that smoothed her features into a reposeful oval. He had risen and was standing too near her for his comfort. He was afraid she would reach out and touch him.

'He made everything? You feel that?'

'Yes.'

'Then who made Him?'

'Why, Man. Man.' The happiness of this answer lit up her face radiantly, until she saw his gesture of disgust. She was so simple, so illogical; such a femme.

'Well, that amounts to saying there is none.'

Her hand reached for his wrist but he backed away. 'David, it's a mystery. A miracle. It's a miracle more beautiful than any Reverend Dobson could have told you about. You don't say houses don't exist because Man made them.'

'No. God has to be different.'

'But, David, you have the *evidence*. Look out the window at the sun; at the fields.'

'Mother, good grief. Don't you see' – he rasped away the roughness in his throat – 'if when we die there's nothing, all your sun and fields and what not are all, ah, *horror*? It's just an ocean of horror.'

'But David, it's not. It's so clearly not that.' And she made an urgent gesture with her hands that expressed, with its suggestion of a willingness to receive his helplessness, all her grace, her gentleness, her love of beauty, gathered into a passive intensity that made him intensely hate her. He would not be wooed away from the truth. *I am the Way, the Truth* . . .

'No,' he told her. 'Just let me alone.'

He found his tennis ball behind the piano and went outside to throw it against the side of the house. There was a patch high up where the brown stucco that had been laid over the sandstone masonry was crumbling away; he kept trying with the tennis ball to chip more pieces off. Superimposed upon his deep ache was a smaller but more immediate worry; that he had hurt his mother. He heard his father's car rattling on the straightaway and went into the house, to make peace before he arrived. To his relief, she was not giving off the stifling damp heat of her anger, but instead, was cool, decisive, maternal. She handed him an old green book, her college text of Plato. 'I want you to read the Parable of the Cave,' she said.

'All right,' he said, though he knew it would do no good. Some story by a dead Greek just vague enough to please her. 'Don't worry about it, Mother.'

'I *am* worried. Honestly, David, I'm sure there will be something for us. As you get older, these things seem to matter a great deal less.'

'That may be. It's a dismal thought, though.'

His father bumped at the door. The locks and jambs stuck here. But before Granmom could totter to the latch and let him in he had knocked it open. He had been in Olinger dithering with trackmeet tickets. Although Mother usually kept her talks with David a confidence, a treasure between them, she called instantly, 'George, David is worried about death!'

He came to the doorway of the living-room, his shirt pocket bristling with pencils, holding in one hand a pint box of melting ice-cream and in the other the knife with which he was about to divide it into four sections, their Sunday treat. 'Is the kid worried about death? Don't give it a thought, David. I'll be lucky if I live till tomorrow, and I'm not worried. If they'd taken a buckshot gun and shot me in the cradle I'd be better off. The *world*'d be better off. Hell, I think death is a wonderful thing. I look forward to it. Get the garbage out of the way. If I had the man here who invented death, I'd pin a medal on him.'

'Hush, George. You'll frighten the child worse than he is.'

This was not true; he never frightened David. There was no harm in his father, no harm at all. Indeed, in the man's steep self-disgust the boy felt a kind of ally. A distant ally. He saw his position with a certain strategic coldness. Nowhere in the world of other people would he find the hint, the nod, he needed to begin to build his fortress against death. They none of them believed. He was alone. In that deep hole. Alone.

Months followed; his position changed little. School was some comfort. All those sexy, perfumed people, wisecracking, chewing gum, all of them doomed to die, and none of them noticing. In their company David felt that they would carry him along into the bright, cheap paradise reserved for them. In any crowd, the fear ebbed a little; he had reasoned that somewhere in the world there must exist a few people who believed what was necessary, and the larger the crowd, the greater the chance that he was near such a soul, within calling distance, if only he was not too ignorant, too ill-equipped, to spot him. The sight of clergymen cheered him; whatever they themselves thought, their collars were still a sign that somewhere, at some time, someone had recognized that we cannot, *cannot*, submit to death. The sermon topics posted outside churches, the flip, hurried pieties of disc jockeys, the cartoons in magazines showing angels or devils – on such scraps he kept alive the possibility of hope.

For the rest, he tried to drown his hopelessness in clatter and jostle. The pinball machine at the luncheonette was a merciful distraction; as he bent over its buzzing, flashing board of flippers and cushions, the weight and constriction in his chest lightened and loosened. He was grateful for all the time his father wasted in Olinger. Every day postponed the moment when they must ride together down the dirt road into the heart of the dark farmland, where the only light was the kerosene lamp waiting on the dining-room table, a light that drowned their food in shadow and made it sinister.

He lost his appetite for reading. He was afraid of being overwhelmed again. In mystery novels people died like dolls being discarded; in science fiction enormities of space and time conspired to crush the humans; and even in P. G. Wodehouse he felt a hollowness, a turning away from reality that was implicitly bitter, and became explicit in the comic figures of futile parsons. All gaiety seemed minced out on the skin of a void. All quiet hours seemed invitations to dread.

Even on weekends, he and his father contrived to escape the farm; and when, some Saturdays, they did stay home, it was to do something destructive – tear down an old henhouse or set huge brush fires that threatened, while Mother shouted and flapped her arms, to spread to the woods. Whenever his father worked, it was with rapt violence; when he chopped kindling, fragments of the old henhouse boards flew like shrapnel and the axe-head was always within a quarter of an inch of flying off the handle. He was exhilarating to watch, sweating and swearing and sucking bits of saliva back into his lips.

School stopped. His father took the car in the opposite direction, to a highway construction job where he had been hired for the summer as a timekeeper, and David was stranded in the middle of acres of heat and greenery and blowing pollen and the strange, mechanical humming that lay invisibly in the weeds and alfalfa and dry orchard grass.

For his fifteenth birthday his parents gave him, with jokes about him being a hillbilly now, a Remington ·22. It was somewhat like a pinball machine to take it out to the old kiln in the woods where they dumped their trash, and set up tin cans on the kiln's sandstone shoulder and shoot them off one by one. He'd take the puppy, who had grown long legs and a rich coat of reddish fur – he was part chow. Copper hated the gun but loved the boy enough to accompany him. When the flat acrid crack rang out, he would race in terrified circles that would tighten and tighten until they brought him, shivering, against David's legs. Depending upon his mood, David would shoot again or drop to his knees and comfort the dog. Giving this comfort to a degree returned comfort to him. The dog's ears, laid flat against his skull in fear, were folded so intricately, so – he groped for the concept – *surely*. Where the dull-studded collar made the fur stand up, each hair showed a root of soft white under the length, black-tipped, of the metal-colour that had lent the dog its name. In his agitation Copper panted through nostrils that were elegant slits, like two healed cuts, or like the keyholes of a dainty lock of black, grained wood. His whole whorling, knotted, jointed body was a wealth of such embellishments. And in the smell of the dog's hair David seemed to descend through many finely differentiated layers of earth: mulch, soil, clay, and the glittering mineral base.

But when he returned to the house, and saw the books arranged on the low shelves, fear returned. The four adamant volumes of Wells like four thin bricks, the green Plato that had puzzled him with its queer softness and tangled purity, the dead Galsworthy and 'Elizabeth', Grandpa's mammoth dictionary, Grandpa's Bible, the Bible that he himself had received on becoming a member of the Firetown Lutheran church – at the sight of these, the memory of his fear reawakened and came around him. He had grown stiff and stupid in its embrace. His parents tried to think of ways to entertain him.

'David, I have a job for you to do,' his mother said one evening at the table.

'What?'

'If you're going to take that tone perhaps we'd better not talk.'

'What tone? I didn't take any tone.'

'Your grandmother thinks there are too many pigeons in the barn.'

'Why?' David turned to look at his grandmother, but she sat there staring at the burning lamp with her usual expression of bewilderment.

Mother shouted, 'Mom, he wants to know why!'

Granmom made a jerky, irritable motion with her bad hand, as if generating the force for utterance, and said, 'They foul the furniture.'

'That's right,' Mother said. 'She's afraid for that old Olinger furniture that we'll never use. David, she's been after me for a month about those poor pigeons. She wants you to shoot them.'

'I don't want to kill anything especially,' David said.

Daddy said, 'The kid's like you are, Elsie. He's too good for this world. Kill or be killed, that's my motto.'

His mother said loudly, 'Mother, he doesn't want to do it.'

'Not?' The old lady's eyes distended as if in horror, and her claw descended slowly to her lap.

'Oh, I'll do it, I'll do it tomorrow,' David snapped, and a pleasant crisp taste entered his mouth with the decision.

'And I had thought, when Boyer's men made the hay, it would be better if the barn doesn't look like a rookery,' his mother added needlessly.

A barn, in a day, is a small night. The splinters of light between the dry shingles pierce the high roof like stars, and the rafters and cross-beams and built-in ladders seem, until your eyes adjust, as mysterious as the branches of a haunted forest. David entered silently, the gun in one hand. Copper whined desperately at the door, too frightened to come in with the gun yet unwilling to leave the boy. David stealthily turned, said, 'Go away', shut the door on the dog, and slipped the bolt across. It was a door within a door; the double door for wagons and tractors was as high and wide as the face of a house.

The smell of old straw scratched his sinuses. The red sofa, half-hidden under its dung-splotched tarpaulin, seemed assimilated into this smell, sunk in it, buried. The mouths of empty bins gaped like caves. Rusty oddments of farming – coils of baling wire, some spare tines for a harrow, a handleless shovel – hung on nails driven here and there in the thick wood. He stood stock-still a minute; it took a while to separate the cooing of the pigeons from the rustling in his ears. When he had focused on the cooing, it flooded the vast interior with its throaty, bubbling outpour: there seemed no other sound. They were up behind the beams. What light there was leaked through the shingles and the dirty glass windows at the far end and the small round holes, about as big as basketballs, high on the opposite stone side walls, under the ridge of the roof.

A pigeon appeared in one of these holes, on the side towards the house. It flew in, with a battering of wings, from the outside, and waited there, silhouetted against its pinched bit of sky, preening and cooing in a throbbing, thrilled, tentative way. David tiptoed four steps to the side, rested his gun against the lowest rung of a ladder pegged between two upright beams, and lowered the gunsight into the bird's tiny, jauntily cocked head. The slap of the report seemed to come off the stone wall behind him, and the pigeon did not fall. Neither did it fly. Instead it stuck in the round hole, pirouetting rapidly and nodding its head as if in frantic agreement. David shot the bolt back and forth and had aimed again before the spent cartridge had stopped jingling on the boards by his feet. He eased the tip of the sight a little lower, into the bird's breast, and took care to squeeze the trigger with perfect evenness. The slow contraction of his hand abruptly sprang the bullet; for a half-second there was doubt, and then the pigeon fell like a handful of rags, skimming down the barn wall into the layer of straw that coated the floor of the mow on this side.

Now others shook loose from the rafters, and whirled in the dim air with a great blurred hurtle of feathers and noise. They would go for the hole; he fixed his sight on the little moon of blue, and when a pigeon came to it, shot him as he was walking the ten inches of stone that would have carried him into the open air. This pigeon lay down in that tunnel of stone, unable to fall either one way or the other, although he was alive enough to lift one wing and cloud the light. It would sink back, and he would suddenly lift it again, the feathers flaring. His body blocked that exit. David raced to the other side of the barn's main aisle, where a similar ladder was symmetrically placed, and rested his gun on the same rung. Three birds came together to this hole; he got one, and two got through. The rest resettled in the rafters.

There was a shallow triangular space behind the cross beams supporting the roof. It was here they roosted and hid. But either the space was too small, or they were curious, for now that his eyes were at home in the dusty gloom David could see little dabs of grey popping in and out. The cooing was shriller now: its apprehensive tremolo made the whole volume of air seem liquid. He noticed one little smudge of a head that was especially persistent in peeking out; he marked the place, and fixed his gun on it, and when the head appeared again, had his finger tightened in advance on the trigger. A parcel of fluff slipped off the beam and fell the barn's height on to a canvas covering some Olinger furniture, and where its head had peeked out there was a fresh prick of light in the shingles.

Standing in the centre of the floor, fully master now, disdaining to steady the barrel with anything but his arm, he killed two more that way. He felt like a beautiful avenger. Out of the shadowy ragged infinity of the vast barn roof these impudent things dared to thrust their heads, presumed to dirty its starred silence with their filthy timorous life, and he cut them off, tucked them back neatly into the silence. He had the sensation of a creator; these little smudges and flickers that he was clever to see and even cleverer to hit in the dim recesses of the rafters – out of each of them he was making a full bird. A tiny peek, probe, dab of life, when he hit it, blossomed into a dead enemy, falling with good, final weight.

The imperfection of the second pigeon he had shot, who was still lifting his wing now and then up in the round hole, nagged him. He put a new clip into the stock. Hugging the gun against his body, he climbed the ladder. The barrel sight scratched his ear; he had a sharp, garish vision, like a colour slide, of shooting himself and being found tumbled on the barn floor among his prey. He locked his arm around the top rung – a fragile, gnawed rod braced between uprights – and shot into the bird's body from a flat angle. The wing folded, but the impact did not, as he had hoped, push the bird out of the hole. He fired again and again, and still the little body, lighter than air when alive, was too heavy to budge from its high grave. From up here he could see green trees and a brown corner of the house through the hole. Clammy with the cobwebs that gathered between the rungs, he pumped a full clip of eight bullets into the stubborn shadow, with no success. He climbed down, and was struck by the silence in the barn. The remaining pigeons must have escaped out the other hole. That was all right; he was tired of it.

He stepped with his rifle into the light. His mother was coming to meet him, and it made him smile to see her shy away from the smoking gun; he held it loosely in one arm, with the expert carelessness of a hillbilly. 'You took a chip out of the house,' she said. 'What were those last shots about?'

'One of them died up in that little round hole and I was trying to shoot it down.'

'Copper's hiding behind the piano and won't come out. I had to leave him.'

'Well don't blame me. *I* didn't want to shoot the poor devils.'

'Don't smirk. You look like your father. How many did you get?'

'Six.'

She went into the barn, and he followed. She listened to the silence. Her hair was scraggly, perhaps from tussling with the dog. 'I don't suppose the others will be back,' she said wearily. 'Indeed, I don't know why I let Mother talk me into it. Their cooing was such a comforting noise.' She began to gather up the dead pigeons. Though he didn't want to touch them, David went into the mow and picked up by its tepid, horny, coral-coloured feet the first bird he had killed. Its wings unfolded disconcertingly, as if the creature had been held together by threads that now were slit. It did not weigh much. He retrieved the one on the other side of the barn; his mother got the three in the middle and led the way across the road to the little southern slope of land that went down toward the foundations of the vanished tobacco shed. The ground was too steep to plant and mow; wild strawberries grew in the tangled grass. She put her burden down and said, 'We'll have to bury them. The dog will go wild.'

He put his two down on her three; the slick feathers let the bodies slide liquidly on one another. He asked, 'Shall I get you the shovel?'

'Get it for yourself; *you* bury them. They're your kill. And be sure to make the hole deep enough so he won't dig them up.' While he went to the tool shed for the shovel, she went into the house. Unlike her, she did not look up, either at the orchard to the right of her or at the meadow on her left, but instead held her head rigidly, tilted a little, as if listening to the ground.

He dug the hole, in a spot where there were no strawberry plants, before he studied the pigeons. He had never seen a bird this close before. The feathers were more wonderful than dog's hair, for each filament was shaped within the shape of the feather, and the feathers in turn were trimmed to fit a pattern that flowed without error across the bird's body. He lost himself in the geometrical tides as the feathers now broadened and stiffened to make an edge for flight, now softened and constricted to cup warmth around the mute flesh. And across the surface of the infinitely adjusted yet somehow effortless mechanics of the feathers played idle designs of colour, no two alike, designs executed, it seemed, in a controlled rapture, with a joy that hung level in the air above and behind him. Yet these birds bred in the millions and were exterminated as pests. Into the fragrant open earth he dropped one broadly banded in slate shades of blue, and on top of it another, mottled all over in rhythms of lilac and grey. The next was almost wholly white, but for a salmon glaze at its throat. As he fitted the last two, still pliant, on the top, and stood up, crusty coverings were lifted from him, and with a feminine, slipping sensation along his nerves that seemed to give the air hands, he was robed in this certainty: that the God who had lavished such craft upon these worthless birds would not destroy His whole Creation by refusing to let David live forever.

Friends from Philadelphia

In the moment before the door was opened to him, he glimpsed her thigh below the half-drawn shade. Thelma was home, then. She was wearing the Camp Winniwoho T-shirt and her quite short shorts.

'Why, my goodness: Janny!' she cried. She always pronounced his name, John, to rhyme with Ann. Earlier that vacation, she had visited in New York City, and tried to talk the way she thought they talked there. 'What on earth ever brings you to me at this odd hour?'

'Hello, Thel,' he said. 'I hope – I guess this is a pretty bad time.' She had been plucking her eyebrows again. He wished she wouldn't do that.

Thelma extended her arm and touched her fingers to the base of John's neck. It wasn't a fond gesture, just a hostess-like one. 'Now, Janny. You know that I – my mother and I – are always happy to be seeing you. Mother, who do you ever guess is here at this odd hour?'

'Don't keep John Nordholm standing there,' Mrs Lutz said. Thelma's mother was settled in the deep red settee watching television and smoking. A coffee cup being used as an ashtray lay in her lap, and her dress was hiked up so that her knees showed.

'Hello, Mrs Lutz,' John said, trying not to look at her broad, pale knees. 'I really hate to bother you at this odd hour.'

'I don't see anything odd about it.' She took a deep-throated drag on her cigarette and exhaled through her nostrils, the way men do. 'Some of the other kids were here earlier this afternoon.'

'I would have come in if anybody had told me.'

Thelma said, 'Oh, Janny! Stop trying to make a martyr of yourself. Keep in touch, they say, if you want to keep up.'

He felt his face grow hot and knew he was blushing, which made him blush all the more. Mrs Lutz shook a wrinkled pack of Herbert Tareytons at him. 'Smoke?' she said.

'I guess not, thanks a lot.'

'You've stopped? It's a bad habit. I wish I had stopped at your age. I'm not sure I even *begun* at your age.'

'No, it's just that I have to go home soon, and my mother would smell the smoke on my breath. She can smell it even through chewing-gum.'

'Why must you go home soon?' Thelma asked.

Mrs Lutz sniffled. 'I have sinus. I can't even smell the flowers in the garden or the food on the table any more. Let the kids smoke if they want, if it makes them feel better. I don't care. My Thelma, she can smoke right in her own home, her own living-room, if she wants to. But she doesn't seem to have the taste for it. I'm just as glad, to tell the truth.'

John hated interrupting, but it was close to five-thirty. 'I have a problem,' he said.

'A problem – how gruesome,' Thelma said. 'And here I thought, Mother, I was being favoured with a social call.'

'Don't talk like that,' Mrs Lutz said.

'It's sort of complex,' John began.

'Talk like what, Mother? Talk like what?'

'Then let me turn this off,' Mrs Lutz said, snapping the right knob on the television set.

'Oh, Mother, and I was listening to it!' Thelma toppled into a chair, her legs flashing. John thought when she pouted she was delicious.

Mrs Lutz had set herself to give sympathy. Her lap was broadened and her hands were laid palms upward in it.

'It's not much of a problem,' John assured her. 'But we're having some people up from Philadelphia.' He turned to Thelma and added, 'If anything is going on tonight, I can't get out.'

'Life is just too, too full of disappointments,' Thelma said.

'Look, is there?'

'Too, too full,' Thelma said.

Mrs Lutz made fluttery motions out of her lap. 'These Philadelphia people.'

John said, 'Maybe I shouldn't bother you about this.' He waited, but she just looked more and more patient, so he went on. 'My mother wants to give them wine, and my father isn't home from teaching school yet. He might not get home before the liquor store closes. It's at six, isn't it? My mother's busy cleaning, so I walked in.'

'She made you walk the whole mile? Poor thing, can't you drive?' Mrs Lutz asked.

'*Sure* I can drive. But I'm not sixteen yet.'

'You look a lot taller than sixteen.'

John looked at Thelma to see how she took that one, but Thelma was pretending to read a rented novel wrapped in cellophane.

'I walked all the way in to the liquor store,' John told Mrs Lutz, 'but they wouldn't give me anything without written permission. It was a new man.'

'Your sorrow has rent me in twain,' Thelma said, as if she was reading it from the book.

'Pay no attention, Johnny,' Mrs Lutz said. 'Now Frank will be home any time. Why not wait until he comes and let him run down with you for a bottle?'

'That sounds wonderful. Thanks an awful lot, really.'

Mrs Lutz's hand descended upon the television knob. Some smiling man was playing the piano. John didn't know who he was; there wasn't any television at his house. They watched in silence until Mr Lutz thumped on the porch outside. The empty milk bottles tinkled, as if they had been nudged. 'Now don't be surprised it he has a bit of a load on,' Mrs Lutz said.

Actually, he didn't act at all drunk. He was like a happy husband in the movies. He called Thelma his little pookie-pie and kissed her on the forehead; then he called his wife his big pookie-pie and kissed her on the mouth. Then he solemnly shook John's hand and told him how very, very happy he was to see him here and asked after his parents. 'Is that goon still on television?' he said finally.

'Daddy, please pay attention to somebody else,' Thelma said, turning off the television set. 'Janny wants to talk to you.'

'And *I* want to talk to *Johnny*,' Thelma's father said. He spread his arms suddenly, clenching and unclenching his fists. He was a big man, with shaved grey hair above his tiny ears. John couldn't think of the word to begin.

Mrs Lutz explained the errand. When she was through, Mr Lutz said, 'People from Philadelphia. I bet their name isn't William L. Trexler, is it?'

'No. I forget their name, but it's not that. The man is an engineer. The woman went to college with my mother.'

'Oh. College people. Then we must get them something very, very nice, I should say.'

'Daddy,' Thelma said. '*Please*. The store will close.'

'Tessie, you hear John. People from college. People with diplomas. And it is very nearly closing time, and who isn't on their way?' He took John's shoulder in one hand and Thelma's arm in the other and hustled them through the door. 'We'll be back in one minute, Mamma,' he said.

'Drive carefully,' Mrs Lutz said from the shadowed porch, where her cigarette showed as an orange star.

Mr Lutz drove a huge blue Buick. 'I never went to college,' he said, 'yet I buy a new car whenever I want.' His tone wasn't nasty, but soft and full of wonder.

'Oh, Daddy, not *this* again,' Thelma said, shaking her head at John, so he could understand what all she had to go through. When she looks like that, John thought, I could bite her lip until it bleeds.

'Ever driven this kind of car, John?' Mr Lutz asked.

'No. The only thing I can drive is my parents' Plymouth, and that not very well.'

'What year car is it?'

'I don't know exactly.' John knew perfectly well it was a 1940 model. 'We got it after the war. It has a gear shift. This is automatic, isn't it?'

'Automatic shift, fluid transmission, directional lights, the works,' Mr Lutz said. 'Now, isn't it funny, John? Here is your father, an educated man, with an old Plymouth, yet at the same time I, who never read more than twenty, thirty books in my life . . . it doesn't seem as if there's justice.' He slapped the fender, bent over to get into the car, straightened up abruptly, and said, 'Do you want to drive it?'

Thelma said, 'Daddy's asking you something.'

'I don't know how,' John said.

'It's very easy to learn, very easy. You just slide in there – come on, its getting late,' John got in on the driver's side. He peered out of the windshield. It was a wider car than the Plymouth; the hood looked wide as a boat.

Mr Lutz asked him to grip the little lever behind the steering-wheel. 'You pull it towards you like *that*, that's it, and fit it into one of these notches. "P" stands for "parking" – I hardly ever use that one. "N", that's "neutral", like on the car you have, "D" means "drive" – just put it in there and the car does all the work for you. You are using that one ninety-nine per cent of the time. "L" is "low", for very steep hills, going up or down. And "R" stands for – what?'

'Reverse,' John said.

'Very, very good. Tessie, he's a smart boy. He'll never own a new car. And when you put them all together, you can remember their order by the sentence, Paint No Dimes Light Red. I thought that up when I was teaching my oldest girl how to drive.'

'Paint No Dimes Light Red,' John said.

'Excellent. Now, let's go.'

A bubble was developing in John's stomach. 'What gear do you want it in to start?' he asked Mr Lutz.

Mr Lutz must not have heard him, because all he said was 'Let's go' again, and he drummed on the dashboard with his finger-tips. They were thick, square fingers, with fur between the knuckles.

Thelma leaned up from the back seat. Her cheek almost touched John's ear. She whispered, 'Put it at "D".'

He did, then he looked for the starter. 'How does he start it?' he asked Thelma.

'I never watch him,' she said. 'There was a button in the last car, but I don't see it in this one.'

'Push on the pedal,' Mr Lutz sang, staring straight ahead and smiling, 'and away we go. And ah, ah, waay we go.'

'Just step on the gas,' Thelma suggested. John pushed down firmly, to keep his leg from trembling. The motor roared and the car bounded away from the kerb. Within a block, though, he could manage the car pretty well.

'It rides like a boat on smooth water,' he told his two passengers. The metaphor pleased him.

Mr Lutz squinted ahead. 'Like a what?'

'Like a boat.'

'Don't go so fast,' Thelma said.

'The motor's so quiet,' John explained. 'Like a sleeping cat.'

Without warning, a truck pulled out of Pearl Street. Mr Lutz, trying to brake, stamped his foot on the empty floor in front of him. John could hardly keep from laughing. 'I see him,' he said, easing his speed so that the truck had just enough room to make its turn. 'Those trucks think they own the road,' he said. He let one hand slide away from the steering-wheel. One-handed, he whipped around a bus. 'What'll she do on the open road?'

'That's a good question, John,' Mr Lutz said. 'And I don't know the answer. Eighty, maybe.'

'The speedometer goes up to a hundred and ten.' Another pause – nobody seemed to be talking. John said, 'Hell. A baby could drive one of these.'

'For instance, you,' Thelma said.

There were a lot of cars at the liquor store, so John had to double-park the big Buick. 'That's close enough, close enough,' Mr Lutz said. 'Don't get any closer, whoa!' He was out of the car before John could bring it to a complete stop. 'You and Tessie wait here,' he said. 'I'll go in for the liquor.'

'Mr Lutz. Say, Mr Lutz,' John called.

'Daddy!' Thelma shouted.

Mr Lutz returned. 'What is it, boys and girls?' His tone, John noticed, was becoming reedy. He was probably getting hungry.

'Here's the money they gave me.' John pulled two wadded dollars from the change pocket of his dungarees. 'My mother said to get something inexpensive but nice.'

'Inexpensive but nice?' Mr Lutz repeated.

'She said something about California sherry.'

'What did she say about it? To get it? Or not to?'

'I guess to get it.'

'You guess.' Mr Lutz shoved himself away from the car and walked backward towards the store as he talked. 'You and Tessie wait in the car. Don't go off somewhere. It's getting late. I'll be only one minute.'

John leaned back in his seat and gracefully rested one hand at the top of the steering-wheel. 'I like your father.'

'You don't know how he acts to Mother,' Thelma said.

John studied the clean line under his wrist and thumb. He flexed his wrist and watched the neat little muscles move in his forearm. 'You know what *I* need?' he said. 'A wrist-watch.'

'Oh, Jan,' Thelma said. 'Stop admiring your own hand. It's really disgusting.'

A ghost of a smile flickered over his lips, but he let his strong nervous fingers remain as they were. 'I'd sell my soul for a drag right now.'

'Daddy keeps a pack in the glove compartment,' Thelma said. 'I'd get them if my fingernails weren't so long.'

'*I'll* get it open,' John said. He leaned over and pushed the recessed button and after a moment of resistance the curved door flopped down. They fished one cigarette out of the old pack of Luckies they found and took alternate puffs. 'Ah,' John said, 'that first drag of the day, clawing and scraping its way down your throat.'

'Be on the look-out for Daddy. They hate my smoking.'

'Thelma.'

'Yes?' She stared deep into his eyes, her face half masked by blue shadow.

'Don't pluck your eyebrows.'

'I think it looks nice.'

'It's like calling me "Jan".' There was a silence, not awkward, between them.

'Get rid of the rette, Jan. Daddy just passed the window.'

Being in the liquor store had put Mr Lutz in a soberer mood. 'Here you be, John,' he said, in a businesslike way. He handed John a tall, velvet-red bottle. 'Better let me drive. You drive like a veteran, but I know the roads.'

'I can walk from your house, Mr Lutz,' John said, knowing Mr Lutz wouldn't make him walk. 'Thanks an awful lot for all you've done.'

'I'll drive you up. Philadelphians can't be kept waiting. We can't make this young man walk a mile, now can we, Tessie?' In the sweeping way the man asked the question there was an energy and a hint of danger that kept the young people quiet all the way out of town, although several things were bothering John.

When the car stopped in front of his house, he forced himself to ask, 'Say, Mr Lutz. I wonder if there was any change?'

'What? Oh. I nearly forgot. You'll have your daddy thinking I'm a crook.' He reached into his pocket and without looking handed John a dollar, a quarter, and a penny.

'This seems like a lot,' John said. The wine must be cheap. His stomach squirmed; maybe he had made a mistake. Maybe he should have let his mother phone his father, like she had wanted to, instead of begging her to let him walk to Thelma's.

'It's your change,' Mr Lutz said.

'Well, thanks an awful lot.'

'Good-bye now,' Mr Lutz said.

'So long.' John slammed the door. 'Good-bye, Thelma. Don't forget what I told you.' He winked.

The car pulled out, and John walked up the path. 'Don't forget what I told you,' he repeated to himself, winking. In his hands the bottle was cool and heavy. He glanced at the label; it read *Château Mouton-Rothschild* 1937.

Flight

At the age of seventeen I was poorly dressed and funny-looking, and went around thinking about myself in the third person. 'Allen Dow strode down the street and home.' 'Allen Dow smiled a thin sardonic smile.' Consciousness of a special destiny made me both arrogant and shy. Years before, when I was eleven or twelve, just on the brink of ceasing to be a little boy, my mother and I, one Sunday afternoon – my father was busy, or asleep – hiked up to the top of the Shale Hill, a child's mountain that formed one side of the valley that held our town. There the town lay under us, Olinger, perhaps a thousand homes, the best and biggest of them climbing Shale Hill towards us, and beyond them the blocks of brick houses, one- and two-family, the homes of my friends, sloping down to the pale thread of the Alton Pike, which strung together the high school, the tennis courts, the movie theatre, the town's few stores and gasoline stations, the elementary school, the Lutheran church. On the other side lay more homes, including our own, a tiny white patch placed just where the land began to rise towards the opposite mountain, Cedar Top. There were rims and rims of hills beyond Cedar Top, and looking south we could see the pike dissolving in other towns and turning out of sight amid the patches of green and brown farmland, and it seemed the entire country was lying exposed under a thin veil of haze. I was old enough to feel embarrassment at standing there alone with my mother, beside a wind-stunted spruce tree, on a long spine of shale. Suddenly she dug her fingers into the hair on my head and announced, 'There we all are, and there we'll all be forever.' She hesitated before the word 'forever', and hesitated again before adding, 'Except you, Allen. You're going to fly.' A few birds were hung far out over the valley, at the level of our eyes, and in her impulsive way she had just plucked the image from them, but it felt like the clue I had been waiting all my childhood for. My most secret self had been made to respond, and I was intensely embarrassed, and irritably ducked my head out from under her melodramatic hand.

She was impulsive and romantic and inconsistent. I was never able to develop this spurt of reassurance into a steady theme between us. That she continued to treat me like an ordinary child seemed a betrayal of the vision she had made me share. I was captive to a hope she had tossed off and forgotten. My shy attempts to justify irregularities in my conduct – reading late at night or not coming back from school on time – by appealing to the image of flight were received with a startled blank look, as if I were talking nonsense. It seemed outrageously unjust. Yes, but, I wanted to say, yes, but it's *your* nonsense. And of course it was just this that made my appeal ineffective: her knowing that I had not made it mine, that I cynically intended to exploit both the privileges of being extraordinary and the pleasures of being ordinary. She feared my wish to be ordinary; once she did respond to my protest that I was learning to fly, by crying with red-faced ferocity, 'You'll never learn, you'll stick and die in the dirt just like I'm doing. Why should you be better than your mother?'

She had been born ten miles to the south, on a farm she and her mother had loved. Her mother, a small fierce woman who looked more like an Arab than a German, worked in the fields with the men, and drove the wagon to market ten miles away every Friday. When still a tiny girl, my mother rode with her, and my impression of those rides is of fear – the little girl's fear of the gross and beery men who grabbed and hugged her, her fear of the wagon breaking, of the produce not selling, fear of her mother's possible humiliation and of her father's condition when at nightfall they returned. Friday was his holiday, and he drank. His drinking is impossible for me to picture; for I never knew him except as an enduring didactic, almost Biblical old man, whose one passion was reading the newspapers and whose one hatred was of the Republican Party. There was something public about him; now that he is dead I keep seeing bits of him attached to famous politicians – his watch chain and his plump square stomach in old films of Theodore Roosevelt, his high-top shoes and the tilt of his head in a photograph of Alfalfa Bill Murray. Alfalfa Bill is turning his head to talk, and holds his hat by the crown, pinching it between two fingers and a thumb, a gentle and courtly grip that reminded me so keenly of my grandfather that I tore the picture out of *Life* and put it in a drawer.

Labouring in the soil had never been congenial to my grandfather, though with his wife's help he prospered by it. Then, in an era when success was hard to avoid, he began to invest in stocks. In 1922 he bought our large white home in the town – its fashionable section had not yet shifted to the Shale Hill side of the valley – and settled in to reap his dividends. He believed to his death that women were foolish, and the broken hearts of his two must have seemed specially so. The dignity of finance for the indignity of farming must have struck him as an eminently advantageous exchange. It strikes me that way, too, and how to reconcile my idea of those fear-ridden wagon rides with the grief that my mother insists she and her mother felt at being taken from the farm? Perhaps prolonged fear is a ground of love. Or perhaps, and likelier, the equation is long and complex, and the few factors I know – the middle-aged woman's mannish pride of land, the adolescent girl's pleasure in riding horses across the fields, their common feeling of rejection in Olinger – are enclosed in brackets and heightened by coefficients that I cannot see. Or perhaps it is not love of land but its absence that needs explaining, in my grandfather's fastidiousness and pride. He believed that as a boy he had been abused, and bore his father a grudge that my mother could never understand. Her grandfather to her was a saintly slender giant, over six feet tall when this was a prodigy, who knew the names of everything, like Adam in Eden. In his old age he was blind. When he came out of the house, the dogs rushed forward to lick his hands. When he lay dying, he requested a Gravenstein apple from the tree on the far edge of the meadow, and his son brought him a Krauser from the orchard near the house. The old man refused it, and my grandfather made a second trip, but in my mother's eyes the outrage had been committed, a savage insult insanely without provocation. What had his father done to him? The only specific complaint I ever heard my grandfather make was that when he was a boy and had to fetch water for the men in the fields, his father would tell him sarcastically, 'Pick up your feet; they'll come down themselves.' How incongruous! As if each generation of parents commits atrocities against their children which by God's decree remain invisible to the rest of the world.

I remember my grandmother as a little dark-eyed woman who talked seldom and who tried to feed me too much, and then as a hook-nosed profile against the lemon cushions of the casket. She died when I was seven. All the rest I know about her is that she was the baby of thirteen children, that while she was alive she made our yard one of the most beautiful in town, and that I am supposed to resemble her brother Pete.

My mother was precocious; she was fourteen when they moved, and for three years had been attending the county normal school. She graduated from Lake College, near Philadelphia, when she was only twenty, a tall handsome girl with a self-deprecatory smile, to judge from one of the curling photographs kept in a shoebox that I was always opening as a child, as if it might contain the clue to the quarrels in my house. My mother stands at the end of our brick walk, beside the elaborately trimmed end of our privet hedge – in shape a thick square column mounted by a rough ball of leaf. The ragged arc of a lilac bush in flower cuts into the right edge of the photograph, and behind my mother I can see a vacant lot where there has been a house ever since I can remember. She poses with a kind of country grace in a long fur-trimmed coat, unbuttoned to expose her beads and a short yet somehow demure flapper dress. Her hands are in her coat pockets, a beret sits on one side of her bangs, and there is a swank about her that seemed incongruous to me, examining this picture on the stained carpet of an ill-lit old house in the evening years of the thirties and in the dark of the warring forties. The costume and the girl in it look so up-to-date, so formidable. It was my grandfather's pleasure, in his prosperity, to give her a generous clothes allowance. My father, the penniless younger son of a Presbyterian minister in Passaic, had worked his way through Lake College by waiting on tables, and still speaks with mild resentment of the beautiful clothes that Lillian Baer wore. This aspect of my mother caused me some pain in high school; she was a fabric snob, and insisted on buying my slacks and sports shirts at the best store in Alton, and since we had little money, she bought me few, when of course what I needed was what my classmates had – a wide variety of cheap clothes.

At the time the photograph was taken, my mother wanted to go to New York. What she would have done there, or exactly what she wanted to do, I don't know; but her father forbade her. 'Forbid' is a husk of a word today, but at that time, in that quaint province, in the mouth of an 'indulgent father', it apparently was still viable, for the great moist weight of that forbidding continued to be felt in the house for years, and when I was a child, as one of my mother's endless harangues to my grandfather screamed towards its weeping peak, I could feel it around and above me, like a huge root encountered by an earthworm.

Perhaps in a reaction of anger my mother married my father, Victor Dow, who at least took her as far away as Wilmington, where he had made a beginning with an engineering firm. But the depression hit, my father was laid off, and the couple came to the white house in Olinger, where my grandfather sat reading the newspapers that traced his stocks' cautious decline into worthlessness. I was born. My grandmother went around as a cleaning lady, and grew things in our quarter-acre yard to sell. We kept chickens, and there was a large plot of asparagus. After she had died, in a frightened way I used to seek her in the asparagus patch. By midsummer it would be a forest of dainty green trees, some as tall as I was, and in their frothy touch a spirit seemed to speak, and in the soft thick net of their intermingling branches a promise seemed to be caught, as well as a menace. The asparagus trees were frightening; in the centre of the patch, far from the house and the alley, I would fall under a spell, and become tiny, and wander among the great smooth green trunks expecting to find a little house with a smoking chimney, and in it my grandmother. She herself had believed in ghosts, which made her own ghost potent. Even now, sitting alone in my own house, a board creaks in the kitchen and I look up fearing she will come through the doorway. And at night, just before I fall asleep, her voice calls my name in a penetrating whisper, or calls, '*Pete.*'

My mother went to work in an Alton department store, selling inferior fabric for $14 a week. During the daytime of my first year of life it was my father who took care of me. He has said since, flattering me as he always does, that it was having me on his hands that kept him from going insane. It may have been this that has made my affection for him so inarticulate, as if I were still a wordless infant looking up into the mothering blur of his man's face. And that same shared year helps account, perhaps, for his gentleness with me, for his willingness to praise, as if everything I do has something sad and crippled in it. He feels sorry for me; my birth coincided with the birth of a great misery, a national misery – only recently has he stopped calling me by the nickname 'Young America'. Around my first birthday he acquired a position teaching arithmetic and algebra in the Olinger high school, and though he was so kind and humorous he couldn't enter a classroom without creating uproarious problems of discipline, he endured it day by day and year by year, and eventually came to occupy a place in this alien town, so that I believe there are now one or two dozen ex-students, men and women nearing middle age, who carry around with them some piece of encouragement my father gave them, or remember some sentence of his that helped shape them. Certainly there are many who remember the antics with which he burlesqued his discomfort in the classroom. He kept a confiscated cap pistol in his desk, and upon getting an especially stupid answer, he would take it out and, wearing a preoccupied, regretful expression, shoot himself in the head.

My grandfather was the last to go to work, and the most degraded by it. He was hired by the borough crew, men who went around the streets shovelling stones and spreading tar. Bulky and ominous in their overalls, wreathed in steam, and associated with dramatic and portentous equipment, these men had grandeur in the eyes of a child, and it puzzled me, as I walked to and from elementary school, that my grandfather refused to wave to me or confess his presence in any way. Curiously strong for a fastidious man, he kept at it well into his seventies, when his sight failed. It was my task then to read his beloved newspapers to him as he sat in his chair by the bay window, twiddling his high-top shoes in the sunshine. I teased him, reading too fast, then maddeningly slow, skipping from column to column to create one long chaotic story; I read him the sports page, which did not interest him, and mumbled the editorials. Only the speed of his feet's twiddling betrayed vexation. When I'd stop, he would plead mildly in his rather beautiful, old-fashioned, elocutionary voice, 'Now just the obituaries, Allen. Just the names to see if anyone I know is there.' I imagined, as I viciously barked at him the list of names that might contain the name of a friend, that I was avenging my mother; I believed that she hated him, and for her sake I tried to hate him also. From her incessant resurrection of mysterious grievances buried far back in the confused sunless earth of time before I was born, I had been able to deduce only that he was an evil man, who had ruined her life, that fair creature in the beret. I did not understand. She fought with him not because she wanted to fight but because *she could not bear to leave him alone.*

Sometimes, glancing up from the sheet of print where our armies swarmed in retreat like harried insects, I would catch the old man's head in the act of lifting slightly to receive the warm sunshine on his face, a dry frail face ennobled by its thick crown of combed corn-silk hair. It would dawn on me then that his sins as a father were likely no worse than any father's. But my mother's genius was to give the people closest to her mythic immensity. I was the phoenix. My father and grandmother were legendary invader-saints, she springing out of some narrow vein of Arab blood in the German race and he crossing over from the Protestant wastes of New Jersey, both of them serving and enslaving their mates with their prodigious powers of endurance and labour. For my mother felt that she and her father alike had been destroyed by marriage, been made captive by people better yet less than they. It was true, my father had loved Mom Baer, and her death made him seem more of an alien than ever. He, and her ghost, stood to one side, in the shadows but separate from the house's dark core, the inheritance of frustration and folly that had descended from my grandfather to my mother to me, and that I, with a few beats of my grown wings, was destined to reverse and redeem.

At the age of seventeen, in the fall of my senior year, I went with three girls to debate at a high school over a hundred miles away. They were, all three, bright girls, A students; they were disfigured by A's as if by acne. Yet even so it excited me to be mounting a train with them early on a Friday morning, at an hour when our schoolmates miles away were slumping into the seats of their first class. Sunshine spread broad bars of dust down the length of the half-empty car, and through the windows Pennsylvania unravelled in a long brown scroll scribbled with industry. Black pipes raced beside the tracks for miles. At rhythmic intervals one of them looped upward, like the Greek letter Ω. 'Why does it do that?' I asked. 'Is it sick?'

'Condensation?' Judith Potteiger suggested in her shy, transparent voice. She loved science.

'No,' I said. 'It's in pain. It's writhing! It's going to grab the train! Look out!' I ducked, honestly a little scared. All the girls laughed.

Judith and Catharine Miller were in my class, and expected me to be amusing; the third girl, a plump small junior named Molly Bingaman, had not known what to expect. It was her fresh audience I was playing to. She was the best dressed of us four, and the most poised; this made me suspect that she was the least bright. She had been substituted at the last moment for a sick member of the debating team; I knew her just by seeing her in the halls and in assembly. From a distance she seemed dumpy and prematurely adult. But close she was gently fragrant, and against the weary purple cloth of the train seats her skin seemed luminous. She had beautiful skin, heartbreaking skin a pencil dot would have marred, and large blue eyes equally clear. Except for a double chin, and a mouth too large and thick, she would have been perfectly pretty, in a little woman's compact and cocky way. She and I sat side by side, facing the two senior girls, who more and more took on the wan slyness of matchmakers. It was they who had forced the seating arrangements.

We debated in the afternoon, and won. Yes, the German Federal Republic *should* be freed from all Allied control. The school, a posh castle on the edge of a miserable coal city, was the site of a state-wide cycle of debates that was to continue into Saturday. There was a dance Friday night in the gym. I danced with Molly mostly, though to my annoyance she got in with a set of Harrisburg boys while I conscientiously pushed Judith and Catharine around the floor. We were stiff dancers, the three of us; only Molly made me seem good, floating backward from my feet fearlessly as her cheek rumpled my moist shirt. The gym was hung with orange and black crêpe paper in honour of Hallowe'en, and the pennants of all the competing schools were fastened to the walls, and a twelve-piece band pumped away blissfully on the year's sad tunes – 'Heartaches', 'Near You', 'That's My Desire'. A great cloud of balloons gathered in the steel girders was released. There was pink punch, and a local girl sang.

Judith and Catharine decided to leave before the dance was over, and I made Molly come too, though she was in a literal sweat of pleasure; her perfect skin in the oval above her neckline was flushed and glazed. I realized, with a little shock of possessiveness and pity, that she was unused to attention back home, in competition with the gorgeous Olinger ignorant.

We walked together to the house where the four of us had been boarded, a large white frame owned by an old couple and standing with lonely decency in a semi-slum. Judith and Catharine turned up the walk, but Molly and I, with a diffident decision that I believe came from her initiative, continued, 'to walk around the block'. We walked miles, stopping off after midnight at a trolley-car-shaped diner. I got a hamburger, and she impressed me by ordering coffee. We walked back to the house and let ourselves in with the key we had been given; but instead of going upstairs to our rooms we sat downstairs in the dark living-room and talked softly for more hours.

What did we say? I talked about myself. It is hard to hear, much less remember, what we ourselves say, just as it might be hard for a movie projector, given life, to see the shadows its eye of light is casting. A transcript, could I produce it, of my monologue through the wide turning-point of that night, with all its word-by-word conceit, would distort the picture: this living-room miles from home, the street light piercing the chinks in the curtains and erecting on the wallpaper rods of light the size of yardsticks, our hosts and companions asleep upstairs, the incessant sigh of my voice, coffee-primed Molly on the floor beside my chair, her stockinged legs stretched out on the rug; and this odd sense in the room, a tasteless and odourless aura unfamiliar to me, as of a pool of water widening.

I remember one exchange. I must have been describing the steep waves of fearing death that had come over me ever since early childhood, about one every three years, and I ended by supposing that it would take great courage to be an atheist. 'But I bet you'll become one,' Molly said. 'Just to show yourself that you're brave enough.' I felt she overestimated me, and was flattered. Within a few years, while I still remembered many of her words, I realized how touchingly gauche our assumption was that an atheist is a lonely rebel; for mobs of men are united in atheism, and oblivion – the dense lead-like sea that would occasionally sweep over me –

is to them a weight as negligible as the faint pressure of their wallets in their hip pockets. This grotesque and tender mis-estimate of the world flares in my memory of our conversation like one of the innumerable matches we struck.

The room filled with smoke. Too weary to sit, I lay down on the floor beside her, and stroked her silver arm in silence, yet still was too timid to act on the wide and negative aura that I did not understand was of compliance. On the upstairs landing, as I went to turn into my room, Molly came forward with a prim look and kissed me. With clumsy force I entered the negative space that had been waiting. Her lipstick smeared in little unflattering flecks into the skin around her mouth; it was as if I had been given a face to eat, and the presence of bone – skull under skin, teeth behind lips – impeded me. We stood for a long time under the burning hall light, until my neck began to ache from bowing. My legs were trembling when we finally parted and sneaked into our rooms. In bed I thought, 'Allen Dow tossed restlessly,' and realized it was the first time that day I had thought of myself in the third person.

On Saturday morning, we lost our debate. I was sleepy and verbose and haughty, and some of the students in the audience began to boo whenever I opened my mouth. The principal came up on the stage and made a scolding speech, which finished me and my cause, untrammelled Germany. On the train back, Catharine and Judith arranged the seating so that they sat behind Molly and me, and spied on only the tops of our heads. For the first time, on that ride home, I felt what it was to bury a humiliation in the body of a woman. Nothing but the friction of my face against hers drowned out the echo of those boos. When we kissed, a red shadow would well under my lids and eclipse the hostile hooting faces of the debate audience, and when our lips parted, the bright inner sea would ebb, and there the faces would be again, more intense than ever. With a shudder of shame I'd hide my face on her shoulder and in the warm darkness there, while a frill of her prissy collar gently scratched my nose, I felt united with Hitler and all the villains, traitors, madmen, and failures who had managed to keep, up to the moment of capture or death, a woman with them. This had puzzled me. In high school, females were proud and remote; in the newspapers they were fantastic monsters of submission. And now Molly administered reassurance to me with small motions and bodily adjustments that had about them a strange flavour of the practical.

Our parents met us at the station. I was startled at how tired my mother looked. There were deep blue dents on either side of her nose, and her hair seemed somehow dissociated from her head, as if it were a ragged, half-grey wig she had put on carelessly. She was a heavy woman, and her weight, which she usually carried upright, like a kind of wealth, had slumped away from her ownership and seemed, in the sullen light of the railway platform, to weigh on the world. I asked, 'How's Grandpa?' He had taken to bed several months before with pains in his chest.

'He still sings,' she said rather sharply. For entertainment in his increasing blindness my grandfather had long ago begun to sing, and his shapely old voice would pour forth hymns, forgotten comic ballads, and camp-meeting songs at any hour. His memory seemed to improve the longer he lived.

My mother's irritability was more manifest in the private cavity of the car; her heavy silence oppressed me. 'You look so tired, Mother,' I said, trying to take the offensive.

'That's nothing to how you look,' she answered. 'What happened up there? You stoop like an old married man.'

'Nothing happened,' I lied. My cheeks were parched, as if her high steady anger had the power of giving sunburn.

'I remember that Bingaman girl's mother when we first moved to town. She was the smuggest little snip south of the pike. They're real old Olinger stock, you know. They have no use for hillbillies.'

My father tried to change the subject. 'Well, you won one debate, Allen, and that's more than I would have done. I don't see how you do it.'

'Why, he gets it from you, Victor. I've never won a debate with you.'

'He gets it from Pop Baer. If that man had gone into politics, Lillian, all the misery of his life would have been avoided.'

'Dad was never a debater. He was a bully. Don't go with little women, Allen. It puts you too close to the ground.'

'I'm not *going* with *any*body, Mother. Really, you're so fanciful.'

'Why, when she stepped off the train from the way her chins bounced I thought she had eaten a canary. And then making my poor son, all skin and bones, carry her bag. When she walked by me I honestly was afraid she'd spit in my eye.'

'I had to carry somebody's bag. I'm sure she doesn't know who you are.' Though it was true I had talked a good deal about my family the night before.

My mother turned away from me. 'You see, Victor – he defends her. When I was his age that girl's mother gave me a cut I'm still bleeding from, and my own son attacks me on behalf of her fat little daughter. I wonder if her mother put her up to catching him.'

'Molly's a nice girl,' my father interceded. 'She never gave me any trouble in class like some of those smug bastards.' But he was curiously listless, for so Christian a man, in pronouncing his endorsement.

I discovered that nobody wanted me to go with Molly Bingaman. My friends – for on the strength of being funny I did have some friends, classmates whose love affairs went on over my head but whom I could accompany, as clown, on communal outings – never talked with me about Molly, and when I brought her to their parties gave the impression of ignoring her, so that I stopped taking her. Teachers at school would smile an odd tight smile when they saw us leaning by her locker or hanging around in the stairways. The eleventh-grade English instructor – one of my 'boosters' on the faculty, a man who was always trying to 'challenge' me, to 'exploit' my 'potential' – took me aside and told me how stupid she was. She just couldn't grasp the principles of syntax. He confided her parsing mistakes to me as if they betrayed – as indeed in a way they did – an obtuseness her social manner cleverly concealed. Even the Fabers, an ultra-Republican couple who ran a luncheonette near the high school, showed malicious delight whenever Molly and I broke up, and persistently treated my attachment as being a witty piece of play, like my pretence with Mr Faber of being a Communist. The entire town seemed ensnarled in my mother's myth, that escape was my proper fate. It was as if I were a sport that the ghostly elders of Olinger had segregated from the rest of the livestock and agreed to donate in time to the air; this fitted with the ambiguous sensation I had always had in the town, of being simultaneously flattered and rejected.

Molly's parents disapproved because in their eyes my family was virtually white trash. It was so persistently hammered into me that I was too good for Molly that I scarcely considered the proposition that, by another scale, she was too good for me. Further, Molly herself shielded me. Only once, exasperated by some tedious, condescending confession of mine, did she state that her mother didn't like me. 'Why not?' I asked, genuinely surprised. I admired Mrs Bingaman – she was beautifully preserved – and I always felt gay in her house, with its white woodwork and matching furniture and vases of iris posing before polished mirrors.

'Oh, I don't know. She thinks you're flippant.'

'But that's not true. Nobody takes himself more seriously than I do.'

While Molly protected me from the Bingaman side of the ugliness, I conveyed the Dow side more or less directly to her. It infuriated me that nobody allowed me to be proud of her. I kept, in effect, asking her, Why was she stupid in English? Why didn't she get along with my friends?

Why did she look so dumpy and smug? – this last despite the fact that she often, especially in intimate moments, looked beautiful to me. I was especially angry with her because this affair had brought out an ignoble, hysterical, brutal aspect of my mother that I might never have had to see otherwise. I had hoped to keep things secret from her, but even if her intuition had not been relentless, my father, at school, knew everything. Sometimes, indeed, my mother said that she didn't care if I went with Molly; it was my father who was upset. Like a frantic dog tied by one leg, she snapped in any direction, mouthing ridiculous fancies – such as that Mrs Bingaman had sicked Molly on me just to keep me from going to college and giving the Dows something to be proud of – that would make us both suddenly start laughing. Laughter in that house that winter had a guilty sound. My grandfather was dying, and lay upstairs singing and coughing and weeping as the mood came to him, and we were too poor to hire a nurse, and too kind and cowardly to send him to a 'home'. It was still his house, after all. Any noise he made seemed to slash my mother's heart, and she was unable to sleep upstairs near him, and waited the nights out on the sofa downstairs. In her desperate state she would say unforgivable things to me even while the tears streamed down her face. I've never seen so many tears as I saw that winter.

Every time I saw my mother cry, it seemed I had to make Molly cry. I developed a skill at it; it came naturally to an only child who had been surrounded all his life by adults ransacking each other for the truth. Even in the heart of intimacy, half-naked each of us, I would say something to humiliate her. We never made love in the final, coital sense. My reason was a mixture of idealism and superstition; I felt that if I took her virginity she would be mine forever. I depended overmuch on a technicality; she gave herself to me anyway, and I had her anyway, and have her still, for the longer I travel in a direction I could not have taken with her, the more clearly she seems the one person who loved me without advantage. I was a homely, comically ambitious hillbilly, and I even refused to tell her I loved her, to pronounce the word 'love' – an icy piece of pedantry that shocks me now that I have almost forgotten the context of confusion in which it seemed wise.

In addition to my grandfather's illness, and my mother's grief, and my waiting to hear if I had won a scholarship to the one college that seemed good enough for me, I was burdened with managing too many petty affairs of my graduating class. I was in charge of year-book write-ups, art editor of the school paper, chairman of the Class Gift Committee, director of the Senior Assembly, and teacher's workhorse.

Frightened by my father's tales of nervous breakdowns he had seen, I kept listening for the sounds of my brain snapping, and the image of that grey, infinitely interconnected mass seemed to extend outward, to become my whole world, one dense organic dungeon, and I felt I had to get out; if I could just get out of this, into June, it would be blue sky, and I would be all right for life.

One Friday night in spring, after trying for over an hour to write thirty-five affectionate words for the year-book about a dull girl in the Secretarial Course I had never spoken a word to, I heard my grandfather begin coughing upstairs with a sound like dry membrane tearing, and I panicked. I called up the stairs, 'Mother! I must go out.'

'It's nine-thirty.'

'I know, but I have to. I'm going insane.'

Without waiting to hear her answer or to find a coat, I left the house and got our old car out of the garage. The weekend before, I had broken up with Molly again. All week I hadn't spoken to her, though I had seen her once in Faber's, with a boy in her class, averting her face while I, hanging by the side of the pinball machine, made wisecracks in her direction. I didn't dare go up to her door and knock so late at night; I just parked across the street and watched the lit windows of her house. Through their living-room window I could see one of Mrs Bingaman's vases of hothouse iris standing on a white mantel, and my open car window admitted the spring air, which delicately smelled of wet ashes. Molly was probably out on a date with that moron in her class. But then the Bingamans' door opened, and her figure appeared in the rectangle of light. Her back was towards me, a coat was on her arm, and her mother seemed to be screaming. Molly closed the door and ran down off the porch and across the street and quickly got into the car, her eyes downcast in their sockets of shadow. *She came.* When I have finally forgotten everything else, her powdery fragrance, her lucid cool skin, the way her lower lip was like a curved pillow of two cloths, the dusty red outer and wet pink inner, I'll still be grieved by this about Molly, that she came to me.

After I returned her to her house – she told me not to worry, her mother enjoyed shouting – I went to the all-night diner just beyond the Olinger town line and ate three hamburgers, ordering them one at a time, and drank two glasses of milk. It was close to two o'clock when I got home, but my mother was still awake. She lay on the sofa in the dark, with the radio sitting on the floor murmuring Dixieland piped up from New

Orleans by way of Philadelphia. Radio music was a steady feature of her insomniac life: not only did it help drown out the noise of her father upstairs but she seemed to enjoy it in itself. She would resist my father's pleas to come to bed by saying that the New Orleans programme was not over yet. The radio was an old Philo we had always had; I had once drawn a fish on the orange disc of its celluloid dial, which looked to my child's eyes like a fishbowl.

Her loneliness caught at me; I went into the living-room and sat on a chair with my back to the window. For a long time she looked at me tensely out of the darkness. 'Well,' she said at last, 'how was little hot-pants?' The vulgarity this affair had brought out in her language appalled me.

'I made her cry,' I told her.

'Why do you torment the girl?'

'To please you.'

'It doesn't please me.'

'Well, then, stop nagging me.'

'I'll stop nagging you if you'll solemnly tell me you're willing to marry her.'

I said nothing to this, and after waiting she went on in a different voice, 'Isn't it funny, that you should show this weakness?'

'Weakness is a funny way to put it when it's the only thing that gives me strength.'

'Does it really, Allen? Well. It may be. I forgot, you were born here.'

Upstairs, close to our heads, my grandfather, in a voice frail but still melodious, began to sing, 'There is a happy land, far, far away, where saints in glory stand, bright, bright as day.' We listened; and his voice broke into coughing, a terrible rending cough growing in fury, struggling to escape, and loud with fear he called my mother's name. She didn't stir. His voice grew enormous, a bully's voice, as he repeated, 'Lillian! Lillian!' and I saw my mother's shape quiver with the force coming down the stairs into her; she was like a dam; and then the power, as my grandfather fell momentarily silent, flowed towards me in the darkness, and I felt intensely angry, and hated that black mass of suffering, even while I realized, with a rapid, light calculation, that I was too weak to withstand it.

In a dry tone of certainty and dislike – how hard my heart had become! – I told her, 'All right. You'll win this one, Mother; but it'll be the last one you'll win.'

My pang of fright following this unprecedently cold insolence seemed to blot my senses; the chair ceased to be felt under me, and the walls and furniture of the room fell away – there was only the dim orange glow of the radio dial down below. In a husky voice that seemed to come across a great distance my mother said, with typical melodrama, 'Good-bye, Allen.'

A Sense of Shelter

Snow fell against the high school all day, wet big-flaked snow that did not accumulate well. Sharpening two pencils, William looked down on a parking lot that was a blackboard in reverse; car tyres had cut smooth arcs of black into the white, and wherever a school bus had backed around, it had left an autocratic signature of two V's. The snow, though at moments it whirled opaquely, could not quite bleach these scars away. The temperature must be exactly 32°. The window was open a crack, and a canted pane of glass lifted outdoor air into his face, coating the cedarwood scent of pencil shavings with the transparent odour of the wet window-sill. With each revolution of the handle his knuckles came within a fraction of an inch of the tilted glass, and the faint chill this proximity breathed on them sharpened his already acute sense of shelter.

The sky behind the shreds of snow was stone-coloured. The murk inside the high classroom gave the air a solidity that limited the overhead radiance to its own vessels; six globes of dull incandescence floated on the top of a thin sea. The feeling the gloom gave him was not gloomy but joyous: he felt they were all sealed in, safe; the colours of cloth were dyed deeper, the sound of whispers was made more distinct, the smells of tablet paper and wet shoes and varnish and face powder pierced him with a vivid sense of possession. These were his classmates sealed in, his, the stupid as well as the clever, the plain as well as the lovely, his enemies as well as his friends, his. He felt like a king and seemed to move to his seat between the bowed heads of subjects that loved him less than he loved them. His seat was sanctioned by tradition; for twelve years he had sat at the rear of classrooms, William Young, flanked by Marsha Wyckoff and Andy Zimmerman. Once there had been two Zimmermans, but one went to work in his father's greenhouse, and in some classes – Latin and Trig – there were none, and William sat at the edge of the class as if on the lip of a cliff, and Marsha Wyckoff became Marvin Wolf or Sandra Wade, but it was always the same desk, whose surface altered from hour to hour but from whose blue-stained ink-hole his mind could extract, like a chain of magicians' handkerchiefs, a continuity of years. As a senior he was a kind of king, and as a teacher's pet another kind, a puppet king, who gathered in appointive posts and even, when the moron vote split between two football heroes, some elective ones. He was not popular, he had never had a girl, his intense friends of childhood had drifted off into teams and gangs, and in large groups – when the whole school, for instance, went in the fall to the beautiful, dung-and-cotton-smelling county fair – he was always an odd man, without a seat on the bus home. But exclusion is itself a form of inclusion. He even had a nickname: Mip, because he stuttered. Taunts no longer much frightened him; he had come late into his physical inheritance, but this summer it had arrived, and he at last stood equal with his enormous, boisterous parents, and had to unbutton his shirt cuffs to get his wrists through them, and discovered he could pick up a basketball with one hand. So, his long legs blocking two aisles, he felt regal even in size and, almost trembling with happiness under the high globes of light beyond whose lunar glow invisible snowflakes were drowning on the gravel roof of his castle, believed that the long delay of unpopularity had been merely a consolidation, that he was at last strong enough to make his move. Today he would tell Mary Landis he loved her.

He had loved her ever since, a fat-faced tomboy with freckles and green eyes, she deftly stole his rubber-lined schoolbag on the walk back from second grade along Jewett Street and outran him – simply had better legs. The superior speed a boy was supposed to have failed to come; his kidneys burned with panic. In front of the grocery store next to her home she stopped and turned. She was willing to have him catch up. This humiliation on top of the rest was too much to bear. Tears broke in his throat; he spun around and ran home and threw himself on the floor of the front parlour, where his grandfather, feet twiddling, perused the newspaper and soliloquized all morning. In time the letter slot rustled, and the doorbell rang, and Mary gave his mother the schoolbag and the two of them politely exchanged whispers. Their voices had been to him, lying there on the carpet with his head wrapped in his arms, indistinguishable. Mother had always liked Mary. From when she had been a tiny girl dancing along the hedge on the end of an older sister's arm, Mother had liked her. Out of all the children that flocked, similar as pigeons, through the neighbourhood, Mother's heart had reached out with claws and fastened on Mary. He never took the schoolbag to school again, had refused to touch it. He supposed it was still in the attic, still faintly smelling of sweet pink rubber.

Fixed high on the plaster like a wren clinging to a barn wall, the buzzer sounded the two-minute signal. In the middle of the classroom Mary

Landis stood up, a Monitor badge pinned to her belly. Her broad red belt was buckled with a brass bow and arrow. She wore a lavender sweater with the sleeves pushed up to expose her forearms, a delicately cheap effect. Wild stories were told about her; perhaps it was merely his knowledge of these that put the hardness in her face. Her eyes seemed braced for squinting and their green was frosted. Her freckles had faded. William thought she laughed less this year; now that she was in the Secretarial Course and he in the College Preparatory, he saw her in only one class a day, this one, English. She stood a second, eclipsed at the thighs by Jack Stephens' zebra-striped shoulders, and looked back at the class with a stiff worn glance, as if she had seen the same faces too many times before. Her habit of perfect posture emphasized the angularity she had grown into. There was a nervous edge, a boxiness in her bones, that must have been waiting all along under the childish fat. Her eye sockets were deeply indented and her chin had a prim square set that seemed in the murky air tremulous and defiant. Her skirt was cut square and straight. Below the waist she was lean; the legs that had outrun him were still athletic; she starred at hockey and cheer-leading. Above, she was abundant: so stacked her spine curved backwards to keep her body balanced. She turned and in switching up the aisle encountered a boy's leg thrown into her path. She coolly looked down until it withdrew. She was used to such attentions. Her pronged chest poised, Mary proceeded out the door, and someone she saw in the hall made her smile, a wide smile full of warmth and short white teeth, and love scooped at William's heart. He would tell her.

In another minute, the second bell rasped. Shuffling through the perfumed crowds to his next class, he crooned to himself, in the slow, overenunciated manner of the Negro vocalist who had brought the song back this year:

> 'Lah-vender blue, dilly dilly,
> Lavendih gree-heen;
> *Eef* I were king, dilly dilly,
> You would be queen.'

The song gave him an exultant sliding sensation that intertwined with the pleasures of his day. He knew all the answers, he had done all the work, the teachers called upon him only to rebuke the ignorance of the others. In Trig and Soc Sci both it was this way. In gym, the fourth hour of the morning, he, who was always picked near the last, startled his side by excelling at volleyball, leaping like a madman, shouting like a bully.

The ball felt light as a feather against his big bones. His hair in wet quills from the shower, he walked in the icy air to Luke's Luncheonette, where he ate three hamburgers in a booth with three juniors. There was Barry Kruppman, a tall, thyroid-eyed boy who came on the school bus from the country town of Bowsville and who was an amateur hypnotist; he told the tale of a Portland, Oregon, businessman who under hypnosis had been taken back through sixteen reincarnations to the condition of an Egyptian concubine in the household of a high priest of Isis. There was his friend Lionel Griffin, a pudgy simp whose blond hair puffed out above his ears in two slick waxed wings. He was rumoured to be a fairy, and in fact did seem most excited by the transvestite aspect of the soul's transmigration. And there was Lionel's girl Virginia, a drab little mystery who chain-smoked Herbert Tareytons and never said anything. She had sallow skin and smudged eyes and Lionel kept jabbing her and shrieking, making William wince. He would rather have sat with members of his own class, who filled the other booths, but he would have had to force himself on them. These juniors admired him and welcomed his company. He asked, 'Wuh-well, was he ever a c-c-c-cockroach, like Archy?'

Kruppman's face grew intense; his furry lids dropped down over the bulge of his eyes, and when they drew back, his pupils were as small and hard as BBs. 'That's the really interesting thing. There was this gap, see, between his being a knight under Charlemagne and then a sailor on a ship putting out from Macedonia – that's where Yugoslavia is now – in the time of Nero; there was this gap, when the only thing the guy would do was walk around the office snarling and growling, see, like this.' Kruppman worked his blotched ferret face up into a snarl and Griffin shrieked. 'He tried to bite one of the assistants and they think that for six hundred years' – the uncanny, unhealthy seriousness of his whisper hushed Griffin momentarily – 'for six hundred years he just was a series of wolves. Probably in the German forests. You see, when he was in Macedonia' – his whisper barely audible – 'he murdered a woman.'

Griffin squealed in ecstasy and cried, 'Oh, Kruppman! Kruppman, how you do go on!' and jabbed Virginia in the arm so hard a Herbert Tareyton jumped from her hand and bobbled across the Formica table. William gazed over their heads in pain.

The crowd at the soda counter had thinned so that when the door to the outside opened he saw Mary come in and hesitate there for a second where the smoke inside and the snow outside swirled together. The mixture made a kind of – Kruppman's ridiculous story had put the phrase in his head – wolf-weather, and she was just a grey shadow caught in it alone.

She bought a pack of cigarettes from Luke and went out again, a kerchief around her head, the pneumatic thing above the door hissing behind her. For a long time, always in fact, she had been at the centre of whatever gang was the one: in the second grade the one that walked home up Jewett Street together, and in the sixth grade the one that went bicycling as far away as the quarry and the Rentschler estate and played touch football Saturday afternoons, and in the ninth grade the one that went roller-skating at Candlebridge Park with the tenth-grade boys, and in the eleventh grade the one that held parties lasting past midnight and that on Sundays drove in caravans as far as Philadelphia and back. And all the while there had been a succession of boy friends, first Jack Stephens and Fritz March in their class and then boys a grade ahead and then Barrel Lord, who was a senior when they were sophomores and whose name was in the newspapers all football season, and then this last summer someone out of the school altogether, a man she met while working as a waitress in the city of Alton. So this year her weekends were taken up, and the party gang carried on as if she had never existed, and nobody saw her much except in school and when she stopped by in Luke's to buy a pack of cigarettes. Her silhouette against the big window had looked wan, her head hooded, her face nibbled by light, her fingers fiddling on the veined counter with her coins. He yearned to reach out, to comfort her, but he was wedged deep in the shrill booths, between the jingling guts of the pin-ball machine and the hillbilly joy of the jukebox. The impulse left him with a disagreeable feeling. He had loved her too long to want to pity her; it endangered the investment of worship on which he had not yet realized any return.

The two hours of the school afternoon held Latin and a study hall. In study hall, while the five people at the table with him played tic-tac-toe and sucked cough drops and yawned, he did all his homework for the next day. He prepared thirty lines of Virgil, Aeneas in the Underworld. The study hall was a huge low room in the basement of the building; its coziness crept into Tartarus. On the other side of the fudge-coloured wall the circular saw in the woodworking shop whined and gasped and then whined again; it bit off pieces of wood with a rising, somehow terrorized inflection – bzzzzzup! He solved ten problems in trigonometry. His mind cut neatly through their knots and separated them, neat stiff squares of answer, one by one from the long but finite plank of problems that connected Plane Geometry with Solid. Lastly, as the snow on a ragged slant drifted down into the cement pits outside the steel-mullioned windows, he read a short story by Edgar Allan Poe. He closed the book softly on the pleasing sonority of its final note of horror, gazed at the red, wet, menthol-scented inner membrane of Judy Whipple's yawn, rimmed with flaking pink lipstick, and yielded his conscience to the snug sense of his work done, of the snow falling, of the warm minutes that walked through their shelter so slowly. The perforated acoustic tiling above his head seemed the lining of a long tube that would go all the way: high school merging into college, college into graduate school, graduate school into teaching at a college – section man, assistant, associate, *full* professor, possessor of a dozen languages and a thousand books, a man brilliant in his forties, wise in his fifties, renowned in his sixties, revered in his seventies, and then retired, sitting in the study lined with acoustical books until the time came for the last transition from silence to silence, and he would die, like Tennyson, with a copy of *Cymbeline* beside him on the moon-drenched bed.

After school he had to go to Room 101 and cut a sports cartoon into a stencil for the school paper. He liked the building best when it was nearly empty, when the casual residents – the rural commuters, the do-nothings, the trash – had cleared out. Then the janitors went down the halls sowing seeds of red wax and making an immaculate harvest with broad brooms, gathering all the fluff and hairpins and wrappers and powder that the animals had dropped that day. The basketball team thumped in the hollow gymnasium; the cheerleaders rehearsed behind drawn curtains on the stage. In Room 101 two empty-headed typists with stripes bleached into their hair banged away between giggles and mistakes. At her desk Mrs Gregory, the faculty sponsor, wearily passed her pencil through misspelled news copy on tablet paper. William took the shadow box from the top of the filing cabinet and the styluses and little square plastic shading screens from their drawer and the stencil from the closet where the typed stencils hung, like fragile scarves, on hooks. B-BALLERS BOW, 57–42, was the headline. He drew a tall b-baller bowing to a stumpy pagan idol, labelled 'W' for victorious Weiserton High, and traced it in the soft blue wax with the fine loop stylus. His careful breath grazed his knuckles. His eyebrows frowned while his heart bobbed happily on the giddy prattle of the typists. The shadow box was simply a black frame holding a pane of glass and lifted at one end by two legs so the light bulb, fitted in a tin tray, could slide under; it was like a primitive lean-to sheltering a fire. As he worked, his eyes smarting, he mixed himself up with the light bulb, felt himself burning under a slanting roof upon which a huge hand scratched. The glass grew hot; the danger in the job was pulling the softened wax with your damp hand, distorting or tearing the typed letters. Sometimes the centre of an *o* stuck to your skin like a bit of blue confetti. But he was expert and cautious. He returned the things to their places feeling airily tall, heightened by Mrs Gregory's appreciation, which she expressed by keeping her back turned, in effect stating that other staff members were undependable but William did not need to be watched.

In the hall outside Room 101 only the shouts of a basketball scrimmage reverberated; the chant of the cheerleaders had been silenced. Though he had done everything, he felt reluctant to leave. Neither of his parents – both worked – would be home yet, and this building was as much his home. He knew all its nooks. On the second floor of the annex, beyond the art room, there was a strange, narrow boys' lavatory that no one ever seemed to use. It was here one time that Barry Kruppman tried to hypnotize him and cure his stuttering. Kruppman's voice purred and his irises turned tiny in the bulging whites and for a moment William felt himself lean backward involuntarily, but he was distracted by the bits of bloodshot pink in the corners of these portentous eyes; the folly of giving up his will to an intellectual inferior occurred to him; he refused to let go and go under, and perhaps therefore his stuttering had continued.

The frosted window at the end of the long room cast a watery light on the green floor and made the porcelain urinals shine like slices of moon. The semi-opacity of this window gave the room's air of secrecy great density. William washed his hands with exaggerated care, enjoying the lavish amount of powdered soap provided for him in this castle. He studied his face in the mirror, making infinitesimal adjustments to attain the absolutely most flattering angle, and then put his hands below his throat to get their strong, long-fingered beauty into the picture. As he walked toward the door he sang, closing his eyes and gasping as if he were a real Negro whose entire career depended upon this recording:

> 'Who – told me so, dilly dilly,
> Who told me soho?
> *Aii* told myself, dilly dilly,
> I told: me so.'

When he emerged into the hall it was not empty: one girl walked down its varnished perspective toward him, Mary Landis, a scarf on her head and books in her arms. Her locker was up here, on the second floor of the annex. His own was in the annex basement. A ticking sensation that existed neither in the medium of sound nor of light crowded against his throat. She flipped the scarf back from her hair and in a conversational voice that carried well down the clean planes of the hall said, 'Hi, Billy.' The name came from way back, when they were both children, and made him feel small but audacious.

'Hi. How are you?'

'Fine.' Her smile broadened out from the *F* of this word.

What was so funny? Was she really, as it seemed, pleased to see him! 'Du-did you just get through cheer-cheer-cheer-leading?'

'Yes. Thank God. *Oh* she's so awful. She makes us do the same stupid locomotives for every cheer; I told her, no wonder nobody cheers any more.'

'This is M-M-Miss Potter?' He blushed, feeling that he made an ugly face in getting past the *M*. When he got caught in the middle of a sentence the constriction was somehow worse. He admired the way words poured up her throat, distinct and petulant.

'Yes, Potbottom Potter,' she said, 'she's just aching for a man and takes it out on us. I wish she would get one. Honestly, Billy, I have half a mind to quit. I'll be so glad when June comes, I'll never set foot in this idiotic building again.'

Her lips, pale with the lipstick worn off, crinkled bitterly. Her face, foreshortened from the height of his eyes, looked cross as a cat's. It a little shocked him that poor Miss Potter and this kind, warm school stirred her to what he had to take as actual anger; this grittiness in her was the first abrasive texture he had struck today. Couldn't she see around teachers, into their fatigue, their poverty, their fear? It had been so long since he had spoken to her, he wasn't sure how coarse she had become. 'Don't quit,' he brought out of his mouth at last. 'It'd be n-n-n-nuh – it'd be nothing without you.'

He pushed open the door at the end of the hall for her and as she passed under his arm she looked up and said, 'Why, aren't you sweet?'

The stairwell, all asphalt and iron, smelled of galoshes. It felt more secret than the hall, more specially theirs; there was something magical in its shifting multiplicity of planes as they descended that lifted the spell on his tongue, so that words came as quickly as his feet pattered on the steps.

'No I mean it,' he said, 'you're really a beautiful cheerleader. But then you're beautiful period.'

'I've skinny legs.'

'Who told you that?'

'Somebody.'

'Well *he* wasn't very sweet.'

'No.'

'Why do you hate this poor old school?'

'Now, Billy. You know you don't care about this junky place any more than I do.'

'I love it. It breaks my heart to hear you say you want to get out, because then I'll never see you again.'

'You don't care, do you?'

'Why sure I care; you *know*' – their feet stopped; they had reached bottom, the first-floor landing, two brass-barred doors and a grimy radiator –'I've always li-loved you.'

'You don't mean that.'

'I do too. It's ridiculous but there it is. I wanted to tell you today and now I have.'

He expected her to laugh and go out the door, but instead she showed an unforeseen willingness to discuss this awkward matter. He should have realized before this that women enjoy being talked to. 'It's a very silly thing to say,' she asserted tentatively.

'I don't see why,' he said, fairly bold now that he couldn't seem more ridiculous, and yet picking his words with a certain strategic care. 'It's not *that* silly to love somebody, I mean what the hell. Probably what's silly is not to do anything about it for umpteen years but then I never had an opportunity, I thought.'

He set his books down on the radiator and she set hers down beside his. 'What kind of opportunity were you waiting for?'

'Well, see, that's it; I didn't know.' He wished, in a way, she would go out the door. But she had propped herself against the wall and plainly awaited more talking. 'Yuh-you were such a queen and I was such a nothing and I just didn't really want to presume.' It wasn't very interesting; it puzzled him that she seemed to be interested. Her face had grown quite stern, the mouth very small and thoughtful, and he made a gesture with his hands intended to release her from the bother of thinking about it; after all, it was just a disposition of his heart, nothing permanent or expensive – maybe it was just his mother's idea anyway. Half in impatience to close the account, he asked, 'Will you marry me?'

'You don't want to marry me,' she said. 'You're going to go on and be a great man.'

He blushed in pleasure; is this how she saw him, is this how they all saw him; as worthless now, but in time a great man? Had his hopes always been on view? He dissembled, saying, 'No I'm not. But anyway, you're great now. You're so pretty, Mary.'

'Oh, Billy,' she said, 'if you were me for just one day you'd hate it.'

She said this rather blankly, watching his eyes; he wished her voice had shown more misery. In his world of closed surfaces a panel, carelessly pushed, had opened, and he hung in this openness paralysed, unable to think what to say. Nothing he could think of quite fit the abruptly immense contest. The radiator cleared its throat; its heat made, in the intimate volume just this side of the doors on whose windows the snow beat limply, a provocative snugness; he supposed he should try, and stepped forward, his hands lifting toward her shoulders. Mary sidestepped between him and the radiator and put the scarf back on. She lifted the cloth like a broad plaid halo above her head and then wrapped it around her chin and knotted it so she looked, in her red galoshes and bulky coat, like a peasant woman in a movie of Europe. With her thick hair swathed, her face seemed pale and chunky, and when she recradled the books in her arms her back bent humbly under the point of the kerchief. 'It's too hot in here,' she said. 'I've got to wait for somebody.' The disconnectedness of the two statements seemed natural in the fragmented atmosphere his stops and starts had produced. She bucked the brass bar with her shoulder and the door slammed open; he followed her into the weather.

'For the person who thinks your legs are too skinny?'

'Uh-huh.' As she looked up at him, a snowflake caught on the lashes of one eye. She jerkily rubbed that cheek on the shoulder of her coat and stamped a foot, splashing slush. Cold water gathered on the back of his thin shirt. He put his hands in his pockets and pressed his arms against his sides to keep from shivering.

'Thuh-then you wo-won't marry me?' His wise instinct told him the only way back was by going forward, through absurdity.

'We don't know each other,' she said.

'My God,' he said. 'Why not? I've known you since I was two.'

'What do you know about me?'

This awful seriousness of hers; he must dissolve it. 'That you're not a virgin.' But instead of making her laugh this made her face go dead and turned it away. Like beginning to kiss her, it was a mistake; in part, he felt grateful for his mistakes. They were like loyal friends who are nevertheless embarrassing. 'What do you know about *me*?' he asked, setting himself up for a finishing insult but dreading it. He hated the stiff feel of his smile between his cheeks; glimpsed, as if the snow were a mirror, how hateful he looked.

'That you're basically very nice.'

Her returning good for evil blinded him to his physical discomfort, set him burning with regret. 'Listen,' he said, 'I did love you. Let's at least get that straight.'

'You never loved anybody,' she said. 'You don't know what it is.'

'O.K.,' he said. 'Pardon me.'

'You better wait in the school,' he called to her. 'He's-eez-eez going to be a long time.'

She didn't answer and walked a little distance, toeing out in the childish Dutch way common to the women in this county, along the slack cable that divided the parking lot from the softball field. One bicycle, rusted as if it has been there for years, leaned in the rack, each of its fenders supporting an airy crescent of white.

The warmth inside the door felt heavy. William picked up his books and ran his pencil along the black ribs of the radiator before going down the stairs to his locker in the annex basement. The shadows were thick at the foot of the steps; suddenly it felt late, he must hurry and get home. He was seized by the irrational fear that they were going to lock him in. The cloistered odours of paper, sweat, and, from the woodshop at the far end of the basement hall, sawdust no longer flattered him. The tall green double lockers appeared to study him critically through the three air slits near their tops. When he opened his locker, and put his books on his shelf, below Marvin Wolf's, and removed his coat from his hook, his self seemed to crawl into the long dark space thus made vacant, the ugly, humiliated, educable self. In answer to a flick of his great hand the steel door weightlessly floated shut and through the length of his body he felt so clean and free he smiled. Between now and the happy future predicted for him he had nothing, almost literally nothing, to do.

The Happiest I've Been

Neil Hovey came for me wearing a good suit. He parked his father's blue Chrysler on the dirt ramp by our barn and got out and stood by the open car door in a double-breasted tan gabardine suit, his hands in his pockets and his hair combed with water, squinting up at a lightning-rod an old hurricane had knocked crooked.

We were driving to Chicago, so I had dressed in worn-out slacks and an outgrown corduroy shirt. But Neil was the friend I had always been most relaxed with, so I wasn't very disturbed. My parents and I walked out from the house, across the low stretch of lawn that was mostly mud after the thaw that had come on Christmas Day, and my grandmother, though I had kissed her good-bye inside the house, came out on to the porch, stooped and rather angry-looking, her head haloed by wild old woman's white hair and the hand more severely afflicted by arthritis waggling at her breast in a worried way. It was growing dark and my grandfather had gone to bed. 'Nev-er trust the man who wears the red necktie and parts his hair in the middle,' had been his final advice to me.

We had expected Neil since middle afternoon. Nineteen, almost twenty, I was a college sophomore home on vacation; that fall I had met in a fine-arts course a girl I had fallen in love with, and she had invited me to the New Year's party her parents always gave and to stay at her house a few nights. She lived in Chicago and so did Neil now, though he had gone to our high school. His father did something – sell steel was my impression, a huge man opening a briefcase and saying 'The I-beams are very good this year' – that required him to be always on the move, so that at about thirteen Neil had been boarded with Mrs Hovey's parents, the Lancasters. They had lived in Olinger since the town was incorporated. Indeed, old Jesse Lancaster, whose sick larynx whistled when he breathed to us boys his shocking and uproarious thoughts on the girls that walked past his porch all day long, had twice been burgess. Meanwhile Neil's father got a stationary job, but he let Neil stay to graduate; after the night he graduated, Neil drove throughout the next day to join his parents.

From Chicago to this part of Pennsylvania was seventeen hours. In the twenty months he had been gone Neil had come east fairly often; he loved driving and Olinger was the one thing he had that was close to a childhood home. In Chicago he was working in a garage and getting his teeth straightened by the Army so they could draft him. Korea was on. He had to go back, and I wanted to go, so it was a happy arrangement. 'You're all dressed up,' I accused him immediately.

'I've been saying good-bye.' The knot of his necktie was loose and the corners of his mouth were rubbed with pink. Years later my mother recalled how that evening his breath to her stank so strongly of beer she was frightened to let me go with him. '*Your* grandfather always thought *his* grandfather was a very dubious character,' she said then.

My father and Neil put my suitcases into the trunk; they contained all the clothes I had brought, for the girl and I were going to go back to college on the train together, and I would not see my home again until spring.

'Well, good-bye, boys,' my mother said. 'I think you're both very brave.' In regard to me she meant the girl as much as the roads.

'Don't you worry, Mrs Nordholm,' Neil told her quickly. 'He'll be safer than in his bed. I bet he sleeps from here to Indiana.' He looked at me with an irritating imitation of her own fond gaze. When they shook hands good-bye it was with an equality established on the base of my helplessness. His being so slick startled me, but then you can have a friend for years and never see how he operates with adults.

I embraced my mother and over her shoulder with the camera of my head tried to take a snapshot I could keep of the house, the woods behind it and the sunset behind them, the bench beneath the walnut tree where my grandfather cut apples into skinless bits and fed them to himself, and the ruts in the soft lawn the bakery truck had made that morning.

We started down the half-mile of dirt road to the highway that, one way, went through Olinger to the city of Alton and, the other way, led through farmland to the Turnpike. It was luxurious, after the stress of farewell, to two-finger a cigarette out of the pack in my shirt pocket. My family knew I smoked but I didn't do it in front of them; we were all too sensitive to bear the awkwardness. I lit mine and held the match for Hovey. It was a relaxed friendship. We were about the same height and had the same degree of athletic incompetence and the same curious lack of whatever force it was that aroused loyalty and compliance in beautiful girls. There was his bad teeth and my skin allergy; these were being remedied now, when they mattered less. But it seemed to me the most important thing – about both our friendship and our failures to become, for all the love we felt for women, actual lovers – was that he and I lived with grandparents. This improved both our backward and forward vistas; we knew about the bedside commodes and midnight coughing fits that awaited most men, and we had a sense of childhoods before 1900, when the farmer ruled the land and America faced west. We had gained a humane dimension that made us gentle and humorous among peers but diffident at dances and hesitant in cars. Girls hate boy's doubts: they amount to insults. Gentleness is for married women to appreciate. (This is my thinking then.) A girl who has received out of nowhere a gift worth all Africa's ivory and Asia's gold wants more than just humanity to bestow it on.

Coming on to the highway, Neil turned right towards Olinger instead of left towards the Turnpike. My reaction was to twist and assure myself through the rear window that, though a pink triangle of sandstone stared through the bare treetops, nobody at my house could possibly see.

When he was again in third gear, Neil asked, 'Are you in a hurry?'

'No. Not especially.'

'Schuman's having his New Year's party two days early so we can go. I thought we'd go for a couple of hours and miss the Friday-night stuff on the Pike.' His mouth moved and closed carefully over the dull, silver, painful braces.

'Sure,' I said. 'I don't care.' In everything that followed there was sensation of my being picked up and carried.

It was four miles from the farm to Olinger; we entered by Buchanan Road, driving past the tall white brick house I had lived in until I was fifteen. My grandfather had bought it before I was born and his stocks became bad, which had happened in the same year. The new owners had strung coloured bulbs all along the front door frame and the edges of the porch roof. Downtown the cardboard Santa Claus still nodded in the drugstore window but the loudspeaker on the undertaker's lawn had stopped broadcasting carols. It was quite dark now, so the arches of red and green lights above Grand Avenue seemed miracles of lift: in daylight you saw the bulbs were just hung from a straight cable by cords of different lengths. Larry Schuman lived on the other side of town, the newer side. Lights ran all the way up the front edges of his house and across the rain gutter. The next-door neighbour had a plywood reindeer-and-sleigh floodlit on his front lawn and a snowman of papier mâché leaning tipsily (his eyes were X's) against the corner of his house. No real snow had fallen yet that winter. The air this evening, though, hinted that harder weather was coming.

The Schumans' living-room felt warm. In one corner a blue spruce drenched with tinsel reached to the ceiling; around its pot surged a drift of wrapping paper and ribbon and boxes, a few still containing presents, gloves and diaries and other small properties that hadn't yet been absorbed into the main-stream of affluence. The ornamental balls were big as base-balls and all either crimson or indigo; the tree was so well dressed I felt self-conscious in the same room with it, without a coat or tie and wearing an old green shirt too short in the sleeves. Everyone else was dressed for a party. Then Mr Schuman stamped in comfortingly, crushing us all into one underneath his welcome, Neil and I and the three other boys who had showed up so far. He was dressed to go out on the town, in a vanilla topcoat and silvery silk muffler, smoking a cigar with the band still on. You could see in Mr Schuman where Larry got the red hair and white eyelashes and the self-confidence, but what in the son was smirking and pushy was in the father shrewd and masterful. What the one used to make you nervous the other used to put you at ease. While Mr was jollying us, Zoe Loessner, Larry's probable fiancée and the only other girl at the party so far, was talking nicely to Mrs, nodding with her entire neck and fingering her Kresge pearls and blowing cigarette smoke through the corners of her mouth, to keep it away from the middle-aged woman's face. Each time Zoe spat out a plume, the shelf of honey hair overhanging her temple bobbed. Mrs Schuman beamed serenely above her mink coat and rhinestone pocketbook. It was odd to see her dressed in the trappings of the prosperity that usually supported her good nature invisibly, like a firm mattress under a bright homely quilt. Everybody loved her. She was a prime product of the county, a Pennsylvania-Dutch woman with sons, who loved feeding her sons and who imagined that the entire world, like her life, was going well. I never saw her not smile, except at her husband. At last she moved him into the outdoors. He turned at the threshold and did a trick with his knees and called in to us, 'Be good and if you can't be good, be careful.'

With them out of the way, the next item was getting liquor. It was a familiar business. Did anybody have a forged driver's licence? If not, who would dare to forge theirs? Larry could provide India ink. Then again, Larry's older brother Dale might be home and would go if it didn't take too much time. However, on weekends he often went straight from work to his fiancée's apartment and stayed until Sunday. If worse came to worse, Larry knew an illegal place in Alton, but they really soaked you. The problem was solved strangely. More people were arriving all the time and one of them, Cookie Behn, who had been held back one year and hence was deposited in our grade, announced that last November he had become in honest fact twenty-one. I at least gave Cookie my share of the money feeling a little queasy, vice had become so handy.

The party was the party I had been going to all my life, beginning with Ann Mahlon's first Hallowe'en party, that I attended as a hot, lumbering, breathless, and blind Donald Duck. My mother had made the costume, and the eyes kept slipping, and were farther apart than my eyes, so that even when the clouds of gauze parted, it was to reveal the frustrating depthless world seen with one eye. Ann, who because her mother loved her so much as a child had remained somewhat childish, and I and another boy and girl who were not involved in any romantic crisis, went down into Schuman's basement to play circular ping-pong. Armed with paddles, we stood each at a side of the table and when the ball was stroked ran around it counter-clockwise, slapping the ball and screaming. To run better the girls took off their heels and ruined their stockings on the cement floor. Their faces and arms and shoulder sections became flushed, and when a girl lunged forwards towards the net the stiff neckline of her semi-formal dress dropped away and the white arcs of her brassière could be glimpsed cupping fat, and when she reached high her shaved armpit gleamed like a bit of chicken skin. An ear-ring of Ann's flew off and the two connected rhinestones skidded to lie near the wall, among the Schumans' power mower and badminton poles and empty bronze motor-oil cans twice punctured by triangles. All these images were immediately lost in the whirl of our running; we were dizzy before we stopped. Ann leaned on me getting back into her shoes.

When we pushed it open the door leading down into the cellar banged against the newel post of the carpeted stairs going to the second floor; a third of the way up these, a couple sat discussing. The girl, Jacky Iselin, cried without emotion – the tears and nothing else, like water flowing over wood. Some people were in the kitchen mixing drinks and making noise. In the living-room others danced to records: 78s then, stiff discs stacked in a ponderous leaning cylinder on the spindle of the Schumans' console. Every three minutes with a click and a crash another dropped and the mood abruptly changed. One moment it would be 'Stay As Sweet As You Are': Clarence Lang with the absolute expression of an idiot standing and rocking monotonously with June Kaufmann's boneless sad brown hand trapped in his and their faces, staring in the same direction, pasted together like the facets of an idol. The music stopped; when they parted, a big squarish dark patch stained the cheek of each. Then the next moment it would be Goodman's 'Loch Lomond' or 'Cherokee' and nobody but Margaret Lento wanted to jitterbug. Mad, she danced by herself, swinging her head recklessly and snapping her backside; a corner of her skirt flipped a Christmas ball on to the rug, where it collapsed into a hundred convex reflectors. Female shoes were scattered in innocent pairs about the room. Some were flats, resting under the sofa shyly toed in; others were high heels lying cock-eyed, the spike of one thrust into its mate. Sitting alone and ignored in a great armchair, I experienced within a warm keen dishevelment, as if there were real tears in my eyes. Had things been less unchanged they would have seemed less tragic. But the girls who had stepped out of these shoes were with few exceptions the ones who had attended my life's party. The alterations were so small: a haircut, an engagement ring, a franker plumpness. While they wheeled above me I sometimes caught from their faces an unfamiliar glint, off of a hardness I did not remember, as if beneath their skins these girls were growing more dense. The brutality added to the features of the boys I knew seemed a more willed effect, more desired and so less grievous. Considering that there was a war, surprisingly many were present, 4-F or at college or simply waiting to be called. Shortly before midnight the door rattled and there, under the porch-light, looking forlorn and chilled in their brief athletic jackets, stood three members of the class ahead of ours who in the old days always tried to crash Schuman's parties. At Olinger High they had been sports stars, and they still stood with that well-coordinated looseness, a look of dangling from strings. The three of them had enrolled together at Melanchthon, a small Lutheran college on the edge of Alton, and in this season played on the Melanchthon basketball team. That is, two did; the third hadn't been good enough. Schuman, out of cowardice more than mercy, let them in, and they hid without hesitation in the basement, and didn't bother us, having brought their own bottle.

There was one novel awkwardness. Darryl Bechtel had married Emmy Johnson and the couple came. Darryl had worked in his father's greenhouse and was considered dull; it was Emmy that we knew. At first no one danced with her, and Darryl didn't know how, but then Schuman, perhaps as host, dared. Others followed, but Schuman had her in his arms most often, and at midnight, when we were pretending the new year began, he kissed her; a wave of kissing swept the room now, and everyone struggled to kiss Emmy. Even I did. There was something about her being married that made it extraordinary. Her cheeks in flame, she kept glancing around for rescue, but Darryl, embarrassed to see his wife dance, had gone into old man Schuman's den, where Neil sat brooding, sunk in mysterious sorrow.

When the kissing subsided and Darryl emerged, I went in to see Neil. He was holding his face in his hands and tapping his foot to a record playing on Mr Schuman's private phonograph: Krupa's 'Dark Eyes'. The arrangement was droning and circular and Neil had kept the record going for hours. He loved saxophones; I guess all of us children of that Depression vintage did. I asked him, 'Do you think the traffic on the Turnpike has died down by now?'

He took down the tall glass off the cabinet beside him and took a convincing swallow. His face from the side seemed lean and somewhat blue. 'Maybe,' he said, staring at the ice cubes submerged in the ochre liquid. 'The girl in Chicago's expecting you?'

'Well, yeah, but we can call and let her know, once *we* know.'

'You think she'll spoil?'

'How do you mean?'

'I mean, won't you be seeing her all the time after we get there? Aren't you going to marry her?'

'I have no idea. I might.'

'Well then: you'll have the rest of Kingdom Come to see her.' He looked directly at me, and it was plain in the blur of his eyes that he was sick-drunk. 'The trouble with you guys that have all the luck,' he said slowly, 'is that you don't give a fuck about us that don't have any.' Such melo-dramatic rudeness coming from Neil surprised me, as had his blarney with my mother hours before. In trying to evade his wounded stare, I discovered there was another person in the room: a girl sitting with her shoes on, reading *Holiday*. Though she held the magazine in front of her face I knew from her clothes and her unfamiliar legs that she was the gir¹ · friend Margaret Lento had brought. Margaret didn't come from Olinger but from Riverside, a section of Alton, not a suburb. She had met Larry Schuman at a summer job in a restaurant and for the rest of high school they had more or less gone together. Since then, though, it had dawned on Mr and Mrs Schuman that even in a democracy distinctions exist, probably welcome news to Larry. In the cruellest and most stretched-out way he could manage he had been breaking off with her throughout the year now nearly ended. I had been surprised to find her at this party. Obviously she had felt shaky about attending and had brought the friend as the only kind of protection she could afford. The other girl was acting just like a hired guard.

There being no answer to Neil, I went into the living-room, where

Margaret, insanely drunk, was throwing herself around as if wanting to break a bone. Somewhat in time to the music she would run a few steps, then snap her body like a whip, her chin striking her chest and her hands flying backward, fingers fanned, as her shoulders pitched forward. In her state her body was childishly plastic; unharmed, she would bounce back from this jolt and begin to clap and kick and hum. Schuman stayed away from her. Margaret was small, not more than 5 ft 3 in., with the smallness ripeness comes to early. She had bleached a section of her black hair platinum, cropped her head all over, and trained the stubble into short hyacinthine curls like those on antique statues of boys. Her face seemed quite coarse from the front, so her profile was classical unexpectedly. She might have been Portia. When she was not putting on her savage pointless dance she was in the bathroom being sick. The pity and the vulgarity of her exhibition made everyone who was sober uncomfortable; our common guilt in witnessing this girl's rites brought us so close together in that room that it seemed never, not in all time, could we be parted. I myself was perfectly sober. I had the impression then that people only drank to stop being unhappy and I nearly always felt at least fairly happy.

Luckily, Margaret was in a sick phase around one o'clock, when the elder Schumans came home. They looked in at us briefly. It was a pleasant joke to see in their smiles that, however corrupt and unwinking we felt, to them we looked young and sleepy: Larry's friends. Things quieted after they went up the stairs. In half an hour people began coming out of the kitchen balancing cups of coffee. By two o'clock four girls stood in aprons at Mrs Schuman's sink, and others were padding back and forth carrying glasses and ashtrays. Another blameless racket pierced the clatter in the kitchen. Out on the cold grass the three Melanchthon athletes had set up the badminton net and in the faint glow given off by the house were playing. The bird, ascending and descending through uneven bars of light, glimmered like a firefly. Now that the party was dying Neil's apathy seemed deliberately exasperating, even vindictive. For at least another hour he persisted in hearing 'Dark Eyes' over and over again, holding his head and tapping his foot. The entire scene in the den had developed a fixity that was uncanny; the girl remained in the chair and read magazines, *Holiday* and *Esquire*, one after another. In the meantime, cars came and went and raced their motors out front; Schuman took Ann Mahlon off and didn't come back; and the athletes carried the neighbour's artificial snowman into the centre of the street and disappeared. Somehow in the arrangements shuffled together at the end, Neil had contracted to drive Margaret and the other girl home. Margaret convalesced in the downstairs

bathroom for most of that hour. I unlocked a little glass bookcase orna-
menting a desk in the dark dining-room and removed a volume of Thack-
eray's Works. It turned out to be Volume II of *Henry Esmond*. I began it,
rather than break another book out of the set, which had been squeezed
in there so long the bindings had sort of interpenetrated.

Henry was going off to war again when Neil appeared in the archway
and said, 'O.K., Norseman. Let's go to Chicago.' 'Norseman' was a vari-
ant of my name he used only when feeling special affection.

We turned off all the lamps and left the hall bulb burning against
Larry's return. Margaret Lento seemed chastened. Neil gave her his arm
and led her into the back seat of his father's car; I stood aside to let the
other girl get in with her, but Neil indicated that I should. I supposed he
realized this left only the mute den-girl to go up front with him. She sat
well over on her side, was all I noticed. Neil backed into the street and
with unusual care steered past the snowman. Our headlights made vivid
the fact that the snowman's back was a hollow right-angled gash; he had
been built up against the corner of a house.

From Olinger, Riverside was diagonally across Alton. The city was
sleeping as we drove through it. Most of the stoplights were blinking
green. Among cities Alton had a bad reputation; its graft and gambling
and easy juries and bawdy houses were supposedly notorious throughout
the Middle Atlantic states. But to me it always presented an innocent face;
row after row of houses built of a local dusty-red brick the shade of
flowerpots, each house fortified with a tiny, intimate, balustraded porch,
and nothing but the wealth of movie houses and beer signs along its main
street to suggest that its citizens loved pleasure more than the run of
mankind. Indeed, as we moved at moderate speed down these hushed
streets bordered with parked cars, a limestone church bulking at every
corner and the hooded street lamps keeping watch from above, Alton
seemed less the ultimate centre of an urban region than itself a suburb of
some vast mythical metropolis, like Pandemonium or Paradise. I was
conscious of evergreen wreaths on door after door and of fanlights of
stained glass in which the house number was embedded. I was also conscious that every block was one block farther from the Turnpike.

Riverside, fitted into the bends of the Schuylkill, was not so regularly
laid out. Margaret's house was one of a short row, composition-shingled,
which we approached from the rear, down a tiny cement alley speckled
with drains. The porches were a few inches higher than the alley. Margaret
asked us if we wanted to come in for a cup of coffee, since we were going

to Chicago; Neil accepted by getting out of the car and slamming his door. The noise filled the alley, alarming me. I wondered at the easy social life that evidently existed among my friends at three-thirty in the morning. Margaret did, however, lead us in stealthily, and she turned on only the kitchen switch. The kitchen was divided from the living-room by a large sofa, which faced into littered gloom where distant light from beyond the alley spilled over the window sill and across the spines of a radiator. In one corner the glass of a television set showed; the screen would seem absurdly small now, but then it seemed disproportionately elegant. The shabbiness everywhere would not have struck me so definitely if I hadn't just come from Schuman's place. Neil and the other girl sat on the sofa: Margaret held a match to a gas burner and, as the blue flame licked an old kettle, doled instant coffee into four flowered cups.

Some man who had once lived in this house had built by the kitchen's one window a breakfast nook, nothing more than a booth, a table between two high-backed benches. I sat in it and read all the words I could see: 'Salt', 'Pepper', 'Have Some LUMPS', 'December', 'Mohn's Milk Inc. – A Very Merry Christmas and Joyous New Year – Mohn's Milk is *Safe* Milk – "Mommy, Make It Mohn's!" ', 'Matches', 'Hotpoint', 'PRESS', 'Magee Stove FEDERAL & Furnace Corp.', 'God Is In This House', 'Ave Maria Gratia Plena', 'SHREDDED WHEAT Benefits Exciting New Pattern KUNGSHOLM'. After serving the two on the sofa, Margaret came to me with coffee and sat down opposite me in the booth. Fatigue had raised two blue welts beneath her eyes.

'Well,' I asked her, 'did you have a good time?'

She smiled and glanced down and made the small sound 'Ch', vestigial of 'Jesus'. With absent-minded delicacy she stirred her coffee, lifting and replacing the spoon without a ripple.

'Rather odd at the end,' I said, 'not even the host there.'

'He took Ann Mahlon home.'

'I know.' I was surprised that she knew, having been sick in the bathroom for that hour.

'You sound jealous,' she added.

'Who does? I do? I don't.'

'You like her, John, don't you?' Her using my first name and the quality of the question did not, although discounting parties we had just met, seem forward, considering the hour and that she had brought me coffee. There is a very little farther to go with a girl who has brought you coffee.

'Oh, I like everybody,' I told her, 'and the longer I've known them the more I like them, because the more they're me. The only people I like

84

better are ones I've just met. Now Ann Mahlon I've known since kindergarten. Every day her mother used to bring her to the edge of the schoolyard for months after all the other mothers had stopped.' I wanted to cut a figure in Margaret's eyes, but they were too dark. Stoically she had got on top of her weariness, but it was growing bigger under her.

'Did you like her then?'

'I felt sorry for her being embarrassed by her mother.'

She asked me, 'What was Larry like when he was little?'

'Oh, bright. Kind of mean.'

'Was he mean?'

'I'd say so. Yes. In some grade or other he and I began to play chess together. I always won until secretly he took lessons from a man his parents knew and read strategy books.'

Margaret laughed, genuinely pleased. 'Then did he win?'

'Once. After that I really tried, and after *that* he decided chess was kid stuff. Besides, I was used up. He'd have these runs on people where you'd be down at his house every afternoon, then in a couple months he'd get a new pet and that'd be that.'

'He's funny,' she said. 'He has a kind of cold mind. He decides on what he wants, then he does what he has to do, you know, and nothing anybody says can change him.'

'He does tend to get what he wants,' I admitted guardedly, realizing that to her this meant her. Poor bruised little girl, in her mind he was all the time cleaving with rare cunning through his parent's objections straight to her.

My coffee was nearly gone, so I glanced towards the sofa in the other room. Neil and the girl had sunk out of sight behind its back. Before this it had honestly not occurred to me that they had a relationship, but now that I saw, it seemed plausible and, at this time of night, good news, though it meant we would not be going to Chicago yet.

So I talked to Margaret about Larry, and she responded, showing really quite an acute sense of him. To me, considering so seriously the personality of a childhood friend, as if overnight he had become a factor in the world, seemed absurd; I couldn't deeply believe that even in her world he mattered much. Larry Schuman, in little more than a year, had become nothing to me. The important thing, rather than the subject, was the conversation itself, the quick agreements, the slow nods, the weave of different memories; it was like one of those Panama baskets shaped underwater around a worthless stone.

She offered me more coffee. When she returned with it, she sat down, not opposite, but beside me, lifting me to such a pitch of gratitude and affection the only way I could think to express it was by *not* kissing her, as if a kiss were another piece of abuse women suffered. She said, 'Cold. Cheap bastard turns the thermostat down to sixty,' meaning her father. She drew my arm around her shoulders and folded my hand around her bare forearm to warm it. The back of my thumb fitted against the curve of one breast. Her head went into the hollow where my arm and chest joined; she was terribly small, measured against your own body. Perhaps she weighed a hundred pounds. Her lids lowered and I kissed her two beautiful eyebrows and then the spaces of skin between the rough curls, some black and some bleached, that fringed her forehead. Other than this I tried to keep as still as a bed would be. It *had* grown cold. A shiver starting on the side away from her would twitch my shoulders when I tried to repress it; she would frown and unconsciously draw my arm tighter. No one had switched the kitchen light off. On Margaret's foreshortened upper lip there seemed to be two pencil marks; the length of wrist my badly fitting sleeve exposed looked pale and naked against the spiralling down of the smaller arm held beneath it.

Outside on the street the house faced there was no motion. Only once did a car go by: around five o'clock, with twin mufflers, the radio on and a boy yelling. Neil and the girl murmured together incessantly; some of what they said I could overhear.

'No. Which?' she asked.

'I don't care.'

'Wouldn't you want a boy?'

'I'd be happy whatever I got.'

'I know, but which would you *rather* have? Don't men want boys?'

'I don't care. You.'

Somewhat later, Mohn's truck passed on the other side of the street. The milkman, well bundled, sat behind headlights in a warm orange volume the size of a phone booth, steering one-handed and smoking a cigar that he set on the edge of the dashboard when, his wire carrier vibrant, he ran out of the truck with bottles. His passing led Neil to decide the time had come. Margaret woke up frightened of her father; we hissed our farewells and thanks to her quickly. Neil dropped the other girl off at her house a few blocks away; he knew where it was. Sometime during that night I must have seen this girl's face, but I have no memory of it. She is always behind a magazine or in the dark or with her back turned. Neil married her years later, I know, but after we arrived in Chicago I never saw him again either.

*

Red dawn light touched the clouds above the black slate roofs as, with a few other cars, we drove through Alton. The moon-sized clock of a beer billboard said ten after six. Olinger was deathly still. The air brightened as we moved along the highway; the glowing wall of my home hung above the woods as we rounded the long curve by the Mennonite dairy. With a .22 I could have had a pane of my parent's bedroom window, and they were dreaming I was in Indiana. My grandfather would be up, stamping around in the kitchen for my grandmother to make him breakfast, or outside, walking to see if any ice had formed on the brook. For an instant I genuinely feared he might hail me from the peak of the barn roof. Then trees interceded and we were safe in a landscape where no one cared.

At the entrance to the Turnpike Neil did a strange thing, stopped the car and had me take the wheel. He had never trusted me to drive his father's car before; he had believed my not knowing where the crankshaft and fuel pump were handicapped my competence to steer. But now he was quite complacent. He hunched under an old mackinaw and leaned his head against the metal of the window frame and soon was asleep. We crossed the Susquehanna on a long smooth bridge below Harrisburg, then began climbing towards the Alleghenies. In the mountains there was snow, a dry dusting like sand, that waved back and forth on the road surface. Farther along there had been a fresh fall that night, about two inches, and the ploughs had not yet cleared all the lanes. I was passing a Sunoco truck on a high curve when without warning the scraped section gave out and I realized I might skid into the fence if not over the edge. The radio was singing 'Carpets of clover, I'll lay right at your feet', and the speedometer said 85. Nothing happened; the car stayed firm in the snow and Neil slept through the danger, his face turned skyward and his breath struggling in his nose. It was the first time I heard a contemporary of mine snore.

When we came into tunnel country the flicker and hollow amplification stirred Neil awake. He sat up, the mackinaw dropping to his lap, and lit a cigarette. A second after the scratch of his match occurred the moment of which each following moment was a slight diminution, as we made the long irregular descent towards Pittsburgh. There were many reasons for my feeling so happy. We were on our way. I had seen a dawn. This far, Neil could appreciate, I had brought us safely. Ahead, a girl waited who, if I asked, would marry me, but first there was a vast trip: many hours and towns interceded between me and that encounter. There was the quality of the 10 a.m. sunlight as it existed in the air ahead of the windshield, filtered by the thin overcast, blessing irresponsibility – you felt you could slice forever through such a cool pure element – and springing, by implying how high these hills had become, a widespreading pride: Pennsylvania, your state – as if you had made your life. And there was knowing that twice since midnight a person had trusted me enough to fall asleep beside me.

The Persistence of Desire

Pennypacker's office still smelled of linoleum. It was a clean, sad scent that seemed to lift from the chequerboard floor in squares of alternating intensity; this pattern had given Clyde as a boy a funny nervous feeling of intersection, and now he stood criss-crossed by a double sense of himself, his present identity extending down from Massachusetts to meet his disconsolate youth in Pennsylvania, projected upward from a distance of years. The enlarged, tinted photograph of a lake in the Canadian wilderness still covered one whole wall, and the walnut-stained chairs and benches continued their vague impersonation of the Shaker manner. The one new thing, set squarely on an orange end table, was a compact black clock constructed like a speedometer; it showed in Arabic numerals the present time – 1.28 – and coiled invisibly in its works the two infinities of past and future. Clyde was early; the waiting-room was empty. He sat down on a chair opposite the clock. Already it was 1.29, and while he watched, the digits slipped again: another drop into the brimming void. He glanced around for the comfort of a clock with a face and gracious, gradual hands. A stopped grandfather matched the other imitation antiques. He opened a magazine and immediately read, 'Science reveals that the cells of the normal human body are replaced *in toto* every seven years.'

The top half of a Dutch door at the other end of the room opened, and, framed in the square, Pennypacker's secretary turned the bright disc of her face towards him. 'Mr Behn?' she asked in a chiming voice. 'Dr Pennypacker will be back from lunch in a minute.' She vanished backwards into the maze of little rooms where Pennypacker, an eye, ear, nose, and throat man, had arranged his fabulous equipment. Through the bay window Clyde could see traffic, gayer in colour than he remembered, hustle down Grand Avenue. On the sidewalk, haltered girls identical in all but name with girls he had known strolled past in twos and threes. Small town perennials, they moved rather mournfully under their burdens of bloom. In the opposite direction packs of the opposite sex carried baseball mitts.

Clyde became so lonely watching his old street that when, with a sucking exclamation, the door from the vestibule opened, he looked up gratefully, certain that the person, this being his home town, would be a friend. When he saw who it was, though every cell in his body had been replaced since he had last seen her, his hands jerked in his lap and blood bounded against his skin.

'Clyde Behn,' she pronounced, with a matronly and patronizing yet frightened finality, as if he were a child and these words the moral of a story.

'Janet.' He awkwardly rose from his chair and crouched, not so much in courtesy as to relieve the pressure on his heart.

'Whatever brings you back to these parts?' She was taking the pose that she was just anyone who once knew him.

He slumped back. 'I'm always coming back. It's just you've never been here.'

'Well, I've' – she seated herself on an orange bench and crossed her plump legs cockily – 'been in Germany with my husband.'

'He was in the Air Force.'

'Yes.' It startled her a little that he knew.

'And he's out now?' Clyde had never met him, but having now seen Janet again, he felt he knew him well – a slight, literal fellow, to judge from the shallowness of the marks he had left on her. He would wear eyebrow-style glasses, be a griper, have some not quite negotiable talent, like playing the clarinet or drawing political cartoons, and now be starting up a drab avenue of business. Selling insurance, most likely. Poor Janet, Clyde felt; except for the interval of himself – his splendid, perishable self – she would never see the light. Yet she had retained her beautiful calm, a sleepless tranquillity marked by that pretty little blue puffiness below the eyes. And either she had grown slimmer or he had grown more tolerant of fat. Her thick ankles and the general *obstinacy* of her flesh used to goad him into being cruel.

'Yes.' Her voice indicated that she had withdrawn; perhaps some ugliness of their last parting had recurred to her.

'I was 4-F.' He was ashamed of this, and his confessing it, though she seemed unaware of the change, turned their talk inward. 'A peacetime slacker,' he went on, 'what could be more ignoble?'

She was quiet a while, then asked, 'How many children do you have?'

'Two. Age three and one. A girl and a boy; very symmetrical. Do you' – he blushed lightly, and brushed at his forehead to hide it – 'have any?'

'No, we thought it wouldn't be fair, until we were more fixed.'

Now the quiet moment was his to hold; she had matched him failing for failing. She recrossed her legs, and in a quaint strained way smiled.

'I'm trying to remember,' he admitted, 'the last time we saw each other. I can't remember how we broke up.'

'I can't either,' she said. 'It happened so often.'

Clyde wondered if with that sarcasm she intended to fetch his eyes to the brink of tears of grief. Probably not; premeditation had never been much of a weapon for her, though she had tried to learn it from him.

He moved across the linoleum to sit on the bench beside her. 'I can't tell you,' he said, 'how much, of all the people in this town, you were the one I wanted to see.' It was foolish, but he had prepared it to say, in case he ever saw her again.

'Why?' This was more like her: blunt, pucker-lipped curiosity. He had forgotten it.

'Well, hell. Any number of reasons. I wanted to say something.'

'What?'

'Well, that if I hurt you, it was stupidity, because I was young. I've often wondered since if I did, because it seems now that you were the only person outside my family who ever, actually, *liked* me.'

'Did I?'

'If you think by doing nothing but asking monosyllabic questions you're making an effect, you're wrong.'

She averted her face, leaving, in a sense, only her body – the pale, columnar breadth of arm, the freckled crescent of shoulder muscle under the cotton strap of her summer dress – with him. 'You're the one who's making effects.' It was such a wan, senseless thing to say to defend herself; Clyde, virtually paralysed by so heavy an injection of love, touched her arm icily.

With a quickness that suggested she had foreseen this, she got up and went to the table by the bay window, where rows of overlapping magazines were laid. She bowed her head to their titles, the nape of her neck in shadow beneath a half-collapsed bun. She had always had trouble keeping her hair pinned.

Clyde's face was burning. 'Is your husband working around here?'

'He's looking for work.' That she kept her back turned while saying this gave him hope.

'Mr Behn?' The petite secretary–nurse, switching like a pendulum, led him back through the sanctums and motioned for him to sit in a high hinged chair padded with black leather. Pennypacker's equipment had always made him nervous; tons of it were marshalled through the rooms. A complex tree of tubes and lenses leaned over his left shoulder, and by his right elbow a porcelain basin was cupped expectantly. An eye chart crisply stated gibberish. In time Pennypacker himself appeared: a tall, stooped man with mottled cheekbones and an air of suppressed anger.

'Now what's the trouble, Clyde?'

'It's nothing; I mean it's very little,' Clyde began, laughing inappropriately. During his adolescence he had developed a joking familiarity with his dentist and his regular doctor, but he had never become intimate with Pennypacker, who remained, what he had seemed at first, an aloof administrator of expensive humiliations. In the third grade he had made Clyde wear glasses. Later, he annually cleaned, with a shrill push of hot water, wax from Clyde's ears, and once had thrust two copper straws up Clyde's nostrils in a futile attempt to purge his sinuses. Clyde always felt unworthy of Pennypacker, felt himself a dirty conduit balking the man's smooth onward flow. 'It's just that for over two months I've had this eyelid that twitters and it makes it difficult to think.'

Pennypacker drew little circles with a pencil-sized flashlight in front of Clyde's right eye.

'It's the left lid,' Clyde said, without daring to turn his head.

'Do you write articles, Clyde?'

'Not usually. I went to a doctor up where I live, and he said it was like a rattle in the fender and there was nothing to do. He said it would go away, but it didn't and didn't, so I had my mother make an appointment for when I came down here to visit.'

Pennypacker moved to the left eye and drew even closer. The distance between the doctor's eyes and the corners of his mouth was very long; the emotional impression of his face close up was like that of those photographs, taken from rockets, in which the earth's curvature was first made apparent. 'How do you like being in your home territory?' Pennypacker asked.

'Fine.'

'Seem a little strange to you?'

The question itself seemed strange. 'A little.'

'Mm. That's interesting.'

'About the eye, there were two things I thought. One was, I got some glasses made in Massachusetts by a man nobody else ever went to, and I thought his prescription might be faulty. His equipment seemed so ancient and kind of full of cobwebs; like a Dürer print.' He never could decide how cultured Pennypacker was; the Canadian lake argued against it, but he was county-famous in his trade, in a county where doctors were as high as the intellectual scale went.

The flashlight, a tepid sun girdled by a grid of optical circles behind which Pennypacker's face loomed dim and colourless, came right to the skin of Clyde's eye, and the vague face lurched forward angrily, and Clyde, blind in a world of light, feared that Pennypacker was inspecting the floor of his soul. Held motionless by fear, he breathed. 'The other was that something might be in it. At night it feels as if there's a tiny speck deep in under the lid.'

Pennypacker reared back and insolently raked the light back and forth across Clyde's face. 'How long have you had this flaky stuff on your lids?'

The insult startled Clyde. 'Is there any?'

'How long have you had it?'

'Some mornings I notice little grains like salt that I thought were what I used to call sleepy-dust –'

'This isn't sleepy-dust,' the doctor said. He repeated, 'This isn't sleepy-dust.' Clyde started to smile at what he took to be kidding of his childish vocabulary, but Pennypacker cut him short with 'Cases of this can lead to loss of the eyelashes.'

'Really?' Clyde was vain of his lashes, which in his boyhood had been exceptionally long, giving his face the alert and tender look of a girl's. 'Do you think it's the reason for the tic?' He imagined his face with the lids bald and the lashes lying scattered on his cheeks like insect legs. 'What can I do?'

'Are you using your eyes a great deal?'

'Some. No more than I ever did.'

Pennypacker's hand, blue after Clyde's dazzlement, lifted an intense brown bottle from a drawer. 'It may be bacteria, it may be allergy; when you leave I'll give you something that should knock it out either way. Do you follow me? Now, Clyde' – his voice became murmurous and consolatory as he placed a cupped hand, rigid as an electrode, on the top of Clyde's head – 'I'm going to put some drops in your eyes so we can check the prescription of the glasses you bought in Massachusetts.'

Clyde didn't remember that the drops stung; so he gasped outright and wept while Pennypacker held the lids apart with his fingers and worked them gently open and shut, as if he were playing with snapdragons. Pennypacker set preposterously small, circular, dark brown glasses on Clyde's face and in exchange took away the stylish horn-rims Clyde had kept in his pocket. It was Pennypacker's method to fill his little rooms with waiting patients and wander from one to another like a dungeon-keeper.

*

Clyde heard, far off, the secretary's voice tinkle, and, amplified by the hollow hall, Pennypacker's rumble in welcome and Janet's response. The one word 'headaches', petulantly emphasized, stood up in her answer. Then a door was shut. Silence.

Clyde admired how matter-of-fact she had sounded. He had always admired this competence in her, her authority in the world of love in which she was so servile. He remembered how she could outface waitresses and how she would bluff her mother when this watchful woman unexpectedly entered the screened porch where they were supposed to be playing cribbage. Potted elephant plants sat in the corners of the porch like faithful dwarfs; robins had built a nest in the lilac outside, inches from the screen. It had been taken as an omen, a blessing, when one evening their being on the swaying glider no longer distressed the birds.

Unlike, say, the effects of Novocain, the dilation of pupils is impalpable. The wallpaper he saw through the open door seemed as distinct as ever. He held his fingernails close to his nose and was unable to distinguish the cuticles. He touched the sides of his nose, where tears had left trails. He looked at his fingers again, and they seemed fuzzier. He couldn't see his fingerprint whorls. The threads of his shirt had melted into an elusive liquid surface.

A door opened and closed, and another patient was ushered into a consulting-room and imprisoned by Pennypacker. Janet's footsteps had not mingled with the others. Without ever quite sacrificing his reputation for good behaviour, Clyde in high school had become fairly bold in heckling teachers he considered stupid or unjust. He got out of his chair, looked down the hall to where a white splinter of secretary showed, and quickly walked past a closed door to a half-closed one. He peeked in.

Janet was sitting in a chair as upright as the one he had left, a two-pronged comb in her mouth, her back arched and her arms up, bundling her hair. As he slipped around the door she plucked the comb from between her teeth and laughed at him. He saw in a little rimless mirror cocked above her head his own head, grimacing with stealth and grotesquely costumed in glasses like two chocolate coins, and appreciated her laughter, though it didn't fit with what he had prepared to say. He said it anyway: 'Janet, are you happy?'

She rose with a practical face and walked past him and clicked the door shut. As she stood facing it, listening for a reaction from outside, he gathered her hair in his hand and lifted it from the nape of her neck, which he had expected to find in shadow but which was instead, to his distended eyes, bright as a candle. He clumsily put his lips to it.

'Don't you love your wife?' she asked.

'Incredibly much,' he murmured into the fine down of her neck.

She moved off, leaving him leaning awkwardly, and in front of the mirror smoothed her mussed hair away from her ears. She sat down again, crossing her wrists in her lap.

'I just got told my eyelashes are going to fall out,' Clyde said.

'Your pretty lashes,' she said sombrely.

'Why do you hate me?'

'Shh. I don't hate you now.'

'But you did once.'

'No, I did *not* once. Clyde what *is* this bother? What are you after?'

'Son of a bitch, so I'm a bother. I knew it. You've just forgotten, all the time I've been remembering; you're so *damn* dense. I come in here a bundle of pain to tell you I'm sorry and I want you to be happy, and all I get is the back of your neck.' Affected by what had happened to his eyes, his tongue had loosened, pouring out impressions; with culminating incoherence he dropped to his knees beside her chair, wondering if the thump would bring Pennypacker. 'I must see you again,' he blurted.

'Shh.'

'I come back here and the only person who was ever pleasant to me I discover I maltreated so much she hates me.'

'Clyde,' she said, 'you didn't maltreat me. You were a good boy to me.'

Straightening up on his knees, he fumbled his fingers around the hem of the neck of her dress and tugged it and looked down into the blurred cavity between her breasts. He had a remembrance of her freckles vanishing like melted snow in the whiteness within her bathing suit. His clumsy glasses hit her cheek.

She stabbed the back of his hand with the points of her comb and he got to his feet, rearing high into a new, less sorrowful atmosphere. 'When?' he asked, short of breath.

'No,' she said.

'What's your married name?'

'Clyde, I thought you were successful. I thought you had beautiful children. Aren't you happy?'

'I am, I am; but' – the rest was so purely inspired its utterance only grazed his lips – 'happiness isn't everything.'

Footsteps ticked down the hall, towards their door, past it. Fear emptied his chest, yet with an excellent imitation of his old high-school flippancy he blew her a kiss, waited, opened the door, and whirled through it. His hand had left the knob when the secretary emerging from the room where he should have been, confronted him in the linoleum-smelling hall. 'Where could I get a drink of water?' he asked plaintively, assuming the hunch and whine of a blind beggar. In truth, he had, without knowing it, become thirsty.

'Once a year I pass through your territory,' Pennypacker intoned as he slipped a growing weight of lenses into the tin frame on Clyde's nose. He had returned to Clyde more relaxed and chatty, now that all his little rooms were full. Clyde had tried to figure out from the pattern of noise if Janet had been dismissed. He believed she had. The thought made his eyelid twitter. He didn't even know her married name. 'Down the Turnpike,' Pennypacker droned on, while his face flickered in and out of focus, 'up the New Jersey Pike, over the George Washington Bridge, up the Merritt, then up Route 7 all the way to Lake Champlain. To hunt the big bass. There's an experience for you to write an article about.'

'I notice you have a new clock in your waiting-room.'

'That's a Christmas present from the Alton Optical Company. Can you read that line?'

'H, L, F, Y, T, something that's either an S or an E –'

'K,' Pennypacker said without looking. The poor devil, he had all those letters memorized, all that gibberish – abruptly, Clyde wanted to love him. The oculist altered one lens. 'Is it better this way? . . . Or this way?'

At the end of the examination, Pennypacker said, 'Though the man's equipment was dusty, he gave you a good prescription. In your right eye the axis of astigmatism has rotated several degrees, which is corrected in the lenses. If you have been experiencing a sense of strain, part of the reason, Clyde, is that these heavy frames are slipping down on your nose and giving you a prismatic effect. For a firm fit you should have metal frames, with adjustable nose pads.'

'They leave such ugly dents on the sides of your nose.'

'You should have them. Your bridge, you see' – he tapped his own – 'is recessed. It takes a regular face to support unarticulated frames. Do you wear your glasses all the time?'

'For the movies and reading. When I got them in the third grade you told me that was all I needed them for.'

'You should wear them all the time.'

'Really? Even just for walking around?'

'All the time, yes. You have middle-aged eyes.'

Pennypacker gave him a little plastic squeeze bottle of drops.

'That is for the fungus on your lids.'

'Fungus? There's a brutal thought. Well, will it cure the tic?'

Pennypacker impatiently snapped, 'The tic is caused by muscular fatigue.'

Thus Clyde was dismissed into a tainted world where things evaded his focus. He went down the hall in his sunglasses and was told by the secretary that he would receive a bill. The waiting-room was full now, mostly with downcast old men and myopic children gnawing at their mothers. From out of this crowd a ripe young woman arose and came against his chest, and Clyde, included in the intimacy of the aroma her hair and skin gave off, felt weak and broad and grand, like a declining rose. Janet tucked a folded note into the pocket of his shirt and said conversationally, 'He's waiting outside in the car.'

The neutral, ominous 'he' opened wide a conspiracy Clyde instantly entered. He stayed behind a minute, to give her time to get away. Ringed by the judging eyes of the young and old, he felt like an actor snug behind the blinding protection of the footlights; he squinted prolongedly at the speedometer-clock, which, like a letter delivered on the stage, in fact was blank. Then, smiling ironically towards both sides, he left the waiting-room, coming into Pennypacker's entrance hall, a cubicle equipped with a stucco umbrella stand and a red rubber mat saying, in letters so large he could read them, WALK IN.

He had not expected to be unable to read her note. He held it at arm's length and slowly brought it towards his face, wiggling it in the light from outdoors. Though he did this several times, it didn't yield even the simplest word. Just wet blue specks. Under the specks, however, in their intensity and disposition, he believed he could make out the handwriting – slanted, open, unoriginal – familiar to him from other notes received long ago. This glimpse, through the skin of the paper, of her plain self quickened and sweetened his desire more than touching her had. He tucked the note back into his shirt pocket and its stiffness there made a shield for his heart. In this armour he stepped into the familiar street. The maples, macadam, shadows, houses, cement, were to his violated eyes as brilliant as a scene remembered; he became a child again in this town, where life was a distant adventure, a rumour, an always imminent joy.

The Blessed Man of Boston,
My Grandmother's Thimble,
and Fanning Island

I saw him only for a moment, and that was years ago. Boston had been beaten by the White Sox. It was a night game, and when it was over, as the crowd, including myself and my friends, pushed with that suppressed Occidental panic up the aisles towards the exit ramps, he, like the heavy pebble of gold that is not washed from the pan, was revealed, sitting alone, immobile and smiling, among the green seats. He was an old Chinese man, solidly fat, like a Chevrolet dealer, and he wore faded black trousers and a white shirt whose sleeves were rolled up. He sat with one arm up on the back of the seat beside him and smiled out towards the field, where the ground crew was unfurling the tarp across the foreshortened clay diamond and the outfield under the arc lights looked as brilliant and flat as a pool-table felt. And it flashed upon me, as I glimpsed this man sitting alone and unperturbed among the drained seats, that here was the happy man, the man of unceasing and effortless blessing. I thought then to write a novel, an immense book, about him, recounting his every move, his every meal, every play, pitch, and hesitation of every ball game he attended, the number of every house he passed as he walked Boston's Indian-coloured slums, the exact position and shape of every cracked and flaking spot on the doorways, the precise scumble and glitter of every floriate and convoluted fancy of ironwork that drifted by his legs, the chalk-marks, the bricks (purple-tinted, ochre-smeared, red), the constellations of lint and stain in his tiny bachelor's room (green walls, painted pipes coughing with steam, telephone wiring stapled along the baseboard), the never-precisely-duplicated curl of the smoke off his rice, the strikes of sound composing the hatchings of noise at his back, every stifled cry, every sizzle of a defective neon sign connexion, every distant plane and train, every roller-skate scratch, everything: all set sequentially down with the bald simplicity of intrinsic blessing, thousands upon thousands of pages; ecstatically uneventful; divinely and defiantly dull.

But we would-be novelists have a reach as shallow as our skins. We walk through volumes of the unexpressed and like snails leave behind a faint thread excreted out of ourselves. From the dew of the few flakes that melt on our faces we cannot reconstruct the snowstorm.

The other night I stumbled downstairs in the dark and kicked my wife's sewing basket from the half-way landing. Needles, spools, buttons, and patches scattered. In gathering the things up, I came upon my grandmother's thimble. For a second I did not know what it was; a stemless chalice of silver weighing a fraction of an ounce had come into my fingers. Then I knew, and the valves of time parted, and after an interval of years my grandmother was upon me again, and it seemed incumbent upon me, necessary and holy, to tell how once there had been a woman who now was no more, how she had been born and lived in a world that had ceased to exist, though its mementos were all about us; how her thimble had been fashioned as if in a magical grotto in the black mountain of time, by workmen dwarfed by remoteness, in a vanished workshop now no larger than the thimble itself and like it soon doomed, as if by geological pressures, to be crushed out of shape. O Lord, bless these poor paragraphs, that would do in their vile ignorance Your work of resurrection.

The thimble was her wedding present to me and my wife. I was her only grandchild. At the time I was married, she was in her late seventies, crippled and enfeebled. She had fought a long battle with Parkinson's disease; in my earliest memories of her she is touched with it. Her fingers and back are bent; there is a tremble about her as she moves about through the dark, odd-shaped rooms of our house in the town where I was born. Crouched in the hall outside my grandparent's room – which I never entered – I can hear her voice, in a whispering mutter that pierces the wall with little snapping stabs, irritably answer a question that my grandfather had asked inaudibly. It is strange; out of their room, he speaks loudest. When she bends over me, I smell a mixture of must, something like cough medicine, and old cloth permeated with dried sunlight. In my childhood she was strong, endowed with possessions and resources. By the time I married, she had become so weak only her piercing will carried her up and down the stairs of the little country house to which we had moved – the very house where she had lived as a bride. She spoke with great difficulty; she would hang impaled in the middle of a sentence, at a loss for the word, her watery eyes and wild white hair transfixed. She had no possessions. Except for her clothes and her bed, the elegant silver thimble – a gift from her father, inscribed with her maiden initials – was her last property, and she gave it to us.

In those days each departure from her I thought was the last. When I left to be married, I did not expect to see her alive again. But when, at the end of the summer, my wife and I returned, it was my grandfather, not she, who had died. He had died minutes before we arrived. His body lay on the floor of their bedroom, his mouth a small black triangle in a face withered beyond recognition. The room was dimly lit by the warm glow of a kerosene lamp. I was afraid that his body would move. I called 'Grandpa' in an experimental whisper and flinched in fear of an answer.

My grandmother sat on the edge of the bed, dazed, smiling slightly to greet me. She was confused, like a craftsman who looks up after a long period of concentration. The sanest of old men, my grandfather had on his last day lost his mind. He had bellowed; she had struggled to restrain him. He thought the bed was on fire and sprang from it; she clung to him and in their fall to the floor he died. But not quite. My mother rushed up the stairs and cried, 'What are you doing?'

'Why, we're on the floor,' her father told her with level sarcasm, and his heart stopped.

My father met our headlights on the lawn; he was panting. 'Jesus,' he said to me, 'you've come at a funny time; we think Pop's died.' My parents-in-law were with us; my wife's father, a surgeon, an intimate of death, went upstairs to the body. He came down, smiling, and said that there was no pulse, though the wrist was still warm. Then when I went upstairs I saw my grandmother smiling in much the same abstracted, considerate way.

She sat, worn and cleansed by her struggle, on the edge of the bed with two hollows. She was a little woman informed by a disproportionate strength. Carrying her husband through his death had been her last great effort. From that moment on, her will tried to arrange itself for defeat, and its power of resistance became an inconvenience to her. I hugged her quickly, afraid of even her body, which had so lately embraced the one on the floor. My mother, behind me, asked her if she wanted to come downstairs with the others. My grandmother refused, saying, 'A little while yet,' and making a tremulous impatient motion of explanation or dismissal.

She knew, perhaps, what I was shocked to discover when, descending the steps with trembling knees, and tingling all over as if from a bath, I went downstairs: that we have no gestures adequate to answer the imperious gestures of nature. Among deaf mountains human life pursues a comic low road. The sherry that my mother had purchased towards our arrival was served; the wait for the undertaker became overlaid with a subdued version of the party she had meant to have. My father-in-law with a chilling professional *finesse* carved the cold ham; my mother, tautly calm, as if at the centre of contradictory tensions, made one or two of her witticisms; my father's telephone conversation with our Lutheran minister was as bewildered and bewildering as his conversations with this young man always were. Without knowing what I had expected instead, I was amazed; the chatter seemed to become unbearably loud and I blurted, thinking of my grandmother listening above our heads, 'Why can't you let the old man rest?' My mother looked at me in startled reproval, and I felt again the security of being her clever but inexperienced boy; there were things I didn't understand.

The minister came with a drawn white face that cracked in relief at finding laughter in the house. At church softball he had broken his ankle sliding into second base, and limped still. His prayers seemed to chip pieces from our hearts and float them away. The undertaker's men, droll wooden figures like the hangmen of old, came and trundled the body out the door. Thus, as if through a series of pressure locks, we were rescued from the tunnel of death.

My grandmother did not attend the funeral. She was wise, for the Masons made it ridiculous with their occult presumption. My grandmother, whose love of activity had been intense, stayed inside the house, and more and more in bed. When my wife and I went away again – I had a year of college left – I said good-bye to her in my heart. But when we returned at Christmas, she was alive, and she was alive in June, though by now completely bedridden.

Blindly her will gave battle. My grandfather had been a vigorous booster of exercise as the key to longevity. Obeying, perhaps, an echo of her husband's voice, my grandmother would ask to be lifted by her hands into a sitting position, and then lowered, and lifted again, until the person doing it for her lost patience and in exasperation quit. She liked company, though almost all power of speech had forsaken her. 'Up. Up,' that fierce and plaintive request, was all I could understand. We knew that the disease touched only her tongue; that in that wordless, glaring head the same alert and appetitive mind lived. But a mind shorn of agency ceases to exist in our world, and we would speak together in her room as if it were empty. Certain, now, this was my last time with her – my wife and

I were going to England for a year – I spent some summer afternoons in my grandmother's room. I knew she could hear, but we had never spoken much to each other, so I would read or write in silence. I remember sitting in the rocking-chair at the foot of the bed, near the spot where my grandfather's body had lain that night in warm lamplight, and writing, while the sun streamed in through the geraniums on the window sill, a piece of light verse about what I imagined the sea voyage I was soon to take would be like.

> That line is the horizon line.
> The blue above it is divine.
> The blue below it is marine.
> Sometimes the blue below is green.

Reading this stanza now, I see, as if over the edge of the paper, my grandmother's nostrils as her head was sunk foreshortened in the pillow. The withering force pressed unevenly on her body, twisted it out of symmetry; one nostril was squeezed into teardrop-shape, and the other was a round black hole through which she seemed to seize the air. The whole delicate frame of her existence seemed suspended from this final hungry aperture, the size of a dime, through which her life was sustained.

In England I hesitated to tear open each letter from home, for fear it would contain the news of her death. But, as if preserved in the unreality of those days that passed without weight on a remote continent whose afternoon was our morning and whose morning was our night, she survived, and was there when we returned. We had had a baby girl. We put the child, too young to creep, on my grandmother's bed beside the hump of her legs, so that for an interval four generations were gathered in one room, and without moving her head my grandmother could see her entire progeny: my mother, myself, and my daughter. At her funeral, my child, by then alive to things around her, smiled and from my arms stretched her hand towards the drained and painted body in the casket, perhaps in some faint way familiar.

My grandmother had died, finally, when I was far away, in Boston. I was at a party; it was a Saturday night. I went to the phone with a cigarette in my hand and Cointreau on my breath; my mother, her voice miniature with the distance, began the conversation with two words, 'Grammy went.' They had found her dead in the morning and had not been able to reach me until now. It was, of course, a blessing; my mother's health had been nearly broken by nursing her. Now we were all released. I returned to the party and told my news, which was received respectfully; it was a small party, of friends. But gaiety cannot be suppressed a whole evening, and when it revived I suppose I joined it. I vowed, groping for some fitness, for the commensurate gesture, to go to a Lutheran church the next morning. But when Sunday morning came, I slept late, and the vow seemed a troublesome whim. I did not go.

I did not go. This refusal seems to be a face at that party and I am about to quarrel with it, but other memories come and touch my elbow and lead me away.

When we were all still alive, the five of us in that kerosene-lit house, on Friday and Saturday nights, at an hour when in the spring and summer there was still abundant light in the air, I would set out in my father's car for town, where my friends lived. I had, by moving ten miles away, at last acquired friends: an illustration of that strange law whereby, like Orpheus leading Eurydice, we achieve our desire by turning our back on it. I had gained a girl, so that the vibrations were as sexual as social that made me jangle with anticipation as I clowned in front of the mirror in our kitchen, shaving from a basin of stove-heated water, combing my hair with a dripping comb, adjusting my reflection in the mirror until I had achieved just that electric angle from which my face seemed beautiful and everlastingly, by the very volumes of air and sky and grass that lay mutely banked about our home, beloved. My grandmother would hover near me, watching fearfully, as she had when I was a child, afraid that I would fall from a tree. Delirious, humming, I would swoop and lift her, lift her like a child, crooking one arm under her knees and cupping the other behind her back. Exultant in my height, my strength, I would lift that frail brittle body weighing perhaps a hundred pounds and twirl with it in my arms while the rest of the family watched with startled smiles of alarm. Had I stumbled, or dropped her, I might have broken her back, but my joy always proved a secure cradle. And whatever irony was in the impulse, whatever implicit contrast between this ancient husk, scarcely female, and the pliant, warm girl I would embrace before the evening was done, direct delight flooded away: I was carrying her who had carried me, I was giving my past a dance, I had lifted the anxious caretaker of my childhood from the floor. I was bringing her with my boldness to the edge of danger, from which she had always sought to guard me.

There is a photograph of my grandmother and me at the side of the first house. There is snow on the ground. The brick walk has been cleared. I am in a snowsuit, and its bulk makes my walking doubly clumsy. We are both of us dark against the snow and the white brick wall of the house. I am unsteady; my grandmother's black shape bends over me with a predatory solicitude, holding one of my hands in a hand that has already become, under the metamorphosis of her disease, a little claw-like. She was worried that I would fall, that I would not eat enough, that the bigger boys of the neighbourhood would harm me, that a cold would strangle me; and her fears were not foolish. There *was* danger in that kind house. Tigers of temper lurked beneath the furniture, and shadows of despair followed my father to the door and flattened themselves against the windows as he walked down the shaded street alone.

I remember watching my mother iron in the dining-room. Suddenly her hand jumps to her jaw; her face goes white; shock unfocuses her eyes. Her teeth had given her a twinge that started tears flowing down her cheeks as she resumed ironing. I must have cried out, for she smiled at my face. I told her she must go to the dentist, and returned to my colouring book. The comforting aroma of heated cloth folded over the glimpsed spark of pain. Now around that cold spark, isolated in memory, the air of that house crystallizes: our neglected teeth, our poor and starchy diet, our worn floors, our musty and haunted halls. I sit on the carpet – which under the dining-table had retained its fresh nap and seemed to me jungle-grass – and my mother stands at the ironing board, and around us, like hieroglyphs haloing the rigid figures of a tomb mural, are the simple shapes of the other three: my grandfather a pyramid sitting re-reading the newspaper in the dwindling light of the front parlour, my father a forked stick striding somewhere in the town, my grandmother, above us in her room or behind us in the kitchen, a crescent bent into some chore. As long as her body carried her, she worked.

The night we moved, my mother and I came through the wet black grass around the edge of the sandstone farmhouse and saw, framed in the doorway, close to us yet far away, like a woman in a Vermeer, my grandmother reaching up with a trembling match to touch the wick of a lamp on the high kitchen mantel. My mother's voice, in recalling that moment to me years later, broke as she added, 'She was always doing things like that.' Like lighting a lamp. Always lighting a lamp.

And through that 'always' I fall into the volume of time that preceded my birth, where my grandmother is a figure of history made deceptively resonant by her persistence into my days. She was the youngest of a dozen children, all of whom, remarkably in that mortal era, lived to maturity. She was the baby, her father's favourite and her brothers' darling. Towards the end of her life, when hallucinations began to walk through the walls of her room and stand silently in the corners, her brothers, all of whom she had long outlived, became again vivid to her. I became one of them; she would ask for me with Pete's name. He was her youngest brother, her own favourite. His brown photograph, mounted on stiff cardboard stamped with gold scrolls, had been set up on the table beside her bed. He displayed a hook nose and the dandified hauteur of a rural buck braced to have his picture taken. Like the eyes of an icon, his snapping black eyes – alone in the photograph unfaded – overlooked her deathbed.

I believe her first language was Pennsylvania German. As some parents speak secrets in French in front of the children, my grandparents used this dialect on my mother. Only two words have descended to me – *ferhuddled* and *dopich*, meaning 'confused' and 'clumsy'. They were frequent words with my grandmother; it is the way other people must have looked to her. Shaped like a sickle, her life whipped through grasses of confusion and ineptitude that in a summer month grew up again as tall as before.

As with the blessed man of Boston, I should here provide a catalogue of her existence; her marriage to a man ten years older, the torment of her one childbirth, the eddies of fortune that contained her constant labour. The fields, the hired men, the horses, the stones of the barn and the fireplace, the three-mile inns on the road to market. The birth of my mother: the lamplight, the simmering water, the buggy clattering for the jesting doctor, fear like a transparent paste on the ceiling, the hours of pain piled higher and higher – my grandmother was a little woman, and the baby was large. Her size at the outset my mother felt as an insult ineradicably delivered to the woman who bore her, the first of a thousand painful awkwardnesses. But to me, from my remote perspective, in which fable, memory, and blood blend, the point of the story is survival. Both survived the ordeal. And in the end all my impressions of my grandmother's life turn on the thin point of her piercing survival.

When we returned to the farm where my mother had been born, my grandmother insisted on fetching the water from the spring. In spite of all our warnings she would sneak off with the bucket and on her unsteady legs tote it back up the slope of grass, brimful, strangely little of it spilled. One summer day my mother and I were standing at the side of the house. The air was vibrating with the noises of nature, the pressing tremolo of insects and birds. Suddenly my mother's face, as if from a twinge of her teeth, went rapt and white: 'Listen!' Before I could listen she ran down the lawn toward the spring, I following, and there we found my grandmother doubled up over the water, hanging, by the pressure of one shoulder, to the sandstone wall that cupped the spring on three sides. The weight of the bucket had pulled her forward; she had thrown herself sideways and, unable to move, had held herself from drowning by sheer adhesion of will until her faint, bird-like whimper for help flew to the attuned ears of her child. Death had to take her while she slept.

She never to my knowledge went outside the boundaries of Pennsylvania. She never saw a movie; I never saw her read. She lived in our nation as a fish lives in the deep sea. One night, when she thought – wrongly – that she was dying, I heard her ask, 'Will I be a little debil?' I had never before heard her curiosity range so far. When presented with disagreeable information, she would look stunned, then with a glimmer of a smile say slowly, 'Ach, I guess not.' Wishing the obstacle away as easily as a child.

Of course, I came upon her late, with a child's unknowing way of seeing. No doubt the innocence of my vision of her is my own innocence, her ignorance mine. I am told that in her day she was sophisticated and formidable. She liked fine clothes, good food, nice things. She was one of the first women in the region to drive a car. This automobile, an Overland, spinning down the orange dirt roads of rural valleys now filled with ranch houses and Philadelphia commuters, recedes into a landscape, a woman whom I must imagine, a woman who is not my grandmother at all.

The initials were K.Z.K. Picking up that thimble, with its crown of stipples like a miniature honeycomb, and its decorative rim of five-petalled flowers tapped into the silver, I felt at my back that night a steep wave about to break over the world and bury us and all our trinkets of survival fathoms down. For I feel that the world is ending, that the mounting mass of people will soon make a blackness in which the glint of this silver will be obliterated; it is this imminent catastrophe that makes it imperative for me to cry now, in the last second when the cry will have meaning, that once there was a woman whom one of the continents in one of its square miles caused to exist. That the land which cast her up was harsher, more sparsely exploited, more fertile than it is now. That she was unique; that she came towards the end of the time when uniqueness was possible. Already identical faces throng the street. She was projected on to my own days by her willed survival; I lived with her and she loved me and I did not understand her, I did not care to. She is gone now because we deserted her; the thimble seems a keepsake pressed into my hand by a forsaken woman as in the company of others I launched out from an island into a wilderness.

Such simplicities bring me to the third of my unwritten stories. It is a simple story, a story of life stripped of the progenitive illusion, perfected out of history: the slam of a door in an empty house. 'Let us imagine', Pascal invites us, 'a number of men in chains, and all condemned to death . . .'

Fanning Island is an isolated Pacific island near the equator. It now supports a relay station for the trans-oceanic telegraph. When Captain Fanning discovered it, it was uninhabited, but bore signs of habitation: a rectangular foundation of coral blocks, a basalt adze, some bone fishhooks, a few raised graves containing drilled porpoise teeth and human bones. All these things were old.

Understand that the Polynesian islands were populated accidentally, as seed in nature is sown. On the wide waste of ocean many canoes and praus were blown astray; short planned voyages were hazardous and extended navigation impossible. Some drifted to other populated islands and thorns there swallowed them. Some starved on the barren ground of the Pacific; some fell southward into antarctic ice. Some washed up on atolls with only the rats in the canoes still alive. A few – a very few; Nature with her mountain of time plays a spendthrift game – survived to reach an uninhabited but inhabitable island. When the company of survivors included a fertile woman, population took place. The souls shed by one nation became the seeds of another. No return was possible. The stars are a far weaker guide than armchair theorists believe. Accident, here as elsewhere, is the generating agency beneath the seemingly achieved surface of things.

What must have happened is this. A company of men in a large canoe, sailing among the Marquesas, were blown away. Eventually they were cast up on Fanning Island. They built a house, fished, and lived. No women were among them, so their numbers could only diminish. The youngest among them may have lived for fifty years. The bones of this man whom no one remained to bury mouldered away and vanished. No sign of disaster is found to explain the disappearance of the men. None is needed.

Qu'on s'imagine un nombre d'hommes dans les chaînes, et tous condamnés à la mort, dont les uns étant chaque jour égorgés à la vue des autres, ceux qui restent voient leur propre condition dans celle de leurs semblables, et, se regardant les uns et les autres avec douleur et sans espérance, attendent à leur tour. C'est l'image de la condition des hommes.

– We came from Hiva Oa, and carried pigs and messages for Nukuhiva, below the horizon. My father was chief. The tabu was strong, and we carried no women in the prau. The wind dropped, and returned from another quarter. The sea grew too smooth, and lustrous like the inside of a coconut; the southern sky merged with the sea. In the storm there were lost many pigs and an old man who had seen Nukuhiva as a boy. When the sky cleared, it was night, and the stars were scrambled. At dawn the horizon all around us was unbroken; we strained to see when the great waves lifted us high. We sang to the sun, and slept in the shade of the bodies of the wakeful. The storm had torn away the hut. The cowards infected us. But the singing gave me comfort, and my father's presence sheltered me. He was the tallest and bravest, yet was among those first to yield up life. We devoured his body; his strength passed into me, though I was young. I long felt the island approaching. It gave the men hope and gaiety to touch me. The island first seemed a cloud; but Marheyo saw birds. Our sails were gone, and we paddled with hands that had lost shape. Our skin shredded in the water. Our throats had become stuck; we were silent. Two days and a night it took us to reach the island; at the second dawn its arms were reaching for us. We saw green bush and coconut palms above the rock. Before our strengths were fully revived, Karnoonoo and I fought. Though he had been a man feared in the village, I won, and killed him, grieving. We took thought to shelter. We built a house of stone, carving the soft rock, like ash, with our axes. We harvested fruit and fish, and learned to make tapa from the strange bark. We buried our dead. We carved a god from a log of the prau. We made women of each other. I was the youngest; I gave myself to those men whom I desired, the best-natured. It was not always the old who died. Demons of apathy seized Mehivi, the clown, and Kory-Kory, who had tended the god. The horizon seemed always about to speak to us; for what had we been brought here? We lived, and though we saw the others turn cold, and the jaws sink, and the body turn stiff and light like a child's canoe, those who remained were not sure that they would die. We buried them with the amulets we brought from the village. Now I am the last. I buried Marheyo, the three-fingered, a season ago, and at night he speaks to me.

This is the outline; but it would be the days, the evocation of the days . . . the green days. The tasks, the grass, the weather, the shades of sea and air. Just as a piece of turf torn from a meadow becomes a *gloria* when drawn by Dürer. Details. Details are the giant's fingers. He seizes the stick and strips the bark and shows, burning beneath, the moist white wood of joy. For I thought that this story, fully told, would become without my willing it a happy story, a story full of joy; had my powers been greater, we would know. As it is, you, like me, must take it on faith.

Packed Dirt, Churchgoing, a Dying Cat, a Traded Car

Different things move us. I, David Kern, am always affected – reassured, nostalgically pleased, even, as a member of my animal species, made proud – by the sight of bare earth that has been smoothed and packed firm by the passage of human feet. Such spots abound in small towns: the furtive break in the playground fence dignified into a thoroughfare, the trough of the dust underneath each swing, the blurred path worn across a wedge of grass, the anonymous little mound or embankment polished by play and strewn with pebbles like the confetti aftermath of a wedding. Such unconsciously humanized intervals of clay, too humble and common even to have a name, remind me of my childhood, when one communes with dirt down among the legs, as it were, of presiding fatherly presences. The earth is our playmate then, and the call to supper has a piercingly sweet eschatological ring.

The corner where I now live was recently widened so that the cars going back and forth to the summer colony on the Point would not be troubled to slow down. My neighbour's house was sold to the town and wrecked and picked clean by salvagers and finally burned in a great bonfire of old notched beams and splintered clapboards that leaped tree-high throughout one whole winter day's cold drizzle. Then bulldozers, huge and yellow and loud, appeared on the street and began to gnaw, it seemed, at the corner of our house. My third child, a boy not yet two, came running from the window in tearful panic. After I tried to soothe him with an explanation, he followed me through the house sobbing and wailing ' 'Sheen! 'Sheen!' while the machines made our rooms shake with the curses of their labour. They mashed my neighbour's foundation stones into the earth and trimmed the levelled lot just as my grandmother used to trim the excess dough from the edge of the pieplate. They brought the curve of the road right to the corner of my property, and the beaten path that does for a sidewalk in front of my home was sheared diagonally by a foot-high cliff.

Last night I was coming back from across the street, fresh from an impromptu civic lamentation with a neighbour at how unsightly, now that the snow was melted, the awkward-shaped vacant lot the bulldozers had left looked, with its high raw embankment gouged by rivulets and littered with old chimney bricks. And soon, we concluded, now that spring was here, it would be bristling with weeds. Crossing from this conversation, I noticed that where my path had been lopped the cliff no longer existed; feet – children's feet, mostly, for mostly children walk in our town – had worn the sharpness away and moulded a little ramp by which ascent was easier.

This small modification, this modest work of human erosion, seemed precious to me not only because it recalled, in the slope and set of the dirt, a part of the path that long ago had led down from my parents' back yard to the high-school softball field. It seemed precious because it had been achieved accidentally, and had about it that repose of grace that is beyond willing. We in America have from the beginning been cleaving and baring the earth, attacking, reforming the enormity of nature we were given, which we took to be hostile. We have explored, on behalf of all mankind, this paradox: the more matter is outwardly mastered, the more it overwhelms us in our hearts. Evidence – gaping right-of-ways, acres mercilessly scraped, bleeding mountains of muddy fill – surrounds us of a war that is incapable of ceasing, and it is good to know that now there are enough of us to exert a counter-force. If craters were to appear in our landscape tomorrow, the next day there would be usable paths threading down the blasted sides. As our sense of God's forested legacy to us dwindles, there grows, in these worn, rubbed, and patted patches, a sense of human legacy – like those feet of statues of saints which have lost their toes to centuries of kisses. One thinks of John Dewey's definition of God as the union of the actual and the ideal.

There was a time when I wondered why more people did not go to church. Taken purely as a human recreation, what could be more delightful, more unexpected than to enter a venerable and lavishly scaled building kept warm and clean for use one or two hours a week and to sit and stand in unison and sing and recite creeds and petitions that are like paths worn smooth in the raw terrain of our hearts? To listen, or not listen, as a poorly paid but resplendently robed man strives to console us with scraps of ancient epistles and halting accounts, hopelessly compromised by words, of those intimations of divine joy that are like pain in that, their instant gone, the mind cannot remember or believe them; to witness the windows donated by departed patrons and the altar flowers arranged by withdrawn hands and the whole considered spectacle lustrous beneath its patina of inheritance; to pay, for all this, no more than we are moved to give – surely in all democracy there is nothing like it. Indeed, it is the most available democratic experience. We vote less than once a year. Only in church and at the polls are we actually given our supposed value, the soul-unit of one, with its noumenal arithmetic of equality: one equals one equals one.

My preaching fouls the words and corrupts me. Belief builds itself unconsciously and in consciousness is spent. Throughout my childhood I felt nothing in church but boredom and an oppressive futility. For reasons my father never explained, he was a dutiful churchman; my mother, who could use her senses, who had read Santayana and Wells, stayed home Sunday mornings, and I was all on her side, on the side of phenomena, in those years, though I went, with the other children, to Sunday school. It was not until we moved from the town and joined a country church that I, an adolescent of fifteen, my head a hotbed of girls and literature, felt a pleasant emotion in church. During Lent – that dull season, those forty suspended days during which spring is gathering the mineral energy to make the resurrection that the church calendar seizes upon as conveniently emblematic – I ushered with my father at the Wednesday-night services. We would arrive in our old car – I think it was the Chevrolet then – on those raw March nights and it pleasantly surprised me to find the building warm, the stoked furnace already humming its devotions in the basement. The nave was dimly lit, the congregation small, the sermon short, and the wind howled a nihilistic counterpoint beyond the black windows blotted with garbled apostles; the empty pews, making the minister seem remote and small and emblematic, intensified our sensation of huddling. There was a strong sepia flavour of early Christianity: a minority flock furtively gathered within the hostile enormity of a dying, sobbing empire. From the rear, the broad back and the baked neck of the occasional dutiful son loomed bullishly above the black straw hats of the mischievous-looking old ladies, gnarled by farmwork, who sat in their rows like withered apples on the shelves of a sweet-smelling cellar. My father would cross and uncross and recross his legs and stare at his thoughts, which seemed distant. It was pleasant to sit beside him in the rear pew. He was not much of a man for sitting still. When my parents and I went to the movies, he insisted on having the aisle seat, supposedly to give his legs room. After about twenty minutes he would leap up and spend the rest of the show walking around in the back of the theatre drinking water and talking to the manager while my mother and I, abandoned, consoled ourselves with the flickering giants of make-believe. He had nothing of the passive in him; a church always became, for him, something he helped run. It was pleasant, and even momentous, when the moment for action came, to walk by his side up the aisle, the thump of our feet the only sound in the church, and to take the wooden, felt-floored plates from a shy blur of white robes and to administer the submission of alms. Coins and envelopes sought to cover the felt. I condescended, stooping gallantly into each pew. The congregation seemed The Others, reaching, with quarters glittering in their \crippled fingers, towards mysteries in which I was snugly involved. Even to usher at a church mixes us with the angels, and is a dangerous thing.

The churches of Greenwich Village had this Second Century quality. In Manhattan, Christianity is so feeble its future seems before it. One walks to church past clattering cafeterias and ravaged newsies in winter weather that is always a shade of Lent, on pavements spangled with last night's vomit. The expectantly hushed shelter of the church is like one of those spots worn bare by a softball game in a weed-filled vacant lot. The presence of the city beats like wind at the glowing windows. One hastens home afterwards, head down, hurrying to assume the disguise – sweaters and suntans – of a non-churchgoer. I tried not to go, but it was not in me not to go. I never attended the same church two Sundays in succession, for fear I would become known, and be expected. To be known by face and name and financial weight robs us of our unitary soul, enrols us against those Others. Devil's work. We are the others. It is of the essence to be a stranger in church.

On the island the very colour of my skin made me strange. This island had been abandoned to the descendants of its slaves. Their church was on a hill; it has since been demolished, I have learned from letters, by a hurricane. To reach it one climbed a steep path made treacherous by the loose rubble of coral rock, jagged grey clinkers that bore no visible relation to the pastel branches that could be plucked, still pliant, from the shallows by Maid's Beach. Dull-coloured goats were tethered along the path; their forelegs were tangled in their ropes so tightly that whenever they nodded the bush anchoring them nodded in answer. For windows the church possessed tall arched apertures filled not with stained glass but with air and outward vision; one could see the goats stirring the low foliage and the brightly dressed little girls who had escaped the service playing on the packed dirt around the church. The service was fatiguingly long. There were exhaustive petitionary prayers (for the Queen, the Prime Minister,

Parliament) and many eight-versed hymns sung with a penetrating, lingering joy and accompanied by a hand-pumped organ. The organ breathed in and out, loud and soft, and the congregation, largely female, followed its ebb and flow at a brief but noticeable distance; their lips moved behind the singing, so I seemed immersed in an imperfectly synchronized movie. Musical stress, the British accent, and Negro elision worked upon the words a triple harmony of distortion. 'Lait eth's waadsa *cull* raio-ind . . .' Vainly seeking my place in the hymn – for without a visual key I was lost – I felt lifted within a sweet, soughing milk, an aspiring chant as patient as the nodding of the goats.

Throughout the service, restless deacons slipped in and out of the windows. Bored myself – for we grow sated even with consolation – I discovered that without moving from my pew I too could escape through those tall portals built to admit the breeze. I rested my eyes on earth's wide circle round. From this height the horizon of the sea was lifted half-way up the sky. The Caribbean seemed a steeply tilted blue plane to which the few fishing boats in the bay below had been attached like magnetized toys. God made the world, Aquinas says, in play.

Matter has its radiance and its darkness; it lifts and it buries. Things compete; a life demands a life. On another English island, in Oxford – it is a strange fact about Americans, that we tend to receive our supernatural mail on foreign soil – I helped a cat die. The incident had the signature: decisive but illegible. For six years I did not tell my wife about it, for fear it would frighten her. Some hours before, I had left her at the hospital in the early stages of labour. Wearing a sterilized gown and mask, I had visited her in a white-tiled room along whose walls gleaming gutters stood ready to drain torrents of blood. Her face, scrubbed and polished, was fervent like a child's, and she seemed, lying there swathed in white, ready for nothing so much as a graduation ceremony. She would break off talking, and listen as if to the distant voice of a schoolmistress, and her face would grow rapt, and when the contraction had passed she would sigh and say, 'That was a good one,' and chatter some more to me of how I would feed myself alone and who I would send the telegrams to.

Shooed from the room, stripped of my mask, I tried to wait, and was told, the comical husband of the American cartoons, to run on home; it would be a time. I went outside and took a bus home. It was the last day of March. I had been born in March and I had looked forward to welcoming my child to the month; but she was late. We lived on Iffley Road, and around midnight for some reason – I think to mail a letter, but what letter could have been that important? – I was out walking a few blocks from our flat. The night was cold enough for gloves. The sensations of turning into a father – or, rather, the lack of sensations; the failure of sympathetic pain, the hesitation of dread, the postponement of pride – made the street seem insubstantial. There was not that swishing company of headlights that along an American road throws us into repeated relief. The brick homes, save for an occasional introverted glow in an upstairs window, were dark in the vehement shadows of privacy behind the dry hedges and spiked walls. The streetlamps – wintry, reserved – drained colour from everything. Myself a shadow, I noticed another in the centre of the road. A puddle of black, as I watched, it curled on itself; its ends lifted from the macadam and seemed to stretch in a yawn. Then it became inert again. I was horrified; the shape was about the size of a baby. When it curled the second time, I went to it, my footsteps the only sound in the street.

It was a cat that had been struck by a car. Struck but not quite killed; a testament to the modest speed and sensible size of English automobiles. By the impersonal witness of lamps burning in the trees I couldn't be sure what colour its fur was – it seemed orange-yellow, tabbied with stripes of dark ginger. The cat was plump and wore a collar. Someone had loved it. Blackness from one ear obscured one side of its head and when I touched here it was like a cup. For the third time, the cat stretched, the tips of its hind feet quivering luxuriously in that way cats have. With a great spastic effort it flipped over on to its other side, but made no cry. The only sound between us was my crooning as I carried it to the side of the street and laid it behind the nearest hedge.

A sallow upstairs light in this home was glowing. I wondered if the cat was theirs. Was it their love invested in my hands? Were they watching as I pushed, crouching, with my burden through their hedge? I wondered if I would be taken for a trespasser, a 'poacher'; as an American, I was nervous of English taboos. In my own brutal country it was a not uncommon insult to kill a cat and throw the body into an enemy's yard, and I was afraid that this would be taken that way. I thought of writing a note to explain everything, but I carried no paper and pen. I explained to the cat, how I was taking her (I felt it was female) out of the street so no more cars would hit her, how I would put her here in the nice safe dirt behind the hedge, where she could rest and get well. I did not believe she would get well; I think she was dead already. Her weight had felt dead in my hands and when I laid her down she did not stretch or twitch again.

Back in my flat, I discovered that one glove was smeared with blood. Most of the palm and three of the fingers were dyed wine-brown. I hadn't realized there was so much blood. I took off my gloves and carefully wrote a note, explaining that I had found this cat in the middle of the street, still alive, and that I put it behind this hedge to be safe. If, as I thought, the cat was dead, I hoped that the finders would bury it. After some deliberation, I signed my name and address. I walked back and tucked the note under the cat's body, which seemed at home behind the hedge; it suffered my intrusion a trifle stiffly. It suggested I was making too much fuss, and seemed to say to me, *Run on home*.

Back in my flat once more, I felt abruptly tired, though my heart was pounding hugely. I went to bed and set the alarm for three and read a book. I remember the title, it was Chesterton's *The Everlasting Man*. I turned off the light and prayed for my wife and, though I did not believe myself capable of it, fell asleep. The alarm at three came crashing into some innocent walk of a dream and my frail head felt like a hollow cup. I dressed and went out to the public phone booth a block away and called the hospital. A chirping voice, after some rummaging in the records, told me that several hours ago, in the first hour of April (in the United States it was still March), a perfect female infant had been born to me.

The next morning, after all the telegrams had been managed, I went back to the hedge, and the cat and my note were gone. Though I had left my address, I never received a letter.

When we returned from England, we bought a car. We had ordered it through my parents from folders they had sent us, and, though its shade of blue was more naïve, more like a robin's egg, than we had expected, this '55 Ford proved an excellent buy. Whether being shuffled from side to side of West Eighty-fifth Street every morning or being rammed in second gear up a washed-out mountain road in Vermont, it never complained. In New York, hot tar from a roof-patching job rained on to its innocent paint, and in Vermont its muffler was racked and rent on a shelf of rock, and in Massachusetts it wallowed, its hot clutch stinking, up from repeated graves of snow. Not only sand and candy wrappers accumulate in a car's interior, but heroisms and instants of communion. We in America make love in our cars, and listen to ball games, and plot our wooing of the dollar: small wonder the landscape is sacrificed to these dreaming vehicles of our ideal and onrushing manhood.

In the beginning, my wife and I would lovingly lave with soap and warm water the unflecked skin of the hood as if it were the thorax of a broad blue baby, and towards the end we let the gallant old heap rust where it would. Its eggshell finish grew grizzled with the stains of dropped maple seeds. Its doors balked at closing; its windows refused to roll down. But I somehow never believed we would ever trade it in, though the little girl born across the ocean in the ominous turning of April, now a vocal and status-conscious democrat of nearly six, applied more and more petulant pressure. The deal was consummated while my soul had its face turned, and Detroit the merciless mother contracted to devour her child. But before the new car arrived, there was a month's grace, and in this grace I enjoyed a final fling with my car, my first, my only – for all the others will be substitutes. It happened this way:

Dancing at a party with a woman not my wife, it seemed opportune to turn her hand in mine and kiss her palm. For some time her thighs had been slithering against mine, and, between dances, she developed a nervous clumsy trick of lurching against me, on tiptoe, and rubbing her breasts against my forearm, which was braced across my chest as I held a cigarette. My first thought was that I might burn her; my second, that Nature in her gruff maternal way had arranged one of her opportunities – as my mother, when I was a child, would unpredictably determine to give me a birthday or Hallowe'en party. Obediently I bowed my head and kissed my friend's moist palm. As her hand withdrew from the advance, her fingertips caressed my chin in the absent-minded manner of one fingering the muzzle of an importunate dog. The exchange transposed us into a higher key; I could hardly hear my own voice, and our dancing lost all connexion with the music, and my hand explored her spine from a great aerial distance. Her back seemed mysteriously taut and hard; the body of a strange woman retains more of its mineral content, not being transmuted, through familiarity, into pure emotion. In a sheltered corner of the room we stopped dancing altogether and talked, and what I distinctly remember is how her hands beneath the steady and opaque appraisal of her eyes, in nervous slurred agitation blindly sought mine and seized and softly gripped, with infantile instinct, my thumbs. Just my thumbs she held, and as we talked she moved them this way and that as if she was steering me. When I closed my eyes, the red darkness inside my lids was trembling, and when I rejoined my wife, and held her to dance, she asked, 'Why are you panting?'

After we got home, and surveyed our four children, and in bed read a few pages made unbearably brilliant by their patina of martinis, and turned out the light, she surprised me by not turning her back. Alcohol, with its loosening effect, touches women more deeply then men in this respect; or perhaps, like a matched pair of tuning forks, I had set her vibrating. Irritated by whatever illicit stimulations, we took it out on each other.

To my regret, I survived the natural bliss of satiety – when each muscle is like a petal snugly curved in a corolla of benediction – and was projected on to the wrinkled, azoic territory of insomnia. That feathery anxious embrace of my erect thumbs tormented me in twenty postures. My stomach turned in love of that woman; I feared I would be physically sick and lay on my back gingerly and tried to soothe myself with the caress of headlights as they evolved from bright slits on the wall into parabolically accelerating fans on the ceiling that then vanished: this phenomenon, with its intimations of a life beyond me, had comforted wakeful nights in my earliest childhood. In Sunday school I had been struck by the passage in which Jesus says that to lust after a woman in thought is the same as committing adultery. Now I found myself helplessly containing the conviction that souls, not deeds, are judged. To feel a sin was to commit it; to touch the brink was to be on the floor of the chasm. The universe that so easily permitted me to commit adultery became, by logical steps each one of which went more steeply down than the one above it, a universe that would easily permit me to die. The enormities of cosmic space, the maddening distension of time, history's forgotten slaughters, the child smothered in the dumped icebox, the recent breakdown of the molecular life-spiral, the proven physiological roots of the mind, the presence in our midst of idiots, Eichmanns, animals, and bacteria – all this evidence piled on, and I seemed already eternally forgotten. The dark vibrating air of my bedroom seemed the dust of my grave; the dust went up and up and I prayed upwards into it, prayed, prayed for a sign, any glimmer at all, any microscopic loophole or chink in the chain of evidence, and saw none. I remembered a movie I had seen as a child in which a young criminal, moaning insanely, is dragged on rubber legs down the long corridor to the electric chair. I became that criminal. My brain in its calcium vault shouted about injustice, thundered accusations into the lustreless and tranquil homogeneity of the air. Each second my agony went unanswered justified it more certainly: the God who permitted me this fear was unworthy of existence. Each instant my horror was extended amplified God's non-existence, so, as the graph of certain equations fluctuates more and more widely as it moves along the lateral coordinate, or as the magnetic motive-power in atom-smashers accelerates itself, I was caught in a gathering vortex whose unbearably shrill pitch moved me at last to drop my weight on my wife's body and beg, 'Wake up. Elaine. I'm so frightened.'

I told her of the centuries coming when our names would be forgotten, of the millennia when our nation would be a myth and our continent an ocean, of the aeons when our earth would be vanished and the stars themselves diffused into a uniform and irreversible tepidity. As, an hour before, I had transferred my lust to her, so now I tried to pass my fear into her. It seemed to offend her sense of good taste that I was jealous of future aeons and frantic because I couldn't live through them; she asked me if I had never been so sick I gave up caring whether I lived or died. This contemptible answer – the decrepit Stoic response – acquired a curious corroboration: eventually, just as I had during the strenuous birth of my fatherhood, I fell asleep, and dreamt of innocent and charming scenes.

The next day, a Saturday, was my birthday. It passed like any day except that underneath the camouflage of furniture and voices and habitual actions I felt death like a wide army invisibly advancing. The newspaper told of nothing but atrocities. My children, wounded and appalled in their competition, came to me to be comforted and I was dismayed to see myself, a gutted shell, appearing to them as the embodiment and pledge of a safe universe. Friends visited, and for the first time truly in my life I realized that each face is suppressing knowledge of an immense catastrophe; our faces are dams that wrinkle under the strain. Around six the telephone rang. It was my mother calling from Pennsylvania; I assumed she had called because of my birthday, so I chattered humorously about the discomforts of growing old for a minute before she could tell me, her voice growing faint, the news. My father was in the hospital. He had been walking around with chest pains for two weeks and suffered shortness of breath at night. She had finally seduced him into a doctor's office; the doctor had taken a cardiogram and driven him to the hospital. He was a seriously sick man.

Instantly I was relieved. The weight on me rolled away. All day death had been advancing under cover and now it had struck, declared its position. My father had engaged the enemy and it would be defeated.

I was restored to crisp health in the play-world of action. That night we had a few friends in for my birthday party and the next day I took the two older children to Sunday school and went myself to church. The faintly lavender lozenge-panes of the white-mullioned windows glowed and dimmed fitfully. It was a spottily overcast day, spitting a little snow. While I was at church my wife had cooked a lamb dinner and as I drank the coffee it became clear that I must drive to Pennsylvania. My mother and I had agreed I would fly down and visit him in a few days; I would have to see about renting a car at the Philadelphia end. This was potentially awkward because, self-employed, I had no credit card. The awkwardness suddenly seemed easy to surmount. I would drive. The car would be traded in a few days, it had just been greased; I had a vision of escaping our foul New England spring by driving south. In half an hour my bag was packed and in my churchgoing suit I abandoned my family. *Run on home.*

Along Route 128 I picked up a young sailor who rode with me all the way to New York and, for two hours through Connecticut, drove my car. I trusted him. He had the full body, the frank and fleshy blue-eyed face of the docile Titans – guileless, competent, mildly earnest – that we have fattened, an ocean removed from the slimming Latin passions and Nordic anxieties of Europe, on our unprecedented abundance of milk and honey, vitamins and protein. He had that instinctive optimism of the young animal that in America is the only generatrix of hope we have allowed ourselves; until recently, it seemed enough. He was incongruously – and somehow reassuringly – tanned. He had got the tan in Key West, where he had spent twenty-four hours, hitching the rides to and from on Navy jets. He had spent the twenty-four hours sleeping on the beach and selecting souvenirs to send back to his parents and girlfriend. His parents lived in Salem, his girlfriend in Peabody. He wanted to marry her, but his parents had old-fashioned ideas, they thought he was too young. And a lot of these guys in the service say, Don't get married, don't ever get married. But she was a nice girl, not so pretty or anything, but really nice: he really wanted to marry her.

I asked him how old he was. He was twenty-two, and was being trained as an airplane mechanic. He wanted at the end of his hitch to come back to Salem and live. He figured an airplane mechanic could find some sort of job. I told him, with a paternal firmness that amazed my ears, to marry her; absolutely; his parents would get used to it. The thing about parents, I told him, was that secretly, no matter what you did, they liked you anyway. I told him I had married at the age of twenty-one and had never for a minute been sorry.

He asked me. 'What do you do? Teach?'

This impressed me. My grandfather had been a teacher, and my father was a teacher, and from my childhood up it had been assumed by the people of our neighbourhood that I in turn would become a teacher.

'No,' I said. 'I'm a writer.'

He seemed less offended than puzzled. 'What do you write?'

'Oh – whatever comes into my head.'

'What's the point?'

'I don't know,' I told him. 'I wish I did.'

We talked less freely after that. At his request I left him off in wet twilight at a Texaco station near the entrance of the New Jersey Turnpike. He hoped to get a ride from there all the way to Washington. Other sailors were clustered out of the rain in the doorways of the station. They hailed him as if they had been waiting for him, and as he went to them he became, from the back, just one more sailor, anonymous, at sea. He did not turn and wave good-bye. I felt I had frightened him, which I regretted, because he had driven for me very well and I wanted him to marry his girl. In the dark I drove down the pike alone. In the first years of my car, when we lived in Manhattan, it would ease up to seventy-five on this wide black stretch without our noticing; now the needle found its natural level at sixty. The windshield wipers beat, and the wonderland lights of the Newark refineries were swollen and broken like bubbles by the raindrops on the side windows. For a dozen seconds a solemn cross of coloured stars was suspended stiffly in the upper part of the windshield: an airplane above me was coming in to land.

I did not eat until I was on Pennsylvania soil. The Howard Johnsons in Pennsylvania are cleaner, less crowded, more home-like in their furnishings. The decorative plants seem to be honestly growing, and the waitresses have just a day ago removed the Mennonite cap from their hair, which is still pulled into a smooth bun flattering to their pallid, sly faces. They served me with that swift grace that comes in a country where food is still one of the pleasures. The familiar and subtle irony of their smiles wakened in me that old sense, of Pennsylvania knowingness – of knowing, that is, that the truth is good. They were the innkeeper's daughters, God had given us crops, and my wagon was hitched outside.

When I returned to the car, the music on the radio had changed colour. The ersatz hiccup and gravel of Atlantic Seaboard hillbilly had turned, inland, backwards into something younger. As I passed the Valley Forge intersection the radio re-lived a Benny Goodman quintet that used to make my scalp freeze in high school. The speedometer went up to seventy without effort.

I left the toll road for our local highway and, turning into our dirt road, I was nearly rammed from behind by a pair of headlights that had been pushing, Pennsylvania style, six feet behind me. I parked beside my father's car in front of the barn. My mother came unseen into the yard, and, two voices calling in the opaque drizzle, while the dogs yapped deliriously in their pen, we debated whether I should move my car farther off the road. 'Out of harm's way,' my grandfather would have said. Complaining, I obeyed her. My mother turned as I carried my suitcase down the path of sandstone stepping-stones, and led me to the back door as if I would not know the way. So it was not until we were inside the house that I could kiss her in greeting. She poured us two glasses of wine. Wine had a ceremonial significance in our family; we drank it seldom. My mother seemed cheerful, even silly, and it took an hour for the willed impetus of gaiety to ebb away. She turned her head and looked delicately at the rug and the side of her neck blushed as she told me, 'Daddy says he's lost all his faith.'

Since I had also lost mine, I could find nothing to say. I remembered, in the silence, a conversation I had had with my father during a vacation from college. With the habitual simplicity of his eagerness to know, he asked me, 'Have you ever had any doubts of the existence of a Divine Being?'

'Sure,' I had answered.

'I never have,' he said. 'It's beyond my ability to imagine it. The divinity of Jesus, yes; but the existence of a Divine Being, never.' He stated this not as an attempt to influence me, but as a moderately curious fact he had that moment discovered about himself.

'He never was much one for faith,' my mother added, hurt by my failure to speak. 'He was strictly a works man.'

I slept badly; I missed my wife's body, that weight of pure emotion, beside me. I was enough of a father to feel lost out of my nest of little rustling souls. I kept looking out of the windows. The three red lights of the chimneys of the plant that had been built some miles away, to mine low-grade iron ore, seemed to be advancing over our neighbour's ridged field towards our farm. My mother had mistaken me for a stoic like my father and had not put enough blankets on the bed. I found an old overcoat of his and arranged it over me; its collar scratched my chin. I tipped into sleep and awoke. The morning was sharply sunny; sheep hustled, heads toppling, through the gauzy blue sky. It was authentic spring in Pennsylvania. Some of the grass in the lawn had already grown shiny and lank. A yellow crocus had popped up beside the BEWARE OF THE DOG sign my father had had a child at school letter for him.

I insisted we drive to Alton in my car, and then was sorry, for it seemed to insult their own. Just a few months ago my father had traded in on yet one more second-hand car; now he owned a '53 Plymouth. But while growing up I had been ambushed by so many mishaps in my father's cars that I insisted we take the car I could trust. Or perhaps it was that I did not wish to take my father's place behind the wheel of his car. My father's place was between me and Heaven; I was afraid of being placed adjacent to that far sky. First we visited his doctor. Our old doctor, a man who believed that people simply 'wore out' and nothing could be done about it, had several years ago himself worn out and died. The new doctor's office, in the centre of the city, was furnished with a certain raw sophistication. Rippling music leaked from the walls, which were hung with semi-professional oils. He himself was a wiry and firm-tongued young man not much older than myself but venerable with competence and witnessed pain. Such are the brisk shepherds who hop us over the final stile. He brought down from the top of a filing cabinet a plaster model of the human heart. 'Your own heart,' he told me, 'is nice and thin like this; but your dad's heart is enlarged. We believe the obstruction is here, in one of these little vessels on the outside, luckily for your dad.'

Outside, in the streets of Alton, my own heart felt enlarged. A white sun warmed the neat façades of painted brick; red chimneys like peony shoots thrust through budding tree-tops. Having grown accustomed to the cramped, improvised cities of New England, I was patriotically exalted by Alton's straight broad streets and superb equipment of institutions. While my mother went off to buy my daughter a birthday present, I returned a book she had borrowed to the Alton Public Library. I had forgotten the deep aroma of that place, mixed of fust and cleaning fluid and binder's glue and sweet pastry baking in the shop next door. I revisited the shelf of P. G. Wodehouse that in one summer I had read straight through. I took down *Mulliner Nights* and looked in the back for the stamped date, in '47 or '48, that would be me. I never thought to look for the section of the shelves where my own few books would be placed. They were not me. They were my children, mysterious and self-willed.

In driving to the hospital on Alton's outskirts, we passed the museum grounds, where every tree and flower-bed wore a name-tag and black swans drifted through flotillas of crumpled bread. As a child I had believed literally that bread cast upon the waters came back doubled. I remembered that within the museum there were mummies with astonished shattered faces; a tiny gilt chair for a baby Pharaoh; an elephant tusk carved into thousands of tiny chinamen and pagodas and squat leafy trees; miniature Eskimo villages that you lit up with a switch and peeped into like an Easter egg; cases of arrowheads; rooms of stuffed birds; and, upstairs, wooden chests decorated with hearts and pelicans and tulips by the pious 'plain people' and iridescent glassware from the kilns of Baron von Steigel and slashing paintings of Pennsylvania woodland by the Shearers and bronze statuettes of wrestling Indians that stirred my first erotic dreams and, in the round skylit room at the head of the marble stairs, a black-rimmed pool in whose centre a naked green lady held to her pursed lips a shell whose lucent contents forever spilled from the other side, filling this whole vast upstairs – from whose Palladian windows the swans in their bready pond could be seen trailing fan-shaped wakes – with the music and chill romance of falling water. The world then seemed an intricate wonder displayed for my delight with no price asked. Above the trees across the pond one saw rose glints of the hospital, an orderly multitude of tall brick rectangles set among levelled and lovingly tended grounds, an ideal city of the ill.

I had forgotten how grand the Alton hospital was. I had not seen its stately entrance, approached down a grassy mall bright with the first flush of green, since, at the age of seven, I had left the hospital unburdened of my tonsils. Then, too, it had been spring, and my mother was with me. I recalled it to her, and she said, 'I felt so guilty. You were so sick.'

'Really? I remember it as so pleasant.' They had put a cup of pink rubber over my nose and there had been a thunderous flood of the smell of cotton candy and I opened my eyes and my mother was reading a magazine beside my bed.

'You were such a hopeful boy,' my mother said, and I did not look at her face for fear of seeing her crying.

I wondered aloud if a certain girl in my high school class were still a nurse here.

'Oh, dear,' my mother said. 'Here I thought you came all this way to see your poor old father and all you care about is seeing –' And she used the girl's maiden name, though the girl had been married as long as I had.

Within the hospital, she surprised me by knowing the way. Usually, wherever we went, it was my father or I who knew the way. As I followed her through the linoleum maze, my mother's shoulders seemed already to have received the responsible shawl of widowhood. Like the halls of a palace, the hospital corridors were lined with patient petitioners. Negro girls electrically dramatic in their starched white uniforms folded bales of cotton sheets; grey men pushed wrung mops. We went through an Exit sign, down a stairway, into a realm where gaunt convalescents in bathrobes shuffled in and out of doorways. I saw my father diagonally through a doorway before we entered his room. He was sitting up in bed, supported sultan-like by a wealth of pillows and clad in red-striped pyjamas.

I had never seen him in pyjamas before; a great man for the shortest distance between two points, he slept in his underclothes. But, having been at last captured in pyjamas, like a big-hearted lion he did not try to minimize his humiliation, but lay fully exposed, without a sheet covering even his feet. Bare, they looked pale, gentle, and oddly unused.

Except for a sullen lymphatic glow under his cheeks, his face was totally familiar. I had been afraid that his loss of faith would show, like the altered shape of his mouth after he had had all his teeth pulled. With grins we exchanged the shy handshake that my going off to college had forced upon us. I sat on the window-sill by his bed, my mother took the chair at the foot of the bed, and my father's room-mate, a tanned and fortyish man flat on his back with a crushed vertebra, sighed and blew smoke towards the ceiling and tried, I suppose, not to hear us. Our conversation, though things were radically changed, followed old patterns. Quite quickly the talk shifted from him to me. 'I don't know how you do it, David,' he said. 'I couldn't do what you're doing if you paid me a million dollars a day.' Embarrassed and flattered, as usual, I tried to shush him, and he disobediently turned to his room-mate and called loudly, 'I don't know where the kid gets his ideas. Not from his old man, I know that. I never gave that poor kid an idea in my life.'

'Sure you did,' I said softly, trying to take pressure off the man with the painful back. 'You taught me two things. Always butter bread towards the edges because enough gets in the middle anyway, and No matter what happens to you, it'll be a new experience.'

To my dismay this seemed to make him melancholy. 'That's right, David,' he said. 'No matter what happens to you, it'll be a new experience. The only thing that worries me is that *she*' – he pointed at my mother – 'will crack up the car. I don't want anything to happen to your mother.'

'The car, you mean,' my mother said, and to me she added, 'It's a sin, the way he worships that car.'

My father didn't deny it. 'Jesus I love that car,' he said. 'It's the first car I've ever owned that didn't go bad on me. Remember all those heaps we used to ride back and forth in?'

The old Chevy was always getting dirt in the fuel pump and refusing to start at awkward hours. Once, going down Fire Hill, the left front wheel had broken off the axle; my father wrestled with the steering-wheel while the tyres screamed and the white posts of the guard fence floated calmly towards my eyes. When the car slid sideways to a stop just short of the embankment my father's face was stunned and the corners of his mouth dribbled saliva. I was surprised; it had not occurred to me to be frightened. The '36 Buick had drunk oil, a quart every fifty miles, and loved to have flat tyres after midnight, when I would be gliding home with a scrubbed brain and the smell of lipstick in my nose. Once, when we had both gone into town and I had dropped him off and taken the car, I had absent-mindedly driven home alone. I came in the door and my mother said, 'Why, where's your father?'

My stomach sank. 'My Lord,' I said, 'I forgot I had him!'

As, smiling, I took in breath and prepared to dip with him into reminiscence of these adventures, my father, staring stonily into the air above his pale and motionless toes, said, 'I love this place. There are a lot of wonderful gentlemen in here. The only thing that worries me is that mother will crack up the car.'

To my horror I saw that my mother, leaning forward red-faced in the chair at the foot of the bed, was silently crying. He glanced at her and said to me, 'It's a funny feeling. The night before we went to see the doctor I woke up and couldn't get my breath and realized I wasn't ready to die. I had always thought I would be. It's a funny feeling.'

'Luckily for your dad', 'all his faith', 'wonderful gentlemen': these phrases were borne in on me with a dreadful weight and my tongue seemed pressed flat on the floor of its grave. The pyjama stripes under my eyes stirred and streamed, real blood. I wanted to speak, to say how I needed him and to beg him not to leave me, but there were no words, no form of words available in our tradition. A pillar of smoke poured upwards from the sighing man in the other bed.

Into this pit hesitantly walked a plain, painfully clean girl with a pad and pencil. She had yellow hair, thick lips, and, behind pink-rimmed glasses, large eyes that looked as if they had been corrected from being crossed. They flicked across our faces and focused straight ahead in that tunnel-vision gaze of those who know perfectly well they are figures of fun. The Jehovah's Witnesses who come to the door wear that funnelled expression. She approached the bed where my father lay barefoot and, suppressing a stammer, explained that she was from Lutheran Home Missions and that they kept accounts of all hospitalized Lutherans and notified the appropriate pastors to make visitations. Clearly she had measured my father for a rebuff; perhaps her eyes, more practised in this respect than mine, spotted the external sign of loss of faith that I had missed. At any rate my father was a Lutheran by adoption; he had been born and raised a Presbyterian and still looked like one.

'That's *aw*fully nice of you,' he told the girl. 'I don't see how you people do it on the little money we give you.'

Puzzled, she dimpled and moved ahead with her routine. 'Your church is – ?'

He told her, pronouncing every syllable meticulously and consulting my mother and me as to whether the word 'Evangelical' figured in the official title.

'That would make your pastor Reverend –'

'Yeah. He'll be in, don't worry about it. Wild horses couldn't keep him away. Nothing he likes better than to get out of the sticks and drive into Alton. I didn't mean to confuse you a minute ago; what I meant was, just last week in church council we were talking about you people. We couldn't figure out how you do anything on the little money we give you. After we've got done feeding the furnace and converting the benighted Hindoo there isn't anything left over for you people that are trying to help the poor devils in our own back yard.'

The grinning girl was lost in this onslaught of praise and clung to the shreds of her routine. 'In the meantime,' she recited, 'here is a pamphlet you might like to read.'

My father took it from her with a swooping gesture so expansive I got down from the window-sill to restrain him physically, if necessary. That he must lie still was my one lever, my one certainty about his situation. 'That's awfully nice of you', he told the girl. 'I don't know where the hell you get the money to print these things.'

'We hope your stay in the hospital is pleasant and would like to wish you a speedy recovery to full health.'

'Thank you; I know you're sincere when you say it. As I was telling my son David here, if I can do what the doctors tell me I'll be all right. First time in my life I've ever tried to do what anybody ever told me to do. The kid was just telling me, "No matter what happens to you, Pop, it'll be a new experience." '

'Now if you will excuse me I have other calls to pay.'

'Of course. You go right ahead, sick Lutherans are a dime a dozen. You're a wonderful woman to be doing what you're doing.'

And she left the room transformed into just that. As a star shines in our heaven though it has vanished from the universe, so my father continued to shed faith upon others. For the remainder of my visit with him his simple presence so reassured me, filled me with such a buoyant humour, that my mother surprised me, when we had left the hospital, by remarking that we had tired him.

'I hadn't noticed,' I said.

'And it worries me,' she went on, 'the way he talks about the movies all the time. You know he never liked them.' When I had offered to stay another night so I could visit him again, he had said, 'No, instead of that why don't you take your mother to the movies?' Rather than do that, I said, I would drive home. It took him a moment, it seemed, to realize that by home I meant a far place, where I had a wife and children; though at the time I was impatient to have his consent, it has since occurred to me and grieved me that during that instant when his face was blank he was swallowing the realization that he was no longer the centre of even his son's universe. Having swallowed, he told me how good I had been to come all this way to see him. He told me I was a good son and a good father; he clasped my hand. I felt I would ascend straight north from his touch.

I drove my mother back to her farm and got my bag and said good-bye on the lawn. The little sandstone house was pink in the declining sunlight; the lawn was a tinkling clutter of shy rivulets. Standing beside the BEWARE OF THE DOG sign with its companion of a crocus, she smiled and said, 'This is like when you were born. Your father drove through a snowstorm all the way from Wheeling in our old Ford.' He had been working with the telephone company then; the story of his all-night ride was the first myth in which I was a character.

Darkness did not fall until New Jersey. The hour of countryside I saw from the Pennsylvania Turnpike looked enchanted – the branches of the trees under-painted with budding russet, the meadows nubbled like new carpets, the bronze sun slanting on Valley Forge and Levittown alike. I do not know what it is that is so welcome to me in the Pennsylvania landscape, but it is the same quality – perhaps of reposing in the certainty that the truth is good – that is in Pennsylvania faces. It seemed to me for this sunset hour that the world is our bride, given to us to love, and the terror and joy of the marriage is that we bring to it a nature not our bride's.

There was no sailor to help me drive the nine hours back. New Jersey began in twilight and ended in darkness, and Manhattan made its gossamer splash at its favourite hour, eight o'clock. The rest of the trip was more and more steeply uphill. The Merritt Turnpike seemed meaninglessly coquettish, the light-controlled stretch below Hartford maddeningly obstinate, and the hour above that frighteningly empty. Distance grew thicker and thicker; the intricate and effortful mechanics of the engine, the stellar infinity of explosive sparks needed to drive it, passed into my body, and wearied me. Repeatedly I stopped for coffee and the hallucinatory comfort of human faces, and after stop, my waiting car, companion and warm home and willing steed, responded to my pressure. It began to seem a miracle that the car could gather speed from my numb foot; the very music on the radio seemed a drag on our effort, and I turned it off, obliterating time. We climbed through a space fretted by scattered brilliance and bathed in a monotonous wind. I had been driving forever; furniture, earth, churches, women, were all things I had innocently dreamed. And through those aeons my car, beginning as a mechanical spiral of molecules, evolved into something soft and organic and consciously brave. I lost, first, heart, then head, and finally any sense of my body. In the last hour of the trip I ceased to care or feel or in any real sense see, but the car, though its soul the driver had died, maintained steady forward motion, and completed the endless journey safely. Above my back yard the stars were frozen in place, and the shapes of my neighbours' houses wore the wonder that children induce by whirling.

Any day now we will trade it in; we are just waiting for the phone to ring. I know how it will be. My father traded in many cars. It happens so cleanly, before you expect it. He would drive off in the old car up the dirt road exactly as usual and when he returned the car would be new, and the old was gone, gone, utterly dissolved back into the mineral world from which it was conjured, dismissed without a blessing, a kiss, a testament, or any ceremony or farewell. We in America need ceremonies, is I suppose, sailor, the point of what I have written.

In Football Season

Do you remember a fragrance girls acquire in autumn? As you walk beside them after school, they tighten their arms about their books and bend their heads forward to give a more flattering attention to your words, and in the little intimate area thus formed, carved into the clear air by an implicit crescent, there is a complex fragrance woven of tobacco, powder, lipstick, rinsed hair, and that perhaps imaginary and certainly elusive scent that wool, whether in the lapels of a jacket or the nap of a sweater, seems to yield when the cloudless fall sky like the blue bell of a vacuum lifts towards itself the glad exhalations of all things. The fragrance, so faint and flirtatious on those afternoon walks through the dry leaves, would be banked a thousandfold and lie heavy as the perfume of a flower shop on the dark slope of the stadium when, Friday nights, we played football in the city.

'We' – we the school. A suburban school, we rented for some of our home games the stadium of a college in the city of Alton three miles away. My father, a teacher, was active in the Olinger High athletic department, and I, waiting for him beside half-open doors of varnished wood and frosted glass, overheard arguments and felt the wind of the worries that accompanied this bold and at that time unprecedented decision. Later, many of the other county high schools followed our lead; for the decision was vindicated. The stadium each Friday night when we played was filled. Not only students and parents came but spectators unconnected with either school, and the money left over when the stadium rent was paid supported our entire athletic programme. I remember the smell of the grass crushed by footsteps behind the end zones. The smell was more vivid than that of a meadow, and in the blue electric glare the green vibrated as if excited, like a child, by being allowed up late. I remember my father taking tickets at the far corner of the wall, wedged into a tiny wooden booth that made him seem somewhat magical, like a troll. And of course I remember the way we, the students, with all of our jealousies and antipathies and deformities, would be – beauty and boob, sexpot and grind – crushed together like flowers pressed to yield to the black sky a concentrated homage, an incense, of cosmetics, cigarette smoke, warmed wool, hot dogs, and the tang, both animal and metallic, of clean hair. In a hoarse olfactory shout, these odours ascended. A dense haze gathered along the ceiling of brightness at the upper limit of the arc lights, whose glare blotted out the stars and made the sky seem romantically void and intimately near, like the death that now and then stooped and plucked one of us out of a crumpled automobile. If we went to the back row and stood on the bench there, we could look over the stone lip of the stadium down into the houses of the city, and feel the cold November air like the black presence of the ocean beyond the rail of a ship; and when we left after the game and from the hushed residential streets of this part of the city saw behind us a great vessel steaming with light, the arches of the colonnades blazing like portholes, the stadium seemed a great ship sinking and we the survivors of a celebrated disaster.

To keep our courage up, we sang songs, usually the same song, the one whose primal verse runs,

> Oh, you can't get to Heaven
> *(Oh, you can't get to Heaven)*
> In a rocking chair
> *(In a rocking chair)*
> 'Cause the Lord don't want
> *('Cause the Lord don't want)*
> No lazy people there!
> *(No lazy people there!)*

And then repeated, double time. It was a song for eternity; when we ran out of verses, I would make them up:

> Oh, you can't get to Heaven
> *(Oh, you can't get to Heaven)*
> In Smokey's Ford
> *(In Smokey's Ford)*
> 'Cause the cylin*ders*
> *('Cause the cylin*ders)
> Have to be rebored
> *(Have to be rebored.)*

Down through the nice residential section, on through the not-so-nice and the shopping district, past dark churches where stained-glass windows, facing inward, warned us with left-handed blessings, down Buchanan Street to the Running Horse Bridge, across the bridge, and two miles out the pike we walked. My invention would become reckless:

Oh, you can't get to Heaven
(*Oh, you can't get to Heaven*)
In a motel bed
(*In a motel bed*)
'Cause the sky is blue
(*'Cause the sky is blue*)
And the sheets are red.
(*And the sheets are red.*)

Few of us had a licence to drive and fewer still had visited a motel. We were at that innocent age, on the borderline of sixteen, when damnation seems a delicious promise. There was Mary Louise Hornberger, who was tall and held herself with such upright and defiant poise that she was Mother in both our class plays, and Alma Bidding, with her hook nose and her smug smile caricatured in cerise lipstick, and Joanne Hardt, whose father was a typesetter, and Marilyn Wenrich, who had a grey front tooth and in study hall liked to have the small of her back scratched, and Nanette Seifert, with her button nose and black wet eyes and peach-down cheeks framed in the white fur frilling the blue hood of her parka. And there were boys, Henny Gring, Leo Horst, Hawley Peters, Jack Lillijed-ahl, myself. Sometimes these, sometimes less or more. Once there was Billy Trupp on crutches. Billy played football and, though only a sopho-more, had made the varsity that year, until he broke his ankle. He was dull and dogged and liked Alma, and she with her painted smile led him on lovingly. We offered for his sake to take the trolley, but he had already refused a car ride back to Olinger, and obstinately walked with us, loping his heavy body along on the crutches, his lifted foot a boulder of plaster. His heroism infected us all; we taunted the cold stars with song, one mile, two miles, three miles. How slowly we went! With what a luxurious sense of waste did we abuse this stretch of time! For as children we had lived in a tight world of ticking clocks and punctual bells, where every minute was an admonition to thrift and where tardiness, to a child running late down a street with his panicked stomach burning, seemed the most mys-terious and awful of sins. Now, turning the corner into adulthood, we found time to be instead a black immensity endlessly supplied, like the wind.

We would arrive in Olinger after the drugstores, which had kept open for the first waves of people returning from the game, were shut. Except for the street lights, the town was dark like a town in a fable. We scattered, each escorting a girl to her door; and there, perhaps, for a moment, you bowed your face into that silent crescent of fragrance, and tasted it, and let it bite into you indelibly. The other day, in a town far from Olinger, I passed on the sidewalk two girls utterly unknown to me and half my age, and sensed, very faintly, that flavour from far-off carried in their bent arms like a bouquet. And I seemed, continuing to walk, to sink into a chasm deeper than the one inverted above us on those Friday nights during football season.

For after seeing the girl home, I would stride through the hushed streets, where the rustling leaves seemed torn scraps scattered in the wake of the game, and go to Mr Lloyd Stephens' house. There, looking in the little square window of his front storm door, I could see down a dark hall into the lit kitchen where Mr Stephens and my father and Mr Jesse Honneger were counting money around a worn porcelain table. Stephens, a local contractor, was the school-board treasurer, and Honneger, who taught social science, the chairman of the high-school athletic department. They were still counting; the silver stacks slipped and glinted among their fingers and the gold of beer stood in cylinders beside their hairy wrists. Their sleeves were rolled up and smoke like a fourth presence, wings spread, hung over their heads. They were still counting, so it was all right. I was not late. We lived ten miles away, and I could not go home until my father was ready. Some nights it took until midnight. I would knock and pull open the storm door and push open the real door and it would be warm in the contractor's hall. I would accept a glass of ginger ale and sit in the kitchen with the men until they were done. It was late, very late, but I was not blamed; it was permitted. Silently counting and expertly tamping the coins into little cylindrical wrappers of coloured paper, the men ordered and consecrated this realm of night into which my days had never extended before. The hour or more behind me, which I had spent so wastefully, in walking when a trolley would have been swifter, and so wickedly, in blasphemy and lust, was past and forgiven me; it had been necessary; it was permitted.

Now I peek into windows and open doors and do not find that air of permission. It has fled the world. Girls walk by me carrying their invisible bouquets from fields still steeped in grace, and I look up in the manner of one who follows with his eyes the passage of a hearse, and remembers what pierces him.

Out in the World

Ace in the Hole

No sooner did his car touch the boulevard heading home than Ace flicked on the radio. He needed the radio, especially today. In the seconds before the tubes warmed up, he said aloud, doing it just to hear a human voice, 'Jesus. She'll pop her lid.' His voice, though familiar, irked him; it sounded thin and scratchy, as if the bones in his head were picking up static. In a deeper register Ace added, 'She'll murder me.' Then the radio came on, warm and strong, so he stopped worrying. The Five Kings were doing 'Blueberry Hill'; to hear them made Ace feel so sure inside that from the pack pinched between the car roof and the sun shield he plucked a cigarette, hung it on his lower lip, snapped a match across the rusty place on the dash, held the flame in the instinctive spot near the tip of his nose, dragged, and blew out the match, all in time to the music. He rolled down the window and snapped the match so it spun end-over-end into the gutter. 'Two points,' he said, and cocked the cigarette towards the roof of the car, sucked powerfully, and exhaled two plumes through his nostrils. He was beginning to feel like himself, Ace Anderson, for the first time that whole day, a bad day. He beat time on the accelerator. The car jerked crazily. 'On Blueberry Hill,' he sang, 'my heart stood still. The wind in the wil-low tree' – he braked for a red light – 'played love's suh-*weet* melodee –'

'Go, Dad, bust your lungs!' a kid's voice blared. The kid was riding in a '52 Pontiac that had pulled up beside Ace at the light. The profile of the driver, another kid, was dark over his shoulder.

Ace looked over at him and smiled slowly, just letting one side of his mouth lift a little. 'Shove it,' he said, good-naturedly, across the little gap of years that separated them. He knew how they felt, young and mean and shy.

But the kid, who looked Greek, lifted his thick upper lip and spat out the window. The spit gleamed on the asphalt like a half-dollar.

'Now isn't that pretty?' Ace said, keeping one eye on the light. 'You miserable wop. You are *mis*erable.' While the kid was trying to think of some smart comeback, the light changed. Ace dug out so hard he smelled burned rubber. In his rear-view mirror he saw the Pontiac lurch forward a few yards, then stop dead, right in the middle of the intersection.

The idea of them stalling their fat tin Pontiac kept him in a good humour all the way home. He decided to stop at his mother's place and pick up the baby, instead of waiting for Evey to do it. His mother must have seen him drive up. She came out on the porch holding a plastic spoon and smelling of cake.

'You're out early,' she told him.

'Friedman fired me,' Ace told her.

'Good for you,' his mother said. 'I always said he never treated you right.' She brought a cigarette out of her apron pocket and tucked it deep into one corner of her mouth, the way she did when something pleased her.

Ace lighted it for her. 'Friedman was O.K. personally,' he said. 'He just wanted too much for his money. I didn't mind working Saturdays, but until eleven, twelve Friday nights was too much. Everybody has a right to some leisure.'

'Well, I don't dare think what Evey will say, but I, for one, thank dear God you had the brains to get out of it. I always said that job had no future to it – no future of any kind, Freddy.'

'I guess,' Ace admitted. 'But I wanted to keep at it, for the family's sake.'

'Now, I know I shouldn't be saying this, but any time Evey – this is just between us – any time Evey thinks she can do better, there's a room for you *and* Bonnie right in your father's house.' She pinched her lips together. He could almost hear the old lady think, *There, I've said it.*

'Look, Mom, Evey tries awfully hard, and anyway you know she can't work that way. Not that *that* – I mean, she's a realist, too . . .' He let the rest of the thought fade as he watched a kid across the street dribbling a basketball around a telephone pole that had a backboard and net nailed on it.

'Evey's a wonderful girl of her own kind. But I've always said, and your father agrees, Roman Catholics ought to marry among themselves. Now I know I've said it before, but when they get out in the greater world –'

'*No*, Mom.'

She frowned, smoothed herself, and said, 'Your name was in the paper today.'

Ace chose to let that go by. He kept watching the kid with the basketball. It was funny how, though the whole point was to get the ball up into the air, kids grabbed it by the sides and squeezed. Kids just didn't think.

'Did you hear?' his mother asked.

'Sure, but so what?' Ace said. His mother's lower lip was coming at him, so he changed the subject. 'I guess I'll take Bonnie.'

His mother went into the house and brought back his daughter, wrapped in a blue blanket. The baby looked dopey. 'She fussed all day,' his mother complained. 'I said to your father, "Bonnie is a dear little girl, but without a doubt she's her mother's daughter." You were the best-natured boy.'

'Well, I *had* everything,' Ace said with an impatience that made his mother blink. He nicely dropped his cigarette into the brown flower-pot on the edge of the porch and took his daughter into his arms. She was getting heavier, solid. When he reached the end of the cement walk, his mother was still on the porch, waving to him. He was so close he could see the fat around her elbow jiggle, and he only lived a half block up the street, yet here she was, waving to him as if he was going to Japan.

At the door of his car, it seemed stupid to him to drive the measly half block home. His old coach, Bob Behn, used to say never to ride where you could walk. Cars were the death of legs. Ace left the ignition keys in his pocket and ran along the pavement with Bonnie laughing and bouncing at his chest. He slammed the door of his landlady's house open and shut, pounded up the two flights of stairs, and was panting so hard when he reached the door of his apartment that it took him a couple of seconds to fit the key into the lock.

The run must have tuned Bonnie up. As soon as he lowered her into the crib, she began to shout and wave her arms. He didn't want to play with her. He tossed some blocks and a rattle into the crib and walked into the bathroom, where he turned on the hot water and began to comb his hair. Holding the comb under the faucet before every stroke, he combed his hair forward. It was so long, one strand curled under his nose and touched his lips. He whipped the whole mass back with a single pull. He tucked in the tufts around his ears, and ran the comb straight back on both sides of his head. With his fingers he felt for the little ridge at the back where the two sides met. It was there, as it should have been. Finally, he mussed the hair in front enough for one little lock to droop over his forehead, like Alan Ladd. It made the temple seem lower than it was. Every day, his hairline looked higher. He had observed all around him how blond men went bald first. He remembered reading somewhere, though, that baldness shows virility.

On his way to the kitchen he flipped the left-hand knob of the television. Bonnie was always quieter with the set on. Ace didn't see how she could understand much of it, but it seemed to mean something to her. He found a can of beer in the refrigerator behind some brownish lettuce and those hot dogs Evey never got around to cooking. She'd be home any time. The clock said 5.12. She'd pop her lid.

Ace didn't see what he could do but try and reason with her. 'Evey,' he'd say, 'you ought to thank God I got out of it. It had no future to it at all.' He hoped she wouldn't get too mad, because when she was mad he wondered if he should have married her, and doubting that made him feel crowded. It was bad enough, his mother always crowding him. He punched the two triangles in the top of the beer can, the little triangle first, and then the big one, the one he drank from. He hoped Evey wouldn't say anything that couldn't be forgotten. What women didn't seem to realize was that there were things you knew but shouldn't say.

He felt sorry he had called the kid in the car a wop.

Ace balanced the beer on a corner where two rails of the crib met and looked under the chairs for the morning paper. He had trouble finding his name, because it was at the bottom of a column on an inside sports page, in a small article about the county basketball statistics.

'Dusty' Tremwick, Grosvenor Park's sure-fingered centre, copped the individual scoring honours with a season's grand (and we do mean grand) total of 376 points. This is within eighteen points of the all-time record of 394 racked up in the 1949– 50 season by Olinger High's Fred Anderson.

Ace angrily sailed the paper into an armchair. Now it was Fred Anderson; it used to be Ace. He hated being called Fred, especially in print, but then the sportswriters were all office boys anyway, Behn used to say.

'Do not just ask for shoe polish,' a man on television said, 'but ask for *Emu Shoe Gloss*, the *only* polish that absolutely *guarantees* to make your shoes look shinier than new.' Ace turned the sound off, so that the man moved his mouth like a fish blowing bubbles. Right away, Bonnie howled, so Ace turned it up loud enough to drown her out and went into the kitchen, without knowing what he wanted there. He wasn't hungry; his stomach was tight. It used to be like that when he walked to the gymnasium alone in the dark before a game and could see the people from town, kids and parents, crowding in at the lighted doors. But once he was inside, the locker room would be bright and hot, and the other guys would be there, laughing it up and towel-slapping, and the tight feeling would leave. Now there were whole days when it didn't leave.

A key scratched at the door lock. Ace decided to stay in the kitchen.

Let *her* find *him*. Her heels clicked on the floor for a step or two; then the television set went off. Bonnie began to cry. 'Shut up, honey,' Evey said. There was a silence.

'I'm home,' Ace called.

'No kidding. I thought Bonnie got the beer by herself.'

Ace laughed. She was in a sarcastic mood, thinking she was Lauren Bacall. That was all right, just so she kept funny. Still smiling, Ace eased into the living-room and got hit with, 'What are *you* smirking about? Another question: What's the idea running up the street with Bonnie like she was a football?'

'You saw that?'

'Your mother told me.'

'You saw her?'

'Of course I saw her. I dropped by to pick up Bonnie. What the hell do you think? – I read her tiny mind?'

'Take it easy,' Ace said, wondering if Mom had told her about Friedman.

'Take it easy? Don't coach *me*. Another question: Why's the car out in front of her place? You give the car to her?'

'Look, I parked it there to pick up Bonnie, and I thought I'd leave it there.'

'Why?'

'Whaddeya mean, why? I just did. I just thought I'd walk. It's not that far, you know.'

'No, I don't know. If you'd been on your feet all day a block would look like one hell of a long way.'

'Okay. I'm sorry.'

She hung up her coat and stepped out of her shoes and walked around the room picking up things. She stuck the newspaper in the wastebasket.

Ace said, 'My name was in the paper today.'

'They spell it right?' She shoved the paper deep into the basket with her foot. There was no doubt; she knew about Friedman.

'They called me Fred.'

'Isn't that your name? What *is* your name anyway? Hero J. Great?'

There wasn't any answer, so Ace didn't try any. He sat down on the sofa, lighted a cigarette and waited.

Evey picked up Bonnie. 'Poor thing stinks. What does your mother do, scrub out the toilet with her?'

'Can't you take it easy? I know you're tired.'

'You should. I'm always tired.'

Evey and Bonnie went into the bathroom; when they came out, Bonnie was clean and Evey was calm. Evey sat down in an easy chair beside Ace and rested her stockinged feet on his knees. 'Hit me,' she said, twiddling her fingers for the cigarette.

The baby crawled up to her chair and tried to stand, to see what he gave her. Leaning over close to Bonnie's nose, Evey grinned, smoke leaking through her teeth, and said, 'Only for grown-ups, honey.'

'Eve,' Ace began, 'there was no future in that job. Working all Saturday, and then Friday nights on top of it.'

'I know. Your mother told *me* all that, too. All I want from you is what happened.'

She was going to take it like a sport, then. He tried to remember how it *did* happen. 'It wasn't my fault,' he said. 'Friedman told me to back this '51 Chevy into the line that faces Church Street. He just bought it from an old guy this morning who said it only had thirteen thousand on it. So in I jump and start her up. There was a knock in the engine like a machine-gun. I almost told Friedman he'd bought a squirrel, but you know I cut that smart stuff out ever since Palotta laid me off.'

'You told me that story. What happens in this one?'

'Look, Eve. I *am* telling ya. Do you want me to go out to a movie or something?'

'Suit yourself.'

'So I jump in the Chevy and snap it back in line, and there was a kind of scrape and thump. I get out and look and Friedman's running over, his arms going like *this*' – Ace whirled his own arms and laughed – 'and here was the whole back fender of a '49 Merc mashed in. Just looked like somebody took a planer and shaved off the bulge, you know, there at the back.' He tried to show her with his hands. 'The Chevy, though, didn't have a dent. It even gained some paint. But *Friedman*, to *hear* him – Boy, they can rave when their pocketbook's hit. He said' – Ace laughed again – 'never mind.'

Evey said, 'You're proud of yourself.'

'No, listen. I'm not happy about it. But there wasn't a thing I could *do*. It wasn't my driving at all. I looked over on the other side, and there was just two or three inches between the Chevy and a Buick. *Nobody* could have gotten into that hole. Even if it had hair on it.' He thought this was pretty good.

She didn't. 'You could have looked.'

'There just wasn't the *space*. Friedman said stick it in; I stuck it in.'

'But you could have looked and moved the other cars to make more room.'

'I guess that would have been the smart thing.'

'I guess, too. Now what?'

'What do you mean?'

'I mean now what? Are you going to give up? Go back to the Army? Your mother? Be a basketball pro? What?'

'You know I'm not tall enough. Anybody under six-six they don't want.'

'Is that so? Six-six? Well, please listen to this, Mr Six-Foot-Five-and-a-Half: I'm fed up. I'm ready as Christ to let you run.' She stabbed her cigarette into an ashtray on the arm of the chair so hard the ashtray jumped to the floor. Evey flushed and shut up.

What Ace hated most in their arguments were these silences after Evey had said something so ugly she wanted to take it back. 'Better ask the priest first,' he murmured.

She sat right up. 'If there's one thing I don't want to hear about from you it's priests. You let the priests to me. You don't know a damn thing about it. Not a damn thing.'

'Hey, look at Bonnie,' he said, trying to make a fresh start with his tone.

Evey didn't hear him. 'If you think,' she went on, 'if for one rotten moment you think, Mr Fred, that the be-all and end-all of my life is you and your hot-shot stunts –'

'Look, Mother,' Ace pleaded, pointing at Bonnie. The baby had picked up the ashtray and put it on her head for a hat and was waiting for praise.

Evey glanced down sharply at the child. 'Cute,' she said. 'Cute as her daddy.'

The ashtray slid from Bonnie's head and she patted where it had been and looked around puzzled.

'Yeah, but watch,' Ace said. 'Watch her hands. They're really terrific hands.'

'You're nuts,' Evey said.

'No, honest. Bonnie's great. She's a natural. Get the rattle for her. Never mind, I'll get it.' In two steps, Ace was at Bonnie's crib, picking the rattle out of the mess of blocks and plastic rings and beanbags. He extended the rattle towards his daughter, shaking it delicately. Made wary by this burst of attention, Bonnie reached with both hands; like two separate animals they approached from opposite sides and touched the smooth rattle simultaneously. A smile bubbled up on her face. Ace tugged weakly. She held on, and tugged back. 'She's a natural,' Ace said, 'and it won't do her any good because she's a girl. Baby, we got to have a boy.'

'I'm not your baby,' Evey said, closing her eyes.

Saying 'Baby' over and over again, Ace backed up to the radio and, without turning around, switched on the volume knob. In the moment before the tubes warmed up, Evey had time to say, 'Wise up, Freddy. What shall we do?'

The radio came in on something slow: dinner music. Ace picked Bonnie up and set her in the crib. 'Shall we dance?' he asked his wife, bowing.

'I want to talk.'

'Baby. It's the cocktail hour.'

'This is getting us no place,' she said, rising from her chair, though.

'Fred Junior. I can see him now,' he said, seeing nothing.

'We will have no Juniors.'

In her crib, Bonnie whimpered at the sight of her mother being seized. Ace fitted his hand into the natural place on Evey's back and she shuffled stiffly into his lead. When, with a sudden injection of saxophones, the tempo quickened, he spun her out carefully, keeping the beat with his shoulders. Her hair brushed his lips as she minced in, then swung away, to the end of his arm; he could feel her toes dig into the carpet. He flipped his own hair back from his eyes. The music ate through his skin and mixed with the nerves and small veins; he seemed to be great again, and all the other kids were around them, in a ring, clapping time.

The Christian Roommates

Orson Ziegler came straight to Harvard from the small South Dakota town where his father was the doctor. Orson, at eighteen, was half an inch under six feet tall, with a weight of 164 and an I.Q. of 152. His eczematous cheeks and vaguely irritated squint – as if his face had been for too long transected by the sight of a level horizon – masked a definite self-confidence. As the doctor's son, he had always mattered in the town. In his high school he had been class president, valedictorian, and captain of the football and baseball teams. (The captain of the basketball team had been Lester Spotted Elk, a full-blooded Chippewa with dirty fingernails and brilliant teeth, a smoker, a drinker, a discipline problem, and the only boy Orson ever had met who was better than he at anything that mattered.) Orson was the first native of his town to go to Harvard, and would probably be the last, at least until his son was of age. His future was firm in his mind: the pre-med course here, medical school either at Harvard, Penn, or Yale, and then back to South Dakota, where he had his wife already selected and claimed and primed to wait. Two nights before he left for Harvard, he had taken her virginity. She had cried, and he had felt foolish, having, somehow, failed. It had been his virginity, too. Orson was sane, sane enough to know that he had lots to learn, and to be, within limits, willing. Harvard processes thousands of such boys and restores them to the world with little apparent damage. Presumably because he was from west of the Mississippi and a Protestant Christian (Methodist), the authorities had given him as a freshman roommate a self-converted Episcopalian from Oregon.

When Orson arrived at Harvard on the morning of Registration Day, bleary and stiff from the series of airplane rides that had begun fourteen hours before, his roommate was already installed. 'H. Palamountain' was floridly inscribed in the upper of the two name slots on the door of Room 14. The bed by the window had been slept in, and the desk by the window was neatly loaded with books. Standing sleepless inside the door, inertly clinging to his two heavy suitcases, Orson was conscious of another presence in the room without being able to locate it; optically and mentally, he focused with a slight slowness.

The roommate was sitting on the floor, barefoot, before a small spinning wheel. He jumped up nimbly. Orson's first impression was of the wiry quickness that almost magically brought close to his face the thick-lipped, pop-eyed face of the other boy. He was a head shorter than Orson, and wore, above his bare feet, pegged sky-blue slacks, a lumberjack shirt whose throat was dashingly stuffed with a silk foulard, and a white cap such as Orson had seen before only in photographs of Pandit Nehru. Dropping a suitcase, Orson offered his hand. Instead of taking it, the roommate touched his palms together, bowed his head, and murmured something Orson didn't catch. Then he gracefully swept off the white cap, revealing a narrow crest of curly blond hair that stood up like a rooster's comb. 'I am Henry Palamountain.' His voice, clear and colourless in the way of West Coast voices, suggested a radio announcer. His handshake was metallically firm and seemed to have a pinch of malice in it. Like Orson, he wore glasses. The thick lenses emphasized the hyperthyroid bulge of his eyes and their fishy, searching expression.

'Orson Ziegler,' Orson said.

'I know.'

Orson felt a need to add something adequately solemn, standing as they were on the verge of a kind of marriage. 'Well, Henry' – he lamely lowered the other suitcase to the floor – 'I guess we'll be seeing a lot of each other.'

'You may call me Hub,' the roommate said. 'Most people do. However, call me Henry if you insist. I don't wish to diminish your dreadful freedom. You may not wish to call me anything at all. Already I've made three hopeless enemies in the dormitory.'

Every sentence in this smoothly enunciated speech bothered Orson, beginning with the first. He himself had never been given a nickname; it was the one honour his classmates had withheld from him. In his adolescence he had coined nicknames for himself – Orrie, Ziggy – and tried to insinuate them in popular usage, without success. And what was meant by 'dreadful freedom'? It sounded sarcastic. And why might he not wish to call him anything at all? And how had the roommate had the time to make enemies? Orson asked irritably, 'How long have you *been* here?'

'Eight days.' Henry concluded every statement with a strange little pucker of his lips, a kind of satisfied silent click, as if to say, 'And what do you think of *that*?'

Orson felt that he had been sized up as someone easy to startle. But he slid helplessly into the straight-man role that, like the second-best bed, had been reserved for him. 'That *long*?'

'Yes. I was totally alone until the day before yesterday. You see, I hitch-hiked.'

'From *Oregon*?'

'Yes. And I wished to allow time enough for any contingency. In case I was robbed, I had sewed a fifty-dollar bill inside my shirt. As it turned out, I made smooth connexions all the way. I had painted a large cardboard sign saying "Harvard". You should try it sometime. One meets some very interesting Harvard graduates.'

'Didn't your parents worry?'

'Of course. My parents are divorced. My father was furious. He wanted me to fly. I told him to give the plane fare to the Indian Relief Fund. He never gives a penny to charity. And, of course, I'm old. I'm twenty.'

'You've been in the Army?'

Henry lifted his hands and staggered back as if from a blow. He put the back of his hand to his brow, whimpered 'Never', shuddered, straightened up smartly, and saluted. 'In fact, the Portland draft board is after me right now.' With a preening tug of his two agile hands – which did look, Orson realized, old: bony and veined and red-tipped, like a woman's – he broadened his foulard. 'They refuse to recognize any conscientious objectors except Quakers and Mennonites. My bishop agrees with them. They offered me an out if I'd say I was willing to work in a hospital, but I explained that this released a man for combat duty and if it came to that I'd just as soon carry a gun. I'm an excellent shot. I mind killing only on principle.'

The Korean War had begun that summer, and Orson, who had been nagged by a suspicion that his duty was to enlist, bristled at such blithe pacifism. He squinted and asked, 'What *have* you been doing for two years, then?'

'Working in a plywood mill. As a gluer. The actual gluing is done by machines, but they become swamped in their own glue now and then. It's a kind of excessive introspection – you've read *Hamlet*?'

'Just *Macbeth* and *The Merchant of Venice*.'

'Yes. Anyway. They have to be cleaned with solvent. One wears long rubber gloves up to one's elbows. It's very soothing work. The inside of a gluer is an excellent place for revolving Greek quotations in your head. I memorized nearly the whole of the *Phaedo* that way.' He gestured towards his desk, and Orson saw that many of the books were green Loeb editions of Plato and Aristotle, in Greek. Their spines were worn; they looked read and reread. For the first time, the thought of being at Harvard frightened him. Orson had been standing between his suitcases and now he moved to unpack. 'Have you left me a bureau?'

'Of course. The better one,' Henry jumped on the bed that had not been slept in and bounced up and down as if it were a trampoline. 'And I've given you the bed with the better mattress,' he said, still bouncing, 'and the desk that doesn't have the glare from the window.'

'Thanks,' Orson said.

Henry was quick to notice his tone. 'Would you rather have my bed? My desk?' He jumped from the bed and dashed to his desk and scooped a stack of books from it.

Orson had to touch him to stop him, and was startled by the tense muscularity of the arm he touched. 'Don't be silly,' he said. 'They're exactly alike.'

Henry replaced his books. 'I don't want any bitterness,' he said, 'or immature squabbling. As the older man, it's my responsibility to yield. Here. I'll give you the shirt off my back.' And he began to peel off his lumberjack shirt, leaving the foulard dramatically knotted around his naked throat. He wore no undershirt.

Having won from Orson a facial expression that Orson himself could not see, Henry smiled and rebuttoned the shirt. 'Do you mind my name being in the upper slot on the door? I'll remove it. I apologize. I did it without realizing how sensitive you would be.'

Perhaps it was all a kind of humour. Orson tried to make a joke. He pointed and asked, 'Do I get a spinning wheel, too?'

'Oh, *that*.' Henry hopped backward on one bare foot and became rather shy. 'That's an experiment. I ordered it from Calcutta. I spin for a half hour a day, after Yoga.'

'You do Yoga, too?'

'Just some of the elementary positions. My ankles can't take more than five minutes of the Lotus yet.'

'And you say you have a bishop.'

The roommate glanced up with a glint of fresh interest. 'Say. You listen, don't you? Yes. I consider myself an Anglican Christian Platonist strongly influenced by Gandhi.' He touched his palms before his chest, bowed, straightened, and giggled. 'My bishop hates me,' he said. 'The one in Oregon, who wants me to be a soldier. I've introduced myself to the bishop here and I don't think he likes me, either. For that matter, I've antagonized my adviser. I told him I had no intention of fulfilling the science requirement.'

'For God's sake, why *not*?'

'You don't really want to know.'

Orson felt this rebuff as a small test of strength. 'Not really,' he agreed.

'I consider science a demonic illusion of human *hubris*. Its phantasmal nature is proved by its constant revision. I asked him, "Why should I waste an entire fourth of my study time, time that could be spent with Plato, mastering a mass of hypotheses that will be obsolete by the time I graduate?" '

'My Lord, Henry,' Orson exclaimed, indignantly defending the millions of lives saved by medical science, 'you can't be serious!'

'Please. Hub. I may be difficult for you, and I think it would help if you were to call me by my name. Now let's talk about you. Your father is a doctor, you received all A's in high school – I received rather mediocre grades myself – and you've come to Harvard because you believe it affords a cosmopolitan Eastern environment that will be valuable to you after spending your entire life in a small provincial town.'

'Who the hell told you all this?' The recital of his application statement made Orson blush. He already felt much older than the boy who had written it.

'University Hall,' Henry said. 'I went over and asked to see your folder. They didn't want to let me at first, but I explained that if they were going to give me a roommate, after I had specifically requested to live alone, I had a right to information about you, so I could minimize possible friction.'

'And they *let* you?'

'Of course. People without convictions have no powers of resistance.' His mouth made its little satisfied click, and Orson was goaded to ask, 'Why did *you* come to Harvard?'

'Two reasons.' He ticked them off on two fingers. 'Raphael Demos and Werner Jaeger.'

Orson did not know these names, but he suspected that 'Friends of yours?' was a stupid question, once it was out of his mouth.

But Henry nodded. 'I've introduced myself to Demos. A charming old scholar, with a beautiful young wife.'

'You mean you just went to his house and pushed yourself *in*?' Orson heard his own voice grow shrill; his voice, rather high and unstable, was one of the things about himself that he liked least.

Henry blinked, and looked unexpectedly vulnerable, so slender and bravely dressed, his ugly, yellowish, flat-nailed feet naked on the floor, which was uncarpeted and painted black. 'That isn't how I would describe it. I went as a pilgrim. He seemed pleased to talk to me.' He spoke carefully, and his mouth abstained from clicking.

That he could hurt his roommate's feelings – that this jaunty apparition had feelings – disconcerted Orson more deeply than any of the surprises he had been deliberately offered. As quickly as he had popped up, Henry dropped to the floor, as if through a trapdoor in the plane of conversation. He resumed spinning. The method apparently called for one thread to be wound around the big toe of a foot and to be kept taut by a kind of absent-minded pedal motion. While engaged in this, he seemed hermetically sealed inside one of the glueing machines that had incubated his garbled philosophy. Unpacking, Orson was slowed and snagged by a complicated mood of discomfort. He tried to remember how his mother had arranged his bureau drawers at home – socks and underwear in one, shirts and handkerchiefs in another. Home seemed infinitely far from him, and he was dizzily conscious of a great depth of space beneath his feet, as if the blackness of the floor were the colour of an abyss. The spinning wheel steadily chuckled. Orson's buzz of unease circled and settled on his room-mate, who, it was clear, had thought earnestly about profound matters, matters that Orson, busy as he had been with the practical business of being a good student, had hardly considered. It was also clear that Henry had thought unintelligently. This unintelligence ('I received rather mediocre grades myself') was more of a menace than a comfort. Bent above the bureau drawers, Orson felt cramped in his mind, able neither to stand erect in wholehearted contempt nor to lie down in honest admiration. His mood was complicated by the repugnance his roommate's physical presence aroused in him. An almost morbidly clean boy, Orson was haunted by glue, and a tacky ambience resisted every motion of his unpacking.

The silence between the roommates continued until a great bell rang ponderously. The sound was near and yet far, like a heartbeat within the bosom of time, and it seemed to bring with it into the room the muffling foliation of the trees in the Yard, which to Orson's prairie-honed eyes had looked tropically tall and lush; the walls of the room vibrated with leaf shadows, and many minute presences – dust motes, traffic sounds, or angels of whom several could dance on the head of a pin – thronged the air and made it difficult to breathe. The stairways of the dormitory rumbled. Boys dressed in jackets and neckties crowded the doorway and entered the room, laughing and calling 'Hub. Hey, Hub.'

'Get up off the floor, dad.'

'Jesus, Hub, put your shoes on.'

'Pee-*yew*.'

'And take off that seductive sarong around your neck.'

'Consider the lilies, Hub. They toil not, neither do they spin, and yet I say unto you that Solomon in all his glory was not arrayed like one of these.'

'Amen, brothers!'

'Fitch, you should be a preacher.'

They were all strangers to Orson. Hub stood and smoothly performed introductions.

In a few days, Orson had sorted them out. That jostling conglomerate, so apparently secure and homogeneous, broke down, under habitual exposure, into double individuals: roommates. There were Silverstein and Koshland, Dawson and Kern, Young and Carter, Petersen and Fitch.

Silverstein and Koshland, who lived in the room overhead, were Jews from New York City. All Orson knew about non-biblical Jews was that they were a sad race, full of music, shrewdness, and woe. But Silverstein and Koshland were always clowning, always wisecracking. They played bridge and poker and chess and Go and went to the movies in Boston and drank coffee in the luncheonettes around the Square. They came from the 'gifted' high schools of the Bronx and Brooklyn respectively, and treated Cambridge as if it were another borough. Most of what the freshman year sought to teach them they seemed to know already. As winter approached, Koshland went out for basketball, and he and his teammates made the floor above bounce to the thump and rattle of scrimmages with a tennis ball and a wastebasket. One afternoon, a section of ceiling collapsed on Orson's bed.

Next door, in Room 12, Dawson and Kern wanted to be writers. Dawson was from Ohio and Kern from Pennsylvania. Dawson had a sulky, slouching bearing, a certain puppyish facial eagerness, and a terrible temper. He was a disciple of Anderson and Hemingway and himself wrote as austerely as a newspaper. He had been raised as an atheist, and no one in the dormitory incited his temper more often than Hub. Orson, feeling that he and Dawson came from opposite edges of that great psychological realm called the Midwest, liked him. He felt less at ease with Kern, who seemed Eastern and subtly vicious. A farm boy driven by an unnatural sophistication, riddled with nervous ailments ranging from conjunctivitis to haemorrhoids, Kern smoked and talked incessantly. He and Dawson maintained between them a battery of running jokes. At night Orson could hear them on the other side of the wall keeping each other awake with improvised parodies and musical comedies based on their teachers, their courses, or their fellow-freshmen. One midnight, Orson distinctly heard Dawson sing, 'My name is Orson Ziegler, I come from South Dakota.' There was a pause, then Kern sang back, 'I tend to be a niggler, and masturbate by quota.'

Across the hall, in 15, lived Young and Carter, Negroes. Carter was from Detroit and very black, very clipped in speech, very well dressed, and apt to collapse, at the jab of a rightly angled joke, into a spastic giggling fit that left his cheeks gleaming with tears; Kern was expert at breaking Carter up. Young was a lean, malt-pale coloured boy from North Carolina, here on a national scholarship, out of his depth, homesick, and cold. Kern called him Br'er Possum. He slept all day and at night sat on his bed playing the mouthpiece of a trumpet to himself. At first, he had played the full horn in the afternoon, flooding the dormitory and its green envelope of trees with golden, tremulous versions of languorous tunes like 'Sentimental Journey' and 'The Tennessee Waltz'. It had been nice. But Young's sombre sense of tact – a slavish drive towards self-effacement that the shock of Harvard had awakened in him – soon cancelled those harmless performances. He took to hiding from the sun, and at night the furtive spitting sound from across the hall seemed to Orson, as he struggled into sleep, music drowning in shame. Carter always referred to his roommate as 'Jonathan', mouthing the syllables fastidiously, as if he were pronouncing the name of a remote being he had just learned about, like Rochefoucauld or Demosthenes.

Cattycorner up the hall, in unlucky 13, Petersen and Fitch kept a strange household. Both were tall, narrow-shouldered, and broad-bottomed; physiques aside, it was hard to see what they had in common, or why Harvard had put them together. Fitch, with dark staring eyes and the flat full cranium of Frankenstein's monster, was a child prodigy from Maine, choked with philosophy, wild with ideas, and pregnant with the seeds of the nervous breakdown he was to have, eventually, in April. Petersen was an amiable Swede with a transparent skin that revealed blue veins in his nose. For several summers he had worked as a reporter for the Duluth *Herald*. He had all the newsman's tricks: the side-of-the-mouth quip, the nip of whisky, the hat on the back of the head, the habit of throwing still-burning cigarettes onto the floor. He did not seem quite to know why he was at Harvard, and in fact did not return at the end of the freshman year. But, while these two drifted towards their respective failures, they made a strangely well-suited couple. Each was strong where the other was helpless. Fitch was so uncoordinated and unorganized he could not even type; he would lie on his bed in pyjamas, writhing and grimacing, and dictate a tangled humanities paper, twice the requested length and mostly about books that had not been assigned, while Petersen, typing with a hectic two-finger system, would obligingly turn this chaotic monologue into 'copy'. His patience verged on the maternal. When Fitch appeared for a meal wearing a coat and tie, the joke ran in the dormitory that Petersen had dressed him. In return, Fitch gave Petersen ideas out of the superabundance painfully cramming his big flat head. Petersen had absolutely no ideas; he could neither compare, contrast, nor criticize St Augustine and Marcus Aurelius. Perhaps having seen, so young, so many corpses and fires and policemen and prostitutes had prematurely blighted his mind. At any rate, mothering Fitch gave him something practical to do, and Orson envied them.

He envied all the roommates, whatever the bond between them – geography, race, ambition, physical size – for between himself and Hub Palamountain he could see no link except forced cohabitation. Not that living with Hub was superficially unpleasant. Hub was tidy, industrious, and ostentatiously considerate. He rose at seven, prayed, did Yoga, spun, and was off to breakfast, often not to be seen again until the end of the day. He went to sleep, generally, at eleven sharp. If there was noise in the room, he would insert rubber plugs in his ears, put a black mask over his eyes, and go to sleep anyway. During the day, he kept a rigorous round of appointments: he audited two courses in addition to taking four, he wrestled three times a week for his physical-training requirement, he wangled tea invitations from Demos and Jaeger and the Bishop of Massachusetts, he attended free evening lectures and readings, he associated himself with the Phillips Brooks House and spent two afternoons a week supervising slum boys in a Roxbury redevelopment house. In addition, he had begun to take piano lessons in Brookline. Many days, Orson saw him only at meals in the Union, where the dormitory neighbours, in those first fall months when their acquaintance was crisp and young and differing interests had not yet scattered them, tended to regroup around a long table. In these months there was often a debate about the subject posed under their eyes: Hub's vegetarianism. There he would sit, his tray heaped high with a steaming double helping of squash and lima beans, while Fitch would try to locate the exact point at which vegetarianism became inconsistent. 'You eat eggs,' he said.

'Yes,' Hub said.

'You realize that every egg, from the chicken's point of reference, is a newborn baby?'

'But in fact is is not unless it has been fertilized by a rooster.'

'But suppose,' Fitch pursued, 'as sometimes happens – which I happen to know, from working in my uncle's henhouse in Maine – an egg that *should* be sterile has in fact been fertilized and contains an embryo?'

'If I see it, I naturally don't eat that particular egg,' Hub said, his lips making that satisfied concluding snap.

Fitch pounced triumphantly, spilling a fork to the floor with a lurch of his hand. 'But *why*? The hen feels the same pain on being parted from an egg whether sterile or fertile. The embryo is unconscious – a vegetable. As a vegetarian, you should eat it with special relish.' He tipped back in his chair so hard he had to grab the table edge to keep from toppling over.

'It seems to me,' Dawson said, frowning darkly – these discussions, clogging some twist of his ego, often spilled him into a vile temper – 'that psychoanalysis of hens is hardly relevant.'

'On the contrary,' Kern said lightly, clearing his throat and narrowing his pink, infected eyes, 'it seems to me that there, in the tiny, dim mind of the hen – the minimal mind, as it were – is where the tragedy of the universe achieves a pinpoint focus. Picture the emotional life of a hen. What does she know of companionship? A flock of pecking, harsh-voiced gossips. Of shelter? A few dung-bespattered slats. Of food? Some flecks of mash and grit insolently tossed on the ground. Of love? The casual assault of a polygamous cock – cock in the Biblical sense. Then, into this heartless world, there suddenly arrives, as if by magic, an egg. An egg of her own. An egg, it must seem to her, that she and God have made. How she must cherish it, its beautiful baldness, its gentle lustre, its firm yet somehow fragile, softly swaying weight.'

Carter had broken up. He bent above his tray, his eyes tight shut, his dark face contorted joyfully. 'Puhleese,' he gasped at last. 'You're making my stomach hurt.'

'Ah, Carter,' Kern said loftily, 'if that were only the worst of it. For then, one day, while the innocent hen sits cradling this strange, faceless, oval child, its little weight swaying softly in her wings' – he glanced hopefully at Carter, but the coloured boy bit his lower lip and withstood the jab – 'an enormous man, smelling of beer and manure, comes and tears the egg from her grasp. And why? Because *he*' – Kern pointed, arm fully extended, across the table, so that his index finger, orange with nicotine, almost touched Hub's nose – '*he*, Saint Henry Palamountain, wants more eggs to eat. "More eggs!" he cries voraciously, so that brutal steers and faithless pigs can continue to menace the children of American mothers!'

Dawson slammed his silver down, got up from the table, and slouched out of the dining room. Kern blushed. In the silence, Petersen put a folded slice of roast beef in his mouth and said, chewing, 'Jesus, Hub, if somebody else kills the animals you might as well eat 'em. They don't give a damn any more.'

'You understand nothing,' Hub said simply.

'Hey, Hub,' Silverstein called down from the far end of the table. 'What's the word on milk? Don't calves drink milk? Maybe you're taking milk out of some calf's mouth.'

Orson felt impelled to speak. '*No*,' he said, and his voice seemed to have burst, its pitch was so unsteady and excited. 'As anybody except somebody from New York would know, milch cows have weaned their calves. What I wonder about, Hub, is your shoes. You wear leather shoes.'

'I do.' The gaiety left Hub's defence of himself. His lips became prim. 'Leather is the skin of a steer.'

'But the animal has already been slaughtered.'

'You sound like Petersen. Your purchase of leather goods – what about your wallet and belt, for that matter? – encourages the slaughter. You're as much of a murderer as the rest of us. More of one – because you think about it.'

Hub folded his hands carefully in front of him, propping them, almost in prayer, on the table edge. His voice became like that of a radio announcer, but an announcer rapidly, softly describing the home stretch of a race. 'My belt, I believe, is a form of plastic. My wallet was given to me by my mother years ago, before I became a vegetarian. Please remember that I ate meat for eighteen years and I still have an appetite for it. If there were any other concentrated source of protein, I would not eat eggs. Some vegetarians do not. On the other hand, some vegetarians eat fish and take liver extract. I would not do this. Shoes are a problem. There is a firm in Chicago that makes non-leather shoes for extreme vegetarians, but they're very expensive and not comfortable. I once ordered a pair. They killed my feet. Leather, you see, "breathes" in a way no synthetic substitute does. My feet are tender; I have compromised. I apologize. For that matter, when I play the piano I encourage the slaughter of elephants, and in brushing my teeth, which I must do faithfully because a vegetable diet is so heavy in carbohydrates, I use a brush of pig bristles. I am covered with blood, and pray daily for forgiveness.' He took up his fork and resumed eating the mound of squash.

Orson was amazed; he had been impelled to speak by a kind of sympathy, and Hub had answered as if he alone were an enemy. He tried to

155

defend himself. 'There are perfectly wearable shoes,' he said, 'made out of canvas, with crêpe-rubber soles.'

'I'll look into them,' Hub said. 'They sound a little sporty to me.'

Laughter swept the table and ended the subject. After lunch Orson walked to the library with the beginnings of indigestion; a backwash of emotion was upsetting his stomach. There was a growing confusion inside him he could not resolve. He resented being associated with Hub, and yet felt attacked when Hub was attacked. It seemed to him that Hub deserved credit for putting his beliefs into practice, and that people like Fitch and Kern, in mocking, merely belittled themselves. Yet Hub smiled at their criticism, took it as a game, and fought back in earnest only at Orson, forcing him into a false position. Why? Was it because in being also a Christian he alone qualified for serious rebuke? But Carter went to church, wearing a blue pin-striped suit with a monogrammed handkerchief peaked in the breast pocket, every Sunday; Petersen was a nominal Presbyterian; Orson had once seen Kern sneaking out of Mem Chapel; and even Koshland observed his holidays, by cutting classes and skipping lunch. Why, therefore, Orson asked himself, should Hub pick on him? And why should he care? He had no real respect for Hub. Hub's handwriting was childishly large and careful and his first set of hour exams, even in the course on Plato and Aristotle, had yielded a batch of C's. Orson resented being condescended to by an intellectual inferior. The knowledge that at the table he had come off second best galled him like an unfair grade. His situation with Hub became in his head a diagram in which all his intentions curved off at right angles and his strengths inversely tapered into nothing. Behind the diagram hung the tuck of complacence in Hub's lips, the fishy impudence of his eyes, and the keenly irksome shape and tint of his hands and feet. These images – Hub disembodied – Orson carried with him into the library, back and forth to classes, and along the congested streets around the Square; now and then the glaze of an eye or the flat yellowish nail of a big toe welled up distinctly through the pages of a book and, greatly magnified, slid with Orson into the unconsciousness of sleep. Nevertheless, he surprised himself, sitting one February afternoon in Room 12 with Dawson and Kern, by blurting, 'I hate him.' He considered what he had said, liked the taste of it, and repeated, 'I hate the bastard. I've never hated anybody before in my life.' His voice cracked and his eyes warmed with abortive tears.

They had all returned from Christmas vacation to plunge into the weird limbo of reading period and the novel ordeal of midyear exams. This was a dormitory, by and large, of public-school graduates, who feel the strain of Harvard most in their freshman year. The private-school boys, launched by little Harvards like Exeter and Groton, tend to glide through this year and to run aground later on strange reefs, foundering in alcohol, or sinking into a dandified apathy. But the institution demands of each man, before it releases him, a wrenching sacrifice of ballast. At Christmas, Orson's mother thought he looked haggard, and set about fattening him up. On the other hand, he was struck by how much his father had aged and shrunk. Orson spent his first days home listening to the mindless music on the radio, hours of it, and driving through farmland on narrow straight roads already banked bright with ploughed snow. The South Dakota sky had never looked so open, so clean; he had never realized before that the high dry sun that made even sub-zero days feel warm at noon was a local phenomenon. He made love to his girl again, and again she cried. He said to her he blamed himself, for ineptitude; but in his heart he blamed her. She was not helping him. Back in Cambridge, it was raining, raining in January, and the entryway of the Coop was full of grey footprints and wet bicycles and Radcliffe girls in slickers and sneakers. Hub had stayed here, alone in their room, and had celebrated Christmas with a fast.

In the monotonous, almost hallucinatory month of rereading, outlining, and memorizing, Orson perceived how little he knew, how stupid he was, how unnatural all learning is, and how futile. Harvard rewarded him with three A's and a B. Hub pulled out two B's and two C's. Kern, Dawson, and Silverstein did well; Petersen, Koshland, and Carter got mediocre grades; Fitch flunked one subject, and Young flunked three. The pale Negro slunk in and out of the dorm as if he were diseased and marked for destruction; he became, while still among them, a rumour. The suppressed whistling of the trumpet mouthpiece was no longer heard. Silverstein and Koshland and the basketball crowd adopted Carter and took him to movies in Boston three or four times a week.

After exams, in the heart of the Cambridge winter, there is a grateful pause. New courses are selected, and even the full-year courses, heading into their second half, sometimes put on, like a new hat, a fresh professor. The days quietly lengthen; there is a snowstorm or two; the swimming and squash teams lend the sports pages of the *Crimson* an unaccustomed note of victory. A kind of foreshadow of spring falls bluely on the snow. The elms are seen to be shaped like fountains. The discs of snow pressed by boots into the sidewalk by Albiani's seem large precious coins; the brick buildings, the arched gates, the archaic lecterns, and the barny mansions along Brattle Street dawn upon the freshman as a heritage he temporarily possesses. The thumb-worn spines of his now familiar text-books seem proof of a certain knowingness, and the strap of the green book bag tugs at his wrist like a living falcon. The letters from home dwindle in importance. The hours open up. There is more time. Experiments are made. Courtships begin. Conversations go on and on; and an almost rapacious desire for mutual discovery possesses acquaintances. It was in this atmosphere, then, that Orson made his confession.

Dawson turned his head away as if the words had menaced him personally. Kern blinked, lit a cigarette, and asked, 'What don't you like about him?'

'Well' – Orson shifted his weight uncomfortably in the black but graceful, shapely but hard Harvard chair – 'it's little things. Whenever he gets a notice from the Portland draft board, he tears it up without opening it and scatters it out the window.'

'And you're afraid that this incriminates you as an accessory and they'll put you in jail?'

'No – I don't know. It seems exaggerated. He exaggerates everything. You should see how he prays.'

'How do you know how he prays?'

'He shows me. Every morning, he gets down on his knees and *throws* himself across the bed, his face in the blanket, his arms way out.' He showed them.

'God,' Dawson said. 'That's marvellous. It's medieval. It's more than medieval. It's Counter-Reformation.'

'I mean,' Orson said, grimacing in realization of how deeply he had betrayed Hub, 'I pray, too, but I don't make a show of myself.'

A frown clotted Dawson's expression, and passed.

'He's a saint,' Kern said.

'He's *not*,' Orson said. 'He's not intelligent. I'm taking Chem 1 with him, and he's worse than a child with the math. And those Greek books he keeps on his desk, they look worn because he bought them second-hand.'

'Saints don't have to be intelligent,' Kern said. 'What saints have to have is energy. Hub has it.'

'Look how he wrestles,' Dawson said.

'I doubt if he wrestles very *well*,' Orson said. 'He didn't make the freshman team. I'm sure if we heard him play the piano, it'd be awful.'

'You seem to miss the point,' Kern said, eyes closed, 'of what Hub's all about.'

'I know goddam well what he thinks he's all about,' Orson said, 'but it's fake. It doesn't go. All this vegetarianism and love of the starving Indian – he's really a terribly cold bastard. I think he's about the coldest person I've ever met in my life.'

'I don't think Orson thinks that; do you?' Kern asked Dawson.

'No,' Dawson said, and his puppyish smile cleared his cloudy face. 'That's not what Orson the Parson thinks.'

Kern squinted. 'Is it Orson the Parson, or Orson the Person?'

'I think Hub is the nub,' Dawson said.

'Or the rub,' Kern added, and both burst into grinding laughter. Orson felt he was being sacrificed to the precarious peace the two roommates kept between themselves, and left, superficially insulted but secretly flattered to have been given, at last, a nickname of sorts: Orson the Parson.

Several nights later they went to hear Carl Sandburg read in New Lecture Hall – the four adjacent roommates, plus Fitch. To avoid sitting next to Hub, who aggressively led them into a row of seats, Orson delayed, and so sat the farthest away from the girl Hub sat directly behind. Orson noticed her immediately; she had a lavish mane of coppery red hair which hung down loose over the back of her seat. The colour of it, and the abundance, reminded him, all at once, of horses, earth, sun, wheat, and home. From Orson's angle she was nearly in profile; her face was small, with a tilted shadowy cheekbone and a pale prominent ear. Towards the pallor of her profile he felt an orgasmic surge; she seemed suspended in the crowd and was floating, a crest of whiteness, towards him. She turned away. Hub had leaned forward and was saying something into her other ear. Fitch overheard it, and gleefully relayed it to Dawson, who whispered to Kern and Orson; '*Hub said to the girl, "You have beautiful hair."* '

Several times during the reading, Hub leaned forward to add something more into her ear, each time springing spurts of choked laughter from Fitch, Dawson, and Kern. Meanwhile, Sandburg, his white bangs as straight and shiny as a doll's wig of artificial fibre, incanted above the lectern and quaintly strummed a guitar. Afterward, Hub walked with the girl into the outdoors. From a distance Orson saw her white face turn and crumple into a laugh. Hub returned to his friends with the complacent nick in the corner of his mouth deepened, in the darkness, to a gash.

It was not the next day, or the next week, but within the month that Hub brought back to the room a heap of red hair. Orson found it lying like a diaphanous corpse on a newspaper spread on his bed. 'Hub, what the hell is this?'

Hub was on the floor playing with his spinning wheel. 'Hair.'

'*Human* hair?'

'Of course.'

'Whose?'

'A girl's.'

'What happened?' The question sounded strange; Orson meant to ask, 'What girl's?'

Hub answered as if he had asked that question. 'It's a girl I met at the Sandburg reading; you don't know her.'

'This is *her* hair?'

'Yes. I asked her for it. She said she was planning to cut it all off this spring anyway.'

Orson stood stunned above the bed, gripped by an urge to bury his face and hands in the hair. 'You've been *seeing* her?' This effeminate stridence in his voice: he despised it and only Hub brought it out.

'A little. My schedule doesn't allow for much social life, but my adviser has recommended that I relax now and then.'

'You take her to movies?'

'Once in a while. She pays her admission, of course.'

'Of *course*.'

Hub took him up on his tone. 'Please remember I'm here on my savings alone. I have refused all financial assistance from my father.'

'Hub' – the very syllable seemed an expression of pain – 'what are you going to do with her hair?'

'Spin it into a rope.'

'A *rope*?'

'Yes. It'll be very difficult; her hair is terribly fine.'

'And what will you do with the rope?'

'Make a knot of it.'

'A *knot*?'

'I think that's the term. I'll coil it and secure it so it can't come undone and give it to her. So she'll always have her hair the way it was when she was nineteen.'

'How the hell did you talk this poor girl into it?'

'I didn't talk her into it. I merely offered, and she thought it was a lovely idea. Really, Orson, I don't see why this should offend your bourgeois scruples. Women cut their hair all the time.'

'She must think you're insane. She was humouring you.'

'As you like. It was a perfectly rational suggestion, and my sanity has never been raised as an issue between us.'

'Well, *I* think you're insane. Hub, you're a *nut*.'

Orson left the room and slammed the door, and didn't return until eleven, when Hub was asleep in his eye mask. The heap of hair had been transferred to the floor beside the spinning wheel, and already some strands were entangled with the machine. In time a rope was produced, a braided cord as thick as a woman's little finger, about a foot long, weightless and waxen. The earthy, horsey fire in the hair's colour had been quenched in the process. Hub carefully coiled it and with black thread and long pins secured and stiffened the spiral into a disc the size of a small saucer. This he presented to the girl one Friday night. The presentation appeared to satisfy him, for, as far as Orson knew, Hub had no further dates with her. Once in a while Orson passed her in the Yard, and without her hair she scarcely seemed female, her small pale face fringed in curt tufts, her ears looking enormous. He wanted to speak to her; some obscure force of pity, or hope of rescue, impelled him to greet this wan androgyne, but the opening word stuck in his throat. She did not look as if she pitied herself, or knew what had been done to her.

Something magical protected Hub; things deflected from him. The doubt Orson had cast upon his sanity bounced back on to himself. As spring slowly broke, he lost the ability to sleep. Figures and facts churned sluggishly in an insomnious mire. His courses became four parallel puzzles. In mathematics, the crucial transposition upon which the solution pivoted consistently eluded him, vanishing into the chinks between the numbers. The quantities in chemistry became impishly unstable; the unbalanced scales clicked down sharply and the system of interlocked elements that fanned from the lab to the far stars collapsed. In the history survey course, they had reached the Enlightenment, and Orson found himself disturbingly impressed by Voltaire's indictment of God, though the lecturer handled it calmly, as one more dead item of intellectual history, neither true nor false. And in German, which Orson had taken to satisfy his language requirement, the words piled on remorselessly, and the existence of languages other than English, the existence of so many, each so vast, intricate, and opaque, seemed to prove cosmic dementia. He felt his mind, which was always more steady than quick, grow slower and slower. His chair threatened to adhere to him, and he would leap up in panic. Sleepless, stuffed with information he could neither forget nor manipulate, he became prey to obsessive delusions; he became convinced that his girl in South Dakota had taken up with another boy and was making love to him happily, Orson having shouldered the awkwardness and blame of taking her virginity. In the very loops that Emily's ballpoint pen described in her bland letters to him he read the pleased rotundity, the inner fatness of a well-loved woman. He even knew the man. It was Spotted Elk, the black-nailed Chippewa, whose impassive nimbleness had so often mocked Orson on the basketball court, whose terrible ease and speed of reaction had seemed so unjust, and whose defence – he recalled now – Emily had often undertaken. His wife had become a whore, a squaw; the scraggly mute reservation children his father had doctored in the charity clinic became, amid the sliding transparencies of Orson's mind, his own children. In his dreams – or in those limp elisions of imagery which in the absence of sleep passed for dreams – he seemed to be rooming with Spotted Elk, and his roommate, who sometimes wore a mask, invariably had won, by underhanded means, the affection and admiration that were rightfully his. There was a conspiracy. Whenever Orson heard Kern and Dawson laughing on the other side of the wall, he knew it was about him, and about his most secret habits. This ultimate privacy was outrageously invaded; in bed, half-relaxed, he would suddenly see himself bodily involved with Hub's lips, Hub's legs, with Hub's veined, vaguely womanish hands. At first he resisted these visions, tried to erase them; it was like trying to erase ripples on water. He learned to submit to them, to let the attack – for it was an attack, with teeth and sharp acrobatic movements – wash over him, leaving him limp enough to sleep. These dives became the only route to sleep. In the morning he would awake and see Hub sprawled flamboyantly across his bed in prayer, or sitting hunched at his spinning wheel, or, gaudily dressed, tiptoeing to the door and with ostentatious care closing it softly behind him; and he would hate him – hate his appearance, his form, his manner, his pretensions with an avidity of detail he had never known in love. The tiny details of his roommate's physical existence – the wrinkles flickering beside his mouth, the slightly withered look about his hands, the complacently polished creases of his leather shoes – seemed a poisonous food Orson could not stop eating. His eczema worsened alarmingly.

By April, Orson was on the verge of going to the student clinic, which had a department called Mental Health. But at this point Fitch relieved him by having, it seemed, his nervous breakdown for him. For weeks, Fitch had been taking several showers a day. Towards the end he stopped going to classes and was almost constantly naked, except for a towel tucked around his waist. He was trying to complete a humanities paper that was already a month overdue and twenty pages too long. He left the dormitory only to eat and to take more books from the library. One night around nine, Petersen was called to the phone on the second-floor landing. The

Watertown police had picked Fitch up as he was struggling through the underbrush on the banks of the Charles four miles away. He claimed he was walking to the West, where he had been told there was enough space to contain God, and proceeded to talk with wild animation to the police chief about the differences and affinities between Kierkegaard and Nietzsche. Hub, ever alert for an opportunity to intrude in the guise of doing good, went to the hall proctor – a spindly and murmurous graduate student of astronomy engaged, under Harlow Shapley, in an endless galaxy count – and volunteered himself as an expert on the case, and even conferred with the infirmary psychologist. Hub's interpretation was that Fitch had been punished for *hubris*. The psychologist felt the problem was fundamentally Oedipal. Fitch was sent back to Maine. Hub suggested to Orson that now Petersen would need a roommate next year. 'I think you and he would hit it off splendidly. You're both materialists.'

'I'm *not* a materialist.'

Hub lifted his dreadful hands in half-blessing. 'Have it your way. I'm determined to minimize friction.'

'Dammit, Hub, all the friction between us comes from *you*.'

'How? What do I do? Tell me, and I'll change. I'll give you the shirt off my back.' He began to unbutton, and stopped, seeing that the laugh wasn't going to come.

Orson felt weak and empty, and in spite of himself he cringed inwardly, with a helpless affection for his unreal, unreachable friend. 'I don't know, Hub,' he admitted. 'I don't know what it is you're doing to me.'

A paste of silence dried in the air between them.

Orson with an effort unstuck himself. 'I think you're right, we shouldn't room together next year.'

Hub seemed a bit bewildered, but nodded, saying, 'I told them in the beginning that I ought to live alone.' And his hurt eyes bulging behind their lenses settled into an invulnerable Byzantine stare.

One afternoon in middle May, Orson was sitting stumped at his desk, trying to study. He had taken two exams and had two to go. They stood between him and release like two towering walls of muddy paper. His position seemed extremely precarious; he was unable to retreat and able to advance only along a very thin thread, a high wire of sanity on which he balanced above an abyss of statistics and formulae, his brain a firmament of winking cells. A push would kill him. There was then a hurried pounding up the stairs, and Hub pushed into the room carrying cradled in his arm a metal object the colour of a gun and the size of a cat. It had a red tongue. Hub slammed the door behind him, snapped the lock, and dumped the object on Orson's bed. It was the head of a parking meter, sheared from its post. A keen quick pain cut through Orson's groin. 'For God's sake,' he cried in his contemptible high voice, 'what's *that*?'

'It's a parking meter.'

'I *know*, I can *see* that. Where the hell did you *get* it?'

'I won't talk to you until you stop being hysterical,' Hub said, and crossed to his desk, where Orson had put his mail. He took the top letter, a special delivery from the Portland draft board, and tore it in half. This time, the pain went through Orson's chest. He put his head in his arms on the desk and whirled and groped in the black-red darkness there. His body was frightening him; his nerves listened for a third psychosomatic slash.

There was a rap on the door; from the force of the knock, it could only be the police. Hub nimbly dashed to the bed and hid the meter under Orson's pillow. Then he pranced to the door and opened it.

It was Dawson and Kern. 'What's up?' Dawson asked, frowning as if the disturbance had been created to annoy him.

'It sounded like Ziegler was being tortured,' Kern said.

Orson pointed at Hub and explained, 'He's castrated a parking meter!'

'I did not,' Hub said. 'A car went out of control on Mass Avenue and hit a parked car, which knocked a meter down. A crowd gathered. The head of the meter was lying in the gutter, so I picked it up and carried it away. I was afraid someone might be tempted to steal it.'

'Nobody tried to stop you?' Kern asked.

'Of course not. They were all gathered around the driver of the car.'

'Was he hurt?'

'I doubt it. I didn't look.'

'You didn't *look*!' Orson cried. 'You're a great Samaritan.'

'I am not prey,' Hub said, 'to morbid curiosity.'

'Where were the police?' Kern asked.

'They hadn't arrived yet.'

Dawson asked, 'Well why didn't you wait till a cop arrived and give the meter to him?'

'Why should I give it to an agent of the State? It's no more his than mine.'

'But it *is*,' Orson said.

'It was a plain act of Providence that placed it in my hands,' Hub said, the corners of his lips dented securely. 'I haven't decided yet which charity should receive the money it contains.'

Dawson asked, 'But isn't that stealing?'

'No more stealing than the State is stealing in making people pay money for space in which to park their own cars.'

'Hub,' Orson said, getting to his feet. 'You give it back or we'll both go to jail.' He saw himself ruined, the scarcely commenced career of his life destroyed.

Hub turned serenely. 'I'm not afraid. Going to jail under a totalitarian regime is a mark of honour. If you had a conscience, you'd understand.'

Petersen and Carter and Silverstein came into the room. Some boys from the lower floors followed them. The story was hilariously retold. The meter was produced from under the pillow and passed around and shaken to demonstrate the weight of pennies it contained. Hub always carried, as a vestige of the lumberjack country he came from, an intricate all-purpose pocket knife. He began to pry open the little money door. Orson came up behind him and got him around the neck with one arm. Hub's body stiffened. He passed the head of the meter and the open knife to Carter, and then Orson experienced sensations of being lifted, of flying, and of lying on the floor, looking up at Hub's face, which was upside down in his vision. He scrambled to his feet and went for him again, rigid with anger and yet, in his heart, happily relaxed; Hub's body was tough and quick and satisfying to grip, though, being a wrestler, he somehow deflected Orson's hands and again lifted and dropped him to the black floor. This time, Orson felt a blow as his coccyx hit the wood; yet even through the pain he perceived, gazing into the heart of this marriage, that Hub was being as gentle with him as he could be. And that he could try in earnest to kill Hub and be in no danger of succeeding was also a comfort. He renewed the attack and again enjoyed the tense defensive skill that made Hub's body a kind of warp in space through which his own body, after an ecstatic instant of contention, was converted to the supine position. He got to his feet and would have gone for Hub the fourth time, but his fellow-freshmen grabbed his arms and held him. He shook them off and without a word returned to his desk and concentrated down into his book, turning the page. The type looked extremely distinct, though it was trembling too hard to be deciphered.

The head of the parking meter stayed in the room for one night. The next day, Hub allowed himself to be persuaded (by the others; Orson had stopped speaking to him) to take it to the Cambridge police headquarters in Central Square. Dawson and Kern tied a ribbon around it, and attached a note: 'Please take good care of my baby.' None of them, however, had the nerve to go with Hub to the headquarters, though when he came back he said the chief was delighted to get the meter, and had thanked him, and had agreed to donate the pennies to the local orphan's home. In another week, the last exams were over. The freshmen all went home. When they returned in the fall, they were different: sophomores. Petersen and Young did not come back at all. Fitch returned, made up the lost credits, and eventually graduated *magna cum* in History and Lit. He now teaches in a Quaker prep school. Silverstein is a biochemist, Koshland a lawyer. Dawson writes conservative editorials in Cleveland, Kern is in advertising in New York. Carter, as if obliged to join Young in oblivion, disappeared between his junior and senior years. The dormitory neighbours tended to lose sight of each other, though Hub, who had had his case shifted to the Massachusetts jurisdiction, was now and then pictured in the *Crimson*, and once gave an evening lecture, 'Why I Am an Episcopalian Pacifist.' As the litigation progressed, the Bishop of Massachusetts rather grudgingly vouched for him, and by the time of his final hearing the Korean War was over, and the judge who heard the case ruled that Hub's convictions were sincere, as witnessed by his willingness to go to jail. Hub was rather disappointed at the verdict, since he had prepared a three-year reading list to occupy him in his cell and was intending to memorize all four Gospels in the original Greek. After graduation, he went to Union Theological Seminary, spent several years as the assistant rector of an urban parish in Baltimore, and learned to play the piano well enough to be the background music in a Charles Street cocktail lounge. He insisted on wearing his clerical collar, and as a consequence gave the bar a small celebrity. After a year of overriding people of less strong convictions, he was allowed to go to South Africa, where he worked and preached among the Bantus until the government requested that he leave the country. From there he went to Nigeria, and when last heard from – on a Christmas card, with French salutations and Negro Magi, which arrived, soiled and wrinkled, in South Dakota in February – Hub was in Madagascar, as a 'combination missionary, political agitator, and soccer coach'. The description struck Orson as probably facetious, and Hub's childish and confident handwriting, with every letter formed individually, afflicted him with some of the old exasperation. Having vowed to answer the card, he mislaid it, uncharacteristically.

Orson didn't speak to Hub for two days after the parking-meter incident. By then, it seemed rather silly, and they finished out the year sitting side by side at their desks as amiably as two cramped passengers who have endured a long bus trip together. When they parted, they shook hands, and Hub would have walked Orson to the subway kiosk except that he had an appointment in the opposite direction. Orson received two A's and two B's on his final exams; for the remaining three years at Harvard, he roomed uneventfully with two other colourless pre-med students, named Wallace and Neuhauser. After graduation, he married Emily, attended the Yale School of Medicine, and interned in St Louis. He is now the father of four children and, since the death of his own father, the only doctor in the town. His life has gone much the way he planned it, and he is much the kind of man he intended to be when he was eighteen. He delivers babies, assists the dying, attends the necessary meetings, plays golf, and does good. He is honourable and irritable. If not as much loved as his father, he is perhaps even more respected. In one particular only – a kind of scar he carries without pain and without any clear memory of the amputation – does the man he is differ from the man he assumed he would become. He never prays.

Still Life

Leonard Hartz, a slender and earnest American with an unromantically round head, came to the Constable School because it was one of three British art schools approved by the Veterans Administration under the new, pruned G.I. Bill. He could not imagine what the V.A. had seen in the place. Constable – 'Connie' to the bird-tongued, red-legged girls who composed half its student body – was at once pedantic and frivolous. The vast university museum which, with a gesture perhaps less motherly than absent-mindedly inclusive, sheltered the school in its left wing was primarily archaeological in interest. Upstairs, room after room was packed with glass cases of Anglo-Saxon rubble; downstairs, a remarkably complete set of casts taken from classical statuary swarmed down corridors and gestured under high archways in a kind of petrified riot. This counterfeit wealth of statues, many of them still decorated with the seams of the casting process and quite swarthy with dust, was only roughly ordered. Beginning in the east with wasp-waisted *kouroi* whose Asiatic faces wore the first faint smile of the Attic dawn, one passed through the jumbled poignance and grandeur of Greece's golden age and ended in a neglected, westerly room where some huge coarse monuments of the Roman–Christian degeneracy rested their hypnotized stares in the shadows. Masterpieces lurked like spies in this mob. His first week, Leonard spent a morning and two afternoons sketching a blackened Amazon leaning half-clad from a dark corner, and only at the end of the second day, struck by a resemblance between his sketch and the trademark of an American pencil manufacturer, did he realize that his silent companion had been the Venus de Milo.

For freshmen at the Constable School were to start off banished from the school itself, with its bright chatter and gay smocks, and sent into these sad galleries to 'draw from the antique'. The newcomers – Leonard and four other resentful American veterans and one wispy English boy and a dozen sturdy English teenage girls – straggled each morning into the museum, gripping a drawingboard under one arm and a bench called a 'horse' under the other, and at dusk, which came early to the interior of the museum, returned with their burdens, increased by the weight of a deity pinned to their boards, in time to see the advanced students jostle at the brush-cleaning sink and the model, incongruously dressed in street clothes, emerge from her closet. The school always smelled of turpentine at this hour.

Its disconsolate scent lingering in his head, Leonard left the school alone, hurrying down the three ranks of shallow steps just in time to miss his bus. Everywhere he turned, those first weeks, he had this sensation of things evading him. When he did board his bus, and climbed to the second deck, the store fronts below sped backwards as if from pursuit – the chemists' shops that were not exactly drugstores, the tea parlours that were by no means luncheonettes. The walls of the college buildings, crusty and impregnable, swept past like an armada of great grey sails, and the little river sung by Drayton and Milton and Matthew Arnold slipped from under him, and at right angles to the curving road red suburban streets plunged down steep perspectives, bristling with hedges and spiked walls and knotted chains. Sometimes, suspended between the retreating brick rows like puffs of flak, a flock of six or so birds was turning and flying, invariably away. The melancholy of the late English afternoon was seldom qualified for Leonard by any expectation of the night. Of the four other Americans, three were married, and although each of these couples in turn had him over for supper and Scrabble, these meals quickly vanished in his evenings' recurrent, thankless appetite. The American movies so readily available reaffirmed rather than relieved his fear that he was out of contact with anything that might give him strength. Even at the school, where he had decided to place himself at least provisionally under the influence of Professor Seabright's musty aesthetic, he began to feel that indeed there was, in the precise contour of a shoulder and the unique shape of space framed between Apollo's legs, something intensely important, which, too – though he erased until the paper tore and squinted till his eyes burned – evaded him.

Seabright tried to visit the students among the casts once a day. Foot-steps would sound briskly, marking the instructor off from any of the rare sightseers, usually a pair of nuns, who wandered, with whispers and a soft slithering step, into this section of the museum. Seabright's voice, its lisp buried in the general indistinctness, would rumble from far away, as if the gods were thinking of thundering. In stages of five minutes each, it would draw nearer, and eventually spoke distinctly with the students on the other side of the pedestals, a tall English girl named, with a pertness that sat somewhat askew on her mature body, Robin.

'Here, here,' Seabright said. 'We're not doing silhouettes.'

'I thought, you know,' Robin replied in an eager voice that to Leonard's American ears sounded also haughty, 'if the outline came right, the rest could be fitted in.'

'Oh no. Oh no. We don't fit *in*; we build *across* the large form. Otherwise all the little pieces will never read. You see, there, we don't even know where the centre of your chest is. Ah – may I?' From the grunts and sighs Leonard pictured Robin rising from straddling her horse and Seabright seating himself. 'Dear me,' he said, 'you've got the outlines so black they rather take my eye. However . . .'

To Leonard it was one of Seabright's charms that, faced with any problem of drawing, he became so engrossed he forgot to teach. He had had to train himself to keep glancing at his watch; else he would sit the whole afternoon attacking a beginner's exercise, frowning like a cat at a mouse hole, while the forgotten student stood by on aching legs.

'There,' Seabright sighed reluctantly. 'I'm afraid I've spent my time with you. It's just one passage, but you can see here, across the thorax, how the little elements already are turning the large surface. And then, as you'd pass into the rib cage, with these two shadows just touched in at first, you see . . . Perhaps I should do a *bit* more . . . There, you see. And then we could pass on to the throat . . . It's a good idea, actually, on these figgers to start with the pit of the throat, and then work the shoulders outward and go up for the head . . .'

'Yes, sir,' Robin said, a shade impatiently.

'The whole thrust of the pose is in those angles, you see? Do you see?'

'Yes, sir, I hope so.'

But her hopes were not enough for him; he came around the pedestals and his plump, solemn, slightly feline figure was in Leonard's view when he turned and said apprehensively to the hidden girl, 'You understand to use the pencil as lightly as you can? Work up the whole form gradually?'

'Oh, yes. Quite,' Robin's bright voice insisted.

Seabright twitched his head and came and stood behind Leonard. 'I don't think,' he said at last, 'we need draw in the casting seams; we can idealize to that extent.'

'It seemed to help in getting the intervals,' Leonard explained.

'Even though these are exercises, you know, there's no advantage in having them, uh, positively ugly.' Leonard glanced around at his teacher, who was not usually sarcastic, and Seabright continued with some embarrassment; his speech impediment was less audible than visible, a fitful effortlessness of the lips. 'I must confess you're not given much help by your subject matter.' His eyes had lifted to the statue Leonard had chosen to draw, for the reason that it had four limbs. Completeness was the crude token by which Leonard preferred one statue to another; he was puzzled by Seabright's offended murmur of 'Wretched thing.'

'Beg pardon, sir?'

'Look here, Hartz,' Seabright exclaimed, and with startling aggressiveness trotted forward, stretched up on tiptoe, and slapped the plaster giant's side. 'The Roman who copied this didn't even understand that this side is constricted by this leg taking the weight!' Seabright himself constricted, then blinked abashedly and returned to Leonard's side with a more cautious voice. 'Nevertheless, you've carried parts of it with admirable intensity. Per, uh, perhaps you've been rather *too* intense; relax a bit at first and aim for the swing of the figger – how that little curve here, you see, sets up against this long lean one.' Leonard expected him to ask for the pencil, but instead he asked, 'Why don't you get yourself a new statue? That charming girl Miss Cox is doing – Venus, really, I suppose she is. At least there you do get some echoes of the Greek grace. I should think you've done your duty by this one.'

'OK. It *was* starting to feel like mechanical drawing.' To dramatize his obedience, Leonard began prying out his thumbtacks, but Seabright, his five minutes not used up, lingered.

'You do see some sense in drawing these at the outset, don't you?' Seabright was troubled by his American students; of the five, Leonard knew he must seem the least rebellious.

'Sure. It's quite challenging, once you get into one.'

The Englishman was not totally reassured. He hovered apologetically, and confided this anecdote: 'Picasso, you know, had a woman come to him for advice about learning how to draw, and he told her right off, "*Dessinez antiques.*" Draw from the antique. There's nothing like it, for getting the big forms.'

Then Seabright left, pattering past threatening athletes and emperors, through the archway, out of the section altogether, into the gayer room where medieval armour, spurs, rings, spoons, and chalices were displayed. The sound of his shoes died. From behind the hedge of pedestals, quite close to Leonard's ear, Robin's clear voice piped, 'Well, isn't Puss in a snorty mood?'

To attack the statue Seabright assigned him, Leonard moved his horse several yards forward, without abandoning the precious light that filtered through a window high behind him. From this new position Robin was in part visible. A plinth still concealed her bulk, but around the plinth's corner her propped drawing-board showed, and her hand when it stabbed at the paper, and even her whole head, massive with floppy hair, when she bent forward into a detail. He was at first too shy to risk meeting her eyes, so her foot, cut off at the ankle, and thus isolated in its blue ballet slipper on the shadowy marble floor, received the brunt of his attention. It was a long foot, with the division of the toes just beginning at the rim of the slipper's blue arc, and the smooth pallor of the exposed oval yielding, above the instep, to the mist-reddened roughness of the Englishwoman's leg. These national legs, thick at the ankles and glazed up to the knees with a kind of weather-proofing, on Robin were not homely; like a piece of fine pink ceramic her ankle kept taking, in Seabright's phrase, his eye.

After an hour he brought out, 'Aren't your feet cold, in just those slippers?'

'*Rather*,' she promptly responded and, with the quick skip that proved to be her custom, went beyond the question: 'Gives me the shivers all over, being in this rotten place.'

It was too quick for him. 'You mean the school?'

'Oh, the school's all right; it's these wretched antiques.'

'Don't you like them? Don't you find them sort of stable, and timeless?'

'If these old things are timeless, I'd rather be timely by a long shot.'

'No, seriously. Think of them as angels.'

'Seriously my foot. You Americans are never serious. Everything you say's a variety of joke; honestly, it's like conversing in a monkey-house.'

On this severe note Leonard feared they had concluded; but a minute later she showed him his silence was too careful by lucidly announcing, 'I have a friend who's an atheist and hopes World War Three blows everything to bits. He doesn't care. He's an atheist.'

Their subsequent conversations sustained this discouraging quality, of two creatures thrown together in the same language exchanging, across a distance wider than it seemed, miscalculated signals. He felt she quite misjudged his earnestness and would have been astonished to learn how deeply and solidly she had been placed in his heart, affording a fulcrum by which he lifted the great dead mass of his spare time, which now seemed almost lighter than air, a haze of quixotic expectations, imagined murmurs, easy undressings, and tourist delights. He believed he was coming to love England. He went to a tailor and bought for four guineas a typical jacket of stiff green wool, only to discover, before the smeary mirror in his digs, that it made his head look absurdly small, like one berry on top of a bush; and he kept wearing his little zippered khaki windbreaker to the Constable School.

On his side, he could not estimate how silly she truly was. She was eighteen, and described looking up as a child and seeing bombs floatingly fall from the belly of a German bomber, yet there was something flat and smooth behind her large eyes that deflected his words oddly; she seemed to be empty of the ragged, absorbent wisdom of girls at home whose war experiences stopped short at scrap drives. Across Robin's incongruities – between her name and body, her experiences and innocence – was braced a certain official austerity, a determined erectness of carriage, as if she were Britannia in the cartoons, and her contours contained nothing erotic but limned a necessarily female symbol of ancient militance. Robin was tall, and her figure, crossing back and forth through the shadows of the casts and the patchy light between, seemed to Leonard to stalk. She was always in and out now. In at nine-thirty, breathless; out at ten for a coffee break; back at eleven; lunch at eleven-thirty; back by one; at two-thirty, out for a smoke; in by three; gone by four. Since the days of their joint attack on the Esquiline Venus, her work habits had grown blithe. She had moved away to another area, to analyse another figure, and he had not been bold enough to follow with his horse, though his next statue took him in her direction. So at least once an hour she came into his eyes, and, though the coffee breaks and long lunches forced him to deduce a lively alien society, he, accustomed by the dragged-out days of army life to patience, still thought of her as partly his. It seemed natural when, three weeks before the Michaelmas term ended, the Puss – Leonard had fallen in with mocking Seabright – promoted them to still life together.

At the greengrocer's on Monday morning they purchased still-life ingredients. The Constable School owned a great bin of inanimate objects, from which Leonard had selected an old mortar and pestle. His idea was then to buy, to make a logical picture, some vegetables that could be ground, and to arrange them in a Chardinesque tumble. But what, really, was ground, except nuts? The grocer did have some Jamaican walnuts.

'Don't be funny, Leonard,' Robin said. 'All those horrid little wrinkles, we'd be at it forever.'

'Well, what else could you grind?'

'We're not going to *grind* anything; we're going to paint it. What we want is something *smooth*.'

'Orange, miss?' the lad in charge offered.

'Oh, oranges. Everyone's doing oranges – looks like a pack of advertisements. What we want . . .' Frowning, she surveyed the produce, and Leonard's heart, plunged in the novel intimacy of shopping with a woman, beat excitedly. 'Onions,' Robin declared. 'Onions are what we want.'

'Onions, miss?'

'Yes, three, and a cabbage.'

'One cabbage?'

'Here, may I pick it out?'

'But, Robin,' Leonard said, having never before called her by name, 'onions and cabbages don't go together.'

'Really, Leonard, you keep talking as if we're going to *eat* them.'

'They're both so round.'

'I dare say. You won't get me doing any globby squashes. Besides, Leonard, ours won't get rotten.'

'Our globby squashes?'

'Our *still* life, sweet. Haven't you seen Melissa's pears? Really, if I had to look at those brown spots all day I think I'd go sick.'

The lad, in his grey apron and muddy boots, gently pushed a paper bag against her arm. 'Tenpence, miss. Five for the onions and four for the head and the bag's a penny.'

'Here,' Leonard said hoarsely, and the action of handing over the money was so husbandly he blushed.

Robin asked, 'Are the onions attractive?'

'Oh yes,' the boy said in a level uncomprehending tone that defended him against any meaning she might have, including that of 'having him on'.

'Did you give us attractive onions?' she repeated. 'I mean, we're not going to eat them.'

'Oh yes. They're good-looking, miss.'

The boy's referring to the cabbage simply as 'the head' haunted Leonard, and he started as if at a ghost when, emerging with Robin into the narrow street, the head of a passer-by looked vividly familiar; it was the head alone, for otherwise Jack Fredericks had quite blended in. He was dressed completely in leather and wool, and even the haircut framing his amazed gape of recognition had the heavy British form. Eerie reunions are common among Americans in Europe, but Leonard had never before been hailed from this far in the past. It offended him to have his privacy, built during so many painful weeks of loneliness, unceremoniously crashed; yet he was pleased to be discovered with a companion so handsome. 'Jack, this is Miss Robin Cox; Robin, Jack Fredericks. Jack is from my home town, Wheeling.'

'Wheeling, in what state?' the girl asked.

'West Virginia,' Jack smiled. 'It's rather like your Black Country.'

'More green than black,' Leonard said.

Jack guffawed. 'Good old literal Len,' he told Robin. His small moist eyes sought in vain to join hers in a joke over their mutual friend. He and Leonard had never been on a 'Len' basis. Had they met on the streets of Wheeling, neither one would have stopped walking.

'What are you doing here?' Leonard asked him.

'Reading Ec at Jesus; but you're the one who baffles me. You're *not* at the university surely?'

'Sort of. We're both at the Constable School of Art. It's affiliated.'

'I've never *heard* of it!' Jack laughed out loud, for which Leonard was grateful, since Robin further stiffened.

'It's in a wing of the museum. It's a very pleasant place.'

'Is it *really*? Well I must come over sometime and see this strange institution. I'm rather interested in painting right now.'

'Sure. Come on over. Anytime. We have to get back now and make a still life out of these onions.'

'Well, aren't you *won*derful? You know,' Jack said to the girl, 'Len was a year older than I in public school and I'm used to looking up at him.'

To this preposterous lie Robin coolly replied with another: 'Oh at Connie we all look up to him.'

The Constable School could not afford to waste its precious space on still lifes, and imposed upon the museum's good nature by setting them up in the Well, a kind of basement with a skylight. Here hard-to-classify casts were stashed. Here a great naturalistic boar reclined on his narrow tufted bottom; the Dying Gaul sunned himself in the soft lighting sifting from above like dust; Winged Victory hoisted her battered feathers; and a tall hermaphrodite, mutilated by Byzantine piety, posed behind a row of brutal Roman portrait busts. The walls were a strange gay blue; even more strangely gay were the five or six students, foreshortened into chipper, quick shapes, chirping around tables of brilliant fruit. As he followed his friend's blonde hair down the reverberating iron of the spiral stairs, Leonard felt he had at last arrived at the radiant heart of the school.

Nowhere in the museum was there as much light as in the Well. Their intimacy of the grocer's shop seemed clarified and enhanced in the fall of light, and pointed by artistic purpose. With much minuteness they arranged the elements upon a yellow cloth. Her white hands fussed imperiously with the cabbage, tearing off leaf after leaf until she had reduced it to a roundness she imagined would be simple to draw. After lunch they began to mark with charcoal their newly bought canvases, which smelled of glue and green wood. To have her, some distance from his side, echoing his task, and to know that her eyes concentrated into the same set of shapes, which after a little concentration took on an unnatural intensity, like fruit in Paradise, curiously enlarged his sense of his physical size; he seemed to tower above the flagstones, and his voice, in responding to her erratic exclamations and complaints, struck into his ears with grave finality, as if his words were being incised into the air. The other students on still life also worked solemnly, and in the afternoon there were few of them. The sounds of museum traffic drifted in from a comparatively dark and cluttered world.

Jack Fredericks paid his visit the very next day. He thumped down the stairs in his little student's gown and stared at the still life over Robin's shoulder and asked, 'Why are you going to grind onions in a mortar?'

'We're not,' she replied in the haughty voice Leonard had first heard.

Jack sauntered over to the hermaphrodite and said, 'Good Lord. What happened to *him*?'

Leonard made no earnest effort to put him at his ease. Embarrassed and hence stubborn, Jack lay down on the shallow ledge designed to set off the exhibits, in a place just behind the table supporting the still life, and smiled up quizzically at the faces of the painters. He meant to look debonair, but in the lambent atmosphere he looked ponderous, with all that leather and wool. The impression of mass was so intense Leonard feared he might move and break one of the casts. Leonard had not noticed on the street how big his fellow West Virginian had grown. The weight was mostly in flesh: broad beefy hands folded on his vest, corpulent legs uneasily crossed on the cold stone floor.

Seabright made no pretence of not being startled at finding him there. 'What uh, what are you doing?'

'I guess I'm auditing.'

The tell-tale 'guess' put the Puss's back up higher. 'We don't generally set aside space for spectators.'

'Oh, I've been very unobtrusive, sir. We haven't been saying a word to each other.'

'Be that as it may, you're right in these people's vision. If you didn't come down here to look at the statues, I'm really afraid there's nothing here for you.'

'Oh. Well. Certainly.' Jack, grimacing with the effort, raised his body to his feet. 'I didn't know there were regulations.'

Leonard did not strenuously follow up this victory. His courtship of Robin continued as subtly as before, though twice he did dare ask her to the movies. The second time, she accepted. The delicately tinted Japanese love tale, so queerly stained with murders, seemed to offer a mutually foreign ground where they might meet as equals, but the strict rules of the girls' house where she stayed, requiring them to scamper directly into a jammed bus, made the whole outing, in the end, seem awkward and foolish. He much preferred the days, full of light and time, when their proximity had the grace of the accidental and before their eyes a constant topic of intercourse was poised. He even wondered if through their one date he hadn't lost some dignity in her eyes. The tone of her talk to him in the Well was respectful; the more so since his painting was coming excellently. Something in those spherical shapes and mild colours spoke to him. Seabright was plainly flattered by his progress. 'Mmm,' he would purr, 'delicious tones on the shadow side here. But I believe you're shading a bit too much towards red. It's really a very distinct violet, you know. If I could have your palette a moment . . . And a clean brush?' Lesson by lesson, Leonard was drawn into Seabright's world, a tender, subdued, world founded on violet, and where violet – pronounced 'vaalet' – at the faintest touch of a shadow, at the slightest hesitation of red or blue, rose to the surface, shyly vibrant. Robin's bluntly polychrome vision caused him to complain, 'Really, Miss Cox, I wish you had got the drawing correct before you began filling in the spaces.' When Puss had gone back up the spiral stair, Robin would transfer his complaint to Leonard as 'Honestly, Len, I can't see all this rotten purple. You'd think my onions were grapes, to see what he's done to them. Tell me, should I scrape his paint right off?'

Leonard walked around to her easel and suggested, 'Why don't you try keying in the rest of it around them?'

'Key it in? Key it in!' She seemed to relish the shrill syllables.

'Sure. Make your cabbage kind of greeny-purple, and the yellow cloth browny-purple, and for the mortar, well, try pure turps.'

'No,' she pouted. 'It's not a joke. You're just being a disgusting silly American. You think I'm stupid at paints.'

Each day he sank deeper into a fatherly role; he welcomed any secure relationship with her, yet wondered if he wasn't being, perhaps, neutralized. She never sought his advice except on technical matters until the day near the end of term when, conceding him in this sense a great stride forward, she asked, 'How well do you know your friend Jack Fredericks?'

'Not well at all. I wouldn't call him my friend. He was a year younger in high school, and we weren't really in the same social class either.'

'The social classes in America – are they very strong?'

'Well – the divisions aren't as great as here, but there're more of them.'

'And he comes from a good class?'

'Fair.' He thought reticence was his best tactic, but when she joined him in silence he was compelled to prod. 'What makes you ask?'

'Now, Leonard. You mustn't breathe a word; if you do, I'll absolutely shrivel. You see, he's asked me to model for him.'

'*Model* for him? He can't paint.'

'Yes he can. He's shown me some of his things and they're rather good.'

'How does he mean "model"? Model in what condition?'

'Yes. In the nude.' High colour burned evenly in her face; she dabbed at the canvas.

'That's ridiculous. He doesn't paint at all.'

'But he *does*, Leonard. He's taken it up very seriously. I've *seen* his things.'

'What do they look like?'

'Oh, rather abstract.'

'I bet.'

'*All* you Americans paint in the abstract.'

'I don't.' He didn't feel this was much of a point to score.

'He says I have a lovely body –'

'Well *I* could have told you *that*.' But he hadn't.

'– and *swears*, absolutely, there would be nothing to it. He's even offered a model's fee.'

'Well I never heard of such an embarrassing awful scheme.'

'Really, Leonard, it's embarrasing only when you talk of it. I *know* he's perfectly serious as a painter.'

Leonard added a fleck of black to a mixture on his palette and sighed. 'Well, Robin. You do whatever you want. It's your life.'

'Oh, I wouldn't *dream* of *do*ing it. Mummy and Daddy would *die*.'

His relief was overwhelmed by a sudden fierce sense of being wronged. 'Don't let *them* stand in your way. Why, this may be the start of a whole career for you.'

'I mean, I never consi*d*ered it. I was just interested in your opinion of the man.'

'My opinion is, he's a *horrible* man. He's a silly spoiled snob and about to get hog fat and I don't see what attracts you in him. Terrible person. Terrible.'

'Well, as you say, you don't know him very well.'

Leonard and the other unmarried veteran went to Europe during the Michaelmas vacation. On the Channel boat, his thoughts, free for the first time from the tangle of departure, returned to Robin, and the certainty of her turning Fredericks down warmed him on the cold, briny deck. In Paris the idea that she even toyed with such a proposition excited him; it suggested an area of willingness, of loneliness, that Leonard could feasibly invade. In Frankfurt he wondered if actually she would turn him down – he knew she was staying around the university during vacation – and by Hamburg he was certain that she had not; she had consented. He grew accustomed to this conviction as he and his companion slowly circled back through the Lowlands. By the time he disembarked at Dover he was quite indifferent to her nakedness.

The school had grown chillier and much older in four weeks. In the Well, the arrangements of fruit had decayed; with the hope that some of the students would continue to work despite the vacation, the things had not been disturbed. Their own still life was least affected by time. The onions were as immutable as the statues; but the cabbage, peeled by Robin to its solid pale heart, had relaxed in wilting, and its outer leaves, grey and almost transparent, rested on the gold cloth. His painting, still standing in its easel, preserved the original appearance of the cabbage, but the pigments had dulled, sinking into the canvas; their hardness made the painting seem finished, though there were several uncovered corners and numerous contrasts his fresh eye saw the need of adjusting. He loaded his palette and touched paint to the canvas reluctantly. The Well was so empty on this Monday morning of resumption, he felt he had made a mistake, by misreading the schedule, or taking it too seriously. At the far end, the little English boy, who was arrogant as well as wispy, noisily dismantled groups, crashing vegetable elements into a paper sack.

After eleven o'clock, Robin appeared on the balcony of the spiral stair. She overlooked the Well with her serene Britannia stance – her bosom a brave chest, her hips and legs a firm foundation – and then descended in a flurry. 'Leonard. Where have you *been*?'

'I told you, I was going to Europe with Max. We went as far east as Hamburg, and came back through Holland and Belgium.'

'You went to *Germany*? Whatever for?'

'Well, I am German, eventually.'

Her attention went sideways. 'I say, the cabbage has taken it hard, hasn't it?' She took her own painting off the easel. 'Are you still going at it? Puss has put me back in antique.'

'Of all the *crust.*'

'Oh, well. He said to me, "You're pretty rotten at this, aren't you?" and I agreed. It's the truth.'

Leonard resented the implication in this blitheness that he, too, the companion of her futile labours, was negligible. His mouth stiff with injury, he sarcastically asked, 'How's your posing for Fredericks coming?'

Her blue eyes squared. 'Posing for *him*? I did nothing of the sort.' Her words might have been 'I love you'; his heart felt a sudden draught and he started to say, 'I'm glad.'

But she went on with surprising intensity, 'Really, Leonard, you refuse to take me *seriously*. I could see all along he was a dreadful bore.' Her arm held her canvas captive against her side and with her free hand she impatiently pushed floppy hair back from her forehead – a rigid, aristocratic gesture that swept his stir of hope quite away. He had been stupid. He had been stupid to think that if Fredericks were eliminated, that left him. Over here, they were two of a kind, and by his own admission he was Fredericks' inferior. She was done with the silly strange lot. After all, boy friends are a serious bit.

Like those flocks of birds seen from the bus window, she had exploded as he watched. Even before she took a backward step, her receding from him seemed so swift he raised his voice in claiming, less in apology than as a fresh basis, 'All Americans are bores.'

Dentistry and Doubt

Burton knew what the dentist would notice first: the clerical collar. People always did. The dentist was standing not quite facing the door, as if it had just occurred to him to turn away. His eyes, grey in a rose, faintly moustached face, clung to Burton's throat a moment too long for complete courtesy before lifting as he said, 'Hello!' Shifting his feet, the dentist thrust out an unexpectedly soft hand.

He noticed next that Burton was an American. In Oxford, Burton had acquired the habit of speaking softly, but susurration alone could not alter the proportionate emphasis of vowel over consonant, the slight drag at the end of each sentence, or any of the diphthongal peculiarities that betray Americans to the twittering English. As soon as Burton had returned the greeting, with an apology for being late (he did not blame the British buses, though they were at fault), he fancied he could hear the other man's mind register 'U.S.A. . . . pioneer piety . . . R.C.? Can't be; no black hat . . . frank enough smile . . . rather heavy tartar on the incisors.'

He motioned Burton to the chair and turned to a sink, where he washed his hands without looking at them. He talked over his shoulder. 'What part are you from?'

'Of the States?' Burton enjoyed saying 'the States'. It sounded so aggregate, so ominous.

'Yes. Are you Canadian?'

'No, I'm from Pennsylvania.' Burton had never had such a good view from a dentist's chair. A great bay window gave on a small back-yard. Black shapes of birds fluttered and jiggled among the twigs of two or three trees – willows, he guessed. Except for the birds, the trees were naked. A wet-wash sky hung, it seemed, a few feet behind the net of limbs. A brick wall looked the shade of rust, and patches of sky hinted at blue, but there was little colour in any of it.

'Pennsylvania,' the dentist mused, the latter syllables of the word amplifying as he drew closer. 'That's in the East?'

'It's a Middle Atlantic state. You know where New York City is?'

'Roughly.'

'It's a little west of that, more or less. It's a neutral sort of state.'

'I see.' The dentist leaned over him, and Burton received two wonderful surprises when he opened his mouth: the dentist said 'Thank you'; and the dentist had something on his breath that, without being either, smelled sweet as candy and spicy as cloves. Peering in, he bumped a mirror across Burton's teeth. An electric reflector like an eye doctor's was strapped to his head. Outside, the black birds did stunts among the twigs. The dentist's eyes were not actually grey; screwed up, they seemed more brown, and then, as they flicked towards the tool tray, rather green, like pebbles on the bed of a fast-running creek. He scraped at an eye-tooth, but with such tact that Burton felt nothing. 'There's certainly one,' he said, turning to make a mark on a clean card.

Burton took the opportunity to rid himself of a remark he had been holding in suspension. 'More than ninety per cent of the world's anthracite comes from Pennsylvania.'

'Really?' the dentist said, obviously not believing him. He returned his hands, the tools in them, to in front of Burton's chin. Burton opened his mouth. 'Thank you,' the dentist said.

As he peered and picked and made notations, a measure of serenity returned to Burton. That morning, possibly because of the scheduled visit to a foreign dentist, the Devil had been very active. Scepticism had mingled with the heat and aroma of his bed; it had dripped from the cold ochre walls of his digs; it had been the substance of his dreams. His slippers, his bathrobe, his face in the mirror, his books – black books, brown ones, C. S. Lewis, Karl Barth, *The Portable Medieval Reader*, Raymond Tully, and Bertrand Russell lying together as nonchalantly as if they had been Belloc and Chesterton – stood witness to a futility that undercut all hope and theory. Even his toothbrush, which on good days presented itself as an acolyte of matinal devotion, today seemed an agent of atheistic hygiene, broadcasting the hideous fact of germs. The faucet's merry gurgle had sounded over Burton's sudden prayers.

The scent of candy and cloves lifted. The dentist, standing erect, was asking. 'Do you take novocain?'

Burton hesitated. He believed that one of the lazier modern assumptions was the identification of pain with evil. Indeed, in so far as pain warned us of corruption, it was good. On the other hand, relieving the pain of others was an obvious virtue – perhaps the *most* obvious virtue. And to court pain was as morbid as to chase pleasure. Yet to flee from pain was clearly cowardice.

The dentist, not hinting by his voice whether he had been waiting for an answer several seconds or no time at all, asked, 'Does your dentist at home give you novocain?'

Ever since Burton was a little boy in crusty dungarees, Dr Gribling had given him novocain. 'Yes.' The answer sounded abrupt, impolite. Burton added, 'He says my nerves are exceptionally large.' It was a pompous thing to say.

'We'll do the eye-tooth,' the dentist said.

Burton's heart beat like a wasp in a jar as the dentist moved across the room, did unseeable things by the sink, and returned with a full hypodermic. A drop of fluid, by some miracle of adhesion, clung trembling to the needle's tip. Burton opened his mouth while the dentist's back was still turned. When at last the man pivoted, his instrument tilting up, a tension beneath his moustache indicated surprise and perhaps amusement at finding things in such readiness. 'Open a little wider, please,' he said. 'Thank you.' The needle moved closer. It was under Burton's nose and out of focus. 'Now, this might hurt a little.' What a kind thing to say! The sharp prick and the consequent slow, filling ache drove Burton's eyes up, and he saw the tops of the bare willow trees, the frightened white sky, and the black birds. As he watched, one bird joined another on the topmost twig, and then a third joined these two and the twig became radically crescent, and all three birds flapped off to where his eyes could not follow them.

'There,' the dentist sighed, in a zephyr of candy and cloves.

Waiting for the novocain to take effect, Burton and the dentist made conversation.

'And what brings you to Oxford?' the dentist began.

'I'm doing graduate work.'

'Oh? What sort?'

'I'm doing a thesis on a man called Richard Hooker.'

'Oh?' The dentist sounded as incredulous as he had about Pennsylvania's anthracite.

Richard Hooker – 'pious, peaceable, primitive', in Walton's phrase – loomed so large in Burton's world that to doubt Hooker's existence was in effect to doubt the existence of Burton's world. But he added the explanatory 'An English divine' without the least bit of irritability or condescension. The lesson of humility was one that had come rather easily to Burton. He recognized, however, that in his very thinking of his own humility he was guilty of pride, and his immediate recognition of it as pride was foundation for further, subtler egotism.

He would have harried the sin to its source had not the dentist said, 'A divine is a church writer?'

'That's right.'

'Could you quote me something he wrote?'

Burton had expected, and was prepared to answer, several questions ('When did he live?' '1554 to 1600.' 'What is the man's claim to fame?' 'He attempted to reconcile Christian – that is, Thomist – political theory with the actual state of things under the Tudor monarchy; he didn't really succeed, but he did anticipate much of modern political thought.' 'What is your thesis?' 'Mostly an attempt to get at reasons for Hooker's failure to come to grips with Renaissance Platonism.'), but he was unprepared for this one. Scraps and phrases – 'visible Church', 'law eternal', 'very slender ability', 'Popish superstition', the odd word 'scrupulosity' – came to mind, but no rounded utterance formed itself. 'I can't think of anything right now,' he apologized, touching his fingers to his collar and, as still sometimes happened, being taken aback by the hard, unbroken edge they met.

The dentist did not seem disappointed. 'Feel numb yet?' he asked.

Burton tested and said, 'Yes.'

The dentist swung the drilling apparatus into place and Burton opened his mouth. 'Thank you.' The novocain had taken. The drilling at the tooth seemed vastly distant, and it hurt no more than the explosion of a star, or the death of an elephant in India, or, Burton realized, the whipping of a child right next door. Pain. The problem presented itself. He slipped into the familiar arguments he used with himself. Creation is His seeking to make souls out of matter. Morally, matter, *per se*, is neutral – with form imposed upon it, good, but in any case its basic nature is competitive. No two things can occupy the same place at the same time. Hence, pain. But we must act with non-material motives. What was His journey on earth but a flouting of competitive values? And then there is the Devil. But with the Devil the whole cosmos became confused, and Burton's attention, by default, rested on the black birds. They kept falling out of the sky and the treetops, but he noticed few ascending.

The dentist changed his drill. 'Thank you.' There were things Burton could comprehend. And then there were things he could not – his aeon-long wait as life struggled up from the atom. With what emotion did He watch all those preposterous, earnest beasts labour up out of the swamp and aimlessly perish on the long and crooked road to Man? And the stars, so far off, the comedy of waste spaces – theologians had always said infinite, but could they have meant *that* infinite? Once, Burton had asked his father if he believed in purgatory. 'Of course I do,' he had snapped, jabbing towards the floor with his pipe-stem. '*This* is purgatory.' Remembering the incident so depressed Burton that when the drill broke through the shell of anaesthetic and bit his nerve, it came in the shape of an answer, and he greeted the pain with something like ecstasy.

'There,' the dentist said. 'Would you care to wash out, please.' He swung the drilling apparatus over to one side, so Burton could see it wouldn't be used any more. He was so kind.

'There seem to be a lot of birds in your back-yard,' Burton said to him.

'We have a feeding station,' the dentist said, grinding the silver for the filling in a thick glass cup.

'What are those black birds?'

'Starlings. A greedy bird. They take everything they can away from the wren.'

For the first time, Burton noticed some smaller shapes among the branches, quicker, but less numerous and less purposeful than the black birds. He watched one in particular, swivelling on his perch, now a formless blob, like a big bud, the next moment in vivid profile, like a Picasso ceramic. As he watched the bird, his mind emptied itself, and nothing, not even the squeaking of the silver, disturbed it.

When he again became conscious, it was of the objects on the tray before him as things in which an unlimited excitement inhered; the tweezers, the picks, the drill burrs, the celluloid container of cotton, the tiny cotton balls, the metal cup where a flame could burn, the enamelled construction beside him housing a hundred useful devices, the tiled walls, the window frame, the things beyond the window – all travelled to his senses burdened with delight and power. The sensation was one that Burton had frequently enjoyed in his childhood and more and more rarely as he aged. His urge to laugh, or to *do* something with the objects, was repressed, and even the smile he gave the dentist was lost, for the man was concerned with keeping a dab of silver on the end of a minute golf-club-shaped tool.

Burton received the silver. He thought of the world as being, like all music, founded on tension. The tree pushing up, gravity pulling down, the bird desiring to fill the air, the air compelled to crush the bird. His head brimmed with irrelevant recollections: a rubber Donald Duck he had owned, and abused, as an infant; the grape arbour in his parents' back yard; the respect his father commanded throughout his town; Shibe Park in sunlight; Max Beerbohm's sentence about there always being a slight shock in seeing an envelope of one's own after it has gone through the post.

The dentist coughed. It was the sound not of a man who has to cough but of one who has done his job, and can cough if he pleases. 'Would you like to wash out, please?' He gestured towards a glass filled with pink fluid, which up to this time Burton had ignored. Burton took some of the liquid into his mouth (it was good, but not as good as the dentist's breath), sloshed it around, and, as silently as possible, spat it into the impeccable basin. 'I'm afraid three or four trips are called for,' the dentist said, studying his card.

'Fine.'

The dentist's moustache stretched fractionally. 'Miss Leviston will give you the appointments.' One by one, he dropped the drill burrs into a compartmented drawer. 'Do you have any idea why your teeth should be so, ah, indifferent?'

Burton concentrated. He yearned to thank the man, to bless him even, but since there was no conventional way to do that, he would show his gratitude by giving everything the dentist said his closest attention. 'I believe Pennsylvania has one of the worst dental records of any state.'

'Really? And why should that be?'

'I don't know. I think the Southern states have the best teeth. They eat fish, or turnip tops, or something with lots of calcium in it.'

'I see.' The dentist moved aside so Burton could climb out of the chair. 'Until next time, then.'

Burton supposed they would not shake hands twice in one visit. Near the doorway, he turned. 'Oh, Doctor, uh . . .'

'Merritt,' the dentist said.

'I just thought of a quotation from Hooker. It's just a short sentence.'

'Yes?'

' "I grant we are apt, prone, and ready, to forsake God; but is God as ready to forsake us? Our minds are changeable; is His so likewise?" '

Dr Merritt smiled. The two men stood in the same position they had hesitated in when Burton entered the room. Burton smiled. Outside the window, two wrens, one by pretending to locate a crumb and the other by flicking a real crumb away, outmanoeuvred a black bird.

A Madman

England itself seemed slightly insane to us. The meadows skimming past the windows of the Southampton–London train seemed green deliriously, seemed so obsessively steeped in the colour that my eyes, still attuned to the exhausted verdure and September rust of American fields, doubted the ability of this landscape to perform useful work. England appeared to exist purely as a context for literature. I had studied this literature for four years, and had been sent here to continue this study. Yet my brain, excited and numbed by travel, could produce only one allusion; 'a' babbled of green fields,' that inconsequential Shakespearian snippet rendered memorable by a classic typographical emendation, kept running through my mind, 'a' babbled, a' babbled,' as the dactylic scansion of the train wheels drew us and our six mute, swaying compartment-mates northward into London. The city overwhelmed our expectations. The Kiplingesque grandeur of Waterloo Station, the Eliotic despondency of the brick row in Chelsea where we spent the night in the flat of a vague friend, the Dickensian nightmare of fog and sweating pavement and besmirched cornices that surrounded us when we awoke – all this seemed too authentic to be real, too corroborative of literature to be solid. The taxi we took to Paddington Station had a high roof and an open side, which gave it to our eyes the shocked, cockeyed expression of a character actor in an Agatha Christie melodrama. We wheeled past mansions by Galsworthy and parks by A. A. Milne; we glimpsed a cobbled eighteenth-century alley, complete with hanging tavern boards, where Dr Johnson might have reeled and gasped the night he laughed so hard – the incident in Boswell so beautifully amplified in the essay by Beerbohm. And underneath all, underneath Heaven knew how many medieval plagues, pageants, and conflagrations, old Londinium itself like a buried Titan lay smouldering in an abyss and tangle of time appalling to eyes accustomed to view the land as a surface innocent of history. We were relieved to board the train and feel it tug us westward.

The train brought us into Oxford at dusk. We had no place to go. We had made no reservations. We got into a cab and explained this to the driver. Middle-aged, his huge ears frothing with hair, he seemed unable to believe us, as if in all his years he had never before carried passengers who had not already visited their destination. He seemed further puzzled by the discovery that, though we claimed to be Americans, we had never been in Stillwater, or even in Tulsa. Fifteen years ago he had spent some months in the depths of Oklahoma learning to fly Lend-Lease planes. Now he repaid his debt by piloting us down a narrow street of brick homes whose windows – queerly, for this was suppertime – were all dark. 'We'll give you a try at the Potts',' he explained briefly, braking. He went with us up to the door and twisted a heavy wrought-iron knob in its centre. A remote, rattling ring sounded on the other side of the opaquely stained panes. At length a tall saturnine man answered. Our driver explained to him, 'Potty, we've two homeless Yanks here. They don't know the score as yet.'

Early in the evening as it was, Mr Pott wore a muttering, fuddled air of having been roused. The BED AND BREAKFAST sign in his window seemed to commit him to no hospitality. Only after impressing us with the dark difficulty of it, with the unprecedented strain we were imposing upon the arrangements he had made with a disobliging and obtusely technical world, did he lead us upstairs and into a room. The room was large, chill, and amply stocked with whatever demigods it is that supervise sleep. I remember that the deliciously cool sheets and coarse blankets were topped by a purple puff smelling of lavender, and that in the morning, dressing, my wife and I skipped in and out of the radiant influence of the electric heater like a nymph and satyr competing at a shrine. The heater's plug was a ponderous and voltish-looking affair of three prongs; plugging it in was my first real work of acclimatization. We appeared for breakfast a bit late. Of all the other boarders, only Mr Robinson (I have forgotten his actual name) had yet to come down. Our places were laid at the dining table, and at my place – I couldn't believe my eyes – was set, an insanity, a half of a cooked tomato on a slice of fried bread.

Mr Robinson came down as Mr Pott was finishing explaining to us why we must quickly find permanent lodgings. Our room would soon be needed by its regular tenant, an Indian undergraduate. Any day now he would take it into his head to show up. It was a thankless job, keeping students' rooms; they were in and out and up and talking and making music at all hours, and the landlord was supposed to enforce the midnight curfew. 'The short of it is,' Mr Pott snarled, 'the university wants me to be a nanny and a copper's nark.' His voice changed tone. 'Ah, Mr Robinson! Good morning, Professor. We have with us two lovebirds from across the Atlantic.'

Mr Robinson ceremoniously shook our hands. Was he a professor? He was of middle size, with a scholar's delicate hunch and long thinning yellowish-white hair brushed straight back. In speech, he was all courtesy, lucid patter, and flattering attention. We turned to him with relief; after our host's dark hints and dour discontents, we seemed to be emerging into the England of light. 'Welcome to Oxford,' he said, and from a bright little tension in his cheeks we could see he was about to quote. ' "That home of lost causes, and forsaken beliefs, and unpopular names, and impossible loyalties." That's Matthew Arnold; if you want to understand Oxford, read Arnold. Student of Balliol, fellow of Oriel, professor of poetry, the highest bird as ever flew with a pedant's clipped wings. Read Arnold, and read Newman. "Whispering from her towers the last enchantments of the Middle Age" – which he did not *mean*, you know, entirely sympathetically; no, not at all. Arnold was not at all church-minded. "The Sea of Faith was once, too, at the full, but now I only hear its melancholy, long, *withdrawing* roar, retreating to the breath of the night-wind down the vast edges drear of the naked shingles of the world." Hah! Mr Pott, what is this I see before me? My customary egg. You are a veritable factotum, a Johannes Factotum, of kindness. Mr Pott of St John's Street,' he confided to us in his quick, twinkling way, 'an institution no less revered by the student body than the church of St Michael's-at-the-northgate, which contains, you should know, and will *see*, the oldest standing structure in' – he cleared his throat, as if to signal something special coming – 'Oxnaford: the old Saxon tower, dating from the ninth century at the least. At the *least*, I insist, though in doing so I incur the certain wrath of the more piddling of local archaeologists, if we can dignify them with the title upon which Schliemann and Sir Leonard Woolley have heaped so much honour.' He set to his egg eagerly, smashing it open with a spoon.

My wife asked him, 'Are you a professor of archaeology?'

'Dear madam,' he said, 'in a manner of speaking, in a manner of speaking, I have taken all knowledge for my province. Do you know Ann Arbor, in, I believe, the very wooded state of Michigan? No? Have no shame, no shame; your country is so vast, a poor Englishman's head reels. My niece, my sister's daughter, married an instructor in the university there. I learn from her letters that the temperature frequently – *frequently* – drops below zero Fahrenheit. Mr Pott, will this charming couple be spending the term with us here?' When it was explained to him, more readily than tactfully, that our presence here was an emergency measure, the result of a merciful impulse which Mr Pott, his implication was, already regretted, Mr Robinson bent his face low over the table to look up at us. He had perfect upper teeth. 'You must know the *way*,' he said, 'the ins and outs, the little short cuts and circumlocutions, circumflexions, the *circumstances*; else you will never find a flat. You have waited long, too long; in a few days the Michaelmas term will be upon us and from Woodstock to Cowley there won't be a room to be *had*. But I, *I*' – he lifted one finger and closed one eye sagely – 'I may be of help. "*Che tu mi segui*," as Virgil said to Dante, "*e io sarò tua guida!*" '

We were of course grateful for a guide. The three of us walked down St John's Street (all the shades were drawn, though this was daylight), up Beaumont past the sooty, leonine sprawl of the Ashmolean, and down Magdalen Street to Cornmarket, where indeed we did see the Saxon tower. Mr Robinson indicated points of interest continuously. His lower jaw seemed abnormally slender, as if a normal jaw had been whittled for greater flexibility and lightness. It visibly supported only one lower tooth, and that one hardly bigger than a fleck of tobacco, and set in the gum sideways; whereas his upper teeth were strikingly even and complete. Through these mismatched gates he poured an incessant stressed stream of words, broken only when, preparatory to some heightened effort of erudition, he preeningly cleared his throat. 'Now we are standing in the centre of town, the very hub and beating heart of Oxfordshire, Carfax, derived – uh-uh-*hem* – from the Norman *carrefor*, the Latin *quadrifurcus*, meaning four forks, or crossroads. Do you know Latin? The last international language, the – uh-hem – Esperanto of Christendom.' He carried an old paper bag, and we found ourselves in a vast roofed market, surrounded by blood-flecked butchers' stalls and bins of raw vegetables smelling of mud. Mr Robinson methodically filled his bag with potatoes. He examined each potato, and hesitated with it, as if it would be his last; but then his anxious parchmenty hand would dart out and seize yet another. When the bag could hold no more, he shrugged and began to wander away. The proprietress of the stall shouted in protest. She was fat; her face looked scorched; and she wore a man's boots and numerous unravelling sweaters. Without a word, Mr Robinson returned and rather grandly dumped all the potatoes back into the bin. Along with the potatoes some papers fluttered out, and these he put back in the bag. He turned to us and smiled. 'Now,' he said, 'it is surely time for lunch. Oxnaford is no town to storm on an empty stomach.'

'But,' I said, 'Mr Robinson, what about the place we have to find?'

He audibly exhaled, as if he had just tasted a superb wine. '*Aaaaah*. I have not forgotten, I have not forgotten. We must tread cautiously; you do not know, you see, the *way*. The ins and outs, the *circumstances*.' He led us to a cafeteria above a furniture store on the Broad and through the chips and custard tried to distract us with a profuse account of Oxford in its medieval heyday – Roger Bacon, Duns Scotus, the 'Mad Parliament' of 1256, the town-gown riots of St Scholastica's Day in 1355. Down on the street once more, he took to plucking our arms and making promises. One more little trip, one harmless excursion that would be *very* useful for us, and then down to business. He escorted us all the way down High Street to the Magdalen Bridge, and thus we received our first glimpse of the Cherwell. No punts were out at this time of year, and swans generally stayed downriver. But looking back towards the centre of town, we were treated to the storybook view of Oxford, all spires and silhouette and flaking stone, under a sky by John Constable, R.A. Weak, distraught, I felt myself succumb; we surrendered the day to Mr Robinson. Triumphantly sensing this, he led us down Rose Lane, through the botanic gardens orange and golden with fall flowers, along Merton Field, and back through a series of crooked alleys to the business district. Here he took us into a bookstore and snatched a little newspaper, the Oxfordshire weekly, out of a rack and indicated to the man behind the counter that I would pay for it. While I rummaged the fourpence out of my pocket, Mr Robinson pranced to the other wall and came back holding a book. It was a collection of essays by Matthew Arnold. 'Don't buy this book,' he told me. '*Don't buy it*. I have it in a superior edition, and will lend it to you. Do you understand? I will *lend* it to you.' I thanked him and, as if all he had wanted from us was a little gratitude, he announced that he would leave us now. He tapped the paper in my hand. He winked. 'Your problems – and don't think, *don't* think they have not been painfully on my mind – are solved; you will find your rooms in here. Very few, *very* few people know about this paper, but all the locals, *all* the locals with *good* rooms advertise in here; they don't *trust* the regular channels. You must know the *way*, you see, the ins and outs.' And he left us, as at the edge of Paradise.

It was growing dark, in that long, slow, tea-shoppe-lit style of English afternoons, and we had tea to clear our heads. Then there seemed nothing to do but return to Mr Pott's house, on St John's Street. Now we noticed for the first time students in the streets, whirring along on their bicycles like bats, their black gowns fluttering. Only we lacked a roost. My wife lay down on top of our purple puff and silently cried. Her legs ached from all the walking. She was – our heavy secret – three months pregnant. We were fearful that if this became known not a landlord in Oxford would have us. I went out in the dusk with my newspaper to a phone booth. In fact, there were few flats advertised in the weekly, and all but one lacked a kitchen; this one was listed as on St Aldate's Street. I called the number and a woman answered. When she heard my voice, she asked, 'Are you an American?'

'I guess, yes.'

'I'm sorry. My husband doesn't like Americans.'

'He doesn't? Why not?' It had been impressed upon me, with the award of my fellowship, that I was to act as an ambassador abroad.

There was a pause, then she said, 'If you must know, our daughter's gone and married an airman from your base at Brize Norton.'

'Oh – well, I'm not an airman. I'm a student. And I'm already married. It would just be me and my wife, we have no children.'

'Hooh, Jack!' The exclamation sounded off focus, as if she had turned her mouth from the receiver. Then she returned close to my ear, confidential, murmurous. 'My husband's this minute come in. Would you like to talk to him?'

'No,' I said, and hung up, trembling but pleased to have encountered a conversation I could end.

The next morning, Mr Robinson had reached the breakfast table before us. Perhaps it had cost him some sleep, for his hair was mussed and its yellow tinge had spread to his face. His eagerness in greeting us was now tipped with a penetrating whine. The falseness of his upper teeth had become painfully clear; spittle sparked from his mouth with the effort of keeping the plate in place. ' "Noon strikes on England," ' he recited at our appearance, ' "noon on Oxford town, Beauty she was statue cold, there's blood upon her gown, proud and godly kings had built her long ago, with her towers and tombs and statues all arow, with her fair and floral air and the love that lingers there, and the streets where the great men go." '

'I thought this morning,' I told him, 'I'd go to my college and see if they could help.'

'Which college?' he asked. His face became abnormally alert.

'Keble.'

'Ah,' he cried, triumphant, 'they won't help. *They won't help.* They know *nothing*. They *wish* to know nothing. *Nihil ex nihilo.*'

'It's a game they play,' Mr Pott muttered sourly, 'called Hands Off.'

'Really?' my wife said, her voice brimming.

'Nevertheless,' I insisted, 'we have to begin somewhere. That weekly you got for us had only one possibility, and the woman's husband didn't like Americans.'

'Your ruddy airmen,' Mr Pott explained, 'from out Norton way have given you a name. They come into town with their powder-blue suits and big shoulders, some of 'em black as shoe polish, and give the local tarts what-for.'

My mention of the weekly had set off a sequence in Mr Robinson's mind, for now he clapped his hands to his head and said, 'That book. I promised to lend you that book. Forgive, *forgive* a rattlebrained old man. I will get it for you *instanter*. No protest, no protest. Youth must be served.'

He went upstairs to his room, and we glanced at Mr Pott inquisitively. He nodded. 'I'd beat it now, in your shoes,' he said.

We had made three blocks and felt safely lost in the crowd along Cornmarket when Mr Robinson caught up with us. He was panting and wearing his bedroom slippers. 'Wait,' he whined, '*wait*, you don't *see*. You can't run blind and headlong into these situations, you don't understand the *circumstances*.' He carried his paper shopping bag and produced from it a book, which he pressed upon me. It was a turn-of-the-century edition of Arnold's essays, with marbled end papers. Right there, on the jostling pavement, I opened it, and nearly slammed it shut in horror, for every page was a spider's web of annotations and underlinings, in many pencils and inks and a wild variety of handwritings. 'Cf.' '*videlicet*,' 'He betrays himself here,' '19th cent. optmsm' – these leaped at me out of the mad swarm. The annotations were themselves annotated, as his argument with the text doubled and redoubled back on itself. 'Is this so?' a firm hand had written in one margin, and below it, in a different slant and fainter pencil, had been added, 'Yes it is so,' with the 'is' triple-underlined; and below this a wobbly ball-point pen had added, without capitals, 'but is it?' It made me dizzy to look into; I shut the book and thanked him.

Mr Robinson looked at me cleverly sideways. 'You thought I had forgotten,' he said. 'You thought an old man's brain didn't hold water. No shame, no shame; in your circumstances you could hardly think otherwise. But no, what I promise, I fulfil; now I will be your guide. A-hem. Everyman, I will go with thee: hah!' He gestured towards the ancient town hall and told us that during the Great Rebellion Oxford had been the Royalist headquarters.

> 'The king, observing with judicious eyes,
> The state of both his universities,
> To Oxford sent a troop of horse, and why?'

he recited, ending with a sweep of his arm that drew eyes to us.

Just as, by being pronounced definitely insane, a criminal curiously obligates the society he has injured, so now Mr Robinson's hold upon us was made perfect. The slither of his shuffling slippers on the pavement, the anxious snagging stress of periodic syllables, the proud little throat clearings were so many filaments that clasped us to him as, all but smothered by embarrassment and frustration, we let him lead us. Our route overlapped much of the route of the day before; but now he began to develop a new theme – that all this while he had been subjecting us to a most meticulous scrutiny and we had passed favourably, with *flying* colours, and that he was going to introduce us to some of his friends, the really *important* people, the grand panjandrums, the people who knew where there were rooms and rooms. He would write letters, perform introductions, secure our admission to secret societies. After lunch, at about the hour when on the day before he had introduced us to the paper seller, he shepherded us into the libary of the Oxford Union Society and introduced us to the fastidious boy behind the desk. Mr Robinson's voice, somehow intensified by whispering, carried to every crusty corner and sacrosanct gallery. The young librarian in his agony did not suppress an ironical smile. When his eyes turned to us, they took on a polite glaze that fell a little short of concealing contempt. But with what a deal of delighted ceremony did Mr Robinson, who evidently really was a member, superintend the signing of our names in a huge old ledger! In return for our signatures we were given, with a sorcerer's flourishes, an application form for membership. There was this to be said for Mr Robinson: he never left you quite empty-handed.

Returning, frantic and dazed, to our room at the Potts', we were able to place the application blank and the annotated Arnold beside our first trophy, the Oxfordshire weekly. I lay down on the bed beside my wife and read through the lead article, a militant lament on the deterioration of the Norman church at Iffley. When I had regained some purpose in my legs, I walked over to Keble and found it was much as I had been warned. The patterns of paternalism did not include those students tasteless enough to have taken a wife. Flats were to be had, though, the underling asserted, absurdly scratching away with a dip pen in his tiny nook with its one Gothic window overlooking a quad; his desk suggested the Tenniel illustration of all the cards flying out of the pack.

I was newly enough married not to expect that my wife, once I was totally drained of hope, would supply some. She had decided in my absence that we must stop being polite to Mr Robinson. Indeed, this did seem the one way out of the maze. I should have thought of it myself. We dressed up and ate a heartily expensive meal at a pseudo-French restaurant that Mr Robinson had told us never, *never* to patronize, because they were brigands. Then we went to an American movie to give us brute strength and in the morning came down to breakfast braced. Mr Robinson was not there.

This was to be, it turned out, our last breakfast at the Potts'. Already we had become somewhat acclimatized. We no longer, for example, glanced around for Mrs Pott; we had accepted that she existed, if she existed at all, on a plane invisible to us. The other boarders greeted us by name now. There were two new faces among them – young students' faces, full of bewilderingly pertinent and respectful questions about the United States. The States, their opinion was, had already gone the way that all countries must eventually go. To be American, we were made to feel, was to be lucky. Mr Pott told us that Karam had written he would be needing his room by the weekend and pushed across the table a piece of paper containing several addresses. 'There's a three-room basement asking four pounds ten off Banbury Road,' he said, 'and if you want to go to five guineas, Mrs Shipley still has her second floor over towards St Hilda's.'

It took us a moment to realize what this meant; then our startled thanks gushed. 'Mr Robinson,' I blurted in conclusion groping for some idiom suitable to Mr Pott and not quite coming up with it, 'has been leading us all around the Maypole.'

'Poor Robbie,' said Mr Pott. 'Daft as a daisy.' He tapped the bony side of his lean dark head.

My wife asked, 'Is he always – like that?'

'Only as when he finds an innocent or two to sink his choppers in; they find him out soon enough, poor Robbie.'

'Does he really have a niece in Michigan?'

'Ah yes, he's not all fancy. He was a learned man before his trouble, but the university never quite took him on.'

' "So poetry, which is in Oxford made an art," ' a familiar voice sweetly insisted behind us, ' "in London only is a trade." Dryden. *Not* a true Oxonian, but an excellent poet and amateur scholar nevertheless. If you enjoy his jingling style. Mr Pott. Can that egg be mine?' He sat down and smashed it neatly with his spoon and turned to us jubilantly. Perhaps the delay in his appearance had been caused by an effort of grooming, for he looked remarkably spruce, his long hair brushed to a tallowish lustre, his tie knotted tightly, his denture snug under his lips, and a plaid scarf draped around his shoulders. 'Today,' he said, 'I will devote myself to your cause wholeheartedly, without intermissions, interruptions, or intercessions. I have spent the last hour preparing a wonderful surprise, *mirabile dictu*, as faithful Aeneas said to his natural mother, Aphrodite.'

'I think,' I said, in a voice constrained by the presence of others around the table, 'we really must do other things today. Mr Pott says that Karam –'

'Wait, *wait*,' he cried, becoming agitated and rising in his chair. 'You do not understand. You are *innocents* – charming, yes, vastly potential, yes, but innocents, you see. You must know the *way*, the ins, the outs –'

'No, honestly –'

'*Wait*. Come with me now. I will show you my surprise *instanter*, if you insist.' And he bustled up from the table, the egg uneaten, and back up the stairs towards his room. My wife and I followed, relieved that what must be done could now be done unwitnessed.

Mr Robinson was already coming out of his room as we met him on the second-floor landing. In his haste he had left the door open behind him. Over his shoulder I glimpsed a chaos of tumbled books and wrinkled papers. He held in his hands a sheet of paper on which he had made a list. 'I have spent the last hour preparing,' he said, 'with a care not incomparable to that of, *ih-ih-humm*, St Jerome transcribing the Vulgate, a list; these are the people that today we will *see*.' I read the list he held to my face. The offices and titles and names at the top meant nothing to me, but halfway down, where the handwriting began to get big and its slant to become inconstant, there was the word 'Chancellor' followed by a huge colon and the name 'Lord Halifax'.

Something in my face made the paper begin to tremble. Mr Robinson took it away and held it at his side. With the other hand he fumbled with his lapel. 'You're terribly kind,' I said. 'You've given us a wonderful introduction to Oxford. But today, really, we must go out on our own. Absolutely.'

'No, no, you don't seem to comprehend; the *circum* –'

'*Please*,' my wife said sharply.

He looked at her, then at me, and an unexpected calm entered his features. The twinkle faded, the jaw relaxed, and his face might have been that of any tired old man as he sighed, 'Very well, very well. No shame.'

'Thank you so much,' my wife said, and made to touch, but did not quite touch, the limp hand that had curled defensively against the breast of his coat.

Knees bent, he stood apparently immobilized on the landing before the door of his room. Yet as we went down the stairs, he did one more gratuitous thing; he came to the banister, lifted his hand and pronounced, as we quickened our steps to dodge his words, 'God bless. God bless.'

Who Made Yellow Roses Yellow?

Of the three telephones in the apartment, the one in the living-room rested on a tabouret given to Fred Platt's grandmother by Henry James, who considered her, the Platts claimed, the only educated woman in the United States. Above this cherrywood gift hung an oval mirror, its frame a patterned involvement of cherubs, acanthus leaves, and half-furled scrolls; its gilt, smooth as butter in the valleys between figures, yielded on the crests of the relief to touches of Watteau brown. Great-Uncle Randy, known for his whims and moustaches, had rescued the mirror from a Paris auction. In the capacious room there was nothing of no intrinsic interest, nothing that would not serve as cause for a narrative, except the three overstuffed pieces installed by Fred's father – two chairs, facing each other at a distance of three strides, and a crescent-shaped sofa, all covered in spandy-new, navy-blue leather. This blue, the dark warm wood of inherited cabinets, the twilight colours of aged books, the scarlet and purple of the carpet from Cairo (where Charlotte, Uncle Randy's wife, had caught a bug and died), and the dismal Sonorities of the Secentistico Transfiguration on the west wall vibrated around the basal shade of plum. Plum: a colour a man can rest in, the one towards which all dressing-gowns tend. Reinforcing the repose and untroubled finality of the interior were the several oval shapes. The mirror was one of a family, kin to the feminine ellipse of the coffee-table; to the burly arc of Daddy's sofa, as they never failed to call it; to the ovoid, palely painted base of a Florentine lamp; to the plaster medallion on the ceiling – the one cloud in the sky of the room – and to the recurrent, tiny gold seal of the Oxford University Press, whose books, monochrome and Latinate as dons, were among the chief of the senior Platt's plum-coloured pleasures.

Fred, his only son, age twenty-five, dialled a Judson number. He listened to five burrs before the receiver was picked up, exposing the tail-end of a girl's giggle. Still tittery, she enunciated, 'Carson Chemi-cal.'

'Hello. Is – ah, Clayton Thomas Clayton there, do you know?'

'Mr Thomas Clayton? Yes he is. Just one moment please.' So poor Clayton Clayton had finally got somebody to call him by his middle name, that 'Thomas' which his parents must have felt made all the difference between the absurd and the sublime.

'Mr Clayton's of-fice,' another girl said. 'About what was it you wished to speak to him?'

'Well nothing really. It's a friend.'

'Just one moment, please.'

After a delay – purely disciplinary, Fred believed – an unexpectedly deep and even melodious voice said, 'Yes?'

'Clayton Clayton?'

A pause. 'Who is this?'

'Good morning, sir. I represent the Society for the Propagation and Eventual Adoption of the A.D. Spooner Graduated Income Tax Plan. As perhaps you know, this plan calls for an income tax which increases in inverse proportion to income, so that the wealthy are exempted and the poor taxed out of existence. Within five years, Mr Spooner estimates, poverty would be eliminated: within ten, a thing not even of memory. Word has come to our office –'

'It's Fred Platt, isn't it?'

'Word has come to our office that in recent years Providence has so favoured thee as to incline thy thoughts the more favourably to the Plan.'

'Fred?'

'Congratulations. You now own the Motorola combination phonograph-and-megaphone. Do you care to try for the Bendix?'

'How long have you been in town? It's damn good to hear from you.'

'Since April first. It's a prank of my father's. Who are all these girls you live in the midst of?'

'Your father called you back?'

'I'm not sure. I keep forgetting to look up "wastrel" in the dictionary.'

That made Clayton laugh. 'I thought you were studying at the Sorbonne.'

'I was. I was.'

'But you're not now.'

'I'm not now. *Moi et la Sorbonne, nous sommes kaput.*' When the other was silent, Fred added, '*Beaucoup kaput.*'

'Look, we must get together,' Clayton said.

'Yes. I was wondering if you eat lunch.'

'When had you thought?'

'Soon?'

'Wait. I'll check.' Some muffled words – a question with his hand over the mouthpiece. A drawer scraped. 'Say, Fred, this is bad. I have something on the go every day this week.'

'So. Well, what about June twenty-first? They say the solstice will be lovely this year.'

'Wait. What about today? I'm free today, they just told me.'

'Today?' Fred had to see Clayton soon, but immediately seemed like a push. '*Comme vous voulez, Monsieur.* Oneish?'

'All right, uh – could you make it twelve thirty? I have a good bit to do . . .'

'Just as easy. There's a Chinese place on East Forty-ninth Street run by Australians. Excellent murals of Li Po embracing the moon in the Yalu, *plus* the coronation of Henri Quatre.'

'I wonder, could that be done some other time? As I say, there's some stuff here at the office. Do you know Shulman's? It's on Third Avenue, a block from here, so that –'

'Press of work, eh?'

'You said it,' Clayton said, evidently sensing no irony. 'Then I'll see you then.'

'In all the old de dum de dumpty that this heart of mine embraces.'

'Pardon?'

'See you then.'

'Twelve thirty at Shulman's.'

'Absolutely.'

'So long.'

'So long.'

The first impulse after a humiliation is to look into a mirror. The heavy Parisian looking-glass, hung on too long a wire, leaned inches from the wall. A person standing would see reflected in it not his head but the carpet, some furniture, and perhaps, in the upper portion of the oval, his shoes and cuffs. By tilting his chair Fred could see his face, flushed like the mask someone momentarily absent from an enervating cocktail party spies in the bathroom mirror. There, the hot-skinned head, backed by pastel tiles and borrowing imperturbability from the porcelain fixtures, strikes the owner as a glamorous symbol of Man, half angel, half beast; and each eye seems the transparent base of a cone luminous with intuitions, secrets, quips, deviltry, and love. Here, in this over-stuffed room, his red face, above his black suit, just looked hot. His excited appearance annoyed him. Between his feverish attempt to rekindle friendship – his mind skidding, his tongue wagging – and

Clayton's response an embarrassing and degrading disproportion had existed.

Until now it had seemed foolishly natural for Clayton to offer him a job. Reportedly he had asked Bim Blackwood to jump Harcourt for a publicity job at Carson Chemical. Bim had said, without seeing anything funny in the word, that Clayton had lots of 'power' at Carson. 'In just three years, he's near the top. He's a *killer*. Really.'

It had been hard to gather from Bim's description exactly what Clayton did. As Bim talked on, flicking with increasing rapidity at the stiff eave of brown hair that overhung his forehead with conceited carelessness, he would say anything to round out a sentence, never surrendering his right to be taken seriously. 'It's an octopus,' he had asserted. 'You know *e*verything is chemicals *ulti*mately. Clayton told me the first thing he was given to do was help design the wrapper for an ammoniated chewing-gum they were just putting out. He said the big question was whether chalk-white or mint-green suggested better a clean feeling in the mouth. They had a survey on it; it cost thousands and *thousands* – thousands of little men going inside people's mouths. Of course he doesn't draw any more; he consults. Can you imagine doing nothing all day but *consult*? On pamphlets, you know, and "flyers" – what *are* flyers anyway? – and motion pictures to show to salesmen to show them how to explain the things they sell. He's *ter*ribly involved with *tel*evision; he told me a *horr*ible story about a play about Irish peasants the Carson Chemical Hour was putting on and the last minute it dawned on everybody that these people were *organic farmers*. Clayton Clayton saw it through. The killer instinct.'

Clayton hadn't had to go into the Army. Troubled knees, or something. That was the thing about poor children; they acquired disabilities which gave them the edge in later life. It's cruel, to expect a man without a handicap to go far.

Fred's position was not desperate. An honourable office in the investments firm (for Father was of the newest school, which sees no wrong in playing favourites) was not, as Father had said, with his arch way of trotting out clichés as if they were moderately obscure literary quotations, 'the fate worse than death'. Furthermore – he was a great man for further-mores – anyone who imagined that the publicity arm of Carson Chemical was an ivory tower compared to Braur, Chappell & Platt lived in a fool's paradise.

Yet viewed allegorically the difference seemed great. Something about all this, perhaps the chaste spring greenery of Central Park, which from these windows was spread out with the falcon's-eye perspective of a medieval map, suggested one of those crossroads in *The Faerie Queene*.

Besides, he had been very kind to Clayton – got him on to the *Quaff*, really. Sans *Quaff*, where would Clayton be? Not that Clayton need consider any of this. Hell, it wasn't as if Fred were asking for something; he was offering something. He pushed back the chair a few feet, so a full view of himself was available in the tilted mirror: a tall, narrow-skulled, smooth-cheeked youth, tightly dressed in darkest grey. A lapsed Episcopalian, Fred was half in love with the clergy.

Entering, late, the appointed restaurant, Fred instantly spotted Clayton Clayton standing at the bar. That three years had passed, that the place was smoky and crowded with interchangeable men, did not matter; an eclipsing head bowed, and the fragment of cheek then glimpsed, though in itself nothing but a daub of white, not only communicated to Fred one human identity but stirred in him warm feelings for the *Quaff*, college, his youth generally, and even America. Fred had inherited that trick of the rich of seeming to do everything out of friendship, but he was three generations removed from the making of the money, and a manner of business had become, in him, a way of life; his dealings were in fact at the mercy of his affections. Grotesquely close to giggling, he walked up to his man and intoned, '*Ego sum via, vita, veritas.*'

Clayton turned, grinned, and pumped Fred's hand. 'How *are* you, Fred?'

Members of the *Quaff* did not ask one another how they were; Fred had supposed ex-members also did not. Finding they did baulked him. He could not think of the joke to turn such a simple attack aside. 'Pretty well,' he conceded and, as if these words were an exorcism enabling the gods of fatuity to descend and dwell in his lips, heard himself add, in what seemed full solemnity. 'How are you?'

'I'm doing' – Clayton paused, nodding once, giving the same words a new import – 'pretty well.'

'Yes, everybody says.'

'I was glad I could make it today. I really am up to my ears this week.' Confidingly: 'I'm in a crazy business.'

On one wall of the restaurant were Revolutionary murals, darkened perhaps by smoke and time but more likely by the painter's timidity. 'Ah,' said Fred, gesturing. 'The Renaissance Popes in Hell.'

'Would you like one of these?' Clayton touched the glass in front of him; it contained that collegiate brew, beer.

How tender of Clayton still to drink beer! By a trick of vision, the liquid stood on the dark bar unbounded by glass. The sight of that suspended amber cylinder, like his magic first glimpse of Clayton's face, conjured in Fred a sensation of fondness. This time he curbed his tendency to babble and said, anxious to be honest, certain that the merest addition of the correct substance – the simple words exchanged by comrades – would reform the alchemy of the relationship, 'Yes. I would like one. Quite a bit.'

'I tell you. Let's grab a table and order from there. They'll let us stand here all day.'

Fred felt not so much frustrated as deflected, as if the glass that wasn't around the beer was around Clayton.

'There's a table.' Clayton picked up his glass, placed a half dollar in the centre of the circle its base had occupied, and shouldered away from the bar. He led the way into a booth, past two old men brandishing their topcoats. Inside, the high partitions shielded them from much of the noise of the place. Clayton took two menus from behind the sugar and handed one to Fred. 'We had better order the food first, then ask for the beer. If you asked for the drinks first, they'll just run off.' He was perfect: the medium-short dry-combed hair, the unimpeachable brown suit, the buttonless collar, the genially dragged vowels, the little edges of efficiency bracing the consonants. Some traces of the scholarship-bothered freshman from Hampton (Md) High School who had come down to the *Quaff* on Candidates' Night with an armful of framed sports cartoons remained – the not smoking, the tucked-in chin and the attendant uplook of the boyishly lucid eyes, and the skin allergy that placed on the flank of each jaw a constellation of red dots. Even these vestiges fitted into the picture, by lending him, until he learned to feign it, the ingratiating uncertainty desired in New York executives. It was just this suggestion of inexperience that in his genuine inexperience Clayton was working to suppress. 'See anything you like?' he asked with a firmness not interrogative.

'I think maybe a lamb chop.'

'I don't see them on the menu.'

'I don't either.'

Raising his hand to the level of his ear and snapping his fingers, Clayton summoned a waiter. 'This gentleman wants a lamb chop. Do you have them?'

The waiter didn't bother to answer, just wrote it down.

'I think I might try,' Clayton went on, 'the chopped sirloin with mushroom sauce. Beans instead of the peas, if you will. And I'm having another glass of Ballantine. Shall I make that two, Fred?'

'Do you have any decent German beer? Würzburger? Or Löwenbräu?'

The request materialized the man, who had been serving them with only his skimpy professional self. Now he smiled, and stood bodied forth as a great-boned Teuton in the prime of his fifties, with the square Bavarian skull, a short hooked nose, and portentous ears covered with a diaphanous fuzz that brought to the dignity they already possessed a certain silky glamour. 'I believe, sir, we have the Löwenbräu. I don't think we have any of the Würzburger, sir.'

'O.K. Anything.' Though Fred truly repented stealing Clayton's show, the evidence of his crime refused to disappear. He had called into being a genie – cloying, zealous, delighted to have his cavernous reserve of attentiveness tapped at last. The waiter bowed and indeed whispered, making an awkward third party of Clayton, 'I think we have the Löwenbräu. If not, would an English stout do? A nice Guinness, sir?'

'Anything is fine.' Trying to bring Clayton back into it, Fred asked him, 'Do you want one? Fewer bubbles than Ballantine. Less tingle for more ferment.'

Clayton's answering laugh would have been agreeable if he had not, while uttering it, lowered his eyelids, showing that he conceived of this as a decision whereby he stood to gain or lose. 'No, I think I'll stick to Ballantine.' He looked Fred needlessly in the eyes. When Clayton felt threatened, the middle sector of his face clouded over; the area between his brows and nostrils queerly condensed.

Fred was both repelled and touched. The expression was exactly that worn by the adolescent Clayton at the *Quaff* candidates' punches, when all the dues members, dead to the magazine, showed up resplendent in black suits and collar pins, eager for Martinis, as full of chatter and strut as a flock of whooping cranes bent on proving they were not extinct yet. Fred pitied Clayton, remembering the days when Fred alone, a respected if sophomore member, was insisting that the kid with the gag name be elected to the *Quaff*. The point was he could draw. Wonky, sure. He was right out of the funny papers. But at least his hands looked like hands. Outrageous, of course, to have the drawings framed, but his parents put him up to that – anybody who'd call a helpless baby Clayton Clayton . . . He wore cocoa-coloured slacks and sport shirts. They'd wear out. If he was sullen, he was afraid. The point was, If we don't get anybody on the magazine who can draw we'll be forced to run daguerreotypes of Chester Arthur and the Conkling Gang.

'Do you see much of Anna Spooner?' Clayton asked, referring back, perhaps unconsciously, to Fred's earlier mistake, his mention of the income-tax plan of their friend A. D. Spooner, nicknamed 'Anno Domini' and eventually 'Anna'.

'Once or twice. I haven't been back that long. He said he kept running into you at the Old Grads' Marching Society.'

'Once in a while.'

'You don't sound too enthusiastic.'

'I hadn't meant to. I mean I hadn't meant not to. He's about the same. Same tie, same jokes. He never thanks me when I buy him a drink. I don't mean the money bothers me. It's one of those absurd little things. I shouldn't even mention it.'

The waiter brought the beers. Fred stared into his Löwenbräu and breathed the word 'Yeah'.

'How long *have* you been back?'

'Two weeks, I guess.'

'That's right. You said. Well, tell me about it. What've you been doing for three years?' His hands were steadily folded on the table, conference-style. 'I'm interested.'

Fred laughed outright at him. 'There isn't that much. In the Army I was in Germany in the Quartermaster Corps.'

'What did you do?'

'Nothing. Typed. Played blackjack, faro, Rook.'

'Do you find it's changed you much?'

'I type faster. And my chest now is a mass of pornographic tattoos.'

Clayton laughed a little. 'It just interests me. I know that psychologically the effect on me of *not* going in is – is genuine. I feel not exactly guilty, but it's something that everyone of our generation has gone through. Not to seems incom*plete*.'

'It should, it should. I bet you can't even rev out a Bowling Bunting H-4 jet-cycle tetrameter. As for shooting a bazooka! Talk of St Teresa's spiritual experiences –'

'It's impressive, how little it's changed you. I wonder if I'm changed. I do like the work, you know. People are always slamming advertising, but I've found out it's a pretty damn essential thing in our economy.'

The waiter came and laid their plates before them. Clayton set to with a disconcerting rapacity, forking in the food as often with his left hand as his right, pausing only to ask questions. 'Then you went back to Europe.'

'Then I went back to Europe.'

'Why? I mean what did you do? Did you do any writing?'

In recent years Fred's literary intelligence had exerted itself primarily in the invention of impeccable but fruitless puns. Parcel Proust. Or Supple Simon. (Supple Simon met a Neiman/Fellow at the Glee Club, gleamin'./Said Supple Simon, 'Tell me, Fellow/Who made yellow roses yellow?') 'Why, yes,' he told Clayton. 'Quite a bit. I've just completed a three-volume biography of the great Hungarian actress, Juxta Pose.'

'No, actually. What did you do in Paris?'

'Actually, I sat in a chair. The same chair whenever I could. It was a straw chair in the sidewalk area of a restaurant on the Boulevard Saint-Michel. In the summer and spring the tables are in the open, but when it gets cold they enclose the area with large windows. It's best then. Everybody except you sits inside the restaurant, where it's warm. It's best of all at breakfast, around eleven of a nippy morning, with your *café* and *croissant avec du beurre* and your copy of *Là-Bas* all on a little table the size of a tray, and people outside the window trying to sell *ballons* to Christmas tourists.'

'You must know French perfectly. It annoys hell out of me that I don't know any.'

'*Oui, pardon, zut!*, and *alors!* are all you need for ordinary conversation. Say them after me: *oui* – the lips so – *par-don* –'

'The reason you probably don't write more,' Clayton said, 'is that you have too much taste. Your critical sense is always a jump ahead of your creative urge.' Getting no response, he went on, 'I haven't been doing much drawing, either. Except roughing out ideas. But I plan to come back to it.'

'I know you do. I know you will.'

That was what Clayton wanted to hear. He loved work; it was all he knew how to do. His type saw competition as the spine of the universe. His *Quaff* career had been all success, all adaptation and productivity, so that in his senior year Clayton was president, and everybody said he alone was keeping silly old *Quaff* alive, when in fact the club, with its fragile ethic of ironic worthlessness, had withered under him.

Clayton had a forkful of hamburger poised between the plate and his mouth. 'What does your father want?' In went the hamburger.

'My father seems to fascinate you. He is a thin man in his late fifties. He sits at one end of an enormous long room filled with priceless things. He is wearing a purple dressing-gown and trying to read a book. But he feels the room is tipping. So he wants me to get in there with him and sit at the other end to keep the balance.'

'No. I didn't mean –'

'He wants me to get a job. Know of one?' So the crucial question was out, stated like a rebuke.

Clayton carefully chewed. 'What sort?'

'I've already been offered a position in Braur, Chappell & Platt. A fine old firm. I'm looking for something with less pay.'

'In publishing?'

Stalling, stalling. 'Or advertising.'

Clayton set down his fork. 'Gee. You should be able to get something.'

'I wouldn't know why. I have no experience. I can't use my father's pull. That wouldn't be the game.'

'I wish you had been here about six months ago. There was an opening up at Carson, and I asked Bim Blackwood, but he didn't want to make the jump. Speaking of Bim, he's certainly come along.'

'Come along? Where to?'

'You know. He seems more mature. I feel he's gotten ahold of himself. His view of things is better proportioned.'

'That's very perceptive. Who else do we know who's come along?'

'Well, I would say Harry Ducloss has. I was talking last week with a man Harry works for.'

'He said he's come along?'

'He said he thought highly of him.'

' "Thought highly." Fermann was always thinking highly of people.'

'I saw Fermann in the street the other day. Boy!'

'Not coming along?'

Clayton lifted his wrists so the waiter could clear away his plate. 'It's just, it's' – with a peculiar intensity, as if Fred had often thought the same thing but never so well expressed it – '*something* to see those tin gods again.'

'Would you young men like dessert?' the waiter asked. 'Coffee?' To Fred: 'We have nice freshly baked strudel. Very nice. It's made right in the kitchen ovens.'

Fred deferred to Clayton. 'Do you have time for coffee?'

Clayton craned his neck to see the clock, 'Eight of two.' He looked at Fred apologetically. 'To tell the truth –'

'No coffee,' Fred told the waiter.

'Oh, let's have it. It'll take just a few minutes.'

'No, it doesn't matter to me and I don't want you to be late.'

'They won't miss me. I'm not *that* indispensable. Are you sure you don't want any?'

'Positive.'

'All right,' Clayton said in the dragged-out, musical tone of a parent acceding to a demand that will only do the child harm. 'Could I have the check, please, waiter?'

'Certainly, sir.' The something sarcastic about that 'sir' was meant for Fred to see.

The check came to $3.80. When Fred reached for his wallet, Clayton said, 'Keep that in your pocket. This is on me.'

'Don't be a fool. The lunch was my idea.'

'No, please. Let me take this.'

Fred dropped a five-dollar bill on the table.

'No, look,' Clayton said. 'I know you have the money –'

'Money! We *all* have *money*.'

Clayton, at last detecting anger, looked up timidly, his irises in the top of his eyes, his chin tucked in. 'Please. You were always quite kind to me.'

It was like a plain girl opening her mouth in the middle of a kiss. Fred wordlessly took back his five. Clayton handed four ones and a quarter to the waiter and said, 'That's right.'

'Thank *you* sir.'

'Thanks a lot,' Fred said to Clayton as they moved towards the door.

'It's –' Clayton shook his head slightly. 'You can get the next one.'

'*Merci beaucoup.*'

'I hope you didn't mind coming to this place.'

'A great place. Vy, sey sought I vuss Cherman.'

Outside, the pavement glittered as if cement were semi-precious; Third Avenue, disencumbered of the el, seemed as spacious and queenly as a South American boulevard. In the harsh light of the two o'clock sun, blemishes invisible in the shadows of the restaurant could be noticed on the skin of Clayton's face – an uneven redness on the flesh of the nose, two spots on his forehead, a flaky area partially hidden beneath an eyebrow. Clayton's feet tended to shuffle backward; he was conscious of his skin, or anxious to get back to work. Fred stood still, making it clear he was travelling in another direction. Clayton did not feel free to go. 'You really want a job in advertising?'

'Forget it. I don't really.'

'I'll keep on the look-out.'

'Don't go to any trouble, but thanks anyway.'

'Thank *you*, for heaven's sake. I really enjoyed this. It's been good.'

For a moment Fred was sorry; he had an impulse to walk a distance with Clayton, to forgive everything, but Clayton, helplessly offensive, smiled and said, 'Well. Back to the salt mines.'

'Well put.' Fred lifted his hand in a benign ministerial gesture startling to passers-by. 'Ye are the salt of the earth. *La lumière du monde*. The light of the world. *Fils de Saint Louis, montez au ciel!*'

Clayton, bewildered by the foreign language, backed a step away and with an uncertain jerk of his hand affirmed, 'See you.'

'*Oui. Allez-en, mon vieux ami. Soyez heureux. Embrassez-moi les fesses douces. Merci. Merci.* Meaning thank you. Thanks again.'

Toward Evening

Waiting for a number five bus in front of St Patrick's Cathedral, Rafe was tired and hence dreamy. When the bus at last came and a short fatty woman in black bounced in front of him and then stopped, apparently paralysed, right at the open doors, with the bus driver tapping the wheel and Rockefeller's towers gathered above them like a thunderhead, Rafe was not very much surprised. The woman made metallic, agitated noises. She seemed unable to step up, to grab the vertical bar, to move away, to do anything. Her hat, black straw strewn with purple berries, quivered, whether with indignation or fright there was no telling. 'Here we go,' Rafe said, grabbing her a few inches below the armpits and hoisting. The woman was filled with sand. The only thing that worried Rafe was, he was carrying in one hand, by a loop of string, a box containing a mobile for the baby and didn't want it crushed.

'Oh, thank you!' a chirping voice beneath the hat cried even before she was safe on the step. 'Thank you so much, whoever you are.' His face seemed to be in her hat; he could see little else. The cloth beneath his fingers turned moist and kept slipping; Rafe had the hideous notion that something would break, and the sack spill, and the woman angrily sink to the pavement as a head in a nest of vacant clothing, like Ray Bolger in *The Wizard of Oz*. Suddenly, when her ascension seemed impossible, she was up, and his freed hands jerked, as if birds had flown from them.

'Wasn't that kind?' the woman asked the bus driver, not turning, though, and never showing Rafe her face.

'Move to the rear,' the driver said in the soft level tones of the poor disciplinarian. Holding the box close to his chest, Rafe edged through the bodies, hunting a porcelain loop. The woman in black had disappeared, yet she couldn't have found a seat. And in the rear of the bus, where there was ample standing-space, a beautiful girl stood. Two ash-blue streaks had been symmetrically dyed into her oloroso-coloured hair. Her topcoat, box-style and black, hung open, half-sheathing her body. Her feet, in grey heels, were planted on the sides of an invisible V. Numberless Vs were visible whenever two edges of the pencil-stripe fabric of her suit met:

in a straight seam down her back, along her sleeves, within her lapels, at the side of her skirt (very acute, these). At the base of her throat, where a V seemed promised, something more complex occurred, involving the sheathed extremities of opposed collarbones, the tapered shelves of their upper edges, the two nervous and rather thoroughbred cords of her neck, and between them a hollow where you could lay a teaspoon. She was less tall than her thinness made her appear; her forehead was level with Rafe's chin.

The bus veered. The standees swung, and her face, until then averted, turned towards his, a fine face, lucid brow. He felt that her mouth could speak French. If her nose had been smaller it would have been too small. The indentation in the centre of the upper lip – the romantic dimple, Rafe's mother had called it, claiming, in the joking, sentimental way she had assumed to raise a child, that in its depth the extent of sexual vigour could be read – was narrow and incisive. Rafe was wondering about her eyes when she turned them up from her book to stare at him for staring, and he lowered his lids too quickly to gain any prize but a meagre impression of bigness. The book in her hand was *A l'ombre des jeunes filles en fleurs*.

After a few moments, he felt that even studying her hand was an intrusion in the ellipse of repose focused on the twin points of face and book. Rafe hugged the box containing the mobile and, stooping down, looked out of the bus window. They had rounded Columbus Circle and were headed up Broadway. The clearly marked numbers on the east side of the street ran: 1832, 1836, 1846, 1850 (Wordsworth dies), 1880 (great Nihilist trial in St Petersburg), 1900 (Rafe's father born in Trenton), 1902 (Braque leaves Le Havre to study painting in Paris), 1914 (Joyce begins *Ulysses*; war begins in Europe), 1926 (Rafe's parents marry in Ithaca), 1936 (Rafe is four years old). Where the present should have stood, a block was torn down, and the numbering began again with 2000, a boring progressive edifice. Rafe diverted his attention from the window to the poster above it. The poster ingeniously advertised Jomar Instant Coffee. The gimmick was a finely corrugated cellulose sheet in which had been embedded two positions of a depicted man's eyeball, arm, and lips. Ideally, from one angle the man was seen holding a cup of coffee to his mouth, smiling, and in flavourful ecstasy rolling his iris to the top of his egg-shaped eye; from another angle he appeared with the cup lowered, his eyeball also lowered, and his lips parted in downright laughter. Rafe's closeness and the curvature of the bus roof prevented the illusion from working with complete success. Both arms, both eyeballs, were always present, though with see-saw intensity as Rafe ducked his head up and down. Either the Jomar man's open-mouthed grin was intersected by the ghost of his close-mouthed smile; or the latter was surrounded by the shadow of the former. Rafe began to feel bus-sick.

He returned to the girl. She was there, beside him, but leaving. Proust jutted from her pocket-book. Her face wore the enamelled look of a person who has emerged from a piece of fiction into the world of decisions. With a whispering touch, her backside eased past his. Having pulled the green cord, she waited in front of the side doors, her profile a brilliant assault on the atmosphere. The doors flapped open. Pursing her mouth, she managed the step, walked south, and was gone.

The entry of some new passengers forced Rafe deeper into the rear of the bus, yards away from where he had stood with the girl. Bit by bit, in confused order, as word of a disaster first filters in over the wires, he became conscious of the young Negress seated beneath him. Her baby-flat nose was a good glossy place for his attention to rest. When she recrossed her legs, he noticed the unpatterned breadth of turquoise skirt, the yellow coat clashing with it, the tense hair painfully pulled straight, the hard-to-read foreshortened curves of her face, the hands folded, with an odd precision, in her turquoise lap. She was wearing blue half-gloves; they stopped at the base of her thumbs. It was the hint of grotesqueness needed to make Rafe lustful. Yet the girl, in becoming desirable, became inaccessible. If Rafe looked at her more steadily than at his previous love, it was because the distance her power established rendered her tactually insensitive to long looks. Likewise, because his imaginings concerning himself and the girl were so plainly fantastic, he could indulge them without limit.

The pure life of the mind, for all its quick distances, is soon tedious. Rafe, dwelling again on the actual Negress, observed the prim secretarial carriage of her head, the orange skin, the sarcastic Caucasian set of her lips. Dress women in sea and sand or pencil lines, they were chapters on the same subject, no more unlike than St Paul and Paul Tillich. In the end, when he alighted at Eighty-fifth Street, the Negress had dwindled to the thought that he had never seen gloves like that before.

Behind him the bus doors closed: pterodactyl wings. A woman standing on the deserted pavement stared at the long box, never guessing a mobile for a baby was in it. The warm air, moistened by the Hudson, guaranteed spring. Rafe went up the rounded, coral-coloured steps, across the chequered lobby floor, and into the tiny scarlet elevator, which was nearly

always waiting for him, like a loyal but not slavish dog. Inside his apartment, the baby had just been fed and was laughing; her mother, flushed
and sleepy, lay in a slip on the sofa bed.

That invisible gas, goodness, stung his eyes and made him laugh, strut,
talk nonsense. He held the baby at arm's height, lowered her until her
belly rested on the top of his head, and walked rapidly around the room
singing. 'I have a little babe, her name is Liz, I think she's better than she
really is, I think she's better than she ever will be, what ev-er will become
of me?'

The baby laughed, 'Gkk, ngk!'

The mobile was not a success. Alice had expected a genuine Calder,
made of beautiful polished woods, instead of seven rubber birds with
celluloid wings, hung from a piece of coarse wire. Elizabeth wanted to put
the birds in her mouth and showed no interest in, perhaps did not even
see, their abstract swinging, quite unlike the rapt infant pictured on the
box.

The baby went to sleep and Alice prepared the dinner in an atmosphere
of let-down.

'I saw some funny gloves today,' Rafe called.

There was no answer from the kitchen, just the disappointed sound of
pans.

When dinner came, it was his favourite everything – peas, hamburger,
baked potato, cooked to avoid his allergies, served on the eccentric tilting
plates in which, newly married, they had sailed the clean seas of sophisticated bliss.

It was growing dark, spottily. A curious illusion was unexpectedly created: his wife, irritated because he had failed to answer some question
of hers – her questions about his life at the office, so well meant, so
understandable in view of her own confined existence, numbed his mind
to the extent that not only his recent doings but her questions themselves
were obliterated – dropped a triangular piece of bread from her fingers,
and the bread, falling to her lap through a width of light, twirled and
made a star.

From where he sat, dinner done, smoking a cigarette, Rafe could look
across the Hudson to the Palisades, surmounted by seeming villages. A
purple sky was being lowered over a yellow one. The Spry sign went on.
The sign, which by virtue of brightness and readability dominated their
night view, had three stages: Spry (red), Spry (white) FOR BAKING (red),
and Spry (white) FOR FRYING (red). Rafe sometimes wondered how it

had come to be there. Some executive, no doubt, had noticed the bare roof of the newly acquired waterfront plant. 'We could use a Spry sign there,' he murmured to his secretary, whom he had kept late at the office and was driving to her home in Riverdale. The following Monday, the secretary made an interdepartmental memo of J.G.'s remark. The man second in charge of Public Relations (the man first in charge was on vacation in the Poconos), new at the job, seven years out of Yale, and not bold enough to take J.G. with a grain of salt, told a man in the Creative End to draw up a sketch. After three days, the man in Creative did this, basing his sketch upon a hundred-and-eighty-six-pound file of past Spry ads. The man in Public Relations had a boy take it into the head office. J.G., flattered to have his suggestion followed up, wrote on the back, 'Turn it slightly south. Nobody at Columbia cooks,' and passed it on, O.K.'d. The two other executives who saw the sketch (both of whom, by an almost supernatural coincidence, had daughters at Sarah Lawrence threatening marriage) suspected that J.G. was developing power among the stockholders and shrewdly strung along. Bids were requested and submitted. One was accepted. The neon people shaped the tubes. Metal-workers constructed a frame. On a November Tuesday, the kind of blowy day that gives you ear-ache, the sign was set in place by eighteen men, the youngest of whom would someday be an internationally known cinema actor. At 3.30, an hour and a half before they were supposed to quit, they knocked off and dispersed, because the damn job was done. Thus the Spry sign (thus the river, thus trees, thus babies and sleep) came to be.

Above its winking, the small cities had disappeared. The black of the river was as wide as that of the sky. Reflections sunk in it existed dimly, minutely wrinkled, below the surface. The Spry sign occupied the night with no company beyond the also uncreated but illegible stars.

Sunday Teasing

Sunday morning: waking, he felt long as a galaxy, and just lacked the will to get up, to unfurl the great sleepy length beneath the covers and go be disillusioned in the ministry by some servile, peace-of-mind-peddling preacher. If it wasn't peace of mind, it was the integrated individual, and if it wasn't the integrated individual, it was the power hidden within each one of us. Never a stern old commodity like sin or remorse, never an open-faced superstition. So he decided, without pretending that it was the preferable course as well as the easier, to stay home and read St Paul.

His wife fussed around the apartment with a too determined silence; whenever he read the Bible, she acted as if he were playing solitaire without having first invited her to play rummy, or as if he were delivering an oblique attack on Jane Austen and Henry Green, whom she mostly read. Trying to bring her into the Sunday-morning club, he said, 'Here's my grandfather's favourite passage, First Corinthians eleven, verse three. "But I would have you know, that the head of every man is Christ; and the head of the woman is the man; and the head of Christ is God." He loved reading that to my mother. It infuriated her.'

A mulish perplexity occupied Macy's usually bland features. '*What*? The head? The head of every man. What does "The head" mean exactly? I'm sorry, I just don't understand.'

If he had been able to answer her immediately, he would have done so with a smile, but, though the sense of 'head' in the text was perfectly clear, he couldn't find a synonym. After a silence he said, 'It's so obvious.'

'Read me the passage again. I really didn't hear it.'

'No,' he said.

'Come on, please. "The head of the man is God . . ." '

'No.'

She abruptly turned and went into the kitchen. 'All you do is tease,' she said from in there. 'You think it's so funny.' He hadn't been teasing her at all, but her saying it put the idea into his head.

They were having a friend to the midday meal that Sunday, Leonard Byrne, a Jewish friend who, no matter what the discussion was about, turned it to matters of the heart and body. 'Do you realize,' he said half-way through the lamb chops, a minute after a round of remarks concerning the movie *Camille* had unexpectedly died, 'that in our home it was nothing for my father to kiss me? When I'd come home from summer camp, he'd actually em*brace* me – physically embrace me. No inhibitions about it at all. In my home, it was *nothing* for men physically to show affection for one another. I remember my uncle when he came to visit had *no* inhibitions about warmly embracing my father. Now that's one thing I find repugnant, personally re*pugnant*, to me about the American home. That there is none of that. It's evident that the American male has some innate fear of being mistaken for a homosexual. But *why*, that's the interesting thing, *why* should he be so protective of his virility? Why shouldn't the American father kiss the American son, when it's done in Italy, in Russia, in France?'

'It's the pioneer,' Macy said: she seldom volunteered her opinions, and in this case, Arthur felt, did it only to keep Leonard from running on and on and eventually embarrassing himself. Now she was stuck with the words 'It's the pioneer,' which, to judge from her face, were beginning to seem idiotic to her. 'Those men *had* to be virile,' she gamely continued, 'they were out there alone.'

'By the way,' Leonard said, resting his elbow on the very edge of the table and tilting his head towards her, for suaveness, 'do you know, it has been established beyond all doubt, that the American pioneer was a drunkard? But that's not the point. Yes, people say, "the pioneer", but I can't quite see how that affects me, as a second-generation American.'

'But that's it,' Arthur told him. 'It doesn't. You just said yourself that your family wasn't American. They kissed each other. Now take me. *I'm* an American. Eleventh-generation German. White, Protestant, Gentile, small-town, middle-class. I am *pure* American. And do you know, I have never seen my father kiss my mother. Never.'

Leonard, of course, was outraged ('That's shocking,' he said. 'That is truly shocking'), but Macy's reaction was what Arthur had angled for. It was hard to separate her perturbation at the announcement from the perturbation caused by her not knowing if he was lying or not. 'That's not true,' she told Leonard, but then asked Arthur, 'Is it?'

'Of course it's true,' he said, talking more to Leonard than to Macy. 'Our family dreaded body contact. Years went by without my touching my mother. When I went to college, she got into the habit of hugging me good-bye, and now does it whenever we go home. But in my teens, when she was younger, there was nothing of the sort.'

'You know, Arthur, that really frightens me,' Leonard said.

'Why? Why should it? It never occurred to my father to manhandle me. He used to carry me when I was little, but when I got too heavy, he stopped. Just like my mother stopped dressing me when I could do it myself.' Arthur decided to push the proposition farther, since nothing he had said since 'I have never seen my father kiss my mother' had aroused as much interest. 'After a certain age, the normal American boy is raised by casual people who just see in him a source of income – movie-house managers, garage attendants, people in luncheonettes. The man who ran the luncheonette where I ate did nothing but cheat us out of our money and crab about the noise we made, but I loved that man like a father.'

'That's *terrible*, Arthur,' Leonard said. 'In my family we didn't really trust anybody outside the family. Not that we didn't have friends. We had lots of friends. But it wasn't quite the *same*. Macy, your mother kissed you, didn't she?'

'Oh, yes. All the time. And my father.'

'Ah, but Macy's parents are atheists,' Arthur said.

'They're Unitarians,' she said.

Arthur continued, 'Now to go back to your *why* this should be so. What do we know about the United States other than the fact that it was settled by pioneers? It is a Protestant country, perhaps the only one. It and Switzerland. Now what *is* Protestantism? A vision of attaining God with nothing but the mind. Nothing but the mind alone on a mountain-top.'

'Yes, yes, of course. We know that,' Leonard said, though in fact Arthur had just stated (he now remembered) not a definition of Protestantism but Chesterton's definition of Puritanism.

'In place of the bureaucratic, interceding Church,' Arthur went on, trying to correct himself, flushing because his argument had urged him into the sacred groves of his mind, 'Luther's notion of Christ is substituted. The reason why in Catholic countries everybody kisses each other is that it's a huge family – God is a family of three, the Church is a family of millions, even heretics are kind of black sheep of the family. Whereas the Protestant lives all by himself, inside of himself. *Sola fide*. Man *should* be lonely.'

'Yes, yes,' Leonard said, puzzling Arthur; he had meant the statements to be debatable.

Arthur felt his audience was bored, because they were eating again, so he said, as a punch, 'I know when we have kids I'm certainly not going to kiss Macy in front of them.'

It was too harsh a thing to say, too bold; he was too excited. Macy said nothing, did not even look up, but her face was tense with an accusatory meekness.

'No, I don't mean that,' Arthur said. 'It's all lies, lies, lies, lies. My family was very close.'

Macy said to Leonard softly, 'Don't you believe it. He's been telling the truth.'

'I know it,' Leonard said. 'I've always felt that about Arthur's home ever since I met him. I really have.'

And though Leonard could console himself with his supposed insight, something uncongenial had been injected into the gathering, and he became depressed; his mood clouded the room, weighed on their temples like smog, and when, hours later, he left, both Arthur and Macy were unwilling to let him go because he had not had a good time. In a guilty spurt of hospitality, they chattered to him of future arrangements. Leonard walked down the stairs with his hat at an angle less jaunty than when he had come up those stairs – a somehow damp angle, as if he had confused his inner drizzle with a state of outer weather.

Supper-time came. Macy mentioned that she didn't feel well and couldn't eat a bite. Arthur put Benny Goodman's 1938 Carnegie Hall Concert on the record-player and, rousing his wife from the Sunday *Times*, insisted that she, who had been raised on Scarlatti and Purcell, take notice of Jess Stacy's classic piano solo on 'Sing, Sing, Sing', which he played twice, for her benefit. He prepared some chicken-with-rice soup for himself, mixing the can with just half a can of water, since it would be for only one person and need not be too much thinned. The soup, heated to a simmer, looked so nutritious that he asked Macy if she really didn't want any. She looked up and thought. 'Just a cupful,' she said, which left him enough to fill a large bowl – plenty, though not a luxurious plenitude.

'Mm. That was so good,' she said after finishing.

'Feel better?'

'Slightly.'

Macy was reading through a collection of short stories, and Arthur brought the rocking-chair from the bedroom and joined her by the lamp, with his paperback copy of *The Tragic Sense of Life*. Here again she misunderstood him; he knew that his reading Unamuno depressed her, and he was reading the book not to depress her but to get the book finished and depress her no longer. She knew nothing of the contents except for his remark one time that according to the author the source of religion is the unwillingness to die, yet she was suspicious.

'Why don't you ever read anything except scary philosophy?' she asked him.

'It isn't scary,' he said. 'The man's a Christian, sort of.'

'You should read some fiction.'

'I will, I will as soon as I finish this.'

Perhaps an hour passed. 'Oh,' Macy said, dropping her book to the floor. 'That's *so* terrible, it's so *aw*ful.'

He looked at her inquiringly. She was close to tears.

'There's a story in here,' she explained. 'It just makes you sick. I don't want to think about it.'

'See, if you'd read Kierkegaard instead of squalid fiction –'

'No, really. I don't even think it's a good story, it's so awful.'

He read the story himself, and Macy moved into the sling chair facing him. He was conscious of her body as clouds of pale colour beyond the edge of the page, stirring with gentle unease, like a dawn. 'Very good,' Arthur said when he was done. 'Quite moving.'

'It's so horrible,' Macy said. 'Why was he so awful to his wife?'

'It's all explained. He was out of his caste. He was trapped. A perfectly nice man, corrupted by bad luck.'

'How can you *say* that? That's so ridiculous.'

'Ridiculous! Why Macy, the whole pathos of the story lies in the fact that the man, for all his selfishness and cruelty, loves the woman. After all, *he's* telling the story, and if the wife emerges as a sympathetic character, it's because that's the way he sees her. The description of her at the train – here. "As the train glided away she turned towards me her face, calm and so sweet and which, in the instant before it vanished, appeared a radiant white heart." ' The story, clumsily translated from the French, was titled *Un Coeur Blanc*. 'And then later, remembering – "It gladdens me that I was able then to simulate a depth of affection that I did not at that time feel. She too generously repaid me, and in that zealous response was there not her sort of victory?" That's absolutely sympathetic, you see. It's a terrific image – this perceptive man caged in his own weak character.'

To his surprise, Macy had begun to cry. Tears mounted from the lower lids of eyes still looking at him. 'Macy,' he said, kneeling by her chair and touching his forehead to hers. He earnestly wished her well at the moment, yet his actions seemed hurried and morbid. 'What is it? Of course I feel sorry for the woman.'

'You said he was a *nice* man.'

'I didn't mean it. I meant that the horror of the story lies in the fact that the man *does* understand, that he does love the woman.'

'It just shows, it shows how *different* we are.'

'No, we're not. We're exactly alike. Our noses' – he touched hers, then his – 'are alike as two peas, our mouths like two turnips, our chins like two hamsters.' She laughed sobbingly, but the silliness of his refutation proved the truth of her remark.

He held her as long as her crying remained strenuous, and when it relented, she moved to the sofa and lay down, saying, 'It's awful when you have an ache and don't know if it's your head or your ear or your tooth.'

He put the palm of his hand on her forehead. He could never tell about fevers. Her skin felt warm, but then human beings were warm things. 'Have you taken your temperature?'

'I don't know where the thermometer is. Broken, probably.' She lay in a forsaken attitude, with one arm, the bluish underside uppermost, extended outward, supported in mid-air by the limits of its flexure. 'Oog,' she said, sticking out her tongue. 'This room is a mess.' The Bible had never been replaced in the row of books; it lay on its side, spanning four secular volumes. Several glasses, drained after dinner, stood like castle sentries on the window-sill, the mantel, and the lowest shelf of the book-case. Leonard had left his rubbers under the table. The jacket of the Goodman record lay on the rug, and the Sunday *Times*, that manifold summation of a week's confusion, was oppressively everywhere. Arthur's soup bowl was still on the table; Macy's cup, cockeyed in the saucer, rested by her chair, along with Unamuno and the collection of short stories. 'It's always so awful,' she said. 'Why don't you ever help to keep the room neat?'

'I will, I will. Now you go to bed.' He guided her into the other room and took her temperature. She kept the thermometer in her mouth as she undressed and got into her nightgown. He read her temperature as 98·8°. 'Very very slight,' he told her. 'I prescribe sleep.'

'I look so pale,' she said in front of the bathroom mirror.

'We never should have discussed *Camille*.' When she was in bed, her face pink against the white pillow and the rest of her covered, he said, 'You and Garbo. Tell me how Garbo says, "You're fooling me." '

'You're fooling me,' she said in a fragile Swedish whisper.

Back in the living-room, Arthur returned the books to the shelves, tearing even strips from the *Times* garden section as bookmarks. He assembled the newspaper and laid it on a window-sill. He stood holding Leonard's rubbers for ten seconds, then dropped them in a corner. He took the record off the phonograph, slipped it into its envelope, and hid it in the closet with the others.

Lastly, he collected the dishes and glasses and washed them. As he stood at the sink, his hands in water which, where the suds thinned and broke, showed a silvery grey, the Sunday's events repeated themselves in his mind, bending like nacreous flakes around a central infrangible irritant, becoming the perfect and luminous thought: *You don't know anything.*

Incest

'I was in a movie house, fairly plush, in a sort of mezzanine, or balcony. It was a wide screen. On it there were tall people – it seemed to be at a dance or at least *function* – talking and bending towards each other gracefully, in that misty Technicolor Japanese pictures have. I *knew* that this was the movie version of *Remembrance of Things Past*, I had the impression sitting there that I had been looking forward to it for a long time, and I felt slightly guilty at not being home, you know. There was a girl sitting down one row, catty-corner from me. She had a small head with a thin, rather touching neck, like Moira Lengel, but it wasn't her, or anyone we know. At any rate there was this feeling of great affection towards her, and it seemed, in the light of the movie – the movie was taking place entirely in a bright yellow ballroom, so the faces of the audience were clear – it seemed somehow that the entire chance to make my life good was wrapped up in this girl, who was strange to me. Then she was in the seat beside me, and I was giving her a back rub.'

'*Uh*-oh,' his wife said, pausing in her stooping. She was grazing the carpet, picking up the toys, cards, matches, and spoons scattered by their daughter Jane, a year and seven months old. Big Jane, as she had dreaded being called when they named the child, held quite still to catch what next he had to tell. Lee had begun the recitation ironically, to register his irritation with her for asking him, her own day had been so dull and wearing, to talk, to tell her of *his* day. Nothing interested him less than his own day, done. It made his jaws ache, as with a smothered yawn, to consider framing one sentence about it. So, part desperation, part discipline, he had begun the account of the dream he had been careful to keep from her at breakfast. He protected his wife here, at the place where he recalled feeling his hands leave the lean girl's comforted shoulder-blades and travel thoughtfully around the cool, strait, faintly ridged sides of the rib case to the always surprising boon in front – sensations momentarily more vivid in the nerves of his fingers than the immediate texture of the bamboo chair he occupied.

'Through the blouse.'

'Good,' she said. 'Good for you both.'

Jane appeared so saucy saying this he was emboldened to add a true detail. 'I think I did undo her bra strap. By pinching through the cloth.' To judge by his wife's expression – tense for him, as if he were bragging before company – the addition was a mistake. He hastened on. 'Then we were standing in back of the seats, behind one of those walls that comes up to your chest, and I was being introduced to her father. I had the impression he was a doctor. He was rather pleasant, really: grey hair, and a firm grip. He seemed cordial, and I had a competent feeling, as if I couldn't help making a good impression. But behind this encounter – with the girl standing off to one side – there was the sadness of the movie itself continuing on the screen; the music soared; Proust's face was shown – a very young face – with the eyelids closed, and this shimmered and spun and turned into a slow pink vortex that then solidified into a huge motionless rose, filling the whole screen. And I thought, *Now I know how the book ends.*'

'How exciting, darley! It's like "The Dream of the Rood".' Jane resumed cleaning up after her daughter. Lee was abruptly oppressed by a belief that he had made her life harder to bear.

He said, 'The girl must have been you because you're the only person I know who likes to have their back rubbed.'

'You find my neck touching?'

'Well for God's sake, I can't be held accountable for the people I meet in dreams. I don't invite them.' He was safe, of course, as long as they stayed away from the real issue, which was why he had told her the dream at all. 'That girl means nothing to me now. In the dream obviously I was still in high-school and hadn't met you. I remember sitting there and wondering, because it was such a long movie, if my mother would give me hell when I got back.'

'I say, it's a very exciting dream. How far *are* you in Proust?'

' "Sodom and Gomorrah".' It occurred to him, what a queer mediocre thing it was, to scorn the English title yet not dare pronunciation of the French, and apropos of this self-revelation he said, 'I'll never get out; I'm just the sort of person who begins Proust and can't finish. Lowest of the low. The humiliated and oppressed. Won't even tell his wife what his day was like.' He changed his tone. 'Which is better – to finish *Remembrance of Things Past*, or to never begin it?'

Unexpectedly, so profound was her fatigue, she did not recognize the question as a piece of sport rhetoric, and, after a moment's thought, seriously answered, 'To finish it.'

Then she turned, and her lovely pale face – in photographs like a white water-smoothed stone, so little did the indentations and markings of it have harshness – lengthened, and the space between her eyebrows creased vertically; into the kitchen she shouted, '*Jane!* What are you *doing?*'

While they had been talking, the child had been keeping herself quiet with the sugar-bowl. It was a new trick of hers, to push a chair and climb up on it; in this way a new world, a fresh stratum of things, was made available to her curiosity. The sugar bowl, plump Swedish pewter, lived casually on the counter of a waist-high cabinet, near the wall. Little Jane had taken and inverted it, and with an eerie, repetitious, patient dabbling motion had reduced the once shining Alp to a system of low ranges. She paid no attention to her mother's shout, but when her parents drew closer and sighed together, she quickly turned her face towards them as if for admiration, her chin and lips frosted. Her upper lip, when she smiled, curved like the handlebar of a bicycle. The sight of her incredibly many, perfect, blue, inturned teeth struck joy into Lee's heart.

With an audience now, little Jane accelerated her work. Her right hand, unattended by her eyes, which remained with her parents, scrabbled in a panicky way among the white drifts and then, palm down, swept a quantity on to the floor, where it hit with a sound like one stroke of a drummer's brush. On the spatter-pattern linoleum the grains of sugar were scarcely visible. The child looked down, wondering where they had gone.

'Damn you,' his wife said to Lee, 'you never do a damn thing to help. Now, why can't you play with her a minute? You're her father. *I'm* not going to clean it up.' She walked out of the kitchen.

'I *do* play with her,' he said, helplessly amiable (he understood his wife so well, divined so exactly what confused pain the scattered sugar caused her heart, as neatness-loving as her mother's), although he recognized that in her distraught state his keeping cheerful figured as mockery of her, one more cross to carry towards the day's end.

Lee asked his daughter, 'Want to run around?'

Jane hunched her shoulders and threw back her head, her sugar-gritty teeth gleefully clenched. 'Pay roun,' she said, waggling her hand on her wrist.

He made the circular motion she had intended, and said, 'In a minute. Now we must help poor Mommy.' With two sheets of typing paper, using one as a brush and the other as a pan, he cleaned up what she had spilled on the counter, reaching around her, since she kept her position standing on the chair. Her breath floated randomly, like a butterfly, on his forearms as he swept. They seemed two conspirators. He folded the pan in a chute and returned the sugar to the bowl. Then there was the sugar on the floor – when you moved your feet, atoms of it crackled. He stooped, the two pieces of paper in his hands, knowing they wouldn't quite do.

Jane whimpered and recklessly jogged her body up and down on her legs, making the chair tip and slap the cabinet. '*Jane*,' he said.

'Pay roun,' the girl whined feebly, her strength sapped by frustration.

'*What?*' his wife answered from the living-room in a voice as cross as his. She had fought giving the baby her name, but he had insisted; there was no other woman's name he liked, he had said.

'Nothing, I was shouting at the kid. She was going to throw herself off the chair. She wants to play Round.'

'Well, why don't you? She's had an awfully dismal day. I don't think we make her happy enough.'

'O.K., dammit. I will.' He crumpled the sheets of paper and stuffed them into the wastepaper can, letting the collected sugar fly where it would.

Round was a simple game. Jane ran from the sofa in one room to the bed in the other, through the high white double doorway, with pilasters, that had persuaded them to take the small apartment. He chased her. When his hands nicked her bottom or touched her swollen waist, she laughed wildly her double laugh, which originated deep in her lungs and ricocheted, shrill, off her palate. Lee's problem was to avoid overtaking her, in the great length of his strides, and stepping on her. When she wobbled or slowed, he clapped twice or thrice, to give her the sense of his hands right behind her ears, like two nipping birds. If she toppled, he swiftly picked her up, tickling her briefly if she seemed stunned or indignant. When she reached the bed – two low couches, box springs on short legs, set side by side and made up as one – he leap-frogged over her and fell full-length on the mattresses. This, for him, was the strenuous part of the game. Jane, finding herself between her father's ankles after the rush of his body above her head, laughed her loudest, pivoted, and ran the other way, flailing her arms, which she held so stiffly the elbows were indentations. At the sofa end of the track there could be no leap-frogging. Lee merely stopped and stood with his back towards her until the little girl calculated she dare make a break for it. Her irises swivelled in their blue whites; it was the first strategy of her life. The instant she decided to move, her bottled excitement burst forth; as she clumped precipitately towards the high white arch laughter threatened to upend her world. The game lasted until the child's bath. Big Jane, for the first time that day free of her daughter, was not hurrying towards this moment.

After four times back and forth Lee was exhausted and damp. He flopped on the bed the fifth time and instead of rising rolled on to his back. This was ruining the crease in his pants. His daughter, having started off, felt his absence behind her and halted. Her mother was coming from the kitchen, carrying washed diapers and a dust brush. Like her own mother, Big Jane held a cigarette in the left corner of her mouth. Her left eye fluttered against the smoke. Lee's mother-in-law was shorter than his wife, paler, more sarcastic – very different, he had thought. But this habit was hers right down to the tilt of the cigarette and the droop of the neglected ash. Looking, Lee saw that as Jane squinted, the white skin at the outside corner of her eye crinkled finely, as dry as her mother's, and that his wife's lids were touched with the lashless, grainy, humiliated quality of the lids of the middle-aged woman he had met not a dozen times, mostly in Indianapolis, where she kept a huge brick house spotlessly clean and sipped sherry from breakfast to bed. All unknowing he had married her.

Jane, as she passed him, glanced down with an untypical, sardonic, cigarette-stitched expression. By shifting his head on the pillow he could watch her in the bathroom. She turned her back to hang the diapers on a grocer's cord strung between mirror and window. This was more his Jane: the rounded shoulders, the back, shaped like a peach, of two halves, the big thighs, the narrow ankles. In the mirror her face, straining up as she attached the clothes-pins, showed age and pallor. It was as if there could exist a coin one side of which wears thin while the other keeps all the gloss and contour of the minting.

'Da-*tee*.' A coral flush had overspread his daughter's face; in another moment she would whimper and throw herself on the floor.

With an ostentatious groan – he didn't know which of his women he was rebuking – Lee rose from the bed and chased his daughter again. Then they played in the living-room with the bolsters, two prism-shaped pieces of foam rubber that served as a back to the sofa, an uncomfortable modernist slab that could, when a relative visited, be used for sleeping. Stood on end, the stiff bolsters were about the baby's height, and little Jane hugged them like brothers, and preferred them to dolls. Though to her human-sized, they were light enough to lift. Especially she loved to unzip the skin of mongrel linen fabric and prod with her finger the greyish, buoyant flesh beneath.

Catching them at this, Big Jane said, 'It kills me, it just is more depressing than anything she does, the way she's always trying to undress those bolsters. Don't en*courage* her at it.'

'I don't. It's not my idea. It was *you* who took the covers to the Launderette so she saw them naked. It made a big impression. It's a state of primal innocence she wants to get them back to.'

Wavering between quarrel and honest discussion – that there was a way of 'talking things out' was an idea she had inherited from her father, a rigorously liberal civic leader and committee-man – she chose discussion. 'It's not just those bolsters, you know. About three times a day she takes all the books out of their jackets. And spills matches in a little heap. You have no idea how much cleaning up I have to do to keep this place from looking like a pig-pen. Yesterday I was in the bathroom washing my hair and when I came out she had gotten our camera open. I guess the whole roll's exposed. I put it back. Today she wanted to get the works out of the music box and threw a tantrum. And I don't know how often she brings those nasty frustrating little Chinese eggs you got her to me and says, "Opo. Opo." '

Reminded of the word, little Jane said, of a bolster, 'Opo, opo.' The zipper was stuck.

'Japanese,' Lee said. 'Those eggs were made in Genuine Occupied Japan. They're antiques.' The child's being baulked by the zipper preyed on his nerves. He hated fiddling with things like zippers caught on tiny strips of cloth. It was like squinting into a specific detail of Hell. Further, as he leaned back on the bolsterless sofa to rest his neck against the wall, he was irritated to feel the glass-capped legs skid on the uneven floor. 'It's a very healthy instinct,' he went on. 'She's an empiricist. She's throwing open doors long locked by superstition.'

Jane said, 'I looked up "unwrapping instinct" in Spock and the only thing in the index was "underweight".' Her tone was listless and humorous, and for the moment this concession put the family, to Lee's mind, as right as three Japanese eggs, each inside the other.

His wife gave his daughter her bath as day turned to evening. He had to go into the bathroom himself and while there studied the scene. The child's silky body, where immersed, was of a graver tint than that of her skin smarting in air. Two new cakes of unwrapped soap drifted around her. When her mother put a washrag to her face, blinding and scratching her, her fingers turned pale green with the pressure of her grip on the edge of the tub. She didn't cry, though. 'She seems to like her bath better now,' he said.

'She loves it. From five on, until you come, she talks about it. Daddy. Bath. Omelet.'

'Omma net,' his daughter said, biting her lower lip in a smile for him.

It had become, in one of those delicate mutations of routine whereby Jane shifted duties to him, his job to feed the little girl. The child's soft mouth had been burned and she was wary; the sample bites Lee took to show her that the food was safe robbed of sharpness his appetite for his own dinner. Foreknowledge of the emotion caused in his wife by the sight of half-clean plates and half-full cups led him to complete little Jane's portion of tomato juice, omelet-with-toast, and, for dessert, apple-sauce. Handling the tiny cup and tiny knife and fork and spoon set his stomach slightly on edge. Though not fussy about food, he was disturbed by eating-implements of improper weight or length. Jane, hidden in the kitchen, was unable to see or, if she had seen, to appreciate – for all their three years of marriage, she had a stunted awareness of his niceties – the discomfort he was giving himself. This annoyed him.

So he was unfortunately brusque with little Jane's bottle. Ideally the bottle was the happiest part of the meal. Steaming and dewy, it soared, white angel, out of the trembling pan, via Mommy's hands, with a kiss, into hers. She grabbed it, and Lee, his hand behind her head, steered her towards the bedroom and her crib.

'Nice maugham,' she said, conscientiously echoing the infinity of times they had told her that the bottle was nice and warm.

Having lifted her into the crib and seen her root the bottle in her mouth, he dropped the fuzzy pink blanket over her and left quickly, gently closing the doors and sealing her into the darkness that was to merge with sleep. It was no doubt this quickness that undid the process. Though the child was drugged with heated milk, she still noticed a slight.

He suspected this at the time. When, their own meal barely begun, the crib springs creaked unmistakably, he said, 'Son of a bitch.' Stan Lomax, on their faint radio, was giving an account of Williams's latest verbal outrage; Lee was desperate to hear every word. Like many Americans he was spiritually dependent on Ted Williams. He asked his wife, 'God damn it, doesn't that kid do anything in the day? Didn't you take her to the park? Why isn't she worn out?'

The one answer to this could be his own getting up, after a silence, and going in to wait out the baby's insomnia. The hollow goodness of the act, like a gift given to a beggar with embarrassment, infuriated his tongue: 'I work like a fool all day and come home and run the kid up and down until my legs ache and I have a headache and then I can't even eat my pork chop in peace.'

In the aquarium of the dark-room his child's face floated spectrally, and her eyes seemed discrete pools of the distant, shy power that had put them all there, and had made these walls, and the single tree outside, showing the first stages of leaf under the yellow night sky of New York. 'Do you want to go on the big bed?'

'Big – *bed*!'

'O.K.'

'Ogay.'

Adjusting to the lack of light, he perceived that the bottle, nested in a crumpled sheet, was drained. Little Jane had been standing in her crib, one foot on the edge, as in ballet school. For two weeks she had been gathering nerve for the time she would climb the crib's wall and drop free outside. He lifted her out, breathing 'Ooh, *heavy*,' and took her to the wide low bed made of two beds. She clung to the fuzzy blanket – with milk, her main soporific.

Beside her on the bed, he began their story. 'Once upon a time, in the big, big woods –' She flipped ecstatically at the known cadence. 'Now you relax. There was a tiny little creature name of Barry Mouse.'

'Mouff!' she cried, and sat straight up, as if she had heard one. She looked down at him for confirmation.

'Barry Mouse,' he said. 'And one day when Barry Mouse was walking through the woods, he came to a great big tree, and in the top of the great big tree what do you think there was?'

At last she yielded to the insistent pressure of his hand and fell back, her heavy blonde head sinking into the pillow. He repeated, 'What do you think there was?'

'Owl.'

'That's right. Up at the top of the tree there was an owl, and the owl said, "I'm going to eat you, Barry Mouse." And Barry Mouse said, "No, no." So Owl said, "O.K., then why don't you *hop* on my *back* and we'll *fly* to the *moon*?" And so Barry Mouse hopped on Owl's back and away they went –'

Jane turned on her side, so her great face was an inch from his. She giggled and drummed her feet against his abdomen, solidly. Neither Lee nor his wife, who shared the one bedtime story, had ever worked out what happened on the moon. Once the owl and the mouse were aloft, their imaginations collapsed. Knowing his voice daren't stop now, when her state was possibly transitional and he felt as if he were bringing to his lips an absolutely brimful glass of liquid, he continued with some nonsense about cinnamon trees and Chinese maidens, no longer bothering to keep within her vocabulary. She began touching his face with her open mouth, a sure sign she was sleepy. 'Hey,' he murmured when one boneless moist kiss landed directly on his lips.

'Jane is so sleepy,' he said, 'because Daddy is sleepy, and Mommy is sleepy, and Bear is ssleepy, and Doll is ssleepy . . .'

She lay quiet, her face in shadow, her fine straight yellow hair fanned across the pillow. Neither he nor his wife was blonde; they had brown hair, rat colour. There was little blondness in either family: just Jane's Aunt Ruth, and Lee's sister Margaret, eight years older than he and married before he had left grade school. She had been the fetching one of the children and he the bright one. So he imagined, though his parents loved them all impeccably.

Presuming his daughter asleep, he lifted himself on one elbow. She kicked his belly, rolled on to her back, and said in a voice loud with drowsiness, 'Baaiy Mouff.'

Stroking her strange hair, he began again, 'Once upon a time, in the deep, deep woods, there lived a little creature,' and this time succeeded.

As he lowered her into her crib, her eyes opened. He said, 'O.K.?'

She pronounced beautifully, 'O.K.'

'Gee, she's practically epileptic with energy,' he said, blinded by the brilliant light of the room where his wife had remained.

'She's a good child,' Jane affirmed, speaking out of her thoughts while left alone rather than in answer to his remark. 'Your dessert is on the table.' She had kept hers intact on the sofa beside her, so they could eat their raspberry whip together. She also had beside her an orange-juice glass half full of sherry.

When the clock said seven-fifty, he said, 'Why don't you run off to the movie? You never have any fun.'

'All right,' she said. 'Go ahead. Go.'

'No, I don't mean that. I mean you should go.' Still, he smiled.

'You can go as a reward for putting her to sleep.'

'Venus, I don't *want* to go,' he said, without great emphasis, since at that moment he was rustling through the paper. He had difficulty finding the theatre section, and decided. 'No, if you're too tired, no one will. I can't leave you. You need me too much.'

'If you want to, go; don't torment me about it,' she said, drawing on her sherry and staring into the *New Republic*. When she had the chance, she worked at being liberal.

'Do you think,' he asked, 'when Jane is sixteen, she'll go around in the back seat of Chevrolets and leave her poor old Daddy?'

'I hope so,' Jane said.

'Will she have your bosom?'

'Not immediately.'

He earnestly tried to visualize his daughter matured, and saw little but a charm bracelet on a slim, fair wrist. The forearms of teenage girls tapered amazingly, towards little cages of bird bones. Charm bracelets were *démodé* already, he supposed.

Lee, committed to a long leisured evening at home, of the type that seemed precious on the nights when they had to go out and be entertained, was made nervous by its wide opportunities. He nibbled at the reading matter closest to hand – an article, 'Is the Individual a Thing of the Past?', and last Sunday's comic section. At Alley Oop he checked himself and went into the kitchen. Thinking of the oatmeal cookies habitual in his parents' home, he opened the cupboard and found four kinds of sugar and seven of cereal, five infants' and two adults'. Jane was always buying some esoteric grind of sugar for a pastry-making project, then discovering she couldn't use it. He smiled at this foible and carried his smile like an egg on a spoon into the living-room, where his wife saw it but, of course, not the point of it, that it was in love of her. He leaned his forehead against the bookcase, by the anthology shelf, and considered all the poetry he had once read evaporating in him, a vast dying sea.

As he stood there, his father floated from behind and possessed him, occupying specifically the curved area of the jawbone. He understood perfectly why that tall stoical man had been a Mason, Booster, deacon, and Scout-troop leader.

Jane, concentrating all the pleasures her day had withheld into the hour remaining before she became too dopey to think, put Bach on the record-player. As she did so, her back and arms made angles signifying to him a whole era of affection and, more, awe.

When she returned to the sofa, he asked, 'What makes you so pretty?' Then, having to answer it, he said, 'Childbearing.'

Preoccupied with some dim speckled thinker in her magazine, she fond-led the remark briefly and set it aside, mistakenly judging it to be a piece of an obscure, ill-tempered substance. He poured a little sherry for himself and struck a pose by the mantel, trying to find with his legs and shoulders angles equivalent in effect to those she had made putting on the record.

As she sat there, studious, he circumscribed her, every detail, with the tidal thought *Mine, mine*. She wasn't watching. She thought she knew what to expect from him, tonight at least.

He resolved, *Later*, and, in a mood of resolution, read straight through the Jones Very section of Matthiessen's anthology. The poet's stubborn sensibility aroused a readerly stubbornness; when Lee had finished, it was too late, the hour had slipped by. By the clock it was 10.30; for his wife, it was after one. Her lids were pink. This was the sort of day when you sow and not reap.

Two hissing, clattering elves working a minor fairy-tale transposition; together they lifted the crib containing the sleeping girl and carried it into the living-room, and shut the doors. Instead of undressing, Jane picked up odds and ends of his – spare shoes and the socks he had worn yesterday and the tie he had worn today. Next she went into the bathroom and emerged wearing a cotton nightie. In bed beside him she read a page of *Swann's Way* and fell asleep under the harsh light. He turned it off and thought furiously, the family's second insomniac. The heat of Jane's body made the bed stuffy. He hated these low beds; he lay miles below the ceiling, deep in the pit. The radiator, hidden in the window-sill by his head, breathed lavishly. High above, through a net of crosses, a few stars strove where the yellow gave out. The child cried once, but, thank God, in her sleep.

He recalled what he always forgot in the interval of day, his insomnia game. Last night he had finished D in a burst of glory: Yvonne Dionne, Zuleika Dobson. He let the new letter be G. Senator Albert Gore, Benny Goodman, Constance Garnett, *David* Garnett, Edvard Grieg. Goethe was Wolfgang and Gorki was Maxim. Farley Granger, Graham Greene (or Greta Garbo, *or* George Gobel), Henry Green. I was always difficult. You kept thinking of Ilka Chase. He wrestled and turned and cursed his wife, her heedless rump way on his side. To choke the temptation to thump her awake, he padded after a glass of water, scowling into the mirror. As he returned his head to the cooled pillow, it came to him, Christian name and surname both at once: Ira Gershwin. Ira Gershwin: he savoured it before proceeding. John Galsworthy, Kathryn Grayson . . . Lou Gehrig, poor devil . . .

He and Jane walked along a dirt road, in high, open-field country, like the farm owned by Mark, his mother's brother. He was glad that Jane was seeing the place, because while he was growing up it had given him a sense of wealth to have an uncle attached to a hundred such well-kept acres. His relationship with Jane seemed to be at that stage when it was important for each side of the betrothal to produce external signs of respectability. 'But I am even richer,' he abruptly announced. She appeared not to notice. They walked companionably but in silence, and seemed responsible for the person with them, a female their height. Lee gathered the impression, despite a veil against his eyes, that this extra girl was blonde and sturdy and docile. His sense of her sullenness may have been nothing but his anxiety to win her approval, reflected; though her features were hard to make out, the emotion he bore her was precise: the coppery, gratified, somewhat adrift feeling he would get when physically near girls he adored in high school. The wind had darkened and grown purposeful.

Jane went back, though the countryside remained the same. Then he was dousing, with a lawn hose attached to the side of the house, the body of this third person. Her head rested on the ground; he held her ankles and slowly, easily turned the light, stiff mass, to wet every area. It was important that water wash over every bit of skin. He was careful; the task, like rinsing an automobile, was more absorbing than pleasant or unpleasant.

A Gift from the City

Like most happy people, they came from well inland. Amid this city's mysteries, they had grown very close. When the phone on his desk rang, he knew it was she. 'Jim? Say. Something awful has happened.'

'What?' His voice had contracted and sounded smaller. He pictured his wife and small daughter attacked by teenagers, derelicts, coal men, beneath the slender sparse trees of Tenth Street; oh if only love were not immaterial! If only there were such a thing as enchantment, and he could draw, with a stick, a circle of safety around them that would hold, though they were on Tenth near Fifth and he forty blocks north.

'I guess it shouldn't be awful but it's so upsetting. Martha and I were in the apartment, we had just come back from the park, and I was making tea for her tea party –'

'Nnn. And?'

'And the doorbell rang. And I didn't know who could be calling, but I pressed the buzzer and went to the stairs, and there was this young Negro. It seemed strange, but then he looked awfully frightened and really smaller than I am. So I stood at the banister and he stood on the middle of the stairs, and he told me this story about how he had brought his family up from North Carolina in somebody else's truck and they had found a landlord who was giving them a room but they had no furniture or food. I couldn't understand half of what he said.' Her voice broke here.

'Poor Liz. It's all right, he didn't expect you to.'

'He kept saying something about his wife, and I *couldn't* understand it.'

'You're O.K. now, aren't you?'

'Yes I'm O.K., let me finish.'

'You're crying.'

'Well it was awfully strange.'

'What did he *do*?'

'He didn't *do* anything. He was very nice. He just wanted to know if there were any odd jobs I could let him do. He'd been all up and down Tenth Street just ringing doorbells, and nobody was home.'

'We don't have any odd jobs.'

'That's what I said. But I gave him ten dollars and said I was sorry but this was all I had in the house. It's all I did have.'

'Good. That was just the right thing.'

'Was it all right?'

'Sure. You say the poor devil came up in a truck?' James was relieved; the shadow of the coal man had passed; the enchantment had worked. It had seemed for a moment, from her voice that the young Negro was right there in the apartment, squeezing Martha on the sofa.

'The point is, though,' Liz said, 'now we don't have any money for the weekend, and Janice is coming tomorrow night so we can go to the movies, and then the Bridges on Sunday. You know how she eats. Did you go to the bank?'

'Dammit, no. I forgot.'

'Well, *darling*.'

'I keep thinking we have lots of money.' It was true; they did. 'Never mind, maybe they'll cash a cheque here.'

'You think? He was really awfully pathetic, and I couldn't tell if he was a crook or not.'

'Well, even if he was he must have needed the money; crooks need money too.'

'You think they *will* cash a cheque?'

'Sure. They love me.'

'The really awful thing I haven't told you. When I gave him the ten dollars he said he wanted to thank you – he seemed awfully interested in you – and I said, Well, fine, but on Saturdays we were in and out all day, so he said he'd come in the evening. He really wants to thank you.'

'He does?'

I told him we were going to the movies and he said he'd come around before we went.'

'Isn't he rather aggressive? Why didn't he let *you* thank me for him?'

'Darley, I don't know *what* to say.'

'Then it's not the Bridges we need the money for; it's him.'

'No, I don't think so. You made me forget the crucial part. He said he has gotten a job that starts Monday, so it's just this weekend he needs furniture.'

'Why doesn't he sleep on the floor?' James could imagine himself, in needful circumstances, doing that. In the Army he had done worse.

'He has this *family*, Jim. Did you want me not to give him anything – to run inside and lock the door? It would have been easy to do, you know.'

'No, no, you were a wonderful Christian. I'm proud of you. Anyway, if he comes before the movie he can't very well stay all night.'

This pleasant logic seemed firm enough to conclude on, yet when she had hung up and her voice was gone, the affair seemed ominous again. It was as if, with the click of the receiver, she had sunk beneath an ocean. His own perch, twenty-two storeys above Park Avenue, swayed slightly, with the roll of too many cigarettes. He ground his present one into a turquoise ashtray, and looked about him, but his beige office at Dudevant & Smith (Industrial and Package Design) offered an inappropriate kind of comfort. His youth's high hopes – he had thought he was going to be a painter – had been distilled into a few practical solids: a steel desk, a sponge chair, a drawing-board the size of a dining-table, infinitely adjustable lighting fixtures, abundant draughtsman's equipment, and a bulletin board so fresh it gave off a scent of cork. Oversized white tacks fixed on the cork several flattering memos from Dudevant, a snapshot, a studio portrait of Liz, and a four-colour ad for the Raydo shaver, a shaver that James had designed, though an asterisk next the object dropped the eye to the right-hand corner, to Dudevant's name, in elegantly modest sans-serif. This was all right; it was in the bargain. James's anonymity had been honestly purchased. Indeed, it seemed they couldn't give him enough; there was always some bonus or adjustment or employee benefit or Christmas present appearing on his desk, in one of those long blue envelopes that spelled 'money' to his mind as surely as green engravings.

His recent fortunes had been so good, James had for months felt that some harsh blow was due. Cautious, he gave Providence few opportunities to instruct him. Its last chance, except for trips in the car, had been childbirth, and Liz had managed that with a poised animal ease, one Thursday at dawn. As the months passed harmlessly, James's suspicion increased that the city itself, with its steep Babylonian surfaces, its black noon shadows, its godless millions, was poised to strike. He placated the circumambient menace the only way he knew – by giving to beggars. He distributed between one and two dollars a day to Salvation Army singers, degraded violinists, husky blind men standing in the centre of the pavement with their beautiful German shepherds, men on crutches offering yellow pencils, mumbling drunks anxious to shake his hand and show him the gash beneath their hats, men noncommittally displaying their metal legs in subway tunnels. Ambulatory ones, given the pick of a large crowd, would approach him; to their vision, though he dressed and looked like anyone else, he must wear, with Byzantine distinctness, the aureole of the soft touch.

*

Saturday was tense. James awoke feeling the exact shape of his stomach, a disagreeable tuber. The night before, he had tried to draw from Liz more information about her young Negro. 'How was he dressed?'

'Not badly.'

'Not badly!'

'A kind of sport coat with a red wool shirt open at the neck, I think.'

'Well, why is he all dolled up if he has no money? He dresses better than I do.'

'It didn't seem *terri*bly strange. You know he *would* have *one* good outfit.'

'And he brought his wife and *seven* children up here in the cab of a truck?'

'I said seven? I just have the feeling it's seven.'

'Sure. Seven dwarfs, seven lively arts, seven levels of Purgatory . . .'

'It couldn't have been in the cab, though. It must have been in the truck part. He said they had no furniture or anything except what they wore.'

'Just the rags on their backs. Son of a bitch.'

'This is so unlike you, darling. You're always sending cheques to Father Flanagan.'

'He only asks me once a year and at least he doesn't come crawling up the stairs after my wife.'

James was indignant. The whole tribe of charity seekers, to whom he had been so good, had betrayed him. On Saturday morning, down on Eighth Street buying a book, he deliberately veered away, off the kerb and into the gutter, to avoid a bum hopefully eyeing his lapels. At lunch the food lacked taste. The interval between the plate and his face exasperated him; he ate too fast, greedily. In the afternoon, all the way to the park, he maintained a repellent frown. When Liz seemed to dawdle, he took over the pushing of the carriage himself. A young coloured man in Levis descended the steps of a brick four-storey and peered up and down the street uncertainly. James's heart tripped. 'There he is.'

'Where?'

'Right ahead, looking at you.'

'Aren't you scary? That's not him. Mine was really short.'

At the park his daughter played in the damp sand by herself. No one seemed to love her; the other children romped at selfish games. The slatted shadow of the fence lengthened as the sun drew closer to the tops of the N.Y.U. buildings. Beneath this orange dying ball a yelping white played tennis with a tall Negro on an asphalt court, beneath the variously papered wall of a torn-down building. Martha tottered from the sandbox to the see-saw to the swings, in her element and fearless. Strange, the fruit of

237

his seed was a native New Yorker; she had been born in a hospital on Twenty-ninth Street. He rescued her at the entry to the swing section, lifted her into one, and pushed her from the front. Her face dwindled and loomed, dwindled and loomed; she laughed, but none of the other parents or children gave a sign of hearing her. The metal of the swing was icy; this was September. A chill, end-of-summer breeze weighed restlessly on the backs of his hands.

When they returned to the apartment, after four, safe, and the Negro was not there, and Liz set about making tea as on any other day, his fears were confounded, and he irrationally ceased expecting anything bad to happen. Of course they gave the baby her bath and ate their dinner in peace; by pure will he was keeping the hateful doorbell smothered. And when it did ring, it was only Janice, their baby-sitter, coming up the stairs with her grandmotherly slowness.

He warned her, 'There's a slight chance a young Negro will be coming here to find us,' and told her, more or less, the story.

'Well don't worry, I won't let him in,' Janice said in the tone of one passing on a particularly frightening piece of gossip. 'I'll tell him you're not here and I don't know when you'll be back.' She was a good-hearted, unfortunate girl, with dusty tangerine hair. Her mother in Rhode Island was being filtered through a series of hopeless operations. Most of her weekends were spent up there, helping her mother die. The salary Janice earned as a stenographer at N.B.C. was consumed by train fares and long-distance phone calls; she never accepted her fee at the end of a night's sitting without saying, with a soft-sided smile wherein ages of Irish wit were listlessly deposited, 'I hate to take it, but I need the money.'

'Well, no, don't be rude or anything. Tell him – and I don't think he'll come, but just in case – we'll be here Sunday.'

'The Bridges, too,' Liz pointed out.

'Yeah, well, I don't think he'll show. If he's as new here as you said he said he was he probably can't find the place again.'

'You know,' Janice said to Liz, 'you really can't be so soft-hearted. I admire you for it, and I feel as sorry for these people as you do, but in this town, believe me, you don't dare trust anybody, literally, *any*body. A girl at work beside me knows a man who's as healthy as you or me, but he goes around on crutches and makes a hundred and twenty dollars a week. Why, that's more than any of us who work honestly make.'

James smiled tightly, insulted twice; he made more than that a week, and he did not like to hear he was being defrauded by pitiable souls on the street who he could see were genuinely deformed or feeble-minded or alcoholic.

After a pause, Liz gently asked the girl, 'How is your mother?'

Janice's face brightened and was not quite so overpowered by the orange hair. 'Oh, on the phone last night she sounded real high and mighty. The P.-T.A. has given her some job with a drive for funds, something she could do with pencil and papers, without getting up. I've told you how active she had been. She was all for getting out of bed. She said she can feel, you know, that it's out of her body now. But when I talked to the doctor last Sunday, he said we mustn't hope too much. But he seemed very proud of the operation.'

'Well, good luck,' James said, jingling the change in his pocket.

Janice shook her finger. 'You have a good time. He isn't going to get in if I'm here, *that* you can depend on,' she assured them, misunderstanding, or perhaps understanding more than necessary.

The picture was excellent, but just at the point where John Wayne, after tracking the Comanches from the snow-bound forests of Montana to the blazing dunes of Border Country, was becoming reconciled to the idea of his niece cohabiting with a brave, James vividly remembered the bum who had wobbled towards him on Eighth Street – the twisted eye, the coat too small to button, the pulpy mouth with pathetic effort trying to frame the first words. The image made him squirm in his seat and pull away from Liz's hand. They decided not to stay for the second feature. Liz said her eyes smarted from the Vistavision. They were reluctant to go home so early; Janice counted on them to last out the double feature. But the service at the luncheonette was swift; the sodas – weak things, scarcely frothy at all, just tan liquid in a paper cone – were quickly drained; and the main streets of the Village, thronged with gangsters and hermaphrodites, seemed to James an unsafe place to stroll with his wife. Liz caught the attention of every thug and teenager they passed. 'Stop it,' he said. 'You'll get me knifed.'

'Darling. There's no law against people's eyes.'

'There should be. They think you're a whore out with her pimp. What makes you stare at everybody?'

'Faces are *interesting*. Why are you so uninterested in people?'

'Because every other day you call up the office and I have to come rescue you from some damn bugaboo you've enticed up the stairs. No wonder Dudevant is getting set to fire me.'

'Let's go home if you want to rave.'

'We can't. Janice needs the money, the bloodsucker.'

'It's nearly ten. She charges a dollar an hour, after all.'

As they advanced down Tenth from Fifth he saw a slight blob by their gate which simply squinting did not erase. He did not expect ever to see Liz's Negro, who had had his chance at dinner. Yet when it was clear that a man *was* standing there, wearing a hat, James hastened forward, glad at last to have the enemy life-size and under scrutiny. They seemed to know each other well; James called 'Hi!' and grasped the quickly offered hand, the palm waxy and cool, like a synthetic fabric.

'I just wanted . . . *thank* . . . such a fine gentleman,' the Negro said, in a voice incredibly thin-spun, the thread of it always breaking.

'Have you been waiting long?' Liz asked.

'No, well . . . the lady upstairs, she said you'd be back. When the man in the taxi let me go from the station . . . came on back to thank such wonderful people.'

'I'm awfully sorry,' James told him. 'I thought you knew we were going off to the movies.' His own voice sounded huge – a magnificent instrument. He must not be too elaborately courteous; Liz was terribly alive to him in regard to vanity or condescension. She was unfair; his natural, heartfelt impulse at this moment was toward elaborate courtesy.

'You were at the police station?' Liz asked. Their previous encounter seemed to have attuned her to the man's speech.

'. . . how I do appreciate.' He was still speaking to James ignoring Liz completely. This assumption that he, as head of the family, superseded all its other elements, and that in finding him the Negro had struck the fountainhead of his good fortune, made James panicky. He had been raised to believe in democratic marriages. Further, the little Negro seemed to need specifically maternal attention. He trembled softly under his coat, and it was not that cold; the night was warmer than the late afternoon had been.

The Negro's clothes, in the dimness of outdoors, did not look as shabby as James would have liked. As for his being young, James could distinguish no marks of either youth or age.

'Well, come on inside,' he said.

'Aaaah . . .?'

'Please,' Liz said.

They entered the little overheated vestibule, and immediately the buzzer rasped at the lock, signalling that Janice had been watching from the window. She ran to the banister and shouted down in a whisper, 'Did he get in? Has he told you about the taxi-driver?'

James, leading the group, attained the top of the stairs. 'How was Martha?' he asked, rather plainly putting first things first.

'An absolute angel. How was the movie?'

'Quite good, really. It really was.'

'I was honestly afraid he'd kill him.'

They shuffled each other into the room. 'I gather you two have met, then,' James said to Janice and the Negro. The girl bared her teeth in a kindly smile that made her look five years older, and the Negro, who had his hat already in his hands and was therefore unable to tip it, bent the brim slightly and swiftly averted his head, confronting a striped canvas Liz had done, titled *Swans and Shadows*.

At this juncture, with these two showing these sinister signs of rapport, Liz deserted him, easing into the bedroom. She was bothered by fears that Martha would stop breathing among the blankets. 'Before the doorbell rang, even,' Janice talked on, 'I could hear the shouting on the street – Oh, it was something. He said terrible things. And then the bell rang, and I answered it, like you had said to, and *he* said –' She indicated the Negro, who was still standing, in a quiet plaid sport coat.

'Sit down,' James told him.

'– and *he* said that the taxi-driver wanted money. *I* said, "I don't have any. I don't have a red cent, honestly." You know when I come over I never think to bring my purse.' James recalled she could never make change. There was usually an amount she was left owing them, 'towards next time'.

'I *tol* him,' the Negro said, 'there were these fine people in this house here. The lady in there, she tol me you'd be *here*.'

James asked, 'Where did you take the taxi *from*?'

The Negro sought refuge in contemplation of his hat, pendent from one quivering hand. 'Please, Mister . . . the lady, she knows about it.' He looked towards the bedroom door.

Janice rescued him, speaking briskly: 'He told me the driver wanted two thirty, and I said, "I don't have a cent." Then I came in here and hunted, you know, to see if you left any around – sometimes there's some tens under the silver bowl.'

'Oh, yes,' James said.

'Then I went to the window to signal – I'm scared to death of going downstairs and locking myself out – and down on the street there was this crowd, from across the street at Alex's and it looked like when he went back to tell the driver, the driver grabbed him; there was a lot of shouting, and some woman kept saying "Cop".'

Liz re-entered the room.

'He grab me here,' the Negro humbly explained. He touched with his little free hand the open collar of his red wool shirt.

'So I guess then they went to the police station,' Janice concluded lamely, disappointed to discover that her information was incomplete.

Liz, assuming that the police-station part of the story had been told when she was out of the room, took this to be the end, and asked, 'Who wants some coffee?'

'No thanks, Betty,' Janice said. 'It keeps me awake.'

'It keeps everybody awake,' James said. 'That's what it's supposed to do.'

'Oh, no, Ma'am,' the Negro said. 'I couldn't do that.' Uneasily shifting his face towards James, though he kept his eyes on the lamp burning above Janice's head, he went on, 'I tolem at the station how there were these people. I had your address, cause the lady wrote it down on a little slip.'

'Uh-huh.' James assumed there was more to come. Why wasn't he still at the police station? Who paid the driver? The pause stretched. James felt increasingly remote; it scarcely seemed his room, with so strange a guest in it. He tilted his chair back, and the Negro sharpened as if through the wrong end of a telescope. There was a resemblance between the Negro's head and the Raydo shaver. The inventive thing about that design – the stroke of mind, in Dudevant's phrase – had been forthrightly paring away the space saved by the manufacturer's improved, smaller motor. Instead of a symmetrical case, then, in form like a tapered sugar sack, a squat, asymmetrical shape was created, which fitted, pleasingly weighty, in the user's hand like a religious stone, full of *mana*. Likewise, a part of the Negro's skull had been eliminated. His eyes were higher in his head than drawing masters teach, and had been set shallowly on the edges where the planes of the face turned sideways. With a smothered start James realized that Janice, and Liz leaning in the doorway of the kitchen, and the Negro too, were expecting him to speak – the man of the situation, the benefactor. 'Well, now, what *is* your trouble?' he asked brutally.

The coffee water sang, and Liz after wrinkling her expressive high forehead at him, turned to the stove.

The Negro feebly rubbed the slant of his skull. 'Aaaah? . . . appreciate the kindness of you and the lady . . . generous to a poor soul like me nobody wanted to help.'

James prompted. 'You and your wife and – how many children?'

'Seven, Mister. The oldest boy ten.'

'– *have* found a place to live. Where?'

'Yessir, the man say he give us this room, but he say he can't put no beds in it, but I found this other man willing to give us on loan, you know, until I go to my job . . . But the wife and children, they don't have no bed to rest their heads. Nothing to eat. My children are tired.'

James put a cigarette in the centre of his mouth and said as it bobbled, 'You say you *have* a job?'

'Oh yes Mister, I went to this place where they're building the new road to the tunnel, you know, and *he* tol *me* as soon as I get in one day's work, he can give me that money, towards my pay. He ast if I could do the work and I said, "Yes, sir, any kind of work you give I can do." He said the pay was two dollar seventy cents for every hour you work.'

'Two seventy? For heaven's sake. Twenty dollars a day just labouring?'

'Yes, pushing the wheelbarrow . . . he said two seventy. I said, "I can do any kind of work you give. I'm a hard worker." '

To James he looked extremely frail, but the happy idea of there existing a broad-shouldered foreman willing to make him a working citizen washed all doubts away. He smiled and insisted, 'So it's really just this weekend you need to get over.'

'Thas right. Starting Monday I'll be making two seventy every hour. The wife, she's as happy as anybody could be.'

The wife seemed to have altered underfoot, but James let it pass; the end was in sight. He braced himself to enter the realm of money. Here Janice, the fool, who should have left the minute they came home, interrupted with, 'Have you tried any agencies, like the Salvation Army?'

'Oh, yes, Miss. All. They don't care much for fellas like me. They say they'll give us money to get *back*, but as for us staying – they won't do a damn thing. Boy, you come up here in a truck, you're on your own. Nobody help me except these people.'

The man he probably was with his friends and family was starting to show. James was sleepy. The hard chair hurt; the Negro had the comfortable chair. He resented the man's becoming at ease. But there was no halting it; the women were at work now.

'Isn't that awful,' Janice said. 'You wonder why they have these agencies.'

'You say you need help, your wife ain't got a place to put her head, they give you money to go *back*.'

Liz entered with two cups of coffee. Hers, James noticed, was just half full; he was to bear the larger burden of insomnia. The cup was too hot to hold. He set it on the rug, feeling soft-skinned and effeminate in the eyes of this hard worker worth twenty dollars a day.

'Why did you decide to leave North Carolina?' Liz asked.

'Missis, a man like me, there's no chance there for him. I worked in the cotton and they give me thirty-five cents an hour.'

'Thirty-five cents?' James said. 'That's illegal, isn't it?'

The Negro smiled sardonically, his first facial expression of the evening. 'Down there you don't tell them what's legal.' To Liz he added, 'The wife, Ma'am, she's the bravest woman. When I say, "Let's go," she said, "Thas right, let's give oursels a chance." So this man promise he'd take us up in the cab of the truck he had . . .'

'With all seven children?' James asked.

The Negro looked at him without the usual wavering. 'We don't have anybody to leave them behind.'

'And you have no friends or relatives here?' Liz asked.

'No, we don't have no friends, and until you were so kind to me it didn't look like we'd find any either.'

Friends! In indignation James rose and, on his feet, had to go through the long-planned action of placing two ten-dollar bills on the table next to the Negro. The Negro ignored them, bowing his head. James made his speech. 'Now, I don't know how much furniture costs – my wife gave me the impression that you were going to make the necessary payment with the ten. But here is twenty. It's all we can spare. This should carry you over until Monday, when you say you can get part of your salary for working on the Lincoln tunnel. I think it was very courageous of you to bring your family up here, and we want to wish you lots of luck. I'm sure you and your wife will make out.' Flushing with shame, he resumed his post in the hard chair.

Janice bit her lip to cure a smile and looked towards Liz, who said nothing.

The Negro said, 'Aeeh . . . Mister . . . can't find words to press, such fine *peo*ple.' And, while the three of them sat there, trapped and stunned, he tried to make himself cry. He pinched the bridge of his nose and shook his head and squeezed soft high animal sounds from his throat, but when he looked up, the grainy whites of his eyes were dry. Uncoordinated with this failure, his lips writhed in grief. He kept brushing his temple as if something were humming there. 'Gee,' he said. 'The wife . . . she tol me, you got to go back and thank that man . . .'

The Negro's sense of exit seemed as defective as his other theatrical skills. He just sat there, shaking his head and touching his nose. The bills on the table remained ignored – taboo, perhaps, until a sufficiently exhausting ritual of gratitude was performed. James, to whom rudeness came hard, teetered in his chair, avoiding all eyes; at the root of the Negro's demonstration there was either the plight he described or a plight that had made him lie. In either case, the man must be borne. Yet James found him all but unbearable; the thought of his life as he described it, swinging from one tenuous vine of charity to the next – the truck driver, the landlord, Liz, the furniture man, the foreman, now James – was sickening, giddying. James said courteously, 'Maybe you'd better be getting back to her.'

'Iiih,' the Negro sighed, on an irrelevant high note, as if he produced the sound with a pitch pipe.

James dreaded that Liz would start offering blankets and food if the Negro delayed further – as he did, whimpering and passing the hatbrim through his hands like an endless rope. While Liz was in the kitchen filling a paper bag for him, the Negro found breath to tell James that he wanted to bring his wife and all his family to see him and his missis, tomorrow, so they could all express gratitude. 'Maybe there's some work . . . washing the floors, anything, she's so happy, until we can pay back. Twenty, gee.' His hand fled to his eyes.

'No, don't you worry about us. That thirty dollars' – the record must be kept straight – 'you can think of as a gift from the city.'

'Oh I wouldn't have it no other way. You let my wife do all your work tomorrow.'

'You and she get settled. Forget us.'

Liz appeared with an awkward paper bag. There were to be no blankets, he deduced; his wife's stance seemed edged with defiance.

Talkative as always when a guest was leaving, James asked, 'Now, do you know how to get back? For heaven's sake don't take a taxi. Take a bus and then the subway. Where is your place?'

'Aaaah . . . right near where that Lexington Avenue is.'

'Where on Lexington? What cross-street?

'Beg pardon, Mister? I'm sorry, I don't make sense I'm so thrilled.'

'What cross street? How far *up* on Lexington?'

'The, ah, hundred twenty-nine.'

As James, with an outlander's simple pride in 'knowing' New York, gave detailed instructions about where to board the Fourteenth Street bus, where to find the subway kiosk after so many stops, and how to put the token in the turnstile, the words seemed to bounce back, as if they were finding identical information already lodged in the Negro's brain.

He concluded, 'Just try to resist the temptation to jump in a taxicab. That would have cost us two thirty if we'd been home. Now here, I'll even give you bus fare and a token.' Dredging a handful of silver from his coat pocket, he placed a nickel and a dime and a token in the svelte little palm and, since the hand did not move, put two more dimes in it, then thought, *Oh hell*, and poured all the coins in – over a dollar's worth.

'Now I'm penniless,' he told the coloured man.

'Thank eh, you too Missis, so much, and you Miss.'

They wished him luck. He shook hands all around, hoisted the bag with difficulty into his arms, and walked murmuring through the door James held open for him.

'Four blocks up, to Fourteenth Street,' James called after him, adding in a normal voice, 'I know damn well he'll take a taxi.'

'It's awfully good-hearted of you,' Janice said, 'but about giving all that money, I – don't – know.'

'Ah, well,' said James, doing a small dance step, 'money is dross.'

Liz said, 'I *was* surprised, darley, that you gave him *two* bills.'

'You *were*? These are times of inflation. You can't buy seven air-conditioned Beautyrest mattresses for ten dollars. He's shown a great gift for spending; he ran through your ten like a little jack-rabbit. We never did find out where it went to.'

Janice, Irishly earnest, still grappled with the moral issue. She spoke more to Liz than to him. 'I don't doubt he needs the money – Oh, you should have heard the things that cabby said, or maybe you shouldn't. But then who doesn't need money? You and I need money, too.'

'Which reminds me,' James said. He looked at the electric clock in the kitchen: 11.20. 'We came home, didn't we, around ten? Seven-thirty to ten – two and a half. Two and a half dollars. You can't change a ten, can you?'

The girl's face fell. 'Honestly, I never remember to bring my purse. But you could owe me to next time . . .'

'I hate to do that. You need the money.' He couldn't believe the girl would take a surplus of $7.50 from him.

'That – I – do,' Janice admitted cheerfully, gathering up her coat and a limp black book stamped simply with a cross. *Her mother*, James thought, and smelled prayers lingering in the room like old smoke.

'Wait,' Liz said. 'I think in my purse. I lied to him when I said I had nothing in the house but the ten.' They found the purse and were indeed able to piece together, out of paper and silver, the fee.

Spited, Janice said, 'For your sakes, I sure hope he doesn't bother you

again. This little island has more different kinds of crooks on it than you
or I could imagine existed. Some of them could out-act old Larry Olivier
himself.'

'I really don't see how he can do this labouring job,' Liz said, with a
tactful appearance of agreeing. 'Why, just that little bag I gave him almost
knocked him over.' When Janice was gone, she asked, 'Do you think she
expected us to pay her for the hour and a half she stayed to watch the
Negro?'

'Heaven knows. I feel vile.'

'Where?'

'Everywhere. I feel like a vile person.'

'Why? You were fine. You were awfully, awfully good.'

From her hasty kiss on his cheek he gathered that, surprisingly, she
meant it.

Sunday, husk among days, was full of fear. Even in gay times James
felt on this day like a nameless statue on an empty plaza. Now he dared
not got out, either to church or to the news-stand. Last night's episode
had the colour of a public disgrace. The Negro was everywhere. James
holed up in his inadequate cave. The walls seemed transparent, the floors
sounding-boards. The Negro's threat to return had smashed the windows
and broken the burglar locks. Never on a morning had he wished so
intensely to be back in Ontauk, Minnesota, his birthplace. The town had
over seven thousand residents now, and a city manager instead of a mayor,
and since the war the creek that ran through its centre and drained its
few mills had been robbed of its Indian name and called the Douglas
MacArthur River; but the cars still parked higgledy-piggledy on the
crooked, shaded streets, and he would still have a place, his father's son.

Liz and James lived four doors down from an Episcopal church. There
was not an inch of air between the masonry of any of the buildings. When
the church bells rang, their apartment quivered sonorously. Enveloped in
this huge dead hum, he fought the picture of seven fuzz-haired children
squeezed into the cab of a truck, roadside lights flickering in their faces,
the dark of the Carolina fields slipping away, great whoring cities bristling
and then falling back, too, and then the children dozing, except for the
oldest, a boy of ten, who remained awake to stare unblinking at the bent-
necked blue lights of the Jersey Turnpike, the jet carpet carrying them to
the sorcerer's palace, where Harlem was choked with Cadillacs and white
men on subways yielded their seats to coloured ladies. James hated the
Negro chiefly because he was tactless. Janice's mother, the sores of street

beggars – this was misery, too, but misery that knew its limits, that kept an orbit and observed manners. But in his perfect ignorance the Negro was like one of those babies born with its heart in front of its ribs. He gave no protection. You touched him and you killed him. Now that he had found this Northern man – the promised man – so free with money, he would be back today, and again tomorrow, with an ever greater gift of mumbled debts. Why not? Thirty was nothing to James. He could give away a flat three thousand, and then thirty every week – more than thirty, fifty – and he and Liz would still be richer than the Negro. Between him and the Negro the ground was unimpeded, and only a sin could be placed there as barrier.

By afternoon the focus of James's discomfort had shifted from the possibility that the Negro had told the truth to the possibility that he had not. Reliving his behaviour in this light was agonizing. He shuddered above the depths of fatuity the Negro must have seen in his clumsy kindness. If the story had been a fraud, the impatience of James's charity was its one saving grace. The bits of abruptness, the gibes about the taxi shone in memory like jewels among refuse. The more he thought, the more he raged, aloud and privately. And the angrier he grew at the Negro, the less he wanted to see him, the more he dreaded him, an opponent invincibly armed with the weapon of having seen him as a fool. And those seven clambering children and the wife bullying Liz.

He only wanted to hide his head in the haven of the Bridges' scheduled visit. They saw him as others saw him and knew his value. He would bask in their lucid external view.

Then mercifully it *was* dark, and his friends had come.

Rudy Bridges was also from Ontauk, Minnesota. He had been two classes ahead of James in high school, a scholastic wonder, the more so because his father was a no-account who died of tuberculosis the year Rudy graduated. In the nine years since, Rudy's buttercup hair had thinned severely, but the spherical head and the chubby lips of the prig had remained constant. *His* great hopes had been boiled down to instructing three sections of Barnard girls in American history. His wife came from Maryland. Augustina was a pale and handsome woman with an uncompromising, uptilted nose that displayed its nostrils. She wore her abundant chestnut hair strictly parted in the middle – a madonna for the Piston Age. They had no children, and with elaborate managing, just enough money. James loved them as guests. In their own home, Rudy talked too much about his special field, domestic fiscal policy between Grant and Wilson, a desert of dullness where the lowliest scholar could be king. And Augustina, careful of the budget, went hungry and thirsty and inhibited everyone. Away from home she drank and ate beautifully, like a belle.

James tiptoed into the bedroom with their heavy coats. Martha was cased in her crib like a piece of apparatus manufacturing sleep. He heard Liz talking and, returning, asked, 'Is she telling you about how we're running the Underground Railway?'

'Why, no, James,' Augustina said slowly.

'I was telling them the accident Martha had in the park,' Liz said.

'Yeah, the poor kid just ran right into the swings,' he said, no doubt duplicating the story.

'Now, James,' Rudy said, 'what is this mad tale about the Underground Rail*road*?' Years of teaching had perfected his speech habit of pronouncing everything, clichés and all, with artificial distinctness. Throughout James's recital of the Negro story he kept saying 'Ah yes', and when it was over and, like Janice the night before, James seemed to have reached an insufficient conclusion, Rudy felt compelled to clarify: 'So the chances are these seven children are going to show up in the middle of supper.'

'Oh dear,' Augustina said with mock alarm. 'Do you have enough food?'

Rudy, beside her on the sofa, attacked the tale pedantically. 'Now. You say he was well dressed?'

'Sort of. But after all it was Saturday night.' James didn't get the smile he expected.

'Did you look at his shoes?'

'Not much.'

'Would you say his accent was Southern or neutral?'

'Well, your wife's the only Southerner I know. His speech was so peculiar and high, I couldn't tell. Certainly he didn't talk like you. Or me.'

'And at one point he used the word "thrilled".'

'Yeah, that got me, too. But look: there were odd things, but when a man is in such a dither anyway –'

Augustina broke in, addressing Liz. 'Did James *really* just hand him thirty dollars?'

'Thirty-one and a token,' James corrected.

Rudy laughed excessively – he had no sense of humour, so when he laughed it was too hard – and lifted his golden glass in toast. Augustina, to back him up, gripped hers, which was already empty. 'James,' Rudy said, 'you're the soul of charity.'

It was flattering, of course, but it wasn't the way he thought they should take it. The point really wasn't the thirty dollars at all; hard as it was to explain without seeming to ridicule Rudy's salary, thirty dollars was nothing.

'It doesn't seem to *me*,' he said, 'that he would have such an unlikely story, with so many authentic overtones, unless it were true. He didn't look at all like a Harlem Negro – his head was uncanny – and he seemed to know about North Carolina and the relief agencies –'

'Nonsense, James. There are a hundred – a thousand – ways of obtaining such information. For instance: he quoted thirty-five cents an hour as his old wage. Well, *you* could research that. *Is* thirty-five cents an hour standard pay in the cotton belt? To be frank, it sounds low to me.'

'That was the thing,' Liz said, 'that made me begin to wonder.'

James turned on her, surprised and stung. 'Damn it, the trouble with people like you who are passed from one happy breadwinner to the next without missing a damn meal is that you refuse to admit that outside your own bubble anybody can be suffering. Of *course* people starve. Of *course* children die. Of *course* a man will pay a quarter an hour if nobody makes him pay more. Jesus.'

'However,' Rudy went on, 'mere dollar-and-cents quotations mean very little; the relative value, purchasewise, of, for instance, ten cents, "a thin dime" –'

James's harangue had agitated Augustina; her nostrils darted this way and that, and when she heard her husband's voice drone, she turned those marvellous staring apertures directly on him. Not insensitive, he slowly climbed out of his brain, sensed the heat in the room, and, the worst thing possible, fell silent.

The silence went on. Liz was blushing. James held his tongue, by way of apology to her. Rudy's brittle gears shifted, his mouth flipped open, and he considerately said. 'No, joke about it as we will, a problem in sheer currency can very seriously affect real people. To take an example, in the states of the Confederacy in the decade after the surrender of Appomattox – that is, from the year eighteen sixty-five to the year eighteen seventy-*four* . . .'

On Monday James's office was waiting for him. The whiteheaded tacks made his personal constellation on the cork. The wastebasket had been emptied. A blue envelope lay on the steel desk. Otherwise, not so much as a pen nib had been disturbed; the drawing he had been working on when Liz called still lay by the telephone, its random placement preserved like the handiwork of a superbly precious being, a god.

He did his work all day with great precision, answering letters, making order. His office encouraged the illusion that each passage of life was on a separate sheet, and could be dropped into the wastebasket, and destroyed by someone else in the night. One job he gave his mind was to keep the phone from ringing. Whether the Negro came or not, with his tattered children or not, from ten to five let the problem belong to Liz. It was of her making. There should be, in a man's life, hours when he has never married, and his wife walks in magic circles she herself draws. It was little enough to ask; he had sold his life, his chances, for her sake. The phone did not ring, except once: Dudevant, effusive.

As he made his way home, through indifferent crowds, the conviction grew that she had wanted to call and had been baulked by the cold pressure he had applied at the other end of the line. He would find her clubbed, and his daughter cut in two. He wondered if he would be able to give enough description of the Negro to the police. He saw himself in the station stammering, blushing, despised by the policemen; had it been their wives, they would have been there, knotting their fists, baring their teeth. Through this daydream ran the cowardly hope that the killer would not still be there, lingering stupidly, so that James would have to struggle with him, and be himself injured.

Liz waited until he was in the apartment and his coat was off before she communicated her news. Her tone was apprehensive. 'He came again, when Martha was having her nap. I went to the stairs – I was terribly busy cleaning up. He said the man who promised to sell him the furniture wouldn't give him the beds if he didn't give him ten dollars more, and I asked him why he wasn't at his job, and he said something about Wednesday, I don't know. I told him we had given him all we could, and I didn't have a dollar – which was true; you went off with all the money and we have nothing for supper. Anyway, he seemed to have expected it, and was really very nice. So I guess he *was* a crook.'

'Thank God,' he said, and they never saw the Negro again, and their happiness returned.

The Stare

Then there it was, in the corner of his eye. He turned, his heart frozen. The incredibility of her being here, now, at a table in this one restaurant on the one day when he was back in the city, did not check the anticipatory freezing of his heart, for when they had both lived in New York they had always been lucky at finding each other, time after time; and this would be one more time. Already, in the instant between recognition and turning, he had framed his first words; he would rise, with the diffidence she used to think graceful, and go to her and say, 'Hey. It's you.'

Her face would smile apologetically, lids lowered, and undergo one of its little shrugs. 'It's me.'

'I'm so glad. I'm sorry about what happened.' And everything would be understood, and the need of forgiveness once again magically put behind them, like a wall of paper flames they had passed through.

It was someone else, a not very young woman whose hair, not really the colour of her hair at all, had, half seen, suggested the way her hair, centrally parted and pulled back into a glossy French roll, would cut with two dark wings into her forehead, making her brow seem low and intense and emphasizing her stare. He felt the eyes of his companions at lunch question him, and he returned his attention to them, his own eyes smarting from the effort of trying to press this unknown woman's appearance into the appearance of another. One of his companions at the table – a gentle grey banker whose affection for him, like a generous cheque, quietly withheld at the bottom a tiny deduction of tact, a modest minus paid as an increment on their mutual security – smiled in such a way as to baulk his impulse to blurt, to confess. His other companion was an elderly female underwriter, an ex-associate, whose statistical insight was remorseless but who in personal manner was all feathers and feigned dismay. 'I'm seeing ghosts,' he explained to her, and she nodded, for they had, all three, with the gay withering credulity of nonbelievers, been discussing ghosts. The curtain of conversation descended again, but his palms tingled, and, as if trapped between two mirrors, he seemed to face a diminishing multiplication of her stare.

The first time they met, in an apartment with huge slablike paintings and fragile furniture that seemed to be tiptoeing, she came to the defence of something her husband had said, and he had irritably wondered how a woman of such evident spirit and will could debase herself to the support of statements so asinine, and she must have felt, across the room, his irritation, for she gave him her stare. It was, as a look, both blunt and elusive: somewhat cold, certainly hard, yet curiously wide, and even open – its essential ingredient shied away from being named. Her eyes were the only glamorous feature of a freckled, bony, tomboyish face, remarkable chiefly for its sharp willingness to express pleasure. When she laughed, her teeth were bared like a skull's, and when she stared, her great, grave, perfectly shaped eyes insisted on their shape as rigidly as a statue's.

Later, when their acquaintance had outlived the initial irritations, he had met her in the Museum of Modern Art, amid an exhibit of old movie stills, and, going forward with the innocent cheerfulness that her presence even then aroused in him, he had been unexpectedly met by her stare. 'We missed you Friday night,' she said.

'You did? What happened Friday night?'

'Oh, nothing. We just gave a little party and expected you to come.'

'We weren't invited.'

'But you *were*. I phoned your wife.'

'She never said anything to me. She must have forgotten.'

'Well, I don't suppose it matters.'

'But it *does*. I'm so sorry. I would have loved to have come. It's very funny that she forgot it; she really just lives for parties.'

'Yes.' And her stare puzzled him, since it was no longer directed at him; the hostility between the two women existed before he had fulfilled its reason.

Later still, at a party they all did attend, he had, alone with her for a moment, kissed her, and the response of her mouth had been disconcerting; backing off, expecting to find her face the moist, formless warmth that had taken his lips, he encountered her stare instead. In the months that unfolded from this, it had been his pleasure to see her stare relax. Her body gathered softness under his; late one night, after yet another party, his wife, lying beside him in the pre-dawn darkness of her ignorance, had remarked, with the cool, fair appraisal of a rival woman, how beautiful she – *she*, the other – had become, and he had felt, half dreaming in the warm bed he had betrayed, justified. Her laugh no longer flashed out so hungrily, and her eyes, brimming with the secret he and she had made, deepened and seemed to rejoin the girlishness that had lingered in the other features of her face. Seeing her across a room standing swathed in the beauty he had given her, he felt a creator's, a father's pride. There existed, when they came together, a presence of tenderness like a ghostly child who when they parted was taken away and set to sleeping. Yet even in those months, in the depths of their secret, lying together as if in an intimate dungeon, discussing with a gathering urgency what they would do when their secret crumbled and they were exposed, there would now and then glint out at him, however qualified by tears and languor, the unmistakable accusatory hardness. It was accusing, yet that was not its essence; his conscience shied away from naming the pressure that had formed it and that, it imperceptibly became apparent, he was helpless to relieve. Each time they parted, she would leave behind, in the last instant before the door closed, a look that haunted him, like the flat persisting ring of struck crystal.

The last time he saw her, all the gentle months had been stripped away and her stare, naked, had become furious. 'Don't you love me?' Two households were in turmoil and the rich instinct that had driven him to her had been reduced to a thin need to hide and beg.

'Not enough.' He meant it simply, as a fact, as something that already had been made plain.

But she took it as a death blow, and in a face whitened and drawn by the shocks of recent days, from beneath dark wings of tensely parted hair, her stare revived into a life so coldly controlled and adamantly hostile that for weeks he could not close his eyes without confronting it – much as a victim of torture must continue to see the burning iron with which he was blinded.

Now, back in New York, walking alone, soothed by food and profitable talk, he discovered himself so healed that his wound ached to be reopened. The glittering city bristled with potential prongs. The pale disc of every face, as it slipped from the edge of his vision, seemed to cup the possibility of being hers. He felt her searching for him. Where would she look? It would be her style simply to walk the streets, smiling and striding in the hope of their meeting. He had a premonition – and yes, there, waiting to cross Forty-third Street between two Puerto Rican messenger boys, it was she, with her back towards him; there was no mistaking the expectant tilt of her head, the girlish curve of her high, taut cheek, the massed roll of hair pulled so glossy he used to imagine that the hairpins gave her pain. He drew abreast, timid and prankish, to surprise her profile, and she became a wrinkled painted woman with a sagging lower lip. He glanced around incredulously, and her stare glimmered and disappeared in the wavering wall-window of a modernistic bank. Crossing the street, he looked into the bank, but there was no one, no one he knew – only some potted tropical plants that looked vaguely familiar.

He returned to work. His company had lent him for this visit the office of a man on vacation. He managed to concentrate only by imagining that each five minutes were the final segment of time he would have to himself before she arrived. When the phone on his desk rang, he expected the receptionist to announce that a distraught woman with striking eyes was asking for him. When he went into the halls, a secretary flickering out of sight battered his heart with a resemblance. He returned to his borrowed office, and was startled not to find her in it, wryly examining the yellowed children's drawings – another man's children – taped to the walls. The bored afternoon pasted shadows on these walls. Outside his window, the skyscrapers began to glow. He went down the elevator and into the cool crowded dusk thankful for her consideration; it was like her to let him finish his day's work before she declared her presence. She had always assumed, in their scattered hours together, a wife's dutiful attitude towards him. But now, now she could cease considerately hiding, and he could take her to dinner with an easy conscience. He checked his wallet to make sure he had enough money. He decided he would refuse to take her to a play, though undoubtedly she would suggest it. She loved the stage. But they had too little time together to waste it in awareness of a third thing.

He had taken a room at what he still thought of as their hotel. To his surprise, she was not waiting for him in the lobby, which seemed filled with a party, a competition of laughter. Charles Boyer was waiting for the elevator. She would have liked that, sitting on the bench before the desk, waiting and watching, her long legs crossed and one black shoe jabbing the air with the prongs of its heel and toe. He had even prepared his explanation to the clerk; this was his wife. They had had (voice lowered, eyebrows lifted, the unavoidable blush not, after all, inappropriate) a fight, and impulsively she had followed him to New York, to make up. Irregular, but . . . women. So could his single reservation kindly be changed to a double? Thank you.

This little play was so firmly written in his head that he looked into the bar to make sure the leading actress was not somewhere in the wings. The bar was bluely lit and amply patronized by fairies. Their drawled, elaborately enunciating voices, discussing musical comedies in tones of peculiar passion, carried to him, and he remembered how she, when he had expressed distaste, had solemnly explained to him that homosexuals were people, too, and how she herself often felt attracted to them, and how it always saddened her that she had nothing, you know – her stare defensively sharpened – to give them. 'That old bag, she's overex*posed* herself,' one of the fairies stridently declared, of a famous actress.

He took the elevator up to his room. It was similar to ones they had shared, but nothing was exactly the same, except the plumbing fixtures, and even these were differently arranged. He changed his shirt and neck-tie. In the mirror, behind him, a slow curve of movement, like a woman's inquisitive step, chilled his spine; it was the door drifting shut. He rushed from the suffocating vacant room into the streets, to inhale the invisible possibility of finding her. He ate at the restaurant he would have chosen for them both. The waiter seemed fussed, seating a solitary man. The woman of a couple at a nearby table adjusted an earring with a gesture that belonged to her; she had never had her ears pierced, and this naïveté of her flesh had charmed him. He abstained from coffee. Tonight he must court sleep assiduously.

He walked to tire himself. Broadway was garish with the clash of mat-ing – sailors and sweethearts, touts and tarts. Spring infiltrates a city through the blood of its inhabitants. The side streets were hushed like the aisles of long Pullman sleepers being drawn forward by their diminishing perspective. She would look for him on Fifth Avenue; her window-shopper's instinct would send her there. He saw her silhouette at a dis-tance, near Rockefeller Center, and up close he spotted a certain momen-tary plane of her face that flew away in a flash, leaving behind the rubble of a face he did not know, had never kissed or tranquilly studied as it lay averted on a pillow. Once or twice, he even glimpsed, shadowed in a doorway, huddled on a bench tipping down towards the Promethean fountain, the ghostly child of their tenderness, asleep; but never her, her in the fragrant solidity he had valued with such a strange gay lightness when it was upon him. Statistically, it began to seem wonderful that out of so many faces not one was hers. It seemed only reasonable that he could skim, like interest, her presence from a sufficient quantity of strangers – that he could refine her, like radium, out of enough pitchblende. She had never been reserved with him; this terrible tact of absence was unlike her.

The moon gratuitously added its stolen glow to the harsh illumination around the iceless skating rink. As if sensing his search, faces turned as he passed. Each successive instant shocked him by being empty of her; he knew so fully how this meeting would go. Her eyes would light on him, and her mouth would involuntarily break into the grin that greeted all her occasions, however grave and dangerous; her stare would pull her body forward, and the gathering nearness of his presence would dissolve away the hardness, the controlled coldness, the – what? What was that element that had been there from the beginning and that, in the end, despite every strenuous motion of his heart, he had intensified, like some wild vague prophecy given a tyrannical authority in its fulfilment? What was the thing he had never named, perhaps because his vanity refused to believe that it could both attach to him and exist before him?

He wondered if he were tired enough now. There was an ache in his legs that augured well. He walked back to the hotel. The air of celebration had left the lobby. No celebrity was in sight. A few well-dressed young women, of the style that bloom and wither by thousands in the city's public places, were standing waiting for an escort or an elevator; as he pressed, no doubt redundantly, the button, a face cut into the side of his vision at such an angle that his head snapped around and he almost said aloud, 'Don't be frightened. Of course I love you.'

The Orphaned Swimming Pool

Marriages, like chemical unions, release upon dissolution packets of the energy locked up in their bonding. There is the piano no one wants, the cocker spaniel no one can take care of. Shelves of books suddenly stand revealed as burdensomely dated and unlikely to be reread; indeed, it is difficult to remember who read them in the first place. And what of those old skis in the attic? Or the doll house waiting to be repaired in the basement? The piano goes out of tune, the dog goes mad. The summer that the Turners got their divorce, their swimming pool had neither a master nor a mistress, though the sun beat down day after day, and a state of drought was declared in Connecticut.

It was a young pool, only two years old, of the fragile type fashioned by laying a plastic liner within a carefully carved hole in the ground. The Turner's side yard looked infernal while it was being done; one bulldozer sank into the mud and had to be pulled free by another. But by mid-summer the new grass was sprouting, the encircling flagstones were in place, the blue plastic tinted the water a heavenly blue, and it had to be admitted that the Turners had scored again. They were always a little in advance of their friends. He was a tall, hairy-backed man with long arms, and a nose flattened by football, and a sullen look of too much blood; she was a fine-boned blonde with dry blue eyes and lips usually held parted and crinkled as if about to ask a worrisome, or whimsical question. They never seemed happier, nor their marriage healthier, than those two summers. They grew brown and supple and smooth with swimming. Ted would begin his day with a swim, before dressing to catch the train, and Linda would hold court all day amid crowds of wet matrons and children, and Ted would return from work to find a poolside cocktail party in progress, and the couple would end their day at midnight, when their friends had finally left, by swimming nude, before bed. What ecstasy! In darkness the water felt mild as milk and buoyant as helium, and the swimmers became giants, gliding from side to side in a single languorous stroke.

The next May, the pool was filled as usual, and the usual after-school gangs of mothers and children gathered, but Linda, unlike her, stayed indoors. She could be heard within the house, moving from room to room, but she no longer emerged, as in the other summers, with a cheerful tray of ice and a brace of bottles, and Triscuits and lemonade for the children. Their friends felt less comfortable about appearing, towels in hand, at the Turners' on weekends. Though Linda had lost some weight and looked elegant, and Ted was cumbersomely jovial, they gave off the faint, sleepless, awkward-making aroma of a couple in trouble. Then, the day after school was out, Linda fled with the children to her parents in Ohio. Ted stayed nights in the city, and the pool was deserted. Though the pump that ran the water through the filter continued to mutter in the lilacs, the cerulean pool grew cloudy. The bodies of dead horseflies and wasps dotted the still surface. A speckled plastic ball drifted into a corner beside the diving board and stayed there. The grass between the flagstones grew lank. On the glass-topped poolside table, a spray can of Off! had lost its pressure and a gin-and-tonic glass held a sere mint leaf. The pool looked desolate and haunted, like a stagnant jungle spring; it looked poisonous and ashamed. The postman, stuffing overdue notices and pornography solicitations into the mailbox, averted his eyes from the side yard politely.

Some June weekends, Ted sneaked out from the city. Families driving to church glimpsed him dolefully sprinkling chemical substances into the pool. He looked pale and thin. He instructed Roscoe Chace, his neighbour on the left, how to switch on the pump and change the filter, and how much chlorine and Algitrol should be added weekly. He explained he would not be able to make it out every weekend – as if the distance that for years he had travelled twice each day, gliding in and out of New York, had become an impossibly steep climb back into the past. Linda, he confided vaguely, had left her parents in Akron and was visiting her sister in Minneapolis. As the shock of the Turners' joint disappearance wore off, their pool seemed less haunted and forbidding. The Murtaugh children – the Murtaughs, a rowdy, numerous family, were the Turners' right-hand neighbours – began to use it, without supervision. So Linda's old friends, with their children, began to show up, 'to keep the Murtaughs from drowning each other'. For if anything were to happen to a Murtaugh, the poor Turners (the adjective had become automatic) would be sued for everything, right when they could least afford it. It became, then, a kind of duty, a test of loyalty, to use the pool.

July was the hottest in twenty-seven years. People brought their own lawn furniture over in station wagons and set it up. Teen-age offspring and Swiss *au-pair* girls were established as lifeguards. A nylon rope with flotation corks, meant to divide the wading end from the diving end of the pool, was found coiled in the garage and reinstalled. Agnes Kleefield contributed an old refrigerator, which was wired to an outlet above Ted's basement workbench and used to store ice, quinine water, and soft drinks. An honour-system shoebox containing change appeared beside it; a little lost-and-found – an array of forgotten sunglasses, flippers, towels, lotions, paperbacks, shirts, even underwear – materialized on the Turners' side steps. When people, that July, said, 'Meet you at the pool,' they did not mean the public pool past the shopping centre, or the country-club pool beside the first tee. They meant the Turners'. Restrictions on admission were difficult to enforce tactfully. A visiting Methodist bishop, two Taiwanese economists, an entire girls' softball team from Darien, an eminent Canadian poet, the archer champion at Hartford, the six members of a black rock group called The Good Intentions, an ex-mistress of Aly Khan, the lavender-haired mother-in-law of a Nixon adviser not quite of Cabinet rank, an infant of six weeks, a man who was killed the next day on the Merritt Parkway, a Filipino who could stay on the pool bottom for eighty seconds, two Texans who kept cigars in their mouths and hats on their heads, three telephone linemen, four expatriate Czechs, a student Maoist from Wesleyan, and the postman all swam, as guests, in the Turners' pool, though not all at once. After the daytime crowd ebbed, and the shoebox was put back in the refrigerator, and the last *au-pair* girl took the last goosefleshed, wrinkled child shivering home to supper, there was a tide of evening activity, trysts (Mrs Kleefield and the Nicholson boy, most notoriously) and what some called, over-dramatically, orgies. True, late splashes and excited guffaws did often keep Mrs Chace awake, and the Murtaugh children spent hours at their attic window with binoculars. And there was the evidence of the lost underwear.

One Saturday early in August, the morning arrivals found an unknown car with New York plates parked in the garage. But cars of all sorts were so common – the parking tangle frequently extended into the road – that nothing much was thought of it, even when someone noticed that the bedroom windows upstairs were open. And nothing came of it, except that around suppertime, in the lull before the evening crowd began to arrive in force, Ted and an unknown woman, of the same physical type as Linda but brunette, swiftly exited from the kitchen door, got into the car, and drove back to New York. The few lingering babysitters and beaux thus unwittingly glimpsed the root of the divorce. The two lovers had been trapped inside the house all day; Ted was fearful of the legal consequences of their being seen by anyone who might write and tell

Linda. The settlement was at a ticklish stage; nothing less than terror of Linda's lawyers would have led Ted to suppress his indignation at seeing, from behind the window screen, his private pool turned public carnival. For long thereafter, though in the end he did not marry the woman, he remembered that day when they lived together like fugitives in a cave, feeding on love and ice water, tiptoeing barefoot to the depleted cupboards, which they, arriving late last night, had hoped to stock in the morning, not foreseeing the onslaught of interlopers that would pin them in. Her hair, he remembered, had tickled his shoulders as she crouched behind him at the window, and through the angry pounding of his own blood he felt her slim body breathless with the attempt not to giggle.

August drew in, with cloudy days. Children grew bored with swimming. Roscoe Chace went on vacation to Italy; the pump broke down, and no one repaired it. Dead dragon-flies accumulated on the surface of the pool. Small deluded toads hopped in and swam around and around hopelessly. Linda at last returned. From Minneapolis she had gone on to Idaho for six weeks, to be divorced. She and the children had burnt faces from riding and hiking; her lips looked drier and more quizzical than ever, still seeking to frame that troubling question. She stood at the window, in the house that already seemed to lack its furniture, at the same side window where the lovers had crouched, and gazed at the deserted pool. The grass around it was green from splashing, save where a long-lying towel had smothered a rectangle and left it brown. Aluminium furniture she didn't recognize lay strewn and broken. She counted a dozen bottles beneath the glass-topped table. The nylon divider had parted, and its two halves floated independently. The blue plastic beneath the colourless water tried to make a cheerful, other-worldly statement, but Linda saw that the pool in truth had no bottom, it held bottomless loss, it was one huge blue tear. Thank God no one had drowned in it. Except her. She saw that she could never live here again. In September the place was sold, to a family with toddling infants, who for safety's sake have not only drained the pool but have sealed it over with iron pipes and a heavy mesh, and put warning signs around, as around a chained dog.

The Witnesses

Fred Prouty, I was told yesterday, is dead – dead, as I imagine it, of cigarettes, confusion, and conscience, though none of these was the *c* my informant named. He died on the West Coast, thousands of miles from both his ex-wives and all his sad expensive children. I pictured him lying in a highly clean hospital bed, smothering in debt, interlaced with tubular machinery, overlooking a sprawling colourless spireless landscape worlds removed from the green and pointed East that had formed him. Though we had come from the same town (New Haven) and the same schools (Hotchkiss, Yale) and the same background (our grandfathers had been ministers and our fathers lawyers), Fred and I never were very close. We belonged to a generation that expressed affection through shades of reticence. The war, perhaps, had made us conservative and cautious; our task had been to bring a society across a chasm and set it down safely on the other side, unchanged. That it changed later was not our affair. After the war Fred had gone into advertising, and I into securities. For a decade, we shared Manhattan and intermittent meals. The last time I had him in my home, there had been a strangeness and, worse, a tactlessness for which I suppose I never quite forgave him. It was the high noon of the Eisenhower era, just before Fred's first divorce. He called me at work and invited himself to our apartment for a drink, and asked, surprisingly, if he might bring a friend.

Jeanne and I had the West Thirteenth Street place then. Of our many apartments, I remember it most fondly. The front windows looked across the street into an elementary school, and the back windows, across some untended yards crammed with trees of heaven, into a mysterious factory. Whatever the factory made, the process entailed great shimmering ribbons and spinning reels of colour being manipulated like giant harps by Negro men and Puerto Rican women. Rising in the morning, we could see them spinning and, eating breakfast in the kitchen, we saw into windows where children were snipping and pasting up, in season, Easter eggs and pumpkins, Christmas trees and hearts and hatchets and cherries. Almost always a breeze flowed through our two large rooms, now from bedroom to living room, from factory to school, and now the other way, bringing with it the sounds of street traffic, which included the drunks on the pavement outside the Original Mario's. Ours was the third floor – the lowest we have ever lived.

Fred came promptly at seven. As he climbed the stairs, I thought the woman behind him was his wife. Indeed, she resembled his wife – an inch taller, perhaps, and a bit more adventurously dressed, but the same physical type, heavy and rounded below the waist, ectomorphically slender above. The two women had the same kind of ears, cupped and protruding, which compelled the same cover-up hairdo and understated earrings. Fred introduced her to us as Priscilla Evans. Jeanne had not known Marjorie Prouty well, yet to ask her to meet and entertain this other woman on no basis beyond the flat implication of her being Fred's mistress was, as perhaps Fred in his infatuation imperfectly understood, a *gaffe*. Jeanne's arm went forward stiffly to take the girl's hand.

A 'girl' more by status than by age, Priscilla was, though unmarried and a year or two younger, one of us – I never knew where Fred met her, but it could have been at work or a party or a crew race, if he still went to them. She had the social grace to be embarrassed, and I wondered how Fred had persuaded her to come. He must have told her I was a very close friend, which perhaps, in his mind, I was. I was New Haven to him, distant and safe; touchingly, his heart had never left that middling town. I would like to reward the loyalty of a ghost by remembering that evening – hour, really, for we did not invite them for dinner – as other than dull. But, in part because Jeanne and I felt constrained from asking them any direct questions, in part because Priscilla put on a shy manner, and in part because Fred seemed sheepishly bewildered by this party he had arranged, our conversation was stilted. We discussed what was current in those departed days: McCarthy's fall, Kefauver's candidacy, Dulles' tactlessness. Dulles had recently called Goa a 'Portuguese province', offending India, and given his 'brinkmanship' interview, offending everyone. Priscilla said she thought Dulles deserved credit for at least his honesty, for saying out loud what everybody knew anyway. It is the one remark of hers that I remember, and it made me look at her again.

She was like Marjorie but with a difference. There was something twisted and wry about her face, some arresting trace of pain endured and wisdom reluctantly acquired. Her life, I felt, had been cracked and mended, and in this her form differed from that of Fred's wife or, for that matter, of my own. My attention, then, for an instant snagged on the irregularity where Fred's spirit had caught, taken root, and hastily flourished. I try to remember them sitting beside each other – he slumped in the canvas sling chair, she upright on the half of the Sheraton settee nearer him. He had bronze hair receding on a brow where the freckles advanced. His nose was thin and straight, his eyes pale blue and slightly bulged behind the silver-frame spectacles that, through some eccentricity of the nose pads, perched too far out from his face. Fred's mouth was one of those sharply cut sets of lips, virtually pretty, that frown down from portraits on bank walls. Something farmerish made his hands heavy; when he clasped his knee, the knuckles were squeezed white. In the awkward sling chair, he clasped his knee; his neck seemed red above the fresh white collar; he was anxious for her. He disagreed with her praise of Dulles, knowing we were liberals. She sat demure, yet with something gaudy and man-catching about her clothes, and there was – I imagine or remember – a static energy imposed on the space between her body and Fred's, as in that visual fooler which now seems two black profiles and now a single white vase, so that the arm of the settee, the mahogany end table inlaid with satinwood, the unlit lamp with the base of beaten copper, the ceramic ashtray full of unfiltered butts shaped like commas, the very shadows and blurs of refraction were charged with a mysterious content, the 'relationship' of these two tense and unwelcome visitors.

I want to believe that Jeanne, however half-heartedly, invited them to dine with us; of course Fred refused, saying they must go, suddenly rising, apologetic, his big hands dangling, his lady looking up at him for leadership. They left before eight, and my embarrassed deafness lifts. I can hear Jeanne complaining distinctly, 'Well, that was strange!'

'Very strange behaviour, from Fred.'

'Was he showing her that he has respectable friends, or what?'

'Surely that's a deduction she didn't need to have proved.'

'She may have a mistrustful nature.'

'What did you make of her?'

'I'm afraid I must say she struck me as very ordinary.'

I said, 'It's hilarious, how much of a copy she is of his wife.'

'Yes, and not as finished as Marjorie. A poor copy.'

'How far,' I said, 'people go out of their way to mess up their lives.' I was trying to agree with some unstated assertion of hers.

'Yes,' Jeanne said, straightening the bent cushions on the settee, 'that was very dismal. Tell me. Are we going to have to see them again? Are we some sort of furniture so they can play house, or what?'

'No, I'm sure not. I'll tell Fred not, if I must.'

'I don't care what people do, but I don't like being used.'

I felt she expected me, though innocent, to apologize. I said, 'I can't imagine what got into Fred. He's usually nothing if not correct.'

For a moment, Jeanne may have considered letting me have the last word. Then she said firmly, 'I found the whole thing extremely dreary.'

The next day, or the day after, Fred called me at the office, and thanked me. He said, with an off-putting trace of the stammering earnestness his clients must have found endearing, that it had meant more to him than I could know, and some day he would tell me why. I may have been incurious and cool. He did not call again. Then I heard he was divorced, and had left Madison Avenue for a consulting outfit starting up in Chicago. His new wife, I was told, came originally from Indianapolis. I tried to remember if Priscilla Evans had had a Midwestern accent and could not.

Years later, but some time ago, when Kennedy Airport was still called Idlewild, Fred and I accidentally met in the main terminal – those acres of white floor where the islands of white waiting chairs cast no shadows. He was on his way back to Los Angeles. He was doing publicity work for one of the studios that can television series. Although he did not tell me, he was on the verge of his second divorce. He seemed heavier, and his hands were puffy. His bronze hair was thinning now on the back of his skull; there were a few freckles in the bald spot. He was wearing horn-rimmed glasses, which did not make him look youthful. He kept taking them off, as if bothered by their fit, exposing, on the bridge of his nose, the red moccasin-shaped dents left by the pads of his old silver frames. He had somehow gone pasty, sheltered from the California sun, and I wondered if I looked equally tired and corrupt to him. Little in my life had changed. We had had one child, a daughter. We had moved uptown, to a bigger, higher, bleaker apartment. Kennedy's bear market had given me a dull spring.

Fred and I sought shelter in the curtained bar a world removed from the sun-stricken airfield and the glinting planes whose rows of rivets and portholes seemed to be spelling a message in punched code. He told me about his life without complaint and let me guess that it was going bad. He had switched to filtered cigarettes but there was a new recklessness in his drinking. I watched his hands and suddenly remembered how those same hands looked squeezed around the handle of a lacrosse stick. He apologized for the night he had brought the girl to our apartment.

I said I had almost forgotten, but that at the time it had seemed out of character.

'How did we look?' he asked.

I didn't understand. 'Worried,' I said. 'She seemed to us much like Marjorie.'

He smiled and said, 'That's how it turned out. Just like Marjorie.' He had had three drinks and took off his glasses. His eyes were still a schoolboy's but his mouth no longer would have looked well on a bank wall; the prim cut of it had been boozed and blurred away, and a dragging cynicism had done something ineradicable to the corners. His lips groped for precision. 'I wanted you to see us,' he said. 'I wanted somebody to see us in love. I loved her so much,' he said, 'I loved her so much it makes me sick to remember it. Whenever I come back to the city, whenever I pass any place we went together when it was beginning, I fall, I kind of drop an inch or so inside my skin. Herbie, do you know what I'm talking about, have you ever had the feeling?'

I did not think it was a correct question or that I was expected to answer it. Perhaps my silence was construed as a rebuke.

Fred rubbed his forehead and closed his bulged blue eyes and said, 'I knew it was wrong. I knew it was going to end in a mess, it had nowhere else to go. That's why I brought her over that time. She hated it, she didn't want to come. But I wanted it. I wanted somebody I knew to see us when it was good. No, I wanted somebody who knew *me* to see me happy. I had never known I could be that happy. God. I wanted you and Jeanne to see us together before it went bad.' He opened his scared eyes and told me, 'So it wouldn't be totally lost.'

The Day of the Dying Rabbit

The shutter clicks, and what is captured is mostly accident – that happy foreground diagonal, the telling expression forever pinned in mid-flight between two plateaus of vacuity. Margaret and I didn't exactly intend to have six children. At first, we were trying until we got a boy. Then, after Jimmy arrived, it was half our trying to give him a brother so he wouldn't turn queer under all those sisters, and half our missing, the both of us, the way new babies are. You know how they are – delicate as film, wrapped in bunting instead of lead foil, but coiled with that same miraculous brimming whatever-it-is: *susceptibility*, let's say. That wobbly hot head. Those navy-blue eyes with the pupils set at f/2. The wrists hinged on silk and the soles of the feet as tender as the eyelids: film that fine-grained would show a doghouse roof from five miles up.

Also, I'm a photographer by trade and one trick of the trade is a lot of takes. In fact, all six kids have turned out pretty well, now that we've got the baby's feet to stop looking at each other and Deirdre fitted out with glasses. Having so many works smoothly enough in the city, where I go off to the studio and they go off to school, but on vacations things tend to jam. We rent the same four-room shack every August. When the cat dragged in as a love-present this mauled rabbit it had caught, it was minutes before I could get close enough even to *see*.

Henrietta – she's the second youngest, the last girl – screamed. There are screams like flashbulbs – just that cold. This one brought Linda out from her murder mystery and Cora up from her Beatles magazine, and they crowded into the corridor that goes with the bedrooms the landlord added to the shack to make it more rentable and that isn't wide enough for two pairs of shoulders. Off this corridor into the outdoors is a salt-pimpled aluminium screen door with a misadjusted pneumatic attachment that snaps like lightning the first two-thirds of its arc and then closes the last third slow as a clock, ticking. That's how the cat got in. It wasn't our cat exactly, just a tattered calico stray the children had been feeding salami scraps to out in the field between our yard and the freshwater pond. Deirdre had been helping Margaret with the dishes, and they piled into the corridor just ahead of me, in time to hear Linda let crash with a collection of those four-letter words that come out of her face more and more. The more pop out, the more angelic her face grows. She is thirteen, and in a few years I suppose it will be liquor and drugs, going in. I don't know where she gets the words, or how to stop them coming. Her cheeks are trimming down, her nose bones edging up, her mouth getting witty in the corners, and her eyes gathering depth; and I don't know how to stop that coming, either. Faces, when you look at them through a lens, are passageways for angels, sometimes whole clouds of them. Jimmy told me the other day – he's been reading books of records, mostly sports – about a man so fat he had been buried in a piano case for a casket, and he asked me what a casket was, and I told him, and a dozen angels overlapped in his face as he mentally matched up casket with fatness, and piano, and earth; and got the picture. Click.

After Linda's swearing, there was the sound of a slap and a second's silence while it developed who had been hit: Henrietta. Her crying clawed the corridor walls, and down among our legs the cat reconsidered its offer to negotiate and streaked back out the screen door, those last ticking inches, leaving the rabbit with us. Now I could see it: a half-grown rabbit huddled like a fur doorstop in the doorway to the bigger girls' room. No one dared touch it. We froze around it in a circle. Henrietta was still sobbing, and Cora's transistor was keeping the beat with static, like a heart stuffed with steel wool. Then God came down the hall from the smaller children's room.

Godfrey is the baby, the second boy. We were getting harder up for names, which was one reason we stopped. Another was, the club feet seemed a warning. He was slow to walk after they took the casts off, and at age four he marches along with an unstoppable sort of deliberate dignity, on these undeformed but somehow distinctly rectangular big feet. He pushed his way through our legs and without hesitation squatted and picked up the rabbit. Cora, the most squeamish of the children – the others are always putting worms down her back – squealed, and God twitched and flipped the bunny back to the floor; it hit neck first, and lay there looking bent. Linda punched Cora, and Henrietta jabbed God, but still none of the rest of us was willing to touch the rabbit, which might be dead this time, so we let God try again. We needed Jimmy. He and Deirdre have the natural touch – middle children tend to. But all month he's been out of the shack, out of our way, playing catch with himself, rowing in the pond, brooding on what it means to be a boy. He's ten. I've missed him. A father is like a dog – he needs a boy for a friend.

This time in God's arms, the rabbit made a sudden motion that felt ticklish, and got dropped again, but the sign of life was reassuring, and Deirdre pushed through at last, and all evening there we were, paying sick calls on this shoebox, whispering, while Deirdre and Henrietta alternately dribbled milk in a dropper, and God kept trying to turn it into a Steiff stuffed animal, and Cora kept screwing up her nerve to look the bunny in its left eye, which had been a little chewed, so it looked like isinglass. Jimmy came in from the pond after dark and stood at the foot of Deirdre's bed, watching her try to nurse the rabbit back to health with a dropper of stale milk. She was crooning and crying. No fuss; just the tears. The rabbit was lying panting on its right side, the bad eye up. Linda was on the next bed, reading her mystery, above it all. God was asleep. Jimmy's nostrils pinched in, and he turned his back on the whole business. He had got the picture. The rabbit was going to die. At the back of my brain I felt tired, damp, and cold.

What was it in the next twenty-four hours that slowly flooded me, that makes me want to get the day on some kind of film? I don't know exactly, so I must put everything in, however under-exposed.

Linda and Cora were still awake when headlights boomed in the driveway – we're a city block from the nearest house and a half mile from the road – and the Pingrees came by. Ian works for an ad agency I've photographed some nudes shampooing in the shower for, and on vacation he lives in boat-neck shirts and cherry-red Bermudas and blue sunglasses, and grows a salt-and-pepper beard – a Verichrome fathead, and nearsighted at that. But his wife, Jenny, is nifty: low forehead, like a fox. Freckles. Thick red sun-dulled hair ironed flat down her back. Hips. And an angle about her legs, the way they're put together, slightly bowed but with the something big and bland and smooth and unimpeachable about the thighs that you usually find only in the fenders of new cars. Though she's very serious and liberal and agitated these days, I could look at her for ever, she's such fun for the eyes. Which isn't the same as being photogenic. The few shots I've taken of her show a staring woman with baby fat, whereas some skinny snit who isn't even a name to me comes over in the magazines as my personal version of Eros. The camera does lie, all the time. It has to.

Margaret doesn't mind the Pingrees, which isn't the same as liking them, but in recent years she doesn't much admit to liking anybody; so it was midnight when they left, all of us giddy with drink and talk under the stars, that seem so presiding and reproachful when you're drunk, shouting good-bye in the driveway, and agreeing on tennis tomorrow. I remembered the rabbit. Deirdre, Linda, and Cora were asleep, Linda with the light still on and the mystery rising and falling on her chest, Cora floating above her, in the upper bunk bed. The rabbit was in the shoebox under a protective lean-to of cookout grilles, in case the cat came back. We moved a grille aside and lit a match, expecting the rabbit to be dead. Photograph by sulphur-glow: undertakers at work. But though the rabbit wasn't hopping, the whiskers were moving, back and forth no more than a millimetre or two at the tips, but enough to signify breathing, life, hope, what else? Eternal solicitude brooding above us, also holding a match, and burning Its fingers. Our detection of life, magnified by liquor, emboldened us to make love for the first time in, oh, days beyond counting. She's always tired, and says the Pill depresses her, and a kind of arms race of avoidance has grown up around her complaints. Moonlight muted by window screens. Great eyesockets beneath me, looking up. To the shack smells of mist and cedar and salt we added musk. Margaret slipped into sleep quick as a fish afterwards, but for an uncertain length of time – the hours after midnight lose their numbers, if you don't remind them with a luminous dial – I lay there, the rabbit swollen huge and oppressive, blanketing all of us, a clenching of the nerves snatching me back from sleep by a whisper, the breathing and rustling all around me precarious, the rumbling and swaying of a ship that at any moment, the next or then the next, might hit an iceberg.

Morning. The rabbit took some milk, and his isinglass eye slightly widened. The children triumphantly crowed. Jubilant sun-sparkle on the sea beyond the sand beyond the pond. We rowed across, six in the rowboat and two in the kayak. The tides had been high in the night, delivering debris dropped between here and Portugal. Jimmy walked far down the beach, collecting light bulbs jettisoned from ships – they are vacuums and will float for ever, if you let them. I had put the 135mm. telephoto on the Nikon and loaded in a roll of Plus-X and took some shots of the children (Cora's face, horrified and ecstatic, caught in the translucent wall of a breaker about to submerge her; Godfrey, his close-cut blond hair shiny as a helmet, a Tritonesque strand of kelp slung across his shoulders) but most of grass and sand and shadows, close-up, using the ultra-violet filter, trying to get, what may be ungettable, the way the shadow edges stagger from grain to grain on the sand, and the way some bent-over grass blades draw circles around themselves, to keep time away.

Jimmy brought the bulbs back and arranged them in order of size, and before I could get to him had methodically smashed two. All I could see was bleeding feet but I didn't mean to grab him so hard. The marks of my hand were still red on his arm a half hour later. Our fight depressed Henrietta; like a seismograph, she feels all violence as hers. God said he was hungry and Deirdre began to worry about the rabbit: there is this puffy look children's faces get that I associate with guilt but that can also signal grief. Deirdre and Jimmy took the kayak, to be there first, and Linda, who maybe thinks the exercise will improve her bosom, rowed the rest of us to our dock. We walked to the house, heads down. Our path is full of poison ivy, our scorched lawn full of flat thistles. In our absence, the rabbit, still lying on its side, had created a tidy little heap of pellet-like faeces. The children were ecstatic; they had a dirty joke and a miracle all in one. The rabbit's recovery was assured. But the eye looked cloudier to me, and the arc of the whisker tips even more fractional.

Lunch: soup and sandwiches. In the sky, the clouding over from the west that often arrives around noon. The level of light moved down, and the hands of the year swept forward a month. It was autumn, every blade of grass shining. August has this tinny, shifty quality, the only month without a holiday to pin it down. Our tennis date was at two. You can picture for yourself Jenny Pingree in tennis whites: whose rounded guileless thighs, and the bobbing, flying hair tied behind with a kerchief of blue gauze, and that humourless, utterly intent clumsiness – especially when catching the balls tossed to her as server – that we love in children, trained animals, and women who are normally graceful. She and I, thanks to my predatory net play, took Ian and Margaret, 6–3, and the next set was called at 4–4, when our hour on the court ran out. A moral triumph for Margaret, who played like the swinger of fifteen years ago, and passed me in the alley half a dozen times. Dazzling with sweat, she took the car and went shopping with the four children who had come along to the courts; Linda had stayed in the shack with another book, and Jimmy had walked to a neighbouring house, where there was a boy his age. The Pingrees dropped me off at our mailbox. Since they were going back to the city Sunday, we had agreed on a beach picnic tonight. The mail consisted of forwarded bills, pencil-printed letters to the children from their friends on other islands or beside lakes, and *Life*. While walking down our dirt road I flicked through an overgorgeous photographic essay on Afghanistan. Hurrying blurred women in peacock-coloured saris, mud palaces, rose dust, silver rivers high in the Hindu Kush. An entire valley – misted, forested earth – filled the centre-page spread. The *lenses* those people have! Nothing beautiful on earth is as selfless as a beautiful lens.

Entering the shack, I shouted out to Linda, 'It's just me,' thinking she would be afraid of rapists. I went into her room and looked in the shoebox. The eye was lustreless and the whiskers had stopped moving, even infinitesimally.

'I think the bunny's had it,' I said.

'Don't make me look,' she said, propped up in the lower bunk, keeping her eyes deep in a paperback titled *A Stitch in Time Kills Nine*. The cover showed a dressmaker's dummy pierced by a stiletto, and bleeding. 'I couldn't *stand it*,' she said.

'What should I do?' I asked her.

'Bury it.' She might have been reading from the book. Her profile, I noticed, was becoming a cameo, with a lovely gentle bulge to the forehead, high like Margaret's. I hoped being intelligent wouldn't cramp her life.

'Deirdre will want to see it,' I argued. 'It's her baby.'

'It will only make her *sad*,' Linda said. 'And dis*gust* me. Already it must be *full* of *vermin*.'

Nothing goads me to courage like some woman's taking a high tone. Afraid to touch the rabbit's body while life was haunting it, I touched it now, and found it tepid, and lifted it from the box. The body, far from stiff, felt unhinged; its back or neck must have been broken since the moment the cat pounced. Blood had dried in the ear – an intricate tunnel leading brainwards, velvety at the tip, oddly muscular at the root. The eye not of isinglass was an opaque black bead. Linda was right; there was no need for Deirdre to see. I took the rabbit out beyond the prickly yard, into the field, and laid it below the least stunted swamp oak, where any child who wanted to be sure that I hadn't buried it alive could come and find it. I put a marsh marigold by its nose, in case it was resurrected and needed to eat, and paused above the composition – fur, flower, and arty shape of fallen oak leaves – with a self-congratulatory sensation that must have carried on my face back to the shack, for Margaret, in the kitchen loading the refrigerator, looked up at me and said, 'Say. I don't mind your being partners with Jenny, but you don't have to toss the balls to her in that cute confiding way.'

'The poor bitch can't catch them otherwise. You saw that.'

'I saw more than I wanted to. I nearly threw up.'

'That second set,' I said, 'your backhand was terrific. The Maggie-O of old.'

Deirdre came down the hall from the bedrooms. Her eyes seemed enormous; I went to her and kneeled to hold her around the waist, and began, 'Sweetie, I have some sad news.'

'Linda told me,' she said, and walked by me into the kitchen. 'Mommy, can I make the cocoa?'

'You did everything you could,' I called after her. 'You were a wonderful nurse and made the bunny's last day very happy.'

'I know,' she called in answer. 'Mommy, I *promise* I won't let the milk boil over this time.'

Of the children, only Henrietta and Godfrey let me lead them to where the rabbit rested. Henrietta skittishly hung back, and never came closer than ten yards. God marched close, gazed down sternly, and said, 'Get up.' Nothing happened, except the ordinary motions of the day: the gulls and stately geese beating home above the pond, the traffic roaring invisible along the highway. He squatted down, and I prevented him from picking up the rabbit, before I saw it was the flower he was after.

Jimmy, then, was the only one who cried. He came home a half hour after we had meant to set out rowing across the pond to the beach picnic, and rushed into the field towards the tree with the tallest silhouette and came back carrying on his cheeks stains he tried to hide by thumping God. 'If *you* hadn't dropped him,' he said. 'You *baby*.'

'It was nobody's fault,' Margaret told him, impatiently cradling her basket of hot dogs and raw hamburger.

'I'm going to kill that cat,' Jimmy said. He added, cleverly, an old grievance: 'Other kids my age have BB guns.'

'Oh, our big man,' Cora said. He flew at her in a flurry of fists and sobs, and ran away and hid. At the dock I let Linda and Cora take the kayak, and the rest of us waited a good ten minutes with the rowboat before Jimmy ran down the path in the dusk, himself a silhouette, like the stunted trees and the dark bar of dunes between two sheets of reflected sunset. Ever notice how sunsets upside down look like stairs?

'Somehow,' Margaret said to me, as we waited, 'you've deliberately dramatized this.' But nothing could fleck the happiness widening within me, to capture the dying light.

The Pingrees had brought swordfish and another, older couple – the man was perhaps an advertising client. Though he was tanned like a tobacco leaf and wore the smartest summer playclothes, a pleading uncertainty in his manner seemed to crave the support of advertisement. His wife had once been beautiful and held herself lightly, lithely at attention – a soldier in the war of self-preservation. With them came two teen-age boys clad in jeans and buttonless vests and hair so long their summer complexions had remained sallow. One was their son, the other his friend. We all collected driftwood – a wandering, lonely, prehistoric task that frightens me. Darkness descended too soon, as it does in the tropics, where the warmth leads us to expect an endless June evening from childhood. We made a game of popping champagne corks, the kids trying to catch them on the fly. Startling, how high they soared, in the open air. The two boys gathered around Linda, and I protectively eavesdropped, and was shamed by the innocence and long childish pauses of what I overheard: 'Philadelphia . . . just been in the airport, on our way to my uncle's, he lives in Virginia . . . wonderful horses, super . . . it's not actually blue, just bluey-green, blue only I guess by comparison . . . was in France once, and went to the races . . . never been . . . I want to go.' Margaret and Jenny, kneeling in the sand to cook, setting out paper plates on tables that were merely wide pieces of driftwood, seemed sisters. The woman of the strange couple tried to flirt with me, talking of foreign places: 'Paris is so dead, suddenly . . . the girls fly over to London to buy their clothes, and then their mothers won't let them wear them . . . Malta . . . Istanbul . . . life . . . sincerity . . . the *people* . . . the poor Greeks . . . a friend absolutely assures me, the C.I.A. engineered . . . apparently used the NATO contingency plan.' Another champagne cork sailed in the air, hesitated, and drifted down, Jimmy diving but missing, having misjudged. A remote light, a lightship, or the promontory of a continent hidden in daylight, materialized on the horizon, beyond the shushing of the surf. Margaret and Jenny served us. Hamburgers and swordfish full of woodsmoke. Celery and sand. God, sticky with things he had spilled upon himself, sucked his thumb and rubbed against Margaret's legs. Jimmy came to me, furious because the big boys wouldn't Indian-wrestle with him, only with Linda and Cora: 'Showing off for their boyfriends . . . whacked me for no reason . . . just because I said "sex bomb".'

We sat in a ring, survivors, around the fire, the heart of a collapsing star, fed anew by paper plates. The man of the older couple, in whose breath the champagne had undergone an acrid chemical transformation, told me about his money – how as a youth just out of business school, in the depths of the Depression, he had made a million dollars in some deal involving Stalin and surplus wheat. He had liked Stalin, and Stalin had liked him. 'The thing we must realize about your Communist is that he's just another kind of businessman.' Across the fire I watched his wife, spurned by me, ardently gesturing with the teen-age boy who was not her son, and wondered how I would take her picture. Tri-X, wide-open, at 1/60; but the shadows would be lost, the subtle events within them, and the highlights would be vapid blobs. There is no adjustment, no darkroom trickery, equivalent to the elastic tolerance of our eyes as they travel.

As my new friend murmured on and on about his money, and the champagne warming in my hand released carbon dioxide to air, exposures flickered in and out around the fire: glances, inklings, angels. Margaret gazing, the nick of a frown erect between her brows. Henrietta's face vertically compressing above an ear of corn she was devouring. The well-preserved woman's face a mask of bronze with cunningly welded seams, but her hand an exclamatory white as it touched her son's friend's arm in some conversational urgency lost in the crackle of driftwood. The halo of hair around Ian's knees, innocent as babies' pates. Jenny's hair an elongated flurry as she turned to speak to the older couple's son; his bearded face was a blur in the shadows, melancholy, the eyes seeming closed, like the Jesus on a faded, drooping veronica. I heard Jenny say, '. . . *must* destroy the system! We've forgotten how to *love*!' Deirdre's glasses, catching the light, leaped like moth wings towards the fire, escaping perspective. Beside me, the old man's face went silent, and suffered a deflation wherein nothing held firm but the reflected glitter of firelight on a tooth his grimace had absent-mindedly left exposed. Beyond him, on the edge of the light, Cora and Linda were revealed sitting together, their legs stretched out long before them, warming, their faces in shadow, sexless and solemn, as if attentive to the sensations of the revolution of the earth beneath them. Godfrey was asleep, his head pillowed on Margaret's thigh, his body suddenly wrenched by a dream sob, and a heavy succeeding sigh.

It was strange, after these fragmentary illuminations, to stumble through the unseen sand and grass, with our blankets and belongings, to the boats on the shore of the pond. Margaret and five children took the rowboat; I nominated Jimmy to come with me in the kayak. The night was starless. The pond, between the retreating campfire and the slowly nearing lights of our neighbours' houses, was black. I could scarcely see his silhouette as it struggled for the rhythm of the stroke: left, a little turn with the wrists, right, the little turn reversed, left. Our paddles occasionally clashed, or snagged on the weeds that clog this pond. But the kayak sits lightly, and soon we put the confused conversation of the rowers, and their wildly careening flashlight beam, behind. Silence widened around us. Steering the rudder with the foot pedals, I let Jimmy paddle alone, and stared upward until I had produced, in the hazed sky overhead, a single, unsteady star. It winked out. I returned to paddling and received an astonishing impression of phosphorescence: every stroke, right and left, called into visibility a rich arc of sparks, animalcula hailing our

passage with bright shouts. The pond was more populous than China. My
son and I were afloat on a firmament warmer than the heavens.

'Hey, Dad.'

His voice broke the silence carefully; my benevolence engulfed him, my
fellow-wanderer, my leader, my gentle, secretive future. 'What, Jimmy?'

'I think we're about to hit something.'

We stopped paddling, and a mass, grey etched on grey, higher than a
man, glided swiftly towards us and struck the prow of the kayak. With
this bump, and my awakening laugh, the day of the dying rabbit ended.
Exulting in homogenous glory, I had steered us into the bank. We pushed
off, and by the lights of our neighbours' houses navigated to the dock,
and waited for the rowboat with its tangle of voices and impatience and
things that would snag. The days since have been merely happy days.
This day was singular in its, let's say, *gallantry*: between the cat's gallant
intentions and my son's gallantly calm warning, the dying rabbit sank like
film in the developing pan, and preserved us all.

The Family Meadow

The family always reconvenes in the meadow. For generations it has been traditional, this particular New Jersey meadow, with its great walnut tree making shade for the tables and its slow little creek where the children can push themselves about in a rowboat and nibble watercress and pretend to fish. Early this morning, Uncle Jesse came down from the stone house that his father's father's brother had built and drove the stakes, with their carefully tied red flags, that would tell the cars where to park. The air was still, inert with the postdawn laziness that foretells the effort of a hot day, and between blows of his hammer Jesse heard the breakfast dishes clinking beneath the kitchen window and the younger collie barking behind the house. A mild man, Jesse moved scrupulously, mildly through the wet grass that he had scythed yesterday. The legs of his grey workman's pants slowly grew soaked with dew and milkweed spittle. When the stakes were planted, he walked out of the lane with the REUNION signs, past the houses. He avoided looking at the houses, as if glancing into their wide dead windows would wake them.

By nine o'clock Henry had come up from Camden with a carful – Eva, Mary, Fritz, Fred, the twins, and, incredibly, Aunt Eula. It is incredible she is still alive, after seven strokes. Her shrivelled head munches irritably and her arms twitch, trying to shake off assistance, as if she intends to dance. They settle her in an aluminium chair beneath the walnut tree. She faces the creek, and the helpless waggle of her old skull seems to establish itself in sympathy with the oscillating shimmer of the sunlight on the slow water. The men, working in silent pairs whose unison is as profound as blood, carry down the tables from the barn, where they are stacked from one year to the next. In truth, it has been three summers since the last reunion, and it was feared that there might never be another. Aunt Jocelyn, her grey hair done up in braids, comes out of her kitchen to say hello on the dirt drive. Behind her lingers her granddaughter, Karen, in white Levis and bare feet, with something shadowy and doubtful about her dark eyes, as if she had been intensely watching television. The girl's father – not here; he is working in Philadelphia – is Italian, and

277

as she matures an alien beauty estranges her, so that during her annual visits to her grandparents' place, which when she was a child had seemed to her a green island, it is now she herself, at thirteen, who seems the island. She feels surrounded by the past, cut off from the images – luncheonette, a civic swimming pool, an auditorium festooned with crêpe paper – that represent life to her, the present, her youth. The air around her feels brown, as in old photographs. These men greeting her seem to have stepped from an album. The men, remembering their original prejudice against her mother's marrying a Catholic, are especially cordial to her, so jovially attentive that Jocelyn suddenly puts her arm around the girl, expressing a strange multitude of things; that she loves her, that she is one of them, that she needs to be shielded, suddenly, from the pronged kidding of men.

By ten-thirty Horace's crowd has come down from Trenton, and the Oranges clan is arriving, in several cars. The first car says it dropped Cousin Claude in downtown Burlington because he was sure that the second car, which had faded out of sight behind them, needed to be told the way. The second car, with a whoop of hilarity, says it took the bypass and never saw him. He arrives in a third car, driven by Jimmy and Ethel Thompson from Morristown, who say they saw this forlorn figure standing along Route 130 trying to thumb a ride and as they were passing him Ethel cried, 'Why, I think that's Claude!' Zealous and reckless, a true believer in good deeds, Claude is always getting into scrapes like this, and enjoying it. He stands surrounded by laughing women, a typical man of this family, tall, with a tribal boyishness, a stubborn refusal to look his age, to lose his hair. Though his face is pitted and gouged by melancholy, Claude looks closer to forty than the sixty he is, and, though he works in Newark, he still speaks with the rural softness and slide of middle New Jersey. He has the gift – the privilege – of making these women laugh; the women uniformly run to fat and their laughter has a sameness, a quality both naïve and merciless, as if laughter meant too much to them. Jimmy and Ethel Thompson, whose name is not the family name, stand off to one side, in the unscythed grass, a fragile elderly couple whose links to the family have all died away but who have come because they received a mimeographed postcard inviting them. They are like those isolated corners of interjections and foreign syllables in a poorly planned crossword puzzle.

The twins bring down from the barn the horseshoes and the quoits. Uncle Jesse drives the stakes and pegs in the places that, after three summers, still show as spots of depressed sparseness in the grass. The sun, reaching towards noon, domineers over the meadow; the shade of the walnut tree grows smaller and more noticeably cool. By noon, all have arrived, including the Dodge station wagon from central Pennsylvania, the young pregnant Wilmington cousin who married an airline pilot, and the White Plains people, who climb from their car looking like clowns, wearing red-striped shorts and rhinestone-studded sunglasses. Handshakes are exchanged that feel to one man like a knobbed wood carving and to the other like a cow's slippery, unresisting teat. Women kiss, kiss stickily, with little overlapping patches of adhesive cheek and clicking conflicts of spectacle rims, under the white unslanting sun. The very insects shrink towards the shade. The eating begins. Clams steam, corn steams, salad wilts, butter runs, hot dogs turn, torn chicken shines in the savage light. Iced tea, brewed in forty-quart milk cans, chuckles when sloshed. Paper plates buckle on broad laps. Plastic butter knives, asked to cut cold ham, refuse. Children underfoot in the pleased frenzy eat only potato chips. Somehow, as the first wave of appetite subsides, the long tables turn musical, and a murmur rises to the blank sky, a cackle rendered harmonious by a remote singleness of ancestor; a kind of fabric is woven and hung, a tapestry of the family fortunes, the threads of which include milkmen, ministers, mailmen, bankruptcy, death by war, death by automobile, insanity – a strangely prevalent thread, the thread of insanity. Never far from a farm or the memory of a farm, the family has hovered in honourable obscurity, between poverty and wealth, between jail and high office. Real-estate dealers, schoolteachers, veterinarians are its noblemen; butchers, electricians, door-to-door salesmen its yeomen. Protestant, teetotalling, and undaring, ironically virtuous and mildly proud, it has added to America's statistics without altering their meaning. Whence, then, this strange joy?

Watermelons smelling of childhood cellars are produced and massively sliced. The sun passes noon and the shadows relax in the intimate grass of this antique meadow. To the music of reminiscence is added the rhythmic chunking of thrown quoits. They are held curiously, between a straight thumb and four fingers curled as a unit, close to the chest, and thrown with a soft constrained motion that implies realms of unused strength. The twins and the children, as if superstitiously, have yielded the game to the older men, Fritz and Ed, Fred and Jesse, who, in pairs, after due estimation and measurement of the fall, pick up their four quoits, clink them together to clean them, and alternately send them back through the air on a high arc, floating with a spin-held slant like that of gyroscopes. The other pair measures, decides, and stoops. When they tap their quoits together, decades fall away. Even their competitive crowing has something measured about it, something patient, like the studied way their shirt-sleeves are rolled up above their elbows. The backs of their shirts are ageless. Generations have sweated in just this style, under the arms, across the shoulder blades, and wherever the suspenders rub. The younger men and the teenage girls play a softball game along the base paths that Jesse has scythed. The children discover the rowboat and, using the oars as poles, bump from bank to bank. When they dip their hands into the calm brown water, where no fish lives, a mother watching from beneath the walnut tree shrieks, 'Keep your hands inside the boat! Uncle Jesse says the creek's polluted!'

And there is a stagnant fragrance the lengthening afternoon strains from the happy meadow. Aunt Eula nods herself asleep, and her false teeth slip down, so her face seems mummified and the children giggle in terror. Flies, an exploding population, discover the remains of the picnic and skate giddily on its odours. The softball game grows boring, except to the airline pilot, a rather fancy gloveman excited by the admiration of Cousin Karen in her tight white Levis. The Pennsylvania and New York people begin to pack their cars. The time has come for the photograph. Their history is kept by these photographs of timeless people in changing costumes standing linked and flushed in a moment of midsummer heat. All line up, from resurrected Aunt Eula, twitching and snapping like a mud turtle, to the unborn baby in the belly of the Delaware cousin. To get them all in, Jesse has to squat, but in doing so he brings the houses into his viewfinder. He does not want them in the picture, he does not want them there at all. They surround his meadow on three sides, raw ranch shacks built from one bastard design but painted in a patchwork of pastel shades. Their back yards, each nurturing an aluminium clothes tree, come right to the far bank of the creek, polluting it, and though a tall link fence holds back the children who have gathered in these yards to watch the picnic as if it were a circus or a zoo, the stare of the houses – mismatched kitchen windows squinting above the gaping cement mouth of a garage – cannot be held back. Not only do they stare, they speak, so that Jesse can hear them even at night. *Sell*, they say. *Sell*.

At a Bar in Charlotte Amalie

Blowfish with light bulbs inside their dried skins glowed above the central fortress of brown bottles. The bar was rectangular; customers sat on all four sides. A slim schoolteacherish-looking girl, without much of a tan and with one front tooth slightly overlapping the other, came in, perched on a corner stool, and asked for a Daiquiri-on-the-rocks. She wore a yellow halter, turquoise shorts, and white tennis sneakers. The bartender, who was not visibly malformed, nevertheless moved like a hunchback, with a sideways bias and the scuttling nimbleness peculiar to cripples. He wore a powder-blue polo shirt, and now and then paused to take a rather avid sip from a tall glass containing perhaps orange juice; his face was glazed with sweat and he kept peering towards the outdoors, as if expecting to be relieved of duty. The green sea was turning grey under round pink clouds. A boat dully knocked against the cement wharf, and suddenly the noise had the subtle importance noises in these latitudes assume at night. A member of the steel band, a tall, long-jawed Negro, materialized in the rear of the place, on a shallow shadowy platform where the cut and dented steel drums were stacked. After unstacking and mounting them, this Negro, who wore a tattered red shirt and held a dead cigarette in the centre of his lips, picked up a mallet and experimentally tapped into the air a succession, a cluster, an overlapping cascade of transparent notes that for a moment rendered everyone at the bar silent.

Then a homosexual with a big head turned to the schoolteacherish girl, who had been served, and said, 'See my pretty hat?' His head seemed big because his body was small, a boy's body, knobby and slack and ill-fitted to his veined man's hands and to his face. His eyes were very close together, making him seem to concentrate, without rest, upon a disagreeable internal problem, and his lips – which in their curt cut somehow expressed New York City – were too quick, snapping in and out of a grin as if he were trying to occupy both sides of his situation, being both the shameless clown and the aloof, if amused, onlooker. He had been talking about his hat, half to himself, since four o'clock this afternoon, and when he held it out to the girl an eddy of sighs and twisted eyebrows passed through the faces in the yellow darkness around the bar. The hat was a cheap broadweave straw with a bird's nest of artificial grass set into the crown, a few glass eggs fixed in the nest, and several toy birds suspended on stiff wires above it, as if in flight. 'I designed it myself,' he explained. 'For the carnival this weekend. Isn't it marvellously uninhibited?' He glanced around, checking on the size of his audience.

He was well known here. If he had scraped, from the surface of indifference, a few shreds of attention, it was because of the girl. Her coming in here, at this twilight hour, alone, bearing herself with such prim determined carelessness, was odd enough to attract notice, even at a tropical bar, where everything is permitted to happen.

'It's lovely,' she said, of the hat, and sipped her drink.

'Do you want to put it on? Please try it.'

'I don't think so, thank you.'

'I designed it myself,' he said, looking around and deciding to make a speech. 'That's the way I am. I just give my ideas away.' He flung up his hands in a gesture of casting away, and a breeze moved in from the street as if to accept his gift. 'If I were like other people, I'd make money with my ideas. Money, mo*nn*ey. It's excrement, but I love it.' A brief anonymous laugh rose and was born off by the breeze. The homosexual returned to the girl with a tender voice. 'You don't have to put it on,' he told her. 'It's really finished. When I get back to my room, where I've been meaning to go all day, if that *fiend*' – he pointed at the bartender, who with his slightly frantic deftness was pouring a rum Collins – 'would let me go. He says I owe him *monnney*! When I get back to my room, I'm going to add a few touches, here, and here. A few spangly things, just a few. It's for the carnival this weekend. Are you down here for the carnival?'

'No,' the girl said. 'I'm flying back tomorrow.'

'You should stay for the carnival. It's wonderfully uninhibited.'

'I'd like to, but I must go back.' Unexpectedly blushing, she lowered her voice and murmured something containing the word 'excursion'.

The homosexual slapped the bar. 'Forgive me, forgive me, dear Lord above' – he rolled his eyes upward, to the glowing blowfish and the great roaches and tarantulas of straw which decorated the walls – 'but I *must* see how my hat looks on you, you're so pretty.'

He reached out and set the hat with its bright hovering birds on her head. She took another sip of her drink, docilely wearing the hat. A child laughed.

The homosexual's eyes widened. This unaccustomed expression was painful to look at; it was as if two incisions were being held open by clamps. The child who had laughed was looking straight at him: a bright round face fine-featured as the moon, rising just barely to the level of the bar and topped by hair so fair it was white. The little boy sat between his parents, a man and woman oddly alike, both wearing white and having stout sun-browned arms, crinkled weather-whipped faces, and irises whose extremely pale blue seemed brittle, baked by days of concentration on a glaring sea. Even their hair matched. The man's had not been cut in months, except across his forehead, and was salt-bleached in great tufts and spirals, like an unravelling rope of half-dark strands. The woman's, finer and longer, was upswept into a tumultuous blond crown that had apparently sheltered the roots enough to leave them, for an inch or two, dark. They looked, this husband and wife, like two sexless chieftains of a thickset, seagoing Nordic tribe. As if for contrast, they were accompanied by a gaunt German youth with swarthy skin, protruding eyes, close-cropped hair, and protruding ears. He stood behind and between them, a shadow uniting three luminaries.

The homosexual crouched down on the bar and fiddled his fingers playfully. 'Hi,' he said. 'Are you laughing at me?'

The child laughed again, a little less spontaneously.

His parents stopped conversing.

'What a gorgeous child,' the homosexual called to them. 'He's so – so *fresh*. So uninhibited. It's wonderful.' He blinked; truly he did seem dazzled.

The father smiled uneasily towards the wife; the pale creases around his eyes sank into his tan, and his face, still young, settled into what it would become – the toughened, complacent, blind face of an old Scandinavian salt, the face that, pipe in teeth, is mimicked on carved bottle stoppers.

'No, really,' the homosexual insisted. 'He's darling. You should take him to Hollywood. He'd be a male Shirley Temple.'

The child, his tiny pointed chin lifting in mute delight, looked upward from one to the other of his parents. His mother, in a curious protective motion, slipped from her stool and placed a sandalled foot on the rung of her child's stool, her tight white skirt riding up and exposing half her thigh. It was stout yet devoid of fat, like the trunk of a smooth-skinned tree.

The father said, 'You think?'

'I *think*?' the homosexual echoed eagerly, crouching further forward and touching his chin to his glass. 'I *know*. He'd be a male Shirley Temple.

My judgement is infallible. If I was willing to leave all you lovely people and go dig in the dung, I'd be a stinking rich talent scout living in Beverly Hills.'

The father's face collapsed deeper into its elderly future. The mother seized her thigh with one hand and ruffled the child's hair with the other. The dark German boy began to talk to them, as if to draw them back into their radiant privacy. But the homosexual had been stirred. 'You know,' he called to the father, 'just looking at you I can feel the brine in my face. You both look as if you've been on the ocean all of your life.'

'Not quite,' the father said, so tersely it wasn't heard.

'I beg your pardon?'

'I haven't been on the sea all my life.'

'You know, I *love* sailing. I love the life of the open sea. It's so' – his lips balked, rejecting 'uninhibited' – 'it's so free, so pure, all that wind, and the waves, and all that jazz. You can just be yourself. No, really. I think it's wonderful. I love Nature. I used to live in Queens.'

'Where do you live now?' the girl beside him asked, setting his hat on the bar between them.

The homosexual didn't turn his head, answering as if the sailing couple had asked the question. 'I live here,' he called. 'In dear old St Thomas. God's own beloved country. Do you need a cook on your boat?'

The child tugged at his mother's waist and pulled her down to whisper something into her ear. She listened and shook her head; a brilliant loop of hair came undone. The father drank from the glass in front of him and in a freshened voice called across, 'Not at the moment.'

'I wish you did, I wish to heaven you did, I'm a beautiful cook, really. I make the *best* omelets. You should see me; I just put in the old eggs and a little bit of milk and a glass of brandy and some of those little green things, what are they called? – chives, I put in the chives and stir until my arm breaks off and it comes out just *won*derful, so light and fluffy. If I cared about money, I'd be a chef in the Waldorf.'

The child's whispered request seemed to recall the group to itself. The father turned and spoke to the German boy, who, in the instant before bowing his head to listen, threw, the whites of his eyes glimmering, a dark glance at the homosexual. Misunderstanding, the homosexual left his stool and hat and drink and went around the corner of the bar towards them. But, not acknowledging his approach, they lifted the child and walked away towards the rear of the place, where there was a jukebox. Here they paused, their brilliant hair and faces bathed in boxed light.

The homosexual returned to his stool and watched them. His head was thrown back like that of a sailor who has suffered a pang at the sight of land. 'Oh dear,' he said aloud, 'I can't decide which I want to have, the man or the woman.'

The schoolteacherish girl sipped her Daiquiri, dipping her head quickly, as if into a bitter birdbath. One stool away from her down the bar, there sat a beefy unshaven customer, perhaps thirty years old, drinking a beer and wearing a T-shirt with a ballpoint pen clipped to the centre of the sweat-soaked neckline. Squinting intently into space and accenting some inner journey with soft grunts, he seemed a truck driver transported, direct and intact, from the counter of an Iowa roadside diner. Next to him, across a space of empty stools, behind an untouched planter's punch, sat a very different man of about the same age, a man who, from his brick-red complexion, his high knobbed forehead, the gallant immobility of his posture, and the striking corruption of his teeth, could only have been English.

Into the space of three stools between them there now entered a dramatic person – tall, gaunt, and sandy. He displayed a decrepit Barrymore profile and a gold ring in one ear. He escorted a squat powdered woman who looked as though she had put on her lipstick by eating it. She carried a dachshund under one arm. The bartender, unsmiling, awkwardly pivoting, asked, 'How's the Baron?'

'Rotten,' the Baron said; and as he eased on to his stool his stiff wide shoulders seemed a huge coat hanger left, out of some savage stubbornness, in his coat. The woman set the dachshund on the bar. When their drinks came, the dog lapped hers, which was a lime rickey. When he tried to lap the Baron's – a straight Scotch – the man gripped the dachshund's thirstily wagging rump, snarled 'Damn alcoholic,' and sent him skidding down the bar. The dog righted himself and sniffed the truck driver's beer; a placid human paw softly closed over the mouth of the glass, blocking the animal's tongue. His nails clicking and slipping on the polished bar, the dog returned to his mistress and curled up at her elbow like a pocketbook. The girl at the corner shyly peeked at the man beside her, but he had resumed staring into space. The pen fixed at his throat had the quality of a threat, or of a scar.

The blond family returned from having put a quarter into the jukebox, which played 'Loco Motion', by Little Eva, 'Limbo Rock', by Chubby Checker, and 'Unchain My Heart', by Ray Charles. The music, like an infusion of letters from home, froze the people at the bar into silence. Beyond the overhang that sheltered the tables, night dominated. The bar lit up a section of pavement where pedestrians flitted like skittish actors

from one wing of darkness into the other. The swish of traffic on the
airport road had a liquid depth. The riding lights of boats by the wharf
bobbed up and down, and a little hard half-moon rummaged for its reflection in the slippery sea. The Baron muttered to the painted old woman an
angry and long story in which the obscene expressions were peculiarly
emphasized, so that only they hung distinct in the air, the connecting
threads inaudible. The Englishman at last moved his forearm and lowered
the level of his planter's punch by a fraction of an inch, making a stoic
face afterwards, as if the sweetness had hurt his teeth. The homosexual,
nettled by the attention received by the drinking dachshund, took off his
hat and addressed the ceiling of the bar as if it were God. 'Hey there,
Great White Father,' he said. 'You haven't been very good to me this
month. I know You love me – how could You help it, I'm so beautiful –
but I haven't seen any money coming out of the sky. I mean, really, You
put us down here in the manure and we need it to live, like. You know?
I mean, don't get too uninhibited up there. Huh?' He listened, and the
Baron, undistracted, set another blue word burning in the hushed air.
'That's O.K.,' the homosexual continued. 'You've kept the sun shining,
and I appreciate it. You just keep the sun shining, Man, and don't send
me back to Queens.' At prayer's end, he put the hat on his head and
looked around, his curt lips pursed defiantly.

Five Negroes, uncostumed, in motley clothes and as various in size as
their instruments, had assembled on the shadowy platform, kidding and
giggling back and forth and teasing the air with rapid, stop-and-start gusts
of tuning up. Abruptly they began to play. The ping-pong, the highest
pan, announced itself with four harsh solo notes, and on the fifth stroke
the slightly deeper guitar pans, the yet deeper cello pans, and the bass
boom, which was two entire forty-four-gallon oil drums, all at once fell
into the tune, and everything – cut and peened drums, rubber-tipped
sticks, tattered shirtsleeves, bobbing heads, munching jaws, a frightened-
looking little black child whipping a triangle as fast as he could – was in
motion, in flight. The band became a great loose-jointed bird feathered
in clashing, rippling bells. It played 'My Basket', and then, with hardly
a break, 'Marengo Jenny', 'How You Come to Get Wet?', and 'Madame
Dracula'. Nobody danced. It was early, and the real tourists, the college
students and Bethlehem Steel executives and Westchester surgeons, had
not yet come down from dinner in the hills to sit at the tables. There was
a small dance floor on one side of the bar. A young Negro appeared here.
He wore canary-yellow trousers and a candy-striped jersey with a boat
neck and three-quarter sleeves. He had a broad, hopeful face and an

athletic, triangular back. From his vaguely agitated air of responsibility, he seemed to be associated with the establishment. He asked the schoolteacherish girl, who looked alone and lost, to dance; but she, with a painted smile and a nervous dip of her head into her second Daiquiri, refused. The young Negro stood stymied on the dance floor, clothed only, it seemed, in music and embarrassment, his pale palms dangling foolishly. When the band, in a final plangent burst cut short as if with a knife, stopped, he went to the leader, the long-jawed red shirt on the ping-pong, and said, 'Ey mon, le peo-*ple* wan I bet "Yel*low* Bird".' He phrased it, as the West Indian accent phrases all statements, like a question.

The leader took offence. He answered deliberately, unintelligibly, as if, the music still ringing in the pan of his skull, he were softly tapping out a melody with his tongue. The man on the bass boom, a coarse thick-lipped mulatto in a blue work shirt unbuttoned down to his navel, joined in the argument and gave the young man a light push that caused him to step backward off the platform. The bass-boom man growled, and the strip of hairy cocoa skin his shirt exposed puffed up like a rooster's throat. No one had danced; the band was defensive and irritable. The leader, biting the butt of his cigarette, rattled a venomous toneless tattoo on the rim of his ping-pong. Then the shadow manning the cello pans – he had a shaved head, and was the oldest of them – spoke an unheard word, and all the Negroes, including the boy with the triangular back, broke into disjointed laughter.

When the band resumed playing, they began with 'Yellow Bird' – played flat, at a grudging tempo. The young Negro approached the blond mother of the little boy. She came with him into the centre of the floor and lifted her fat fair arms. They danced delicately, sleepily, the preening shuffle of the mambo, her backside switching in its tight white dress, his broad face shining as his lips silently mouthed the words: *Ye-ell-o-oh bi-ird, up in the tree so high, ye-ell-o-oh bi-ird, you sit alone like I*. Her thick waist seemed at home in the wide curve of his hand.

When the song finished, he bowed thank you and she returned to her family by the bar and, as if sighing, let down her hair. Apparently it had been held by one pin; she pulled this pin, the fluffy sun-bleached crown on the top of her head cascaded down her back in a blinding stream, and she looked, with her weather-pinched face, like a negative of a witch, or what relates to witches as angels relate to devils. The little boy, as if his heart were climbing the golden rope she had let down, whispered up to her, and she, after bowing her head to listen, glanced up at the homosexual, who was complaining to the bartender that his vodka-and-tonic had gone watery.

'You owe me,' the bartender said, 'a dollar-fifty, and if you let the drink sit there hour after hour, damn right it'll melt.'

'I don't have a dollar-fifty,' was the answer. 'I have washed my hands, forever and ever, amen, of filthy lucre. People want me to get a job but I won't; that's the way I am. It's a matter of principle with me. Why should I work all day for a pittance and starve when I can do nothing whatsoever and starve anyway?'

Now the whole blond family was staring at him fascinated. The glow of their faces caught the corner of his eye, and he turned towards them inquisitively; memory of the snub they had given him made his expression shy.

'I want one dollar and fifty cents from you,' the bartender insisted, with unconvincing emphasis; his anxious sweat and obscurely warped posture seemed that of a warden trapped in his own prison, among inmates he feared. He gulped some orange from his glass and looked towards the outdoors for relief. Pale square clouds rested above the sea, filtering stars. Laughter like spray was wafted from a party on a yacht.

The homosexual called, 'Really, he is the most cunning little boy I have ever seen in my *life*. In Hollywood he could be a male Shirley Temple, honestly, and when he grows up a little he could be a male what's-her-name – oh, what *was* her name? Jane Withers. I have a beautiful memory. If I cared, I could go back to New York and get on a quiz show and make a million dollars.'

The German boy spoke for the group. 'He vunts – your hatt.'

'Does he? Does he really? The little angel wants to wear my hat. I designed it myself for the carnival this weekend.' He left his stool, scrambled around the corner, set the hat with its glade of decoration squarely on the child's spherical head, and, surprisingly, knelt on the floor. 'Come on,' he said, 'come on, darling. Get on my shoulders. Let's go for a ride.'

The father looked a question at his wife, shrugged, and lifted his son onto the stranger's shoulders. The birds on their wires bobbed unsteadily, and fear flickered not only in the child's face but in the grown face to which he clung. The homosexual, straightening up, seemed startled that the child was a real weight. Then, like a frail monster overburdened with two large heads, one on top of the other and the upper one sprouting a halo of birds, he began to jog around the rectangular bar, his shaved legs looking knobbed and bony in their shorts. The steel band broke into a pachanga. Some tourist families had come down from the hills to occupy the tables, and the athletic young Negro, whose flesh seemed akin to rubber, successfully invited a studiously tanned girl with orange hair, a beauty, to dance. She had long green eyes and thin lips painted paler than her skin, and an oval of nakedness displayed her fine shoulder-bones. The Baron cursed and yanked his own lady on to the floor; as they danced, the dachshund nipped worriedly at their stumbling feet. The Baron kicked the dog away, and in doing so turned his head, so that, to the dizzy little boy riding by, the gold ring in his ear flashed like the ring on a merry-go-round. A stately bald man, obviously a North American doctor, rose, and his wife, a midget whose Coppertone face was wrinkled like a walnut, rose to dance with him. The homosexual's shoulders hurt. He galloped one last lap around the bar and lifted the child back on to the stool. The airy loss of pressure around his neck led him to exhale breathlessly into the bright round face framed by straw, 'You know, Mark Twain wrote a lovely book *just* about you.' He took the hat from the child's head and replaced it on his own. The child, having misunderstood the bargain, burst into tears, and soon his mother carried him from the bar.

The dancing gathered strength. The floor became crowded. From her high vantage at the corner of the bar, the schoolteacherish girl studied with downcast eyes the dancing feet. They seemed to be gently tamping smooth a surface that was too hot to touch for more than an instant. Some females, of both races, had removed their shoes; their feet looked ugly and predatory, flickering, spread-toed, in and out of shadows and eclipses of cloth. When the music stopped, black hands came and laid, on the spot of floor where her eyes were resting, two boards hairy with upright rusty nails. A spotlight was focused on them. The band launched into a fierce limbo. The young Negro with the handsome rubbery back leaped, nearly naked, into the light. His body was twitching in rhythm, he was waving two flaming torches, and he was clad in knit swimming trunks and orange streamers representing, she supposed, Caribbean slave dress. His eyes shut, he thrust the torches alternately into his mouth and spit out flame. Indifferent applause rippled through the tables.

The Baron, drunker than anyone had suspected, pushed off from the bar and, as the young Negro lay down on a board of nails and stroked the skin of his chest with the sticks of fire, lay down beside him and kicked his trousered legs high in parody. No one dared laugh, the Baron's face was so impassive and rapt. The young Negro, his back resting on the nails, held one torch at arm's length, so that the flame rested on the Baron's coat lapel and started a few sparks there; but the Baron writhed on obliviously, and the smouldering threads winked out. When the Negro stood, now clearly shaken, and with a great mock-primitive grimace leaped on one board of nails with his bare feet, the Baron leaped in his sandals on the other, and through sandy eyelashes blindly peered into the surrounding darkness of applause, his earring glinting, his shoulders still seeming to have a coat hanger in them. Two black waiters, nervous as deer, ventured into the spotlight and seized his upraised arms; as they led him out of the light, the tall figure of the white man, gasping as if he had surfaced after a shipwreck, yet expressed, in profile, an incorrigible dignity. There was murmuring at the tables as the tourists wondered if this had been part of the act.

The music pitched into an even fiercer tempo. The young Negro, handing away his torches, was given a cloth sack, which he dropped on the floor. It fell open to reveal a greenish heap of smashed bottles. He trod on the heap with both feet. He got down and rolled in it as a dog rolls ecstatically in the rotten corpse of woodchuck. He rested his back on the pillow of shards and the heavy mulatto left the bass boom and stood on his chest. There was applause. The mulatto jumped off and walked away. The Negro got up on his knees, cupped a glittering quantity of broken glass in his palms, and scrubbed his face with it. When he stood to take the applause, the girl observed that his back, which gleamed, heaving, a foot from her eyes, indeed did bear a few small unbleeding cuts. The applause died, the music halted, and the bright lights went on before the slave, hugging his nail-boards and bag of glass, had reached the haven of the door behind the platform. As he passed among them, the members of the steel band cackled.

Now there was an intermission. The bartender, his hands trembling and his eyes watering, it seemed, on the edge of tears, scuttled back and forth mixing a new wave of drinks. More tourists drifted in, and the families containing adolescents began to leave. The traffic on the airport road had diminished, and the bumping of the boats on the wharf, beneath the moon that had lost its reflection, regained importance. The people on the decks of these boats could see the windows burning in the dry hills above Charlotte Amalie, lights spread through the middle of the night sky like a constellation about to collide with our Earth but held back, perpetually poised in the just bearable distance, by that elusive refusal implicit in tropical time, which like the soft air seems to consist entirely of circles. Within the bar, the German boy wandered over and spoke to the homosexual, who looked up from under the brim of his hat with alert lips and no longer preoccupied eyes, all business. The very English-appearing man left his place behind the undiminishing planter's punch, sauntered around the bar, and commenced a conversation with the now deserted Nordic father; the Englishman's first words betrayed a drawling American accent. The Baron laid his handsome head on the bar and fell asleep. The dachshund licked his face, because it smelled of alcohol. The woman slapped the dog's nose. The beefy man abruptly pulled the pen from the neck of his T-shirt, removed the cardboard coaster from under his beer, and wrote something on it, something very brief – one word, or a number. It was as if he had at last received a message from the ghostly trucking concern that had misplaced him here. The ping-pong sounded; the music resumed. The young Negro, changed out of costume back into his yellow pants and candy-striped boat-necked shirt, returned. Flexing his back and planting his palms on his hips, he again asked the strange girl at the corner of the bar to dance. This time, with a smile that revealed her slightly overlapping front teeth, she accepted.

Under the Microscope

It was not his kind of pond; the water tasted slightly acid. He was a Cyclops, the commonest of copepods, and this crowd seemed exotically cladoceran – stylish water-fleas with transparent carapaces, all shimmer and bubbles and twitch. His hostess, a magnificent Daphnia fully an eighth of an inch tall, her heart and cephalic ganglion visibly pulsing, welcomed him with

 a lavish gesture of her ciliate, branching antennae; for a moment he feared she would eat him. Instead she offered him a platter of living desmids. They were bright green in colour and shaped like crescents, hourglasses, omens. 'Who do you know here?' Her voice was a distant constant above the din. 'Everybody knows *you*, of course. They've read your books.' His books, taken all together, with generous margins, would easily have fitted on the period that ends this sentence.

The Cyclops modestly grimaced, answered 'No one,' and turned to a young specimen of water-mite, probably *Hydrachna geographica*, still bearing ruddy traces of the larval stage. 'Have you been here long?' he asked, meaning less the party than the pond.

'Long enough.' Her answer came as swiftly as a reflex. 'I go back to the surface now and then; we breathe air, you know.'

'Oh I know. I envy you.' He noticed she had only six legs. She was newly hatched, then. Between her eyes, arranged in two pairs, he counted a fifth, in the middle, and wondered if in her he might find his own central single optic amplified and confirmed. His antennules yearned to touch her red spots; he wanted to ask her, *What do you see?* Young as she was, partially formed, she appeared, alerted by his abrupt confession of envy, ready to respond to any question, however presuming.

But at that moment a monstrous fairy shrimp, an inch in length and extravagantly tinted blue, green, and bronze, swam by on its back, and

the water shuddered. Furious, the Cyclops asked the water-mite, 'Who invites *them*? They're not even in our scale.'

She shrugged permissively, showing that indeed she had been here long enough. 'They're entomostracans,' she said, 'just like Daphnia. They amuse her.'

'They're going to eat her up,' the Cyclops predicted.

Though she laughed, her fifth eye gazed steadily into his wide lone one. 'But isn't that what we all want? Subconsciously, of course.'

'Of course.'

An elegant, melancholy flat-worm was passing *hors d'oeuvres*. The Cyclops took some diatoms, cracked their delicate shells of silica, and ate them. They tasted golden brown. Growing hun-

grier, he pushed through to the serving table and had a Volvox in algae dip. A shrill little rotifer, his head cilia whirling, his three-toothed mastax chattering, leaped up before him, saying, with the mixture of put-on and pleading characteristic of this pond, 'I wead all your wunnaful books, and I have a wittle bag of pomes I wote myself, and I would wove it, *wove* it if you would wead them and wecommend them to a big bad pubwisher!' At a loss for a civil answer, the Cyclops considered the rotifer silently, then ate him. He tasted slightly acid.

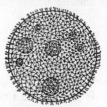

The party was thickening. A host of protozoans drifted in on a raft of sphagnum moss: a trumpet-shaped Stentor, apparently famous and interlocked with a lanky, bleached Spirostomum; a

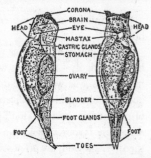

Labels in diagram: CORONA, BRAIN, HEAD, EYE, HEAD, MASTAX, GASTRIC GLANDS, STOMACH, OVARY, BLADDER, FOOT GLANDS, FOOT, FOOT, TOES

claque of paramœcia, swishing back and forth tickling the crustacea on the backs of their knees; an old Vorticella, a plant-like animalcule as dreary, the Cyclops thought, as the batch of puffs rooted to the flap of last year's *succès d'estime*. The kitchen was crammed with ostracods and flagellates engaged in mutually consuming conversation, and over in a

corner, beneath an African mask, a great brown hydra, the real thing, attached by its sticky foot to the hissing steam radiator, rhythmically swung its tentacles here and there until one of them touched, in the circle of admirers, something appetizing; then the poison sacs exploded, the other tentacles contracted, and the prey was stuffed into the hydra's swollen coelenteron, which gluttony had stretched to a transparency that veiled the preceding meals like polyethylene film protecting a rack of drycleaned suits.

Hairy with bacteria, a Simocephalus was munching a rapt nematode. The fairy shrimps, having multiplied, their crimson tails glowing with haemoglobin, came cruising in from the empty bedrooms. The party was thinning.

Suddenly fearful, fearing he had lost her for ever, the Cyclops searched for the water-mite, and found her miserably crouching in a corner, quite drunk, her seventh and eighth legs almost sprouted. 'What do you see?' he now dared ask.

'Too much,' she answered swiftly. 'Everything. Oh, it's horrible, horrible.'

Out of mercy as much as appetite, he ate her. She felt prickly inside him. Hurriedly – the rooms were almost depleted, it was late – he sought his hostess. She was by the doorway, her antennae frazzled from waving good-bye, but still magnificent, Daphnia, her carapace a liquid shimmer of psychedelic pastel. 'Don't go,' she commanded, expanding, 'I have a *minus*cule favour to ask. Now that my children, all thirteen billion of them, thank God, are off at school, I've taken a part-time editing job, and my first real break is this manuscript I'd be *so* grateful to have you read and comment on, whatever comes into your head, I admit it's a little long, maybe you can skim the part where Napoleon invades Russia, but it's the first *effort* by a perfectly delightful midge larva I know you'd enjoy meeting –'

'I'd adore to, but I can't,' he said, explaining, 'my eye. I can't afford to strain it, I have only this one . . .' He trailed off, he felt feebly. He was beginning to feel permeable, acidic.

'You poor dear,' Daphnia solemnly pronounced, and ate him.

And the next instant, a fairy shrimp, oaring by inverted, casually gathered her into the trough between his eleven pairs of undulating gill-feet and passed her towards his brazen mouth. Her scream, tinier than even the dot on this 'i', was unobserved.

During the Jurassic

Waiting for the first guests, the iguanodon gazed along the path and beyond, towards the monotonous cycad forests and the low volcanic hills. The landscape was everywhere interpenetrated by the sea, a kind of metallic blue rottenness that daily breathed in and out. Behind him, his wife was assembling the *hors d'oeuvres*. As he watched her, something unintended, something grossly solemn, in his expression made her laugh, displaying the leaf-shaped teeth lining her cheeks. Like him, she was an ornithischian, but much smaller – a compsognathus. He wondered, watching her race bipedally back and forth among the scraps of food

(dragonflies wrapped in ferns, cephalopods on toast), how he had ever found her beautiful. His eyes hungered for size; he experienced a rage for sheer blind size.

The stegosauri, of course, were the first to appear. Among their many stupid friends these were the most stupid, and the most punctual. Their front legs bent outward and their little filmy-eyed faces virtually skimmed the ground; the upward sweep of their backs was gigantic, and the double rows of giant bone plates  along the spine clicked together in the sway of their cumbersome gait. With hardly a greeting, they dragged their tails, quadruply spiked, across the threshold and manoeuvred themselves towards the bar, which was tended by a minute and shapeless mammal hired for the evening.

Next came the allosaurus, a carnivorous bachelor whose dangerous aura and needled grin excited the female herbivores; then Rhamphorhynchus, a pterosaur whose much admired 'flight' was in reality a clumsy brittle glide ending in an embarrassed bump and trot. The iguanodon despised these pterosaurs' pretensions, thought grotesque the precarious elongation of the single finger from which their levitating membranes were stretched, and privately believed that the less handsomely underwritten archaeopteryx, though sneered at as unstable and feathered, had more of a future. The hypsilophodon, with her graceful hands and branch-gripping feet, arrived escorted by the timeless crocodile – an incongruous pair, but both were recently divorced. Still the iguanodon gazed down the path.

Behind him, the conversation gnashed on a thousand things – houses, mortgages, lawns, fertilizers, erosion, boats, winds, annuities, capital gains, recipes, education, the day's tennis, last night's party. Each party was consumed by discussion of the previous one. Their lives were subject to constant cross-check. When did you leave? When did *you* leave? We'd been out every night this week. We had an amphibious babysitter who had to be back in the water by one. Gregor had to meet a client in town, and now they've reduced the Saturday schedule, it means the 7:43 or nothing. Trains? I thought they were totally extinct. Not at all. They're coming back, it's just a matter of time until the government . . . In the long range of evolution, they are still the most efficient . . . Taking into account the heat-loss/weight ratio and assuming there's no more glaciation . . . Did you know – I think this is fascinating – did you know that in the financing of those great ornate stations of the eighties and nineties, those real monsters, there was no provision for amortization? They weren't amortized at all, they were financed on the basis of eternity! The railroad was conceived of as the end of Progress! *I* think – though not an expert – that the key word in this overall industrio-socio-what-have-you-oh nexus or syndrome or bag or whatever is *overextended*. Any competitor-less object *bloats*. Personally, I miss the trolley cars. Now don't tell me I'm the only creature in the room old enough to remember the trolley cars!

The iguanodon's high pulpy heart jerked and seemed to split; the brontosaurus was coming up the path.

Her husband, the diplodocus, was with her. They moved together, rhythmic twins, buoyed by the hollow assurance of the huge. She paused to tear with her lips a clump of leaf from an overhanging palaeocycas. From her deliberate grace the iguanodon received the impression that she knew he was watching her. Indeed, she had long guessed his love, as had her husband. The two saurischians entered his party with the languid confidence of the specially cherished. In the teeth of the iguanodon's ironic stance, her bulk, her gorgeous size, enraptured him, swelled to fill the massive ache he carried when she was not there. She rolled outward across his senses – the dawn-pale underparts, the reticulate skin, the vast bluish muscles whose management required a second brain at the base of her spine.

Her husband, though even longer, was more slenderly built, and per-haps weighed less than twenty-five tons. His very manner was attenuated and tabescent. He had recently abandoned an orthodox business career to enter the Episcopalian seminary. This regression – as the iguanodon felt it – seemed to make his wife more prominent, less supported, more access-ible.

How splendid she was! For all the lavish solidity of her hips and legs, the modelling of her little flat diapsid skull was delicate. Her facial essence appeared to narrow, along the diagrammatic points of her auricles and eyes and nostrils, towards a single point, located in the air, of impermutable refinement and calm. This irreducible point was, he realized, in some sense her mind; the focus of the minimal interest she brought to play upon the inchoate and edible green world flowing all about her, buoying her, bathing her. The iguanodon felt himself as an upright speckled stain in this world. He felt himself, under her distant dim smile, impossibly

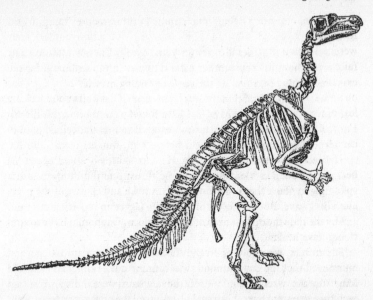

ugly: his mouth a sardonic chasm, his throat a pulsing curtain of scaly folds, his body a blotched bulb. His feet were heavy and horny and three-toed and his thumbs – strange adaptation! – were erect rigidities of pointed bone. Wounded by her presence, he savagely turned on her husband.

'*Comment va le bon Dieu?*'

'Ah?' The diplodocus was maddeningly good-humoured. Minutes elapsed as stimuli and reactions travelled back and forth across his length.

The iguanodon insisted. 'How are things in the supernatural?'

'The supernatural? I don't think that category exists in the new theology.'

'*N'est-ce pas?* What *does* exist in the new theology?'

'Love. Immanence as opposed to transcendence. Works as opposed to faith.'

'Work? I had thought you had quit work.'

'That's an unkind way of putting it. I prefer to think that I've changed employers.'

The iguanodon felt in the other's politeness a detestable aristocracy, the unappealable oppression of superior size. He said gnashingly, 'The Void pays wages?'

'Ah?'

'You mean there's a living in nonsense? I said nonsense. Dead, foetid nonsense.'

'Call it that it if makes it easier for you. Myself, I'm not a fast learner. Intellectual humility came rather natural to me. In the seminary, for the first time in my life, I feel on the verge of finding myself.'

'Yourself? That little thing? *Cette petite chose*? That's all you're looking for? Have you tried pain? Myself, I have found pain to be a great illuminator. *Permettez-moi.*' The iguanodon essayed to bite the veined base of the serpentine throat lazily upheld before him; but his teeth were too specialized and could not tear flesh. He abraded his lips and tasted his own salt blood. Disoriented, crazed, he thrust one thumb deep into a yielding grey flank that hove through the smoke and chatter of the party like a dull wave. But the nerves of his victim lagged in reporting the pain, and by the time the distant head of the diplodocus was notified, the wound would have healed.

The drinks were flowing freely. The mammal crept up to him and murmured that the dry vermouth was running out. The iguanodon told him to use the sweet. Behind the sofa the stegosauri were Indian-wrestling; each time one went over, his spinal plates raked the recently papered wall. The hypsilophodon, tipsy, perched on a banister; the allosaurus darted forward suddenly and ceremoniously nibbled her tail. On the far side of the room, by the great slack-stringed harp, the compsognathus and the brontosaurus were talking. He was drawn to them: amazed that his wife would presume to delay the much larger creature; to insert herself, with her scrabbling nervous motions and chattering leaf-shaped teeth, into the crevices of that queenly presence. As he drew closer to them, music began. His wife confided to him, 'The salad is running out.' He murmured to the brontosaurus, '*Chère madame, voulez-vous danser avec moi?*'

Her dancing was awkward, but even in this awkwardness, this ponderous stiffness, he felt the charm of her abundance. 'I've been talking to your husband about religion,' he told her, as they settled into the steps they could do.

'I've given up,' she said. 'It's such a deprivation for me and the children.'

'He says he's looking for himself.'

'It's so selfish,' she blurted. 'The children are teased at school.'

'Come live with me.'

'Can you support me?'

'No, but I would gladly sink under you.'

'You're sweet.'

'*Je t'aime.*'

'Don't. Not here.'

'Somewhere, then?'

'No. Nowhere. Never.' With what delightful precision did her miniature mouth encompass these infinitesimal concepts!

'But I,' he said, 'but I lo –'

'Stop it. You embarrass me. Deliberately.'

'You know what I wish? I wish all these beasts would disappear. What
do we see in each other? Why do we keep getting together?'

She shrugged. 'If they disappear, we will too.'

'I'm not so sure. There's something about us that would survive. It's
not in you and not in me but between us, where we almost meet. Some
vibration, some enduring cosmic factor. Don't you feel it?'

'Let's stop. It's too painful.'

'Stop dancing?'

'Stop being.'

'That is a beautiful idea. *Une belle idée.* I will if you will.'

'In time,' she said, and her fine little face precisely fitted this laconic
promise; and as the summer night yielded warmth to the multiplying
stars, he felt his blood sympathetically cool and grow thunderously, fruit-
fully slow.

Tarbox Tales

The Indian

The town, in New England, of Tarbox, restrained from embracing the sea by a margin of tawny salt marshes, locates its downtown four miles inland up the Musquenomenee River, which ceased to be tidal at the waterfall of the old hosiery mill, now given over to the manufacture of plastic toys. It was to the mouth of this river, in May of 1634, that the small party of seventeen men, led by the younger son of the Governor of the Massachusetts Bay Colony – Jeremiah Tarbox being only his second in command – came in three rough skiffs with the purpose of establishing amid such an unpossessed abundance of salt hay a pastoral plantation. This, with God's forbearance, they did. They furled their sails and slowly rowed, each boat being equipped with four oarlocks, in search of firm land, through marshes that must appear, now that their grass is no longer harvested by men driving horses shod in great wooden discs, much the same today as they did then – though undoubtedly the natural abundance of ducks, cranes, otter, and deer has been somewhat diminished. Tarbox himself, in his invaluable diary, notes that the squealing of the livestock in the third skiff attracted a great cloud of 'protestating sea-fowl'. The first houses (not one of which still stands, the oldest in town dating, in at least its central timbers and fireplace, from 1642) were strung along the base of the rise of firm land called Near Hill, which, with its companion Far Hill, a mile away, in effect bounds the densely populated section of the present township. In winter the population of Tarbox numbers something less than seven thousand; in summer the figure may be closer to nine thousand. The width of the river mouth and its sheltered advantage within Tarbox Bay seemed to promise the makings of a port to rival Boston; but in spite of repeated dredging operations the river has proved incorrigibly silty, and its shallow winding channels, rendered especially fickle where the fresh water of the river most powerfully clashes with the restless saline influx of the tide, frustrate all but pleasure craft. These Chris-Craft and Kit-Kats, skimming seaward through the exhilarating avenues of wild hay, in the early morning may pass, as the fluttering rust-coloured horizon abruptly yields to the steely blue monotone of the open water, a few dour clammers in hip boots patiently harrowing the tidewater floor. The intent posture of their silhouettes distinguishes them from the few bathers who have drifted down from the dying campfires by whose side they have dozed and sung and drunk away a night on the beach – one of the finest and least spoiled, it should be said, on the North Atlantic coast. Picturesque as Millet's gleaners, their torsos doubled like playing cards in the rosy mirror of the dawn-stilled sea, these sparse representatives of the clamming industry, founded in the eighteen-eighties by an immigration of Greeks and continually harassed by the industrial pollution upriver, exploit the sole vein of profit left in the name of old Musquenomenee. This shadowy chief broke the bread of peace with the son of the Governor, and within a year both were dead. The body of the one was returned to Boston to lie in the King's Chapel graveyard; the body of the other is supposedly buried, presumably upright, somewhere in the woods on the side of Far Hill where even now no houses have intruded, though the tract is rumoured to have been sold to a divider. Until the postwar arrival of Boston commuters, still much of a minority, Tarbox lived (discounting the summer people, who came and went in the marshes each year like the migrations of mallards) as a town apart. A kind of curse has kept its peace. The handmade-lace industry, which reached its peak just before the American Revolution, was destroyed by the industrial revolution; the textile mills, never numerous, were finally emptied by the industrialization of the South. They have been succeeded by a scattering of small enterprises, electronic in the main, which have staved off decisive depression.

Viewed from the spur of Near Hill where the fifth edifice, now called Congregationalist, of the religious society incorporated in 1635 on this identical spot thrusts its spire into the sky, and into a hundred coloured postcards purchasable at all four local drug-stores – viewed from this eminence, the business district makes a neat and prosperous impression. This is especially true at Christmastide, when coloured lights are strung from pole to pole, and at the height of summer, when girls in shorts and bathing suits decorate the pavements. A one-hour parking limit is enforced during business hours, but the traffic is congested only during the evening homeward exodus. A stoplight has never been thought quite necessary. A new Woolworth's with a noble façade of corrugated laminated Fiberglas has been erected on the site of a burned-out tenement. If the building which it vacated across the street went begging nearly a year for a tenant, and if some other properties along the street nervously change hands and wares now and then, nevertheless there is not that staring stretch of blank shopwindows which desolates the larger mill towns to the north and west. Two hardware stores confront each other without apparent rancour; three banks vie in promoting solvency; several luncheonettes withstand waves of factory workers and high-school students; and a small proud army of *petit-bourgeois* knights – realtors and lawyers and jewellers – parades up and down in clothes that would not look quaint on Madison Avenue. The explosive thrust of superhighways through the land has sprinkled on the town a cosmopolitan garnish; one resourceful divorcée has made a good thing of selling unabashedly smart women's clothes and Scandinavian kitchen accessories, and, next door, a foolish young matron nostalgic for Vassar has opened a combination paperback bookstore and art gallery, so that now the Tarbox town derelict, in sneaking with his cherry-red face and tot of rye from the liquor store to his home above the shoe-repair nook, must walk a garish gauntlet of abstract paintings by a minister's wife from Gloucester. Indeed, the whole street is laid open to an accusatory chorus of brightly packaged titles by Freud, Camus, and those others through whose masterworks our civilization moves towards its dark climax. Strange to say, so virulent is the spread of modern culture, some of these same titles can be had, seventy-five cents cheaper, in the homely old magazine-and-newspaper store in the middle of the block. Here, sitting stoically on the spines of the radiator behind the large left-hand window, the Indian can often be seen.

He sits in this window for hours at a time, politely waving to any passerby who happens to glance his way. It is hard always to avoid his eye, his form is so unexpected, perched on the radiator above cards of pipes and pyramids of Prince Albert tins and fanned copies of *True* and *Male* and *Sport*. He looks, behind glass, somewhat shadowy and thin, but outdoors he is solid enough. During other hours he takes up a station by Leonard's Pharmaceutical on the corner. There is a splintered telephone pole here that he leans against when he wearies of leaning against the brick wall. Occasionally he even sits upon the fire hydrant as if upon a campstool, arms folded, legs crossed, gazing across at the renovations on the face of Poirier's Liquor Mart. In cold or wet weather he may sit inside the drugstore, expertly prolonging a coffee at the counter, running his tobacco-dyed fingertip around and around the rim of the cup as he watches the steam fade. There are other spots – untenanted doorways, the benches halfway up the hill, idle chairs in the barbershops – where he loiters, and indeed there cannot be a square foot of the downtown pavement where he has not at some time or other paused; but these two spots, the window of the news store and the wall of the drugstore, are his essential habitat.

It is difficult to discover anything about him. He wears a plaid lumberjack shirt with a grey turtleneck sweater underneath, and chino pants, olive rather than khaki in colour, and remarkably white tennis sneakers. He smokes and drinks coffee, so he must have some income, but he does not, apparently, work. Inquiry reveals that now and then he is employed – during the last Christmas rush he was seen carrying baskets of Hong Kong shirts and Italian crèche elements through the aisles of the five-and-ten – but he soon is fired or quits, and the word 'lazy', given somehow more than its usual force of disapproval, sticks in the mind, as if this is the clue. Disconcertingly, he knows your name. Even though you are a young mutual-fund analyst newly bought into a neo-saltbox on the beach road and downtown on a Saturday morning to rent a wallpaper steamer, he smiles if he catches your eye, lifts his hand lightly, and says 'Good morning, Mr —,' supplying your name. Yet his own name is impossible to learn. The simplest fact about a person, identity's very seed, is in his case utterly hidden. It can be determined, by matching consistencies of hearsay, that he lives in that tall, speckle-shingled, disreputable hotel overlooking the atrophied railroad tracks, just down from the Amvets, where shuffling Polish widowers and one-night-in-town salesmen hang out, and in whose bar, evidently, money can be wagered and women may be approached. But his name, whether it is given to you as Tugwell or Frisbee or Wiggleworth, even if it were always the same name would be in its almost parodic Yankeeness incredible. 'But he's an Indian!'

The face of your informant – say, the chunky Irish dictator of the School Building Needs Committee, a dentist – undergoes a faint rapt transformation. His voice assumes its habitual whisper of extravagant discretion. 'Don't go around saying that. He doesn't like it. He prides himself on being a typical run-down Yankee.'

But he *is* an Indian. This is, alone, certain. Who but a savage would have such an immense capacity for repose? His cheek-bones, his never-faded skin, the delicate little jut of his scowl, the drooping triangularity of his eye sockets, the way his vertically lined face takes the light, the lustreless black of his hair are all so profoundly Indian that the imagination, surprised by his silhouette as he sits on the hydrant gazing across at the changing face of the liquor store, effortlessly plants a feather at the back of his head. His air of waiting, of gazing; the softness of his motions; the odd sense of proprietorship and ease that envelops him; the good humour that makes his vigil gently dreadful – all these are totally foreign to the shambling shy-eyes and moist lower lip of the failed Yankee. His age and status are too peculiar. He is surely older than forty and younger than sixty – but *is* this sure? And, though he greets everyone by name with a light wave of his hand, the conversation never passes beyond a greeting, and even in the news store, when the political contention and convivial obscenity literally drive housewives away from the door, he does not seem to participate. He witnesses, and now and then offers in a gravelly voice a debated piece of town history, but he does not participate.

It is caring that makes mysteries. As you grow indifferent, they lift. You live longer in the town, season follows season, the half-naked urban people arrive on the beach, multiply, and like leaves fall away again, and you have ceased to identify with them. The marshes turn green and withdraw through gold into brown, and their indolent, untouched, enduring existence penetrates your fibre. You find you must drive down towards the beach once a week or it is like a week without love. The ice cakes pile up along the banks of the tidal inlets like the rubble of ruined temples. You begin to meet, without seeking them out, the vestigial people: the unmarried daughters of vanished mill owners, the retired high-school teachers, the senile deacons in their unheated seventeenth-century houses with attics full of old church records in spidery brown ink. You enter, by way of an elderly baby-sitter, a world where at least they speak of him as 'the Indian'. An appalling snicker materializes in the darkness on the front seat beside you as you drive dear Mrs Knowlton home to her shuttered house on a back road. 'If you knew what they say, Mister, if you knew what they say.' And at last, as when in a woods you break through miles of underbrush into a clearing, you stand up surprised, taking a deep breath of the obvious, agreeing with the trees that of course this is the case. Anybody who is anybody knew all along. The mystery lifts, with some impatience, here, in Miss Horne's low-ceilinged front parlour, which smells of warm fireplace ashes and of peppermint balls kept ready in red-tinted knobbed glass goblets for whatever open-mouthed children might dare to come visit such a very old lady, all bent double like a little gripping rose clump, Miss Horne, a fable in her lifetime. Her father had been the sixth minister before the present one (whom she does *not* care for) at the First Church, and *his* father the next but one before him. There had been a Horne among those first seventeen men. Well – where was she? – yes, the Indian. The Indian had been loitering – waiting, if you prefer – in the centre of town when she was a tiny girl in gingham. And he is no older now than he was then.

The Hillies

The town of Tarbox was founded, in 1634, on the way north from Boston, by men fearful of attack. They built their fortified meeting-house on a rocky outcropping commanding a defensive view of the river valley, where a flotilla of canoes might materialize and where commerce and industry, when they peaceably came, settled of their own gravity. Just as the functions of the meeting-house slowly split between a town hall and a Congregational church, the town itself evolved two centres: the hilltop green and the downtown. On the green stands the present church, the sixth successive religious edifice on this site, a marvel (or outrage, depending upon your architectural politics) of poured concrete, encircled by venerable clapboarded homes that include the tiny old tilting post office (built 1741, decommissioned 1839) and its companion the one-time jail, recently transformed into a kinetic-art gallery by a young couple from Colorado. Downtown, a block or more of false fronts and show windows straggles towards the factory – once productive of textiles, now of plastic 'recreational products' such as inflatable rafts and seamless footballs. The street holds two hardware stores, three banks, a Woolworth's with a new façade of corrugated Fibreglass, the granite post office (built 1933) with its Japanese cherry trees outside and its Pilgrim murals inside, the new two-storey Town Hall of pre-rusted steel and thick brown glass, and a host of retail enterprises self-proclaimed by signs ranging in style from the heartily garish to the timidly tasteful, from 3-D neo-Superman to mimicry of the pallid script incised on Colonial tombstones. This downtown is no uglier than most, and its denizens can alleviate their prospect by lifting their eyes to the hill, where the church's parabolic peak gleams through the feathery foliage of the surviving elms. Between the green and the downtown lies an awkward steep area that has never been, until recently, settled at all. Solid ledge, this slope repelled buildings in the early days and by default became a half-hearted park, a waste tract diagonally skewered by several small streets, dotted with various memorial attempts – obelisks and urns – that have fallen short of impressiveness, and feebly utilized by a set of benches where, until recently, no one ever sat. For lately these leaden, eerily veined rocks and triangular patches of parched grass *have* been settled, by flocks of young people; they sit and lie here overlooking downtown Tarbox as if the spectacle is as fascinating as Dante's rose. Dawn finds them already in position, and midnight merely intensifies the murmur of their conversation, marred by screams and smashed bottles. The town, with the wit anonymously secreted within the most pedestrian of populations, has christened them 'the hillies'.

They are less exotic than hippies. Many are the offspring of prominent citizens; the son of the bank president is one, and the daughter of the meatmarket man is another. But even children one recognizes from the sidewalk days when they peddled lemonade or pedalled a tricycle stare now from the rocks with the hostile strangeness of marauders. Their solidarity appears absolute. Their faces, whose pallor is accented by smears of dirt, repel scrutiny; returning their collective stare is as difficult as gazing into a furnace or the face of a grieving widow. In honesty, some of these effects – of intense embarrassment, of menace – may be 'read into' the faces of the hillies; apart from lifting their voices in vague mockery, they make no threatening moves. They claim they want only to be left alone.

When did they arrive? Their advent merges with the occasional vagrant sleeping on a bench, and with the children who used to play here while their mothers shopped. At first, they seemed to be sunning; the town is famous for its beach, and acquiring a tan falls within our code of coherent behaviour. Then, as the hillies were seen to be sitting up and clothed in floppy costumes that covered all but their hands and faces, it was supposed that their congregation was sexual in motive; the rocks were a pickup point for the lovers' lanes among the ponds and pines and quarries on the dark edges of the town. True, the toughs of neighbouring villages swarmed in, racing their Hondas and Mustangs in a preening, suggestive fashion. But our flaxen beauties, if they succumbed, always returned to dream on the hill; and then it seemed that the real reason was drugs. Certainly their torpitude transcends normal physiology. And certainly the afternoon air is sweet with pot, and pushers of harder stuff come out from Boston at appointed times. None of our suppositions has proved entirely false, even the first, for on bright days some of the young men do shuck their shirts and lie spread-eagled under the sun, on the brown grass by the Civil War obelisk. Yet the sun burns best at the beach, and sex and dope can be enjoyed elsewhere, even – so anxious are we parents to please – in the hillies' own homes.

With the swift pragmatism that is triumphantly American, the town now tolerates drugs in its midst. Once a scandalous rumour on the rim of possibility, drugs moved inward, became a scandal that must be faced, and now loom as a commonplace reality. The local hospital proficiently treats fifteen-year-old girls deranged by barbiturates, and our family doctors matter-of-factly counsel their adolescent patients against the dangers, such as infectious hepatitis, of dirty needles. That surprising phrase woven into our flag, 'the pursuit of happiness', waves above the shaggy, dazed heads on the hill; a local parson has suggested that the community sponsor a 'turn-on' centre for rainy days and cold weather. Yet the hillies respond with silence. They pointedly decline to sit on the green that holds the church, though they have been offered sanctuary from police harassment there. The town discovers itself scorned by a mystery beyond drugs, by an implacable 'no' spoken between its two traditional centres. And the numbers grow; as many as seventy were counted the other evening.

We have spies. The clergy mingle and bring back reports of intelligent, uplifting conversations; the only rudeness they encounter is the angry shouting ('Animals!' 'Enlist!') from the passing carfuls of middle–aged bourgeoisie. The guidance director at the high school, wearing a three days' beard and blotched blue jeans, passes out questionnaires. Two daring young housewives have spent an entire night on the hill, with a tape recorder concealed in a picnic hamper. The police, those bone-chilled sentries on the boundaries of chaos, have developed their expertise by the intimate light of warfare. They sweep the rocks clean every second hour all night, which discourages cooking fires, and have instituted, via a few quisling hillies, a form of self-policing. Containment, briefly, is their present policy. The select-men cling to the concept of the green as 'common land', intended for public pasturage. By this interpretation, the hillies graze, rather than trespass. Nothing is simple. Apparently there are strata and class animosities within the hillies – the 'grassies', for example, who smoke marijuana in the middle area of the slope, detest the 'beeries', who inhabit the high rocks, where they smash their no-return bottles, fist-fight, and bring the wrath of the town down upon them all. The grassies also dislike the 'pillies', who loll beneath them, near the kerb, and who take harder drugs, and who deal with the sinister salesmen from Boston. It is these pillies, stretched bemused between the Spanish-American War memorial urns, who could tell us, if we wished to know, how the trashy façades of Poirier's Liquor Mart and Leonard's Pharmaceutical Store appear when deep-dyed by LSD and ballooned by the Eternal. In a sense, they see an America whose glory is hidden from the rest of us.

The guidance director's questionnaires reveal some surprising statistics. Twelve per cent of the hillies favour the Vietnam war. Thirty-four per cent have not enjoyed sexual intercourse. Sixty-one per cent own their own automobiles. Eighty-six per cent hope to attend some sort of graduate school.

Each week, the Tarbox *Star* prints more of the vivacious correspondence occasioned by the hillies. One taxpayer writes to say that God has forsaken the country, that these young people are fungi on a fallen tree. Another, a veteran of the Second World War, replies that on the contrary they are harbingers of hope, super-Americans dedicated to saving a mad world from self-destruction; if he didn't have a family to support, he would go and join them. A housewife writes to complain of loud obscenities that wing outward from the hill. Another housewife promptly rebuts all such 'credit-card hypocrites, instalment-plan lechers, and Pharisees in plastic curlers'. A hillie writes to assert that he was driven from his own home by 'the stench of ego' and 'heartbreaking lasciviousness'. The father of a hillie, in phrases broken and twisted by the force of his passion, describes circumstantially his child's upbringing in an atmosphere of love and plenty and in conclusion hopes that other parents will benefit from the hard lesson of his present disgrace - a punishment he 'nightly embraces with grateful prayer'. Various old men write in to reminisce about their youths. Some remember hard work, bitter winters, and penny-pinching; others depict a lyrically empty land where a boy's natural prankishness and tendency to idle had room to 'run their course'. One 'old-timer' states that 'there is nothing new under the sun'; another sharply retorts that *everything* is new under the sun, that these youngsters are 'subconsciously seeking accommodation' with unprecedented overpopulation and 'hyper-technology'. The Colorado couple write from their gallery to agree, and to suggest that salvation lies in Hindu reposefulness, 'free-form creativity', and wheat germ. A downtown businessman observes that the hillies have become something of a tourist attraction and should not be disbanded 'without careful preliminary study'. A minister cautions readers to 'let him who is without sin cast the first stone'. The editor editorializes to the effect that 'our' generation has made a 'mess' of the world and that the hillies are registering a 'legitimate protest'; a letter signed by sixteen hillies responds that they protest nothing, they just want to sit and 'dig'. 'Life as it is,' the letter (a document mimeographed and distributed by the local chapter of PAX) concludes, 'truly grooves.'

The printed correspondence reflects only a fraction of the opinions expressed orally. The local sociologist has told a luncheon meeting of the

Rotary Club that the hillies are seeking 'to re-employ human-ness as a non-relative category'. The local Negro, a crack golfer and horseman whose seat on his chestnut mare is the pride of the local hunt club, cryptically told the Kiwanis that 'when you create a slave population, you must expect a slave mentality'. The local Jesuit informed an evening meeting of the Lions that drugs are 'the logical end product of the pernicious Protestant heresy of the "inner light" '. The waitresses at the local restaurant tell customers that the sight of the hillies through the plate-glass windows gives them 'the creeps'. 'Why don't they go to *work*?' they ask; their own legs are blue-veined from the strain of work, of waiting and hustling. The local Indian, who might be thought sympathetic, since some of the hillies affect Pocahontas bands and bead necklaces, is savage on the subject: 'Clean the garbage out,' he tells the seedy crowd that hangs around the liquor mart. 'Push 'em back where they came from.' But this ancient formula, so often invoked in our history, no longer applies. They came from our own homes. And in honesty do we want them back? How much a rural myth is parental love? The Prodigal Son no doubt became a useful overseer; they needed his hands. We need our self-respect. That is what is eroding on the hill – the foundations of our lives, the identities our industry and acquisitiveness have heaped up beneath the flag's blessing. The local derelict is the only adult who wanders among them without self-consciousness and without fear.

For fear is the mood. People are bringing the shutters down from their attics and putting them back on their windows. Fences are appearing where children used to stray freely from back yard to back yard, through loose hedges of forsythia and box. Locksmiths are working overtime. Once we parked our cars with the keys dangling from the dashboard, and a dog could sleep undisturbed in the middle of the street. No more. Fear reigns, and impatience. The downtown seems to be tightening like a fist, a glistening clot of apoplectic signs and sunstruck, stalled automobiles. And the hillies are slowly withdrawing upward, and clustering around the beeries, and accepting them as leaders. They are getting ready for our attack.

A & P

In walks these three girls in nothing but bathing suits. I'm in the third checkout slot, with my back to the door, so I don't see them until they're over by the bread. The one that caught my eye first was the one in the plaid green two-piece. She was a chunky kid, with a good tan and a sweet broad soft-looking can with those two crescents of white just under it, where the sun never seems to hit, at the top of the backs of her legs. I stood there with my hand on a box of HiHo crackers trying to remember if I rang it up or not. I ring it up again and the customer starts giving me hell. She's one of these cash-register-watchers, a witch about fifty with rouge on her cheekbones and no eyebrows, and I know it made her day to trip me up. She'd been watching cash registers for fifty years and probably never seen a mistake before.

By the time I got her feathers smoothed and her goodies into a bag – she gives me a little snort in passing, if she'd been born at the right time they would have burned her over in Salem – by the time I get her on her way the girls had circled around the bread and were coming back, without a pushcart, back my way along the counters, in the aisle between the checkouts and the Special bins. They didn't even have shoes on. There was this chunky one, with the two-piece – it was bright green and the seams on the bra were still sharp and her belly was still pretty pale so I guessed she just got it (the suit) – there was this one, with one of those chubby berry-faces, the lips all bunched together under her nose, this one, and a tall one, with black hair that hadn't quite frizzed right, and one of these sunburns right across under the eyes, and a chin that was too long – you know, the kind of girl other girls think is very 'striking' and 'attractive' but never quite makes it, as they very well know, which is why they like her so much – and then the third one, that wasn't quite so tall. She was the queen. She kind of led them, the other two peeking around and making their shoulders round. She didn't look around, not this queen, she just walked straight on slowly, on these long white prima-donna legs. She came down a little hard on her heels, as if she didn't walk in her bare feet that much, putting down her heels and then letting the weight move along to her toes as if she was testing the floor with every step, putting a little deliberate extra action into it. You never know for sure how girls' minds work (do you really think it's a mind in there or just a little buzz like a bee in a glass jar?) but you got the idea she had talked the other two into coming in here with her, and now she was showing them how to do it, walk slow and hold yourself straight.

She had on a kind of dirty-pink – beige maybe, I don't know – bathing suit with a little nubble all over it and, what got me, the straps were down. They were off her shoulders looped loose around the cool tops of her arms, and I guess as a result the suit had slipped a little on her, so all around the top of the cloth there was this shining rim. If it hadn't been there you wouldn't have known there could have been anything whiter than those shoulders. With the straps pushed off, there was nothing between the top of the suit and the top of her head except just *her*, this clean bare plane of the top of her chest down from the shoulder bones like a dented sheet of metal tilted in the light. I mean, it was more than pretty.

She had sort of oaky hair that the sun and salt had bleached, done up in a bun that was unravelling, and a kind of prim face. Walking into the A & P with your straps down, I suppose it's the only kind of face you *can* have. She held her head so high her neck, coming up out of those white shoulders, looked kind of stretched, but I didn't mind. The longer her neck was, the more of her there was.

She must have felt in the corner of her eye me and over my shoulder Stokesie in the second slot watching, but she didn't tip. Not this queen. She kept her eyes moving across the racks, and stopped, and turned so slow it made my stomach rub the inside of my apron, and buzzed to the other two, who kind of huddled against her for relief, and then they all three of them went up the cat-and-dog-food-breakfast-cereal-macaroni-rice-raisins-seasonings-spreads-spaghetti-soft-drinks-crackers-and-cookies aisle. From the third slot I look straight up the aisle to the meat counter, and I watched them all the way. The fat one with the tan sort of fumbled with the cookies, but on second thought she put the package back. The sheep pushing their carts down the aisle – the girls were walking against the usual traffic (not that we have one-way signs or anything) – were pretty hilarious. You could see them, when Queenie's white shoulders dawned on them, kind of jerk, or hop, or hiccup, but their eyes snapped back to their own baskets and on they pushed. I bet you could set off dynamite in an A & P and the people would by and large keep reaching and checking oatmeal off their lists and muttering 'Let me see, there was a third thing, began with A, asparagus, no, ah, yes, apple-sauce!' or whatever it is they do mutter. But there was no doubt, this jiggled them. A few houseslaves in pin curlers even looked around after pushing their carts past to make sure what they had seen was correct.

You know, it's one thing to have a girl in a bathing suit down on the beach, where what with the glare nobody can look at each other much anyway, and another thing in the cool of the A & P, under the fluorescent lights, against all those stacked packages, with her feet paddling along naked over our checkerboard green-and-cream rubber-tile floor.

'Oh Daddy,' Stokesie said beside me. 'I feel so faint.'

'Darling,' I said. 'Hold me tight.' Stokesie's married, with two babies chalked up on his fuselage already, but as far as I can tell that's the only difference. He's twenty-two, and I was nineteen this April.

'Is it done?' he asks, the responsible married man finding his voice. I forgot to say he thinks he's going to be manager some sunny day, maybe in 1990 when it's called the Great Alexandrov and Petrooshki Tea Company or something.

What he meant was, our town is five miles from a beach, with a big summer colony out on the Point, but we're right in the middle of town, and the women generally put on a shirt or shorts or something before they get out of the car into the street. And anyway these are usually women with six children and varicose veins mapping their legs and nobody, including them, could care less. As I say, we're right in the middle of town, and if you stand at our front doors you can see two banks and the Congregational church and the newspaper store and three real-estate offices and about twenty-seven old freeloaders tearing up Central Street because the sewer broke again. It's not as if we're on the Cape; we're north of Boston and there's people in this town haven't seen the ocean for twenty years.

The girls had reached the meat counter and were asking McMahon something. He pointed, they pointed, and they shuffled out of sight behind a pyramid of Diet Delight peaches. All that was left for us to see was old McMahon patting his mouth and looking after them sizing up their joints. Poor kids, I began to feel sorry for them, they couldn't help it.

Now here comes the sad part of the story, at least my family says it's sad, but I don't think it's so sad myself. The store's pretty empty, it being Thursday afternoon, so there was nothing much to do except lean on the register and wait for the girls to show up again. The whole store was like a pinball machine and I didn't know which tunnel they'd come out of. After a while they come around out of the far aisle, around the light bulbs, records at discount of the Caribbean Six or Tony Martin Sings or some such gunk you wonder they waste the wax on, sixpacks of candy bars, and plastic toys done up in cellophane that fall apart when a kid looks at them anyway. Around they come, Queenie still leading the way, and holding a little grey jar in her hand. Slots Three through Seven are unmanned and I could see her wondering between Stokesie and me, but Stokesie with his usual luck draws an old party in baggy grey pants who stumbles up with four giant cans of pineapple juice (what do these bums *do* with all that pineapple juice? I've often asked myself) so the girls come to me. Queenie puts down the jar and I take it into my fingers icy cold. Kingfish Fancy Herring Snacks in Pure Sour Cream: 49c. Now her hands are empty, not a ring or a bracelet, bare as God made them, and I wonder where the money's coming from. Still with that prim look she lifts a folded dollar bill out of the hollow at the centre of her nubbled pink top. The jar went heavy in my hand. Really, I thought that was so cute.

Then everybody's luck begins to run out. Lengel comes in from haggling with a truck full of cabbages on the lot and is about to scuttle into that door marked MANAGER behind which he hides all day when the girls touch his eye. Lengel's pretty dreary, teaches Sunday school and the rest, but he doesn't miss much. He comes over and says, 'Girls, this isn't the beach.'

Queenie blushes, though maybe it's just a brush of sunburn I was noticing for the first time, now that she was so close. 'My mother asked me to pick up a jar of herring snacks.' Her voice kind of startled me, the way voices do when you see the people first, coming out so flat and dumb yet kind of tony, too, the way it ticked over 'pick up' and 'snacks'. All of a sudden I slid right down her voice into her living room. Her father and the other men were standing around in ice-cream coats and bow ties and the women were in sandals picking up herring snacks on toothpicks off a big glass plate and they were all holding drinks the colour of water with olives and sprigs of mint in them. When my parents have somebody over they get lemonade and if it's a real racy affair Schlitz in tall glasses with 'They'll Do It Every Time' cartoons stencilled on.

'That's all right,' Lengel said. 'But this isn't the beach.' His repeating this struck me as funny, as if it had just occurred to him, and he had been thinking all these years the A & P was a great big dune and he was the head lifeguard. He didn't like my smiling – as I say he doesn't miss much – but he concentrates on giving the girls that sad Sunday-school-superintendent stare.

Queenie's blush is no sunburn now, and the plump one in plaid, that I liked better from the back – a really sweet can – pipes up, 'We weren't doing any shopping. We just came in for the one thing.'

'That makes no difference,' Lengel tells her, and I could see from the way his eyes went that he hadn't noticed she was wearing a two-piece before. 'We want you decently dressed when you come in here.'

'We *are* decent,' Queenie says suddenly, her lower lip pushing, getting sore now that she remembers her place, a place from which the crowd that runs the A & P must look pretty crummy. Fancy Herring Snacks flashed in her very blue eyes.

'Girls, I don't want to argue with you. After this come in here with your shoulders covered. It's our policy.' He turns his back. That's policy for you. Policy is what the kingpins want. What the others want is juvenile delinquency.

All this while, the customers had been showing up with their carts but, you know, sheep, seeing a scene, they had all bunched up on Stokesie, who shook open a paper bag as gently as peeling a peach, not wanting to miss a word. I could feel in the silence everybody getting nervous, most of all Lengel, who asks me, 'Sammy, have you rung up their purchase?'

I thought and said 'No' but it wasn't about that I was thinking. I go through the punches, 4, 9, GROC, TOT – it's more complicated than you think, and after you do it often enough, it begins to make a little song, that you hear words to, in my case 'Hello (*bing*) there, you (*gung*) hap-py *pee*-pul (*splat*)!' – the *splat* being the drawer flying out. I uncrease the bill, tenderly as you may imagine, it just having come from between the two smoothest scoops of vanilla I had ever known were there, and pass a half and a penny into her narrow pink palm, and nestle the herrings in a bag and twist its neck and hand it over, all the time thinking.

The girls, and who'd blame them, are in a hurry to get out, so I say 'I quit' to Lengel quick enough for them to hear, hoping they'll stop and watch me, their unsuspected hero. They keep right on going, into the electric eye; the door flies open and they flicker across the lot to their car, Queenie and Plaid and Big Tall Goony-Goony (not that as raw material she was so bad), leaving me with Lengel and a kink in his eyebrow.

'Did you say something, Sammy?'

'I said I quit.'

'I thought you did.'

'You didn't have to embarrass them.'

'It was they who were embarrassing us.'

I started to say something that came out 'Fiddle-de-doo.' It's a saying of my grandmother's, and I know she would have been pleased.

'I don't think you know what you're saying,' Lengel said.

'I know you don't,' I said. 'But I do.' I pull the bow at the back of my apron and start shrugging it off my shoulders. A couple of customers that had been heading for my slot begin to knock against each other, like scared pigs in a chute.

Lengel sighs and begins to look very patient and old and grey. He's been a friend of my parents for years. 'Sammy, you don't want to do this to your Mom and Dad,' he tells me. It's true, I don't. But it seems to me that once you begin a gesture it's fatal not to go through with it. I fold the apron, 'Sammy' stitched in red on the pocket, and put it on the counter, and drop the bow tie on top of it. The bow tie is theirs, if you've ever wondered. 'You'll feel this for the rest of your life,' Lengel says, and I know that's true, too, but remembering how he made that pretty girl blush makes me so scrunchy inside I punch the No Sale tab and the machine whirs 'pee-pul' and the drawer splats out. One advantage to this scene taking place in summer, I can follow this up with a clean exit, there's no fumbling around getting your coat and galoshes, I just saunter into the electric eye in my white shirt that my mother ironed the night before, and the door heaves itself open, and outside the sunshine is skating around on the asphalt.

I look around for my girls, but they're gone, of course. There wasn't anybody but some young married screaming with her children about some candy they didn't get by the door of a powder-blue Falcon station wagon. Looking back in the big windows, over the bags of peat moss and aluminium lawn furniture stacked on the pavement, I could see Lengel in my place in the slot, checking the sheep through. His face was dark grey and his back stiff, as if he'd just had an injection of iron, and my stomach kind of fell as I felt how hard the world was going to be to me hereafter.

Lifeguard

Beyond doubt, I am a splendid fellow. In the autumn, winter, and spring, I execute the duties of a student of divinity; in the summer I disguise myself in my skin and become a lifeguard. My slightly narrow and gingerly hirsute but not necessarily unmanly chest becomes brown. My smooth back turns the colour of caramel, which, in conjunction with the whipped cream of my white pith helmet, gives me, some of my teenage satellites assure me, a delightfully edible appearance. My legs, which I myself can study, cocked as they are before me while I repose on my elevated wooden throne, are dyed a lustreless maple walnut that accentuates their articulate strength. Correspondingly, the hairs of my body are bleached blond, so that my legs have the pointed elegance of, within the flower, umber anthers dusted with pollen.

For nine months of the year, I pace my pale hands and burning eyes through immense pages of Biblical text barnacled with fudging commentary; through multi-volumed apologetics couched in a falsely friendly Victorian voice and bound in subtly abrasive boards of finely ridged, pre-faded red; through handbooks of liturgy and histories of dogma; through the bewildering duplicities of Tillich's divine politicking; through the suave table talk of Father D'Arcy, Étienne Gilson, Jacques Maritain, and other such moderns mistakenly put at their ease by the exquisite furniture and overstuffed larder of the hospitable St Thomas; through the terrifying attempts of Kierkegaard, Berdyaev, and Barth to scourge God into being. I sway appalled on the ladder of minus signs by which theologians would surmount the void. I tiptoe like a burglar into the house of naturalism to steal the silver. An acrobat, I swing from wisp to wisp. Newman's iridescent cobwebs crush in my hands. Pascal's blackboard mathematics are erased by a passing shoulder. The cave drawings, astoundingly vital by candlelight, of those aboriginal magicians, Paul and Augustine, in daylight fade into mere anthropology. The diverting productions of literary flirts like Chesterton, Eliot, Auden, and Greene – whether they regard Christianity as a pastel forest designed for a fairyland romp or a deliciously miasmic pit from which chiaroscuro can be mined with mechanical buckets – in the end all infallibly strike, despite the comic variety of gongs and mallets, the note of the rich young man who on the coast of Judaea refused in dismay to sell all that he had.

Then, for the remaining quarter of the solar revolution, I rest my eyes on a sheet of brilliant sand printed with the runes of naked human bodies. That there is no discrepancy between my studies, that the texts of the flesh complement those of the mind, is the easy burden of my sermon.

On the back rest of my lifeguard's chair is painted a cross – true, a red cross, signifying bandages, splints, spirits of ammonia, and sunburn unguents. Nevertheless, it comforts me. Each morning, as I mount into my chair, my athletic and youthfully fuzzy toes expertly gripping the slats that make a ladder, it is as if I am climbing into an immense, rigid, loosely fitting vestment.

Again, in each of my roles I sit attentively perched on the edge of an immensity. That the sea, with its multiform and mysterious hosts, its savage and senseless rages, no longer comfortably serves as a divine metaphor indicates how severely humanism has corrupted the apples of our creed. We seek God now in flowers and good deeds, and the immensities of blue that surround the little scabs of land upon which we draw our lives to their unsatisfactory conclusions are suffused by science with vacuous horror. I myself can hardly bear the thought of stars, or begin to count the mortalities of coral. But from my chair the sea, slightly distended by my higher perspective, seems a misty old gentleman stretched at his ease in an immense armchair which has for arms the arms of this bay and for an antimacassar the freshly laundered sky. Sailboats float on his surface like idle and unrelated but benevolent thoughts. The soughing of the surf is the rhythmic lifting of his ripple-stitched vest as he breathes. Consider. We enter the sea with a shock; our skin and blood shout in protest. But, that instant, that leap, past, what do we find? Ecstasy and buoyance. Swimming offers a parable. We struggle and thrash, and drown; we succumb, even in despair, and float, and are saved.

With what timidity, with what a sense of trespass, do I set forward even this obliquely a thought so official! Forgive me. I am not yet ordained; I am too disordered to deal with the main text. My competence is marginal, and I will confine myself to the gloss of flesh with which this particular margin, this one beach, is annotated each day.

Here the cinema of life is run backwards. The old are the first to arrive. They are idle, and have lost the gift of sleep. Each of our bodies is a clock that loses time. Young as I am, I can hear in myself the protein acids ticking; I wake at odd hours and in the shuddering darkness and silence feel my death rushing towards me like an express train. The older we get, and the fewer the mornings left to us, the more deeply dawn stabs us awake. The old ladies wear wide straw hats and, in their hats' shadows, smiles as wide, which they bestow upon each other, upon salty shells they discover in the morning-smooth sand, and even upon me, downy-eyed from my night of dissipation. The gentlemen are often incongruous; withered white legs support brazen barrel chests, absurdly potent, bustling with white froth. How these old roosters preen on their 'condition'! With what fatuous expertness they swim in the icy water – always, however, prudently parallel to the shore, at a depth no greater than their height.

Then come the middle-aged, burdened with children and aluminium chairs. The men are scarred with the marks of their vocation – the red forearms of the gasoline-station attendant, the pale X on the back of the overall-wearing mason or carpenter, the clammer's nicked ankles. The hair on their bodies has as many patterns as matted grass. The women are wrinkled but fertile, like the Iraqi rivers that cradled the seeds of our civilization. Their children are odious. From their gaunt faces leer all the vices, the greeds, the grating urgencies of the adult, unsoftened by maturity's reticence and fatigue. Except that here and there, a girl, the eldest daughter, wearing a knit suit striped horizontally with green, purple, and brown, walks slowly, carefully, puzzled by the dawn enveloping her thick smooth body, her waist not yet nipped but her throat elongated.

Finally come the young. The young matrons bring fat and fussing infants who gobble the sand like sugar, who toddle blissfully into the surf and bring me bolt upright on my throne. My whistle tweets. The mothers rouse. Many of these women are pregnant again, and sluggishly lie in their loose suits like cows tranced in a meadow. They gossip politics, and smoke incessantly, and lift their troubled eyes in wonder as a trio of flat-stomached nymphs parades past. These maidens take all our eyes. The vivacious redhead, freckled and white-footed, pushing against her boy and begging to be ducked; the solemn brunette, transporting the vase of herself with held breath; the dimpled blonde in the bib and diapers of her Bikini, the lambent fuzz of her midriff shimmering like a cat's belly. Lust stuns me like the sun.

You are offended that a divinity student lusts? What prigs the unchurched are. Are not our assaults on the supernatural lascivious, a kind of indecency? If only you knew what de Sadian degradations, what frightful psychological spelunking, our gentle transcendentalist professors set us to, as preparation for our work, which is to shine in the darkness.

I feel that my lust makes me glow; I grow cold in my chair, like a torch of ice, as I study beauty. I have studied much of it, wearing all styles of bathing suit and facial expression, and have come to this conclusion; a woman's beauty lies, not in any exaggeration of the specialized zones, nor in any general harmony that could be worked out by means of the *sectio aurea* or a similar aesthetic superstition; but in the arabesque of the spine. The curve by which the back modulates into the buttocks. It is here that grace sits and rides a woman's body.

I watch from my white throne and pity women, deplore the demented judgement that drives them towards the braggart muscularity of the meso-morph and the prosperous complacence of the endomorph when it is we ectomorphs who pack in our scrawny sinews and exacerbated nerves the most intense gift, the most generous shelter, of love. To desire a woman is to desire to save her. Anyone who has endured intercourse that was neither predatory nor hurried knows how through it we descend, with a partner, into the grotesque and delicate shadows that until then have remained locked in the most guarded recess of our soul: into this harbour we bring her. A vague and twisted terrain becomes inhabited; each shadow, touched by the exploration, blooms into a flower of act. As if we are an island upon which a woman, tossed by her labouring vanity and blind self-seeking, is blown, and there finds security, until, an instant before the anticlimax, Nature with a smile thumps down her trump, and the island sinks beneath the sea.

There is great truth in those motion pictures which are slandered as true neither to the Bible nor to life. They are – written though they are by demons and drunks – true to both. We are all Solomons lusting for Sheba's salvation. The God-filled man is filled with a wilderness that cries to be populated. The stony chambers need jewels, furs, tints of cloth and flesh, even though, as in Samson's case, the temple comes tumbling. Women are an alien race of pagans set down among us. Every seduction is a conversion.

Who has loved and not experienced that sense of rescue? It is not true that our biological impulses are tricked out with ribands of chivalry; rather, our chivalric impulses go clanking in encumbering biological armour. Eunuchs love. Children love. I would love.

My chief exercise, as I sit above the crowds, is to lift the whole mass into immortality. It is not a light task; the throng is so huge, and its members so individually unworthy. No *memento mori* is so clinching as a photograph of a vanished crowd. Cheering Roosevelt, celebrating the Armistice, there it is, wearing its ten thousand straw hats and stiff collars, a fearless and wooden-faced bustle of life: it is gone. A crowd dies in the street like a derelict; it leaves no heir, no trace, no name. My own persist-ence beyond the last rim of time is easy to imagine; indeed, the effort of imagination lies the other way – to conceive of my ceasing. But when I study the vast tangle of humanity that blackens the beach as far as the sand stretches, absurdities crowd in on me. Is it as maiden, matron, or crone that the females will be eternalized? What will they do without children to watch and gossip to exchange? What of the thousand deaths of memory and bodily change we endure – can each be redeemed at a final Adjustments Counter? The sheer numbers involved make the mind scream. The race is no longer a tiny clan of simian aristocrats lording it over an ocean of grass; mankind is a plague racing like fire across the exhausted continents. This immense clot gathered on the beach, a fraction of a fraction – can we not say that this breeding swarm is its own immortality and end the suspense? The beehive in a sense survives; and is each of us not proved to be a hive, a galaxy of cells each of whom is doubtless praying, from its pew in our thumbnail or oesophagus, for personal resurrection? Indeed, to the cells themselves cancer may seem a revival of faith. No, in relation to other people oblivion is sensible and sanitary.

This sea of others exasperates and fatigues me most on Sunday mornings. I don't know why people no longer go to church – whether they have lost the ability to sing or the willingness to listen. From eight-thirty onwards they crowd in from the parking lot, ants each carrying its crumb of baggage, until by noon, when the remote churches are releasing their gallant and gaily dressed minority, the sea itself is jammed with hollow heads and thrashing arms like a great bobbing backwash of rubbish. A transistor radio somewhere in the sand releases in a thin, apologetic gust the closing peal of a transcribed service. And right here, here at the very height of torpor and confusion, I slump, my eyes slit, and the blurred forms of Protestantism's errant herd seem gathered by the water's edge in impassioned poses of devotion. I seem to be lying dreaming in the infinite rock of space before Creation, and the actual scene I see is a vision of impossibility: a Paradise. For had we existed before the gesture that split the firmament, could we have conceived of our most obvious possession, our most platitudinous blessing, the moment, the single ever-present moment that we perpetually bring to our lips brimful?

So: be joyful. Be Joyful is my commandment. It is the message I read in your jiggle. Stretch your skins like pegged hides curing in the miracle of the sun's moment. Exult in your legs' scissoring, your waist's swivel. Romp; eat the froth; be children. I am here above you; I have given my youth that you may do this. I wait. The tides of time have treacherous under-currents. You are borne continually towards the horizon. I have prepared myself; my muscles are instilled with everything that must be done. Someday my alertness will bear fruit; from near the horizon there will arise, delicious, translucent, like a green bell above the water, the call for help, the call, a call, it saddens me to confess, that I have yet to hear.

The Deacon

He passes the plate, and counts the money afterwards – a large dogged-looking man, wearing metal-framed glasses that seem tight across his face and that bite into the flesh around his eyes. He wears for Sunday morning a clean white shirt, but a glance downward, as you lay on your thin envelope and pass the golden plate back to him, discovers fallen socks and scuffed shoes. And as he with his fellow-deacons strides forward towards the altar, his suit is revealed as the pants of one suit (grey) and the coat of another (brown). He is too much at home here. During the sermon, he stares towards a corner of the nave ceiling, which needs repair, and slowly, reverently, yet unmistakably chews gum. He lingers in the vestibule, with his barking, possessive laugh, when the rest of the congregation has passed into the sunshine and the dry-mouthed minister is fidgeting to be out of his cassock and home to lunch. The deacon's car, a dusty Dodge, is parked outside the parish hall most evenings. He himself wonders why he is there so often, how he slipped into this ceaseless round of men's suppers, of Christian Education Committee meetings, choir rehearsals, emergency sessions of the Board of Finance where hours churn by in irrelevant argument and prayerful silences that produce nothing. 'Nothing,' he says to his wife on returning, waking her. 'The old fool refuses to amortize the debt.' He means the treasurer. 'His Eminence tells us foreign missions can't be applied to the oil bill even if we make it up in the summer at five per cent interest.' He means the minister. 'It was on the tip of my tongue to ask whence he derives all his business expertise.'

'Why don't you resign?' she asks. 'Let the young people get involved before they drop away.'

'One more peace in Vietnam sermon, they'll drop away anyway.' He falls heavily into bed, smelling of chewing gum. As with men who spend nights away from home drinking in bars, he feels guilty, but the motion, the brightness and excitement of the place where he has been continues in him: the varnished old tables, the yellowing Sunday-school charts, the folding chairs and pocked linoleum, the cork bulletin board, the giggles of the children's choir leaving, the strange constant sense of dark sacred space surrounding their lit meeting room like the void upholding a bright planet. 'One more blessing on the damn Vietcong,' he mumbles, and the young minister's face, white and worriedly sucking a pipestem, skids like a vision of the Devil across his plagued mind. He has a headache. The sides of his nose, the tops of his cheeks, the space above his ears – wherever the frames of his glasses dig – dully hurt. His wife snores, neglected. In less than seven hours, the alarm clock will ring. This must stop. He must turn over a new leaf.

His name is Miles. He is over fifty, an electrical engineer. Every seven years or so, he changes employers and locations. He has been a member of the board of deacons of a prosperous Methodist church in Iowa, a complex of dashing blond brick-and-glass buildings set in acres of parking lot carved from a cornfield; then of a Presbyterian church in San Francisco, goldrush Gothic clinging to the back of Nob Hill, attended on Sundays by a handful of Chinese businessmen and prostitutes in sunglasses and whiskery, dazed dropout youths looking for a warm place in which to wind up their Saturday-night trips; then of another Presbyterian church in New York State, a dour granite chapel in a suburb of Schenectady; and most recently, in southeastern Pennsylvania, of a crypt-like Reformed church sunk among clouds of foliage so dense that the lights were kept burning in midday and the cobwebbed balconies swarmed all summer with wasps. Though Miles has travelled far, he has never broken out of the loose net of Calvinist denominations that places almost every American within sight of a spire. He wonders why. He was raised in Ohio, in a village that had lost the tang of the frontier but kept its bleak narrowness, and was confirmed in the same colourless, bean-eating creed that millions in his generation have dismissed forever. He was not, as he understood the term, religious. Ceremony bored him. Closing his eyes to pray made him dizzy. He distinctly heard in the devotional service the overamplified tone of voice that in business matters would signal either ignorance or dishonesty. His profession prepared him to believe that our minds, with their crackle of self-importance, are merely collections of electrical circuits. He saw nothing about his body worth resurrecting. God, concretely considered, had a way of merging with that corner of the church ceiling that showed signs of water leakage. That men should be good, he did not doubt, or that social order demands personal sacrifice; but the Heavenly hypothesis, as it had fallen upon his ears these forty years of Sundays, crushes us all to the same level of unworthiness, and redeems us all indiscriminately, elevating especially, these days, the irresponsible – the unemployable, the riotous, the outrageous, the one in one hundred that strays. Neither God nor His Ministers displayed love for deacons – indeed, Pharisees were the first objects of their wrath. Why persist, then, in work so thoroughly thankless, begging for pledges, pinching and scraping to save degenerate old buildings, facing rings of Sunday-school faces baked to adamant cynicism by hours of television-watching, attending fruitless meetings where the senile and the frustrated dominate, arguing, yawning, missing sleep, the company of his wife, the small, certain joys of home. Why? He had wanted to offer his children the Christian option, to begin them as citizens as he had begun; but all have left home now, are in college or married, and, as far as he can tactfully gather, are unchurched. So be it. He has done his part.

A new job offer arrives, irresistible, inviting him to New England. In Pennsylvania the Fellowship Society gives him a farewell dinner; his squad of Sunday-school teachers presents him with a pen set; he hands in his laborious financial records, his neat minutes of vague proceedings. He bows his head for the last time in that dark sanctuary smelling of mouldering plaster and buzzing with captive wasps. He is free. Their new house is smaller, their new town is white. He does not join a church; he stays home reading the Sunday paper. Wincing, he flicks past religious news. He drives his wife north to admire the turning foliage. His evenings are immense. He reads through Winston Churchill's history of the Second World War; he installs elaborate electrical gadgets around the house, which now and then give his wife a shock. They go to drive-in movies, and sit islanded in a sea of fornication. They go bowling and square dancing, and feel ridiculous, too ponderous and slow. His wife, these years of evenings alone, has developed a time-passing pattern – television shows spaced with spells of sewing and dozing – into which he fits awkwardly. She listens to him grunt and sigh and grope for words. But Sunday mornings are the worst, blighted times haunted by the giddy swish and roar of churchward traffic on the road outside. He stands by the window; the sight of three little girls, in white beribboned hats, bluebird coats, and dresses of starched organdie, scampering home from Sunday school gives him a pang unholy in its keenness.

Behind him his wife says, 'Why don't you go to church?'

'No, I think I'll wash the Dodge.'

'You washed it last Sunday.'

'Maybe I should take up golf.'

'You want to go to church. Go. It's no sin.'

'Not the Methodists. Those bastards in Iowa nearly worked me to death.'

'What's the pretty white one in the middle of town? Congregational. We've never been Congregationalists; they'd let you alone.'

'Are you sure you wouldn't like to take a drive?'

'I get carsick with all that starting and stopping. To tell the truth, it would be a relief to have you out of the house.'

Already he is pulling off his sweater, to make way for a clean shirt. He puts on a coat that doesn't match his pants. 'I'll go,' he says, 'but I'll be damned if I'll join.'

He arrives late, and sits staring at the ceiling. It is a wooden church, and the beams and ceiling boards in drying out have pulled apart. Above every clear-glass window he sees the dried-apple-coloured stains of leakage. At the door, the minister, a very young pale man with a round moon face and a know-it-all pucker to his lips, clasps Miles' hand as if never to let it go. 'We've been looking for you, Miles. We received a splendid letter about you from your Reformed pastor in Pennsylvania. As you know, since the U.C.C. merger you don't even need to be reconfirmed. There's a men's supper this Thursday. We'll hope to see you there.' Some ministers' hands, Miles has noticed, grow fatty under the pressure of being so often shaken, and others dwindle to the bones; this one's, for all his fat face, is mostly bones.

The church as a whole is threadbare and scrawny; it makes no resistance to his helpless infiltration of the Men's Club, the Board of Finance, the Debt Liquidation and Building Maintenance Committee. He and a few shaggy Pilgrim Youth paint the Sunday-school chairs Chinese red. He and one grimy codger and three bottles of beer clean the furnace room of forgotten furniture and pageant props, of warped hymnals and unused programmes still tied in the printer's bundles, of the gilded remnants of a dozen abandoned projects. Once he attends a committee meeting to which no one else comes. It is a gusty winter night, a night of cold rain from the sea, freezing on the roads. The minister has been up all night with the family of a suicide and cannot himself attend; he has dropped off the church keys with Miles.

The front door key, no bigger than a car key, seems magically small for so large a building. Is it the only one? Miles makes a mental note: have duplicates made. He turns on a light and waits for the other committee members – a retired banker and two maiden ladies. The furnace is running gamely, but with an audible limp in its stride. It is a coal burner converted to oil twenty years ago. The old cast-iron clinker grates are still heaped in a corner, too heavy to throw out. Should be sold for scrap. Every penny counts. Pinching and scraping. Miles thinks, as upon a mystery, upon the prodigality of heating a huge vacant barn like this with such an inefficient burner. Hot air rises direct from the basement to the ceiling, drying and spreading the wood. Fuel needle half gummed up. Waste. Nothing but waste, salvage and waste. And weariness.

Miles removes his glasses and rubs the chafed spots at the bridge of his nose. He replaces them to look at his watch. His watch has stopped, its small face wet from the storm like an excited child's. The electric clock in the minister's study has been unplugged. Bogus thrift. There are books: concordances, daily helps, through the year verse by verse, great sermons, best sermons, sermon hints, all second-hand, no, third-hand, worse, hundredth-hand, thousandth-hand, a coin rubbed blank. The books are leaning on their sides and half the shelves are empty. Empty. The desk is clean. No business conducted on it. He tests the minister's fountain pen and it is dry. Dry as an old snakeskin, dry as a locust husk that still clings to a tree.

In search of the time, Miles goes into the sanctuary. The 1880 pendulum clock on the choir balustrade still ticks. He can hear it in the dark, overhead. He switches on the nave lights. A moment passes before they come on. Some shaky connection in the toggle, the wiring doubtless rotten throughout the walls, a wonder it hasn't burnt down. Miles has never belonged to a wooden church before. Around and above him, like a stiff white forest, the hewn frame creaks and groans in conversation with the wind. The high black windows, lashed as if by handfuls of sand, seem to flinch, yet do not break, and Miles feels the timbers of this ark, with its ballast of tattered pews, give and sway with the fierce weather, yet hold; and this is why he has come, to share the pride of this ancient thing that will not quite die, to have it all to himself. Warm air from a grilled duct breathes on his ankles. Miles can see upward past the clock and the organ to the corner of the unused gallery where souvenirs of the church's past – Puritan pew doors, tin footwarmers, velvet collection bags, Victorian commemorative albums, cracking portraits of wigged pastors, oval photographs of deceased deacons, and inexplicable unlabelled ferrotypes of chubby cross children and picnics past – repose in dusty glass cases that are in themselves antiques. All this anonymous treasure Miles possesses by being here, like a Pharaoh hidden with his life's rich furniture, while the rain like a robber rattles to get in.

Yes, the deacon sees, it is indeed a preparation for death – an emptiness where many others have been, which is what death will be. It is good to be at home here. Nothing now exists but himself, this shell, and the storm. The windows clatter; the sand has turned to gravel, the rain has turned to sleet. The storm seizes the church by its steeple and shakes, but the walls were built with love, and withstand. The others are very late, they will not be coming; he is not displeased, he is serene. He turns out the lights. He locks the door.

The Carol Sing

Surely one of the natural wonders of Tarbox was Mr Burley at the Town Hall carol sing. How he would jubilate, how he would God-rest those merry gentlemen, how he would boom out when the male voices became Good King Wenceslas:

> Mark my footsteps, good my page;
> Tread thou in them boldly:
> Thou shalt find the winter's rage
> Freeze thy blood less co-*oh*-ldly.

When he hit a good 'oh', standing beside him was like being inside a great transparent Christmas ball. He had what you'd have to call a God-given bass. This year, we other male voices just peck at the tunes: Wendell Huddlestone, whose hardware store has become the pizza place where the dropouts collect after dark; Squire Wentworth, who is still getting up petitions to protect the marsh birds from the atomic power plant; Lionel Merson, lighter this year by about three pounds of gallstones; and that selectman whose freckled bald head looks like the belly of a trout; and that fireman whose face is bright brown all the year round from clamming; and the widow Covode's bearded son, who went into divinity school to avoid the draft; and the Bisbee boy, who no sooner was back from Vietnam than he grew a beard and painted his car every colour of the rainbow; and the husband of the new couple that moved this September into the Whitman place on the beach road. He wears thick glasses above a little mumble of a mouth tight as a keyhole, but his wife appears perky enough.

> The-ey lo-oked up and sa-haw a star,
> Shining in the east, beyond them far;
> And to the earth it ga-ave great light,
> And so it continued both da-hay and night.

She is wearing a flouncy little Christmassy number, red with white polka dots, one of those dresses so short that when she sits down on the old plush deacon's bench she has to help it with her hand to tuck

332

under her bottom, otherwise it wouldn't. A lively bit of a girl with long thighs glossy as pond ice. She smiles nervously up over her cup of cinnamon-stick punch, wondering why she is here, in this dusty draughty public place. We must look monstrous to her, we Tarbox old-timers. And she has never heard Mr Burley sing, but she knows something is missing this year; there is something failed, something hollow. Hester Hartner sweeps wrong notes into every chord: arthritis – arthritis and indifference.

> The first good joy that Mary had,
>   It was the joy of one;
> To see the blessed Jesus Christ
>   When he was first her son.

The old upright, a Pickering, for most of the year has its keyboard turned to the wall, beneath the town zoning map, its top piled high with rolled-up plot plans filing for variances. The Town Hall was built, strange to say, as a Unitarian church, around 1830, but it didn't take around here, Unitarianism; the sea air killed it. You need big trees for a shady mystic mood, or at least a lake to see yourself in like they have over to Concord. So the town bought up the shell and ran a second floor through the air of the sanctuary, between the balconies: offices and the courtroom below, more offices and this hall above. You can still see the Doric pilasters along the walls, the top halves. They used to use it more; there were the Tarbox Theatricals twice a year, and political rallies with placards and straw hats and tambourines, and get-togethers under this or that local auspice, and town meetings until we went representative. But now not even the holly the ladies of the Grange have hung around can cheer it up, can chase away the smell of dust and must, of cobwebs too high to reach and rats' nests in the hot-air ducts and, if you stand close to the piano, that faint sour tang of blueprints. And Hester lately has taken to chewing eucalyptus drops.

> And him to serve God give us grace,
> *O lux beata Trinitas.*

The little wife in polka dots is laughing now: maybe the punch is getting to her, maybe she's getting used to the look of us. Strange people look ugly only for a while, until you begin to fill in those tufty monkey features with a little history and stop seeing their faces and start seeing their lives. Regardless, it does us good, to see her here, to see young people at the carol sing. We need new blood.

This time of the year is spent in good cheer,
   And neighbours together do meet,
To sit by the fire, with friendly desire,
   Each other in love to greet.
Old grudges forgot are put in the pot,
   All sorrows aside they lay;
The old and the young doth carol this song,
   To drive the cold winter away.

At bottom it's a woman's affair, a chance in the darkest of months to iron some man-fetching clothes and get out of the house. Those old holidays weren't scattered around the calendar by chance. Harvest and seedtime, seedtime and harvest, the elbows of the year. The women do enjoy it; they enjoy jostle of most any kind, in my limited experience. The widow Covode as full of rouge and purple as an old-time Scollay Square tart, when her best hope is burial on a sunny day, with no frost in the ground. Mrs Hortense broad as a barn door, yet her hands putting on a duchess's airs. Mamie Nevins sporting a sprig of mistletoe in her neck brace. They miss Mr Burley. He never married and was everybody's gallant for this occasion. He was the one to spike the punch and this year they let young Covode do it, maybe that's why Little Polka Dots can't keep a straight face and giggles across the music like a pruning saw.

> *Adeste, fideles,*
> *Laeti triumphantes;*
> *Venite, venite*
> *In Bethlehem.*

Still that old tussle, 'v' versus 'wenite', the 'th' as hard or soft. Education is what divides us. People used to actually resent it, the way Burley, with his education, didn't go to some city, didn't get out. Exeter, Dartmouth, a year at the Sorbonne, then thirty years of Tarbox. By the time he hit fifty he was fat and fussy. Arrogant, too. Last sing, he two or three times told Hester to pick up her tempo. 'Presto, Hester, not andante!' Never married, and never really worked. Burley Hosiery, that his grandfather had founded, was shut down and the machines sold South before Burley got his manhood. He built himself a laboratory instead and was always about to come up with something perfect: the perfect synthetic substitute for leather, the harmless insecticide, the beer can that turned itself into mulch. Some said at the end he was looking for a way to turn lead into gold. That was just malice. Anything high attracts lightning, anybody with a name attracts malice. When it happened, the papers in Boston gave him six inches and a photograph ten years old. 'After a long illness.' It wasn't a long illness, it was cyanide, the Friday after Thanksgiving.

> The holly bears a prickle,
> As sharp as any thorn,
> And Mary bore sweet Jesus Christ
> On Christmas day in the morn.

They said the cyanide ate out his throat worse than a blow-torch. Such a detail is satisfying but doesn't clear up the mystery. Why? Health, money, hobbies, that voice. Not having that voice makes a big hole here. Without his lead, no man dares take the lower parts; we just wheeze away at the melody with the women. It's as if the floor they put in has been taken away and we're standing in air, halfway up the old sanctuary. We peek around guiltily, missing Burley's voice. The absent seem to outnumber the present. We feel insulted, slighted. The dead turn their backs. The older you get, the more of them snub you. He was rude enough last year, Burley, correcting Hester's tempo. At one point, he even reached over, his face black with impatience, and slapped her hands that were still trying to make sense of the keys.

> Rise, and bake your Christmas bread:
> Christians, rise! The world is bare,
> And blank, and dark with want and care,
> Yet Christmas comes in the morning.

Well, why anything? Why do *we*? Come every year sure as the solstice to carol these antiquities that if you listened to the words would break your heart. Silence, darkness, Jesus, angels. Better, I suppose, to sing than to listen.

The Music School

My name is Alfred Schweigen and I exist in time. Last night I heard a young priest tell of a change in his Church's attitude towards the Eucharistic wafer. For generations nuns and priests, but especially (the young man said) nuns, have taught Catholic children that the wafer must be held in the mouth and allowed to melt; that to touch it with the teeth would be (and this was never doctrine, but merely a nuance of instruction) in some manner blasphemous. Now, amid the flowering of fresh and bold ideas with which the Church, like a tundra thawing, responded to that unexpected sun the late Pope John, there has sprung up the thought that Christ did not say *Take and melt this in your mouth* but *Take and eat.* The word is *eat*, and to dissolve the word is to dilute the transubstantiated metaphor of physical nourishment. This demiquaver of theology crystallizes with a beautiful simplicity in the material world; the bakeries supplying the Mass have been instructed to unlearn the science of a dough translucent to the tongue and to prepare a thicker, tougher wafer – a host, in fact, so substantial it *must* be chewed to be swallowed.

This morning I read in the newspaper that an acquaintance of mine had been murdered. The father of five children, he had been sitting at the dinner table with them, a week after Thanksgiving. A single bullet entered the window and pierced his temple; he fell to the floor and died there in minutes, at the feet of his children. My acquaintance with him was slight. He has become the only victim of murder I have known, and for such a role anyone seems drastically miscast, though in the end each life wears its events with a geological inevitability. It is impossible, today, to imagine him alive. He was a computer expert, a soft-voiced, broad-set man from Nebraska, whose intelligence, concerned as it was with matters so arcane to me, had a generous quality of reserve, and gave him, in my apprehension of him, the dignity of an iceberg, which floats so serenely on its hidden mass. We met (I think only twice) in the home of a mutual friend, a professional colleague of his who is my neighbour. We spoke, as people do whose fields of knowledge are miles apart, of matters where all men are ignorant – of politics, children, and, perhaps, religion. I have the impression, at any rate, that he, as is often the case with scientists and Midwesterners, had no use for religion, and I saw in him a typical specimen of the new human species that thrives around scientific centres, in an environment of discussion groups, outdoor exercise, and cheerful husbandry. Like those vanished gentlemen whose sexual energy was exclusively spent in brothels, these men confine their cleverness to their work, which, being in one way or another for the government, is usually secret. With their sufficient incomes, large families, Volkswagen buses, hi-fi phonographs, half-remodelled Victorian homes, and harassed, ironical wives, they seem to have solved, or dismissed, the paradox of being a thinking animal and, devoid of guilt, apparently participate not in this century but in the next. If I remember him with individual clarity, it is because once I intended to write a novel about a computer programmer, and I asked him questions, which he answered agreeably. More agreeably still, he offered to show me around his laboratories any time I cared to make the hour's trip to where they were. I never wrote the novel – the moment in my life it was meant to crystallize dissolved too quickly – and I never took the trip. Indeed, I don't believe I thought of my friend once in the year between our last encounter and this morning, when my wife at breakfast put the paper before me and asked, 'Don't we know him?' His pleasant face with its eyes set wide like the eyes of a bear gazed from the front page. I read that he had been murdered.

I do not understand the connection between last night and this morning, though there seems to be one. I am trying to locate it this afternoon, while sitting in a music school, waiting for my daughter to finish her piano lesson. I perceive in the two incidents a common element of nourishment, of eating transfigured by a strange irruption, and there is a parallel movement, a flight immaculately direct and elegant, from an immaterial phenomenon (an exegetical nicety, a maniac hatred) to a material one (a bulky wafer, a bullet in the temple). About the murder I feel certain, from my knowledge of the victim, that his offence was blameless, something for which he could not have felt guilt or shame. When I try to picture it, I see only numbers and Greek letters, and conclude that from my distance I have witnessed an almost unprecedented crime, a crime of unalloyed scientific passion. And there is this to add: the young priest plays a twelve-string guitar, smokes mentholated cigarettes, and seemed unembarrassed to find himself sitting socially in a circle of Protestants and nonbelievers – like my late computer friend, a man of the future.

But let me describe the music school. I love it here. It is the basement of a huge Baptist church. Golden collection plates rest on the table beside me. Girls in their first blush of adolescence, carrying fawn-coloured flute cases and pallid folders of music, shuffle by me; their awkwardness is lovely, like the stance of a bather testing the sea. Boys and mothers arrive and leave. From all directions sounds – of pianos, oboes, clarinets – arrive like hints of another world, a world where angels fumble, pause, and begin again. Listening, I remember what learning music is like, how impossibly difficult and complex seem the first fingerings, the first decipherings of that unique language which freights each note with a double meaning of position and duration, a language as finicking as Latin, as laconic as Hebrew, as surprising to the eye as Persian or Chinese. How mysterious appears that calligraphy of parallel spaces, swirling clefs, superscribed ties, subscribed decrescendos, dots and sharps and flats! How great looms the gap between the first gropings of vision and the first stammerings of percussion! Vision, timidly, becomes percussion, percussion becomes music, music becomes emotion, emotion becomes – vision. Few of us have the heart to follow this circle to its end. I took lessons for years, and never learned, and last night, watching the priest's fingers confidently prance on the neck of his guitar, I was envious and incredulous. My daughter is just beginning the piano. These are her first lessons, she is eight, she is eager and hopeful. Silently she sits beside me as we drive the nine miles to the town where the lessons are given; silently she sits beside me, in the dark, as we drive home. Unlike her, she does not beg for a reward of candy or a Coke, as if the lesson itself has been a meal. She only remarks – speaking dully, in a reflex of greed she has outgrown – that the store windows are decorated for Christmas already. I love taking her, I love waiting for her, I love driving her home through the mystery of darkness towards the certainty of supper. I do this taking and driving because today my wife visits her psychiatrist. She visits a psychiatrist because I am unfaithful to her. I do not understand the connection, but there seems to be one.

In the novel I never wrote, I wanted the hero to be a computer programmer because it was the most poetic and romantic occupation I could think of, and my hero had to be extremely romantic and delicate, for he was to die of adultery. Die, I mean, of knowing it was possible; the possibility crushed him. I conceived of him, whose professional life was spent in the sanctum of the night (when, I was told, the computers, too valuable to be unemployed by industry during the day, are free, as it were, to frolic and to be loved), devising idioms whereby problems might be fed to the machines and emerge, under binary percussion, as the music of truth –

I conceived of him as being too fine, translucent, and scrupulous to live in our coarse age. He was to be, if the metaphor is biological, an evolutionary abortion, a mammalian mutation crushed underfoot by dinosaurs, and, if the metaphor is mathematical, a hypothetical ultimate, one digit beyond the last real number. The title of the book was to be $N + 1$. Its first sentence went, *As Echo passed overhead, he stroked Maggy Johns' side through her big-flowered dress*. Echo is the artificial star, the first, a marvel; as the couples at a lawn party look upward at it, these two caress one another. She takes his free hand, lifts it to her lips, warmly breathes on, kisses, his knuckles. *His halted body seemed to catch up in itself the immense slow revolution of the earth, and the firm little white star, newly placed in space, calmly made its way through the older points of light, which looked shredded and faint in comparison*. From this hushed moment under the ominous sky of technological miracle, the plot was to develop more or less downhill, into a case of love, guilt, and nervous breakdown, with physiological complications (I had to do some research here) that would kill the hero as quietly as a mistake is erased from a blackboard. There was to be the hero, his wife, his love, and his doctor. In the end the wife married the doctor, and Maggy Johns would calmly continue her way through the comparatively faint . . . Stop me.

My psychiatrist wonders why I need to humiliate myself. It is the habit, I suppose, of confession. In my youth I attended a country church where, every two months, we would all confess; we kneeled on the uncarpeted floor and propped the books containing the service on the seats of the pews. It was a grave, long service, beginning, *Beloved in the Lord! Let us draw near with a true heart and confess our sins unto God, our Father* . . . There was a kind of accompanying music in the noise of the awkward fat Germanic bodies fitting themselves, scraping and grunting, into the backwards-kneeling position. We read aloud, *But if we thus examine ourselves, we shall find nothing in us but sin and death, from which we can in no wise set ourselves free*. The confession complete, we would stand and be led, pew by pew, to the altar rail, where the young minister, a black-haired man with very small pale hands, would feed us, murmuring, *Take, eat; this is the true body of our Lord and Saviour Jesus Christ, given unto death for your sins*. The altar rail was of varnished wood, and ran around three sides, so that, standing (oddly, we did not kneel here), one could see, one could not help but see, the faces of one's fellow-communicants. We were a weathered, homely congregation, sheepish in our Sunday clothes, and the faces I saw while the wafer was held in my mouth were strained; above their closed lips their eyes held a watery look of pleading to be rescued from the depths of this mystery. And it distinctly seems, in the reaches of this memory so vivid it makes my saliva flow, that it was necessary, if not to chew, at least to touch, to embrace and tentatively shape, the wafer with the teeth.

We left refreshed. *We give thanks to thee, Almighty God, that Thou hast refreshed us through this salutary gift.* The church smelled like this school, glinting with strange whispers and varnished highlights. I am neither musical nor religious. Each moment I live, I must think where to place my fingers, and press them down with no confidence of hearing a chord. My friends are like me. We are all pilgrims, faltering towards divorce. Some get no further than mutual confession, which becomes an addiction, and exhausts them. Some move on, into violent quarrels and physical blows; and succumb to sexual excitement. A few make it to the psychiatrists. A very few get as far as the lawyers. Last evening, as the priest sat in the circle of my friends, a woman entered without knocking; she had come from the lawyers, and her eyes and hair were flung wide with suffering, as if she had come in out of a high wind. She saw our black-garbed guest, was amazed, ashamed perhaps, and took two backward steps. But then, in the hush, she gained her composure and sat down among us. And in this grace note, of the two backward steps and then again the forward movement, a coda seems to be urged.

The world is the host; it must be chewed. I am content here in this school. My daughter emerges from her lesson. Her face is fat and satisfied, refreshed, hopeful; her pleased smile, biting her lower lip, pierces my heart, and I die (I think I am dying) at her feet.

Leaves

The grape leaves outside my window are curiously beautiful. 'Curiously' because it comes upon me as strange, after the long darkness of self-absorption and fear and shame in which I have been living, that things are beautiful, that independent of our catastrophes they continue to maintain the casual precision, the effortless abundance of inventive 'effect', which is the hallmark and specialty of Nature. Nature: this morning it seems to me very clear that Nature may be defined as that which exists without guilt. Our bodies are in Nature; our shoes, their laces, the little plastic tips of the laces – everything around us and about us is in Nature, and yet something holds us away from it, like the upward push of water which keeps us from touching the sandy bottom, ribbed and glimmering with crescental fragments of oyster shell, so clear to our eyes.

A blue jay lights on a twig outside my window. Momentarily sturdy, he stands astraddle, his dingy rump towards me, his head alertly frozen in silhouette, the predatory curve of his beak stamped on a sky almost white above the misting tawny marsh. See him? I do, and, snapping the chain of my thought, I have reached through glass and seized him and stamped him on this page. Now he is gone. And yet, there, a few lines above, he still is, 'astraddle', his rump 'dingy', his head 'alertly frozen'. A curious trick, possibly useless, but mine.

The grape leaves where they are not in each other's shadows are golden. Flat leaves, they take the sun flatly, and turn the absolute light, sum of the spectrum and source of all life, into the crayon yellow with which children render it. Here and there, wilt transmutes this lent radiance into a glowing orange, and the green of the still tender leaves – for green persists long into autumn, if we look – strains from the sunlight a fine-veined chartreuse. The shadows these leaves cast upon each other, though vagrant and nervous in the wind that sends friendly scavenging rattles scurrying across the roof, are yet quite various and definite, containing innumerable barbaric suggestions of scimitars, flanged spears, prongs, and menacing helmets. The net effect, however, is innocent of menace. On the contrary, its intricate simultaneous suggestion of shelter and openness, warmth and breeze, invites me

341

outward; my eyes venture into the leaves beyond. I am surrounded by leaves. The oak's are tenacious claws of purplish rust; the elm's, scant feathers of a feminine yellow; the sumac's, a savage, toothed blush. I am upheld in a serene and burning universe of leaves. Yet something plucks back, returns me to that inner darkness where guilt is the sun.

The events need to be sorted out. I am told I behaved wantonly, and it will take time to integrate this unanimous impression with the unqualified righteousness with which our own acts, however admittedly miscalculated, invest themselves. And once the events are sorted out – the actions given motivations, the actors assigned psychologies, the miscalculations tabulated, the abnormalities named, the whole furious and careless growth pruned by explanation and rooted in history and returned, as it were, to Nature – what then? Is not such a return spurious? Can our spirits really enter Time's haven of mortality and sink composedly among the mulching leaves? No: we stand at the intersection of two kingdoms, and there is no advance and no retreat, only a sharpening of the edge where we stand.

I remember most sharply the black of my wife's dress as she left our house to get her divorce. The dress was a soft black sheath, with a V neckline, and Helen always looked handsome in it; it flattered her pallor. This morning she looked especially handsome, her face utterly white with fatigue. Yet her body, that natural thing, ignored our catastrophe, and her shape and gestures were incongruously usual. She kissed me lightly in leaving, and we both felt the humour of this trip's being insufficiently unlike any other of her trips to Boston – to Symphony, to Bonwit's. The same search for the car keys, the same harassed instructions to the complacent baby-sitter, the same little dip and thrust of her head as she settled behind the wheel of her car. And I, satisfied at last, divorced, studied my children with the eyes of one who had left them, examined my house as one does a set of snapshots from an irrevocable time, drove through the turning landscape as a man in asbestos cuts through a fire, met my wife-to-be – weeping yet smiling, stunned yet brave – and felt, unstoppably, to my horror, the inner darkness burst my skin and engulf us both and drown our love. The natural world, where our love had existed, ceased to exist. My heart shied back; it shies back still. I retreated. As I drove back, the leaves of the trees along the road stated their shapes to me. There is no more story to tell. By telephone I plucked my wife back; I clasped the black of her dress to me, and braced for the pain.

It does not stop coming. The pain does not stop coming. Almost every day, a new instalment arrives by mail or face or phone. Every time the telephone rings, I expect it to uncoil some new convolution of consequence. I have come to hide in this cottage, but even here, there is a telephone, and the scraping sounds of wind and branch and unseen animal are charged with its electronic silence. At any moment, it may explode, and the curious beauty of the leaves will be eclipsed again.

In nervousness, I rise, and walk across the floor. A spider like a white asterisk hangs in air in front of my face. I look at the ceiling and cannot see where its thread is attached. The ceiling is smooth plasterboard. The spider hesitates. It feels a huge alien presence. Its exquisite white legs spread warily and of its own dead weight it twirls on its invisible thread. I catch myself in the quaint and antique pose of the fabulist seeking to draw a lesson from a spider, and become self-conscious. I dismiss self-consciousness and do earnestly attend to this minute articulated star hung so pointedly before my face; and am unable to read the lesson. The spider and I inhabit contiguous but incompatible cosmoses. Across the gulf we feel only fear. The telephone remains silent. The spider reconsiders its spinning. The wind continues to stir the sunlight. In walking in and out of this cottage, I have tracked the floor with a few dead leaves, pressed flat like scraps of dark paper.

And what are these pages but leaves? Why do I produce them but to thrust, by some subjective photosynthesis, my guilt into Nature, where there is no guilt? Now the marsh, level as a carpet, is streaked with faint green amid the shades of brown – russet, ochre, tan, *marron* – and on the far side, where the land lifts above tide level, evergreens stab upwards sullenly. Beyond them, there is a low blue hill; on this coastal region, the hills are almost too modest to bear names. But I *see* it; for the first time in months I see it. I see it as a child, fingers gripping and neck straining, glimpses the roof of a house over a cruelly high wall. Under my window, the lawn is lank and green and mixed with leaves shed from a small elm, and I remember how, the first night I came to this cottage, thinking I was leaving my life behind me, I went to bed alone and read, in the way one reads stray books in a borrowed house, a few pages of an old edition of *Leaves of Grass*. And my sleep was a loop, so that in awaking I seemed still in the book, and the light-struck sky quivering through the stripped branches of the young elm seemed another page of Whitman, and I was entirely open, and lost, like a woman in passion, and free, and in love, without a shadow in any corner of my being. It was a beautiful awakening, but by the next night I had returned to my house.

The precise barbaric shadows on the grape leaves have shifted. The angle of illumination has altered. I imagine warmth leaning against the door, and open the door to let it in; sunlight falls flat at my feet like a penitent.

Four Sides of One Story

Tristan

MY LOVE:

Forgive me, I seem to be on a boat. The shock of leaving you numbed me rather nicely to the usual humiliations of boarding – why is it that in a pier shed everyone, no matter how well-born and self-confident, looks like a Central European immigrant, and is treated accordingly? – and even though we are now two days out to sea, and I can repose, technically, in your utter inaccessibility, I still am unable to focus on my fellow-passengers, though for a split second of, as it were, absent-minded sanity, I did prophetically perceive, through a chink in my obsession, that the waiter, having sized me up as one of the helpless solitaries of the world, would give me arrogant service and expect in exchange, at journey's end, an apologetically huge tip. No matter. The next instant, I unfolded the napkin, and your sigh, shaped exactly like a dove, the blue tint of its throat visibly clouding for a moment the flame of the candle on the table, escaped; and I was plunged back into the moist murmurs, the eclipsed whispers, the vows instantly hissingly retracted, the exchanged sweats, of our love.

The boat shakes. The vibration is incessant and ubiquitous; it has sniffed me out even here, in the writing room, a dark nook staffed by a dour young Turinese steward and stocked, to qualify as a library, with tattered copies of *Paris Match* and, behind glass, seventeen gorgeously bound and impeccably unread volumes of D'Annunzio, in of course Italian. So that the tremor in my handwriting is a purely motor affair, and the occasional splotches you may consider droplets of venturesome spray. As a matter of fact, there is a goodly roll, though we have headed into sunny latitudes. When they try to fill the swimming pool, the water thrashes and pitches so hysterically that I peek over the edge expecting to see a captured mermaid. In the bar, the bottles tinkle like some immensely dainty Swiss gadget, and the Daiquiris come to you aquiver, little circlets of agitation spinning back and forth between the centre and the rim. The first day, having forgotten, in my landlocked days with you, the feel of an

344

ocean voyage, I was standing in the cabin-class lobby, waiting to try to buy my way towards a higher deck and if possible a porthole, when, without any visible change in the disposition of furniture, lighting fixtures, potted palms, or polylingual bulletin board, the floor like a great flat magnet suddenly rendered my blood heavy – extraordinarily heavy. There were people around me, and their facial expressions did not alter by one millimetre. It was quite comic, for as the ship rolled back the other way my blood absolutely *swung* upward in my veins – do you remember how your arm feels in the first instant after a bruise? – and it seemed imminent that I, and, if I, all these dead-panned others too, would lift like helium balloons and be bumpingly pasted to the ceiling, from which the ship's staff would have to rescue us, irritably, with broom handles. The vision passed. The ship rolled again. My blood went heavy again. It seemed that you were near.

Iseult. I must write your name. Iseult. I am bleeding to death. Certainly I feel bloodless, or, more precisely, diluted, diluted by half, since everything around me – the white ropes, the ingenious little magnetic catches that keep the doors from swinging, the charmingly tessellated triangular shower stall in my cabin, the luxurious and pampered textures on every side – I seem to see, or touch, or smile over, with you, which means, since you are not here, that I only half-see, only half-exist. I keep thinking what a pity all this luxury is wasted on me, Tristan the Austere, the Perpetually Grieving, the Orphaned, the Homeless. The very pen I am writing this with is an old-fashioned dip, or nib, pen, whose flexibility irresistibly invites flourishes that sit up wet and bluely gleaming for minutes before finally deigning to dry. The holder is some sort of polished Asiatic wood. Teak? Ebony? You would know. It was enchanting for me, how you knew the names of surfaces, how you had the innocence to stroke a pelt and not flinch from the panicked little quick-eyed death beneath; for me, who have always been on the verge of becoming a vegetarian, which Mark, I know, would say was a form of death-wish (I can't describe to you how stupid that man seems to me; unfairly enough, even what tiny truth there is in him seems backed by this immense capital – these armies, this downright kingdom – of stupidity, so that even when he says something intelligent it affects me like Gospel quoted in support of social injustice. This parenthesis has gotten out of all control. If it seems ugly to you, blame it on jealousy. I am not sure, however, if I hate your husband because he – if only legally – possesses you, or if, more subtly, because he senses my own fear of just such legal possession, which gives him, for all his grossness, his grotesque patronization and prattling, a curious moral hold over me which I cannot, writhe as I will, break. End parenthesis).

An especially, almost maliciously, prolonged roll of the boat just slid the ink bottle, unspilled, the width of my cubbyhole and gave me the choice of fixing my eyes on the horizon or beginning to be seasick.

Where was I?

For me it was wonderful to become a partner in your response to textures. Your shallowness, as my wife calls it – and like everything she says, there is something in it which, at the least, gives dismissal pause – broke a new dimension into my hitherto inadequately superficial world. Now, adrift in this luxurious island universe, where music plays like a constant headache, I see everything half through your eyes, conduct circular conversations with you in my head, and rest my hand on the wiped mahogany of the bar as if the tremor beneath the surface is you, a mermaid rising. What are our conversations about? I make, my mind tediously sifting the rubble of the emotional landslide, small discoveries about us that I hasten to convey to you, who are never quite as impressed by them as I thought you would be. Yesterday, for example, at about 3.30 p.m., when the sallow sun suddenly ceased to justify sitting in a deck chair, I discovered, in the act of folding the blanket, that I had never, in my heart, taken your suffering as seriously as my own. That you were unhappy, I knew. I could diagram the mechanics of the bind you were in, could trace the vivacious contours and taste the bright flat colours of your plight – indeed I could picture your torment so clearly that I felt I was feeling it with you. But no, there was a final kind of credence I denied your pain, that cheated it of dimension and weight, and for this I belatedly apologized. In my head you accepted the apology with a laugh, and then wished to go on and discuss the practical aspects of our elopement. Two hours later, pinning a quivering Daiquiri to the bar with my fingers, I rather jerkily formulated this comforting thought: however else I failed you, I never pretended to feel other than love for you, I never in any way offered to restrict, or control, the love you felt for me. Whatever sacrifices you offered to make, whatever agony you volunteered to undergo for me, I permitted. In the limitless extent of my willingness to accept your love, I was the perfect lover. Another man, seeing you flail and lacerate yourself so mercilessly, might have out of timid squeamishness (calling it pity) pretended to turn his back, and saved your skin at the price of your dignity. But I, whether merely hypnotized or actually suicidal, steadfastly kept my face turned towards the blaze between us, though my eyes watered, my nose peeled, and my eyebrows disappeared in twin whiffs of smoke. It took all the peculiar strength of my egotism not to flinch and flaw the purity of your generous fury. No? For several hours I discussed this with you, or rather vented exhaustive rewordings upon your silent phantom, whose comprehension effortlessly widened, like ringing water, to include every elaboration.

Then, at last weary, brushing my teeth while the shower curtains moved back and forth beside me like two sluggish, rustling pendulums, I received, as if it were a revelation absolutely gravitational in importance, the syllogism that (major premise) however much we have suffered because of each other, it is quite out of the question for me to blame you for my pain, though strictly speaking you were the cause; and, since (minor premise) you and I as lovers were mirrors and always felt the same, therefore (conclusion) this must also be the case with you. Ergo, my mind is at peace. That is, it is a paradoxical ethical situation to be repeatedly wounded by someone *because he or she is beloved*. Those small incidentals within my adoration, those crumbs of Mark's influence that I could never digest, those cinders from past flames unswept from your corners, the flecks of mediocrity, glimpses of callousness, even moments of physical repulsiveness – it was never these that hurt me. It was your *perfection* that destroyed me, demented my logical workings, unmanned my healthy honour, bled me white. But I bear no grudge. And thus know that you bear none; and this knowledge, in the midst of my restless misery, gives me ease. As if what I wish to possess forever is not your presence but your good opinion.

I was rather disturbed to learn, from Brangien, just before I left, that you are seeing a psychiatrist. I cannot believe there is anything abnormal or curable about our predicament. We are in love. The only way out of it is marriage, or some sufficiently pungent piece of overexposure equivalent to marriage. I am prepared to devote my life to avoiding this death. As you were brave in creating our love, so I must be brave in preserving it. My body aches for the fatal surfeit of you. It creaks under the denial like a strained ship. A hundred times a day I consider casting myself loose from this implacable liner and giving myself to the waves on the implausible chance that I might again drift to you as once I drifted, pustular, harping, and all but lifeless, into Whitehaven. But I who slew the Morholt slay this Hydra of yearning again and again. My ship plows on, bleeding a straight wake of aquamarine, heading Heaven knows where, but away, away from the realms of compromise and muddle wherein our love, like a composted flower, would be returned to the stupid earth. Yes, had we met as innocents, we could have indulged our love and let it run its natural course of passion, consummation, satiety, contentment, boredom, betrayal. But, being guilty, we can seize instead a purity that will pass without interruption through death itself. Do you remember how, by the river, staking your life on a technicality, you seized the white-hot iron, took nine steps, and showed all Cornwall your cold clean palms? It is from you that I take my example. Do you remember in the Isak Dinesen book I gave you the story in which God is described as He who says No? By saying No to our love we become you and I, gods. I feel this is blasphemy and yet I write it.

The distance between us increases. Bells ring. The Turinese steward is locking up the bookcase. I miss you. I am true to you. Let us live, forever apart, as a shame to the world where everything is lost save what we ourselves deny.

T.

Iseult of the White Hands

DEAR KAHERDIN:

Sorry not to have written before. This way of life we've all been living doesn't conduce to much spare time. I haven't read a book or magazine in weeks. Now the brats are asleep (I think), the dishes are chugging away in the washer, and here I sit with my fifth glass of Noilly Prat for the day. You were the only one he ever confided in, so I tell you. He's left me again. On the other hand, he's also left her. What do you make of it? She is taking it, from appearances, fairly well. She was at a castle do Saturday night and seemed much the same, only thinner. Mark kept a heavy eye on her all evening. At least she has *him*; all I seem to have is a house, a brother, a bank account, and a ghost. The night before he sailed, he explained to me, with great tenderness, etc., that he married me as a kind of pun. That the thing that drew him to me was my having her name. It was all – seven years, three children – a kind of Freudian slip, and he was really charmingly boyish as he begged to be excused. He even made me laugh about it.

If I had any dignity I'd be dead or insane. I don't know if I love him or what love is or even if I want to find out. I tried to tell him that if he loved her and couldn't help it he should leave me and go to her, and not torment us both indefinitely. I've never much liked her, which oddly enough offends him, but I really do sympathize with what he must have put her through. But he seems to think there's something so beautiful about hanging between us that he won't let go with either hand. He's rapidly going from the sublime to the ridiculous. Mark, who in his bullying way wants to be sensible and fair, had his lawyer on the move, and I was almost looking forward to six weeks on a ranch somewhere. But no. After spending the whole summer climbing fences, faking appointments, etc., anything that looks like real action terrifies him and he gets on a boat. And through it all, making life a hell for everybody concerned, including the children, he wears this saintly pained look and insists he's trying to do the right thing. What was really annihilating wasn't his abuse of me, but his kindness.

I've mentally fiddled with your invitation to come back to Carhaix, but there seems no point. The children are in school, I have friends here, life goes on. I've explained his absence as a business trip, which everybody accepts and nobody believes. The local men are both a comfort and a menace – I guess it's their being a menace that makes them a comfort. My virtue is reasonably safe. It all comes back to me, this business of managing suitors, keeping each at the proper distance, not too close and not too far, trying to remember exactly what has been said to each. Mark's eye, for that matter, was heavy on *me* for a few moments at the party. It's essentially disgusting. But nothing else is keeping my ego afloat.

I could never get out of him what she had that I didn't. If you know, as a man, don't tell me, please. But I can't see that it was our looks, or brains, or even in bed. The better I was in bed, the worse it made him. He took it as a reproach, and used to tell me I was beautiful as if it were some cruel joke I had played on him. The harder I tried, the more I became a kind of distasteful parody. But of what? She is really too shallow and silly even for me to hate. Maybe that's it. I feel I'm dropped, *bump*, as one drops any solid object, but she, she is sought in her abandonment. His heart rebounds from shapeless surfaces – the sky, the forest roof, the sea – and gives him back a terror which is her form. The worst of it is, I sympathize. I'm even jealous of his misery. At least it's a kind of pointed misery. His version is that they drank from the same cup. It has nothing to do with our merits but she loves him and I don't. I just think I do. But if I don't love him, I've never loved anything. Do you think this is so? You've known me since I was born, and I'm frightened of your answer. I'm frightened. At night I take one of the children into bed with me and hold him/her for hours. My eyelids won't close, it scalds when I shut them. I never knew what jealousy was. It's an endlessly hungry thing. It really just consumes and churns and I can't focus on anything. I remember how I used to read a newspaper and care and it seems like another person.

In the day I can manage, and on the nights when I go out, but in the evenings when I'm alone, there is an hour, right now, when everything is so hollow there is no limit on how low I and my Noilly Prat can go. I didn't mean to put this into a letter. I wanted to be cheerful, and brave, and funny about it. You have your own life. My love to your family. The physical health here is oddly good. Please, *please* don't say anything to Mother and Daddy. They wouldn't understand and their worrying would just confuse me. I'm really all right, except right now. My fundamental impression I think is of the incredible wastefulness of being alive.

Love,

Iseult

Iseult the Fair (Unsent)

TRISTAN:

Tristan

Tristan Tristan

flowers – books –

Your letter confused and dismayed me – I showed it to Mark – he is thinking of suing you again – pathetic – his attempts to make himself matter. Between words I listen for his knock on the door – if he knew what I was writing he would kick me out – and he's right.

my king brought low

forgive?????

an easy word for you

I wanted to grow fat in your arms and sleep – you ravished me with absences – enlarged our love at our expense – tore me every time we parted – I have lost 12 pounds and live on pills – I dismay myself.

Your wife looks well.

Trist

Mr

Mrs

the flowers are dead and the books hidden and heavy winter here – his knock on the door –

Kill You. I must kill you in my heart – shut you out – don't knock even if I listen. Return to your wife – try – honestly try with her. She hates me but I love her for the sorrow I have brought her – no – I hate her because she would not admit what everybody could see – she had given you up. I had earned you.

the pen in my hand

the whiteness of the paper

a draught on my ankles the stone floor – the sounds of the castle – your step?

Beware of Mark – he is strong – pathetic – my king brought low – he protects me. I am teaching myself to love him.

I would have loved the boat.

Love is too painful.

If the narcissi you planted come up next spring I will dig them out.

What a funny thing to write – I can't tell if this is a letter to you or not – I dismay myself – Mark thinks I should be committed – he is more mature than you and I

do you remember the flowers and the books you gave me?

For my sake end it – your knock never comes – the winter is heavy – children sledding – the mountains are sharp through the window – I have a scratchy throat – Mark says psychosomatic – I hear you laugh.

Tr

Please return – nothing matters

King Mark

MY DEAR DENOALEN:

Your advice has been followed with exemplary success. Confronted with the actuality of marriage, the young man bolted even sooner than we had anticipated. The Queen is accordingly disillusioned and satisfactorily tractable.

Therefore I think that the several legal proceedings against them both may be for the time being halted at this time. By no means, however, do I wish to waive all possibility of further legal action. I am in possession of an interminable, impudent, and incriminating letter written by the confessed lover subsequent to his defection. If you desire, I will forward it to you for photostatic reproduction as a safeguard.

In the case that, through some event or events unforeseen, the matter were after all to come to court, I agree wholeheartedly that their plea of having accidentally partaken of a magic potion will not stand up. Yet your strong suggestion that execution should be the punishment for both does not seem to me to allow for what possible extenuating circumstances there are. It is indisputable, for example, that throughout the affair Tristan continued to manifest, in battle, perfect loyalty to me, and prowess quite in keeping with the standards he had set in the days prior to his supposed enchantment. Also, their twin protestations of affection for me, despite their brazen and neurotic pursuance of physical union, did not ring entirely falsely. It was, after all, Tristan's feat (i.e., slaying the dragon of Whitehaven) that brought her to Tintagel; and, while of course this is in no sense a legally defensible claim, I can appreciate that, in immature and excitable minds, it might serve as a shadow of a claim. It will do us both good, as fair-minded Englishmen, to remember that we are dealing here with a woman of Irish blood and a man whose upbringing was entirely Continental. In addition, there is the Queen herself as a political property to consider. Alive, she adorns my court. The populace is fond of her. Further, the long peace between Ireland and Cornwall which our marriage has assured should not be rashly jeopardized.

Weighing all these factors, then, and not excluding the private dispositions of my heart, I have settled on a course of action more moderate than that which you now advise. Tristan's banishment we may assume to be permanent. Return will result in recapture, trial, and death. The Queen will remain by my side. Her long sojourn in the Wood of Morois has without doubt heightened her appreciation of the material advantages she enjoys in my palace. My power and compassion have been manifested to her, and she is essentially too rational to resist their imperative appeal. As long as her present distracted state obtains, I am compelling her to submit to psychoanalysis. If her distraction persists without improvement, I will have her committed. I am confident this will not be necessary. On the remote chance that the 'magic potion' is more than a fable, I have instructed my alchemists to develop an antidote. I am fully in control of matters at last.

All the best,
(*Dictated but not signed*)
MARK: REX

I Will Not Let Thee Go,
Except Thou Bless Me

At the farewell party for the Bridesons, the Bridesons themselves were very tired. Lou (for Louise) had been sorting and packing and destroying for days, and her sleep was gouged by nightmares of trunks that would not close, of doors that opened to reveal forgotten secret rooms crammed with yet more debris of ten years' residence – with unmended furniture and outgrown toys and stacked *Life*s and *National Geographic*s and hundreds, thousands, of children's drawings, each one a moment, a memory, impossible to keep, impossible to discard. And there was another dream, recurrent, in which she and the children arrived in Texas. Brown horizon on all sides enclosed a houseless plain. They wheeled the aeroplane stairway away, and Tom was not there, he was not with them. Of course: he had left them. He had stayed behind, in green Tarbox. 'Now, children' – she seemed to be shouting into a sandstorm – 'we must keep together, together . . .' Lou would awake, and the dark body beside hers in the bed was an alien presence, a visitor from another world.

And Tom, hurriedly tying up loose ends in the city, lunching one day with his old employers and the next day with representatives of his new, returning each evening to an emptier house and increasingly apprehensive children, slept badly also. The familiar lulling noises – car horn and dog bark, the freight train's echoing shunt and the main drag's murmur – had become irritants; the town had unravelled into tugging threads of love. Departure rehearses death. He lay staring with open sockets, a void where thoughts swirled until the spell was broken by the tinkle of the milkman, who also, it seemed, had loved him. Fatigue lent to everything the febrile import of an apparition. At the farewell party, his friends of nearly a decade seemed remote, yet garish. Linda Cotteral, that mouse, was wearing green eyeshadow. Bugs Leonard had gone Mod – turquoise shirt, wide pink tie – and had come already drunk from cocktails somewhere else. Maggie Aldridge, as Tom was carrying the two coats to the bedroom, swung down the hall in a white dress with astonishingly wide sleeves.

Taken unawares, Tom uttered the word 'Lovely!' to hide his loud heart-beat. She grinned, and then sniffed, as if to erase the grin. Her grin, white above white, had been a momentary flash of old warmth, but in the next moment, as she brushed by him, her eyes were cast ahead in stony pretence of being just another woman. He recognized his impulse to touch her, to seize her wrist, as that of a madman, deranged by lack of sleep.

Drinks yielded to dinner, dinner to dancing. Gamely they tried to Frug (or was it Monkey?) to the plangent anthems of a younger generation. Then the rock music yielded, as their host dug deeper into his strata of accumulated records, to the reeds and muted brass and foggy sighing that had voiced the furtive allegiances of their own, strange, in-between generation – too young to be warriors, too old to be rebels. Too tired to talk, Tom danced. The men with whom he had shared hundreds of athletic Sunday afternoons had become hollow-voiced ghosts inhabiting an infinite recession of weekends when he would not be here. His field was computer software (indeed, he *was* the software); theirs was advertising or securities or the law, and though they all helped uphold the Boston tent pole of a nationwide canopy of rockets and promises, they spoke different languages when there was no score to shout. 'If I was John Lindsay,' a man began, and rather than listen Tom seized a woman, who whirled him around. These women: he had seen their beauty pass from the smooth bodily complacence of young motherhood to the angular self-possession, slightly grey and wry, of veteran wives. To have witnessed this, to have seen in the sides of his vision so many pregnancies and births and quarrels and near-divorces and divorces and affairs and near-affairs and arrivals in vans and departures in vans, loomed, in retrospect, as the one accomplishment of his tenancy here – a heap of organic incident that in a village of old would have mouldered into wisdom. But he was not wise, merely older. The thought of Texas frightened him: a desert of strangers, barbecues on parched lawns, in the gaunt shade of oil rigs and radar dishes.

'We'll miss you,' Linda Cotteral dutifully said. Mouselike, she nestled when dancing; all men must look alike to her – a wall of damp shirt.

'I doubt it,' he responded, stumbling. It surprised him that he didn't dance very well. He had danced a lot in Tarbox, rather than make conversation, yet his finesse had flattened along one of those hyperbolic curves that computers delight in projecting. Men had been wrong ever to imagine the universe as a set of circles; in reality, nothing closes, everything approaches, but never quite touches, its asymptote.

'Have you danced with Maggie?'

'Not for years. As you know.'

'Don't you think you should?'

'She'd refuse.'

'Ask her,' Linda said, and left him for the arms of a man who would be here next weekend, who was real.

Maggie liked living rooms; they flattered her sense of courtesy and display. She had spread herself with her sleeves on the big curved white sofa, white on white. Lou's voice tinkled from the kitchen. Lou always gravitated, at parties, to the kitchen, just as others, along personal magnetic lines, drifted outside to the screened porch, or sought safety in the bathroom. Picturing his wife perched on a kitchen stool, comfortably showing her thighs and tapping her ashes into the sink, Tom approached Maggie and, numb as a moth, asked her to dance.

She looked up. Her eyes had been painted to look startled. 'Really?' she asked, and added, 'I'm terribly tired.'

'Me too.'

She looked down to where her hands were folded in her white lap. Her contemplative posture appeared to express the hope that he, like an unharmonious thought, would melt away.

Tom told her, 'I'll never ask you again.'

With a sigh, then sniffing as if to erase the sigh, Maggie rose and went with him into the darkened playroom, where other adults were dancing, folding each other into old remembered music. She lifted her arms to accept him; her wide sleeves made her difficult to grasp. Her body in his arms, unexpectedly, felt wrong: something had unbalanced her – her third drink, or time. Her hand in his felt overheated.

'You're taller,' she said.

'I am?'

'I believe you've grown, Tom.'

'No, it's just that your memory of me has shrunk.'

'Please, let's not talk memories. You asked me to dance.'

'I've discovered I don't dance very well.'

'Do your best.'

'I always have.'

'No.'

'Don't you believe it was my best?'

'Of course I don't believe that.'

Her hot hand was limp, but her body, as he tried to contain and steer it, seemed faintly resistant, as perhaps any idea does when it is embodied. He did not feel that she was rigid deliberately, as a rebuke to him, but that they both, once again, were encountering certain basic factors of gravity and inertia. She did not resist when, trying to solve their bad fit – trying to devise, as it were, an interface – he hugged her closer to his chest. Nor, however, did he feel her infuse this submission with conscious willingness, as lovers do when they transmute their bodies into pure sensitivity and volition. She held mute. While he sought for words to fill their grappling silence, she sniffed.

He said, 'You have a cold.'

She nodded.

He asked, 'A fever?'

Again she nodded, more tersely, with a touch of the automatic, a touch he remembered as intrinsic to her manner of consent.

Surer of himself, he glided then across waxed squares of vinyl and heard his voice emerge enriched by a paternal, protective echo. 'You shouldn't have come if you're sick.'

'I wanted to.'

'Why?' He knew the answer: because of him. He feared he was holding her so close she had felt his heart thump; he might injure her with his heart. He relaxed his right arm, and she accepted the inch of freedom as she had surrendered it, without spirit – a merely metric adjustment. And her voice, when she used it, swooped at the start and scratched, like an old record.

'Oh Tom,' Maggie said, 'you know me. I can't say no. If I'm invited to a party, I come.' And she must have felt, as did he, that her shrug insufficiently broke the hold his silence would have clinched, for she snapped her head and said with angry emphasis, 'Anyway, I *had* to come and say good*bye* to the Bridesons.'

His silence had become a helpless holding on.

'Who have been so *kind*,' Maggie finished. The music stopped. She tried to back out of his arms, but he held her until, in the little hi-fi cabinet with its sleepless incubatory glow, another record flopped from the stack. Softly fighting to be free, Maggie felt to him, with her great sleeves, like a sumptuous heavy bird that has evolved into innocence on an island, that can be seized by any passing sailor, and that will shortly become extinct. Facing downward to avoid her beating wings, he saw her thighs, fat in net tights, and had to laugh, not so much at this befuddled struggle as at the comedy of the female body, that kind white clown, all greasepaint and bounce. To have seized her again, to feel her contending, was simply jolly.

'Tom, let go of me.'

'I can't.'

Music released them from struggle. An antique record carried them back to wartime radio they had listened to as children, children a thousand miles apart. Maggie smoothed her fluffed cloth and formally permitted herself to be danced with. Her voice had become, with its faint bronchial rasp, a weapon cutting across the involuntary tendency of her body to melt, to glide. She held her face averted and downcast, so that her shoulders were not quite square with his; if he could adjust this nagging misalignment, perhaps by bringing her feverish hand closer to his shoulder, the fit would be again perfect, after a gap of years. He timidly tugged her hand, and she said harshly, 'What do you want me to say?'

'Nothing. Something inoffensive.'

'There's nothing to say, Tommy.'

'O.K.'

'You said it all, five years ago.'

'Was it five?'

'Five.'

'It doesn't seem that long.'

'It does if you live it, minute after minute.'

'I lived it too.'

'No.'

'O.K. Listen –'

'No. You promised we'd just dance.'

But only a few bars of music, blurred saxophones and a ruminating clarinet, passed before she said, in a dangerously small and dreaming voice, 'I was thinking, how funny . . . Five years ago you were my life and my death, and now . . .'

'Yes?'

'No, it wouldn't be fair. You're leaving.'

'Come on, sweet Maggie, say it.'

'. . . you're just nothing.'

He was paralysed, but his body continued to move, and the music flowed on, out of some infinitely remote U.S.O. where doomed sailors swayed with their clinging girls.

She sniffed and repeated, 'You're *nothing*, Tommy.'

He heard himself laugh. 'Thank you. I got the bit the first time.'

Being nothing, he supposed, excused him from speech; his silence wrested an embarrassed giggle from her. She said, 'Well, I suppose it proves I've grown.'

'Yes,' he agreed, trying to be inoffensive, 'you are a beautifully growing girl.'

'You were always full of compliments, Tommy.'

Turquoise and pink flickered in the side of his vision; his shoulder was touched. Bugs Leonard asked to cut in. Tom backed off from Maggie, relieved to let go, yet hoping, as he yielded her, for a yielding glance. But her stare was stony, as it had been in the hall, except that there it had been directed past him, and here fell full upon him. He bowed.

Those hours after midnight, usually weightless, bent his bones in a strained curve that pressed against the inside of his forehead. Too weary to leave, he stood in the darkened playroom watching the others dance, and observed that Bugs and Maggie danced close, in wide confident circles that lifted her sleeves like true wings. A man sidled up to him and said, 'If I was John Lindsay, I'd build a ten-foot wall across Ninety-sixth Street and forget it,' and lurched away. Tom had known this man once. He went into the living room and offered here and there to say good-bye, startling conspiracies of people deep in conversation. They had forgotten he was leaving. He went into the kitchen to collect Lou; she recognized him, and doused her cigarette in the sink, and stepped down from the stool, smoothing her skirt. On his way from the bedroom with their coats, he ducked into the bathroom to see if he had aged; he was one of those who gravitated, at parties, to the bathroom. Of these Connecticut homes he would remember best the bright caves of porcelain fixtures: the shower curtains patterned in antique automobiles, the pastel towelling, the shaggy toilet-seat coverlets, the inevitable cartoon anthology on the water closet. The lecherous gleam of hygiene. Good-bye, Crane. Good-bye, Kleenex. See you in Houston.

Lou was waiting in the foyer. A well-rehearsed team, they pecked the hostess farewell, apologized in unison for being party poops, and went into the green darkness. Their headlights ransacked the bushes along this driveway for the final time.

Safely on the road, Lou asked, 'Did Maggie kiss you goodbye?'

'No. She was quite unfriendly.'

'Why shouldn't she be?'

'No reason. She should be. She should be awful and she was.' He was going to agree, agree, all the way to Texas.

'She kissed *me*,' Lou said.

'When?'

'When you were in the bathroom.'

'Where did she kiss you?'

'I was standing in the foyer waiting for you to get done admiring yourself or whatever you were doing. She swooped out of the living-room.'

'I mean where *on* you?'

'On the mouth.'

'Warmly?'

'Very. I didn't know how to respond. I'd never been kissed like that, by another woman.'

'*Did* you respond?'

'Well, a little. It happened so quickly.'

He must not appear too interested, or seem to gloat. 'Well,' Tom said, 'she may have been drunk.'

'Or else very tired,' said Lou, 'like the rest of us.'

The Corner

The town is one of those that people pass through on the way to somewhere else; so its inhabitants have become expert in giving directions. Ray Blandy cannot be on his porch five minutes before a car, baffled by the lack of signs at the corner, will shout to him, 'Is this the way to the wharf?' or 'Am I on the right road to East Mather?' Using words and gestures that have become rote, Ray heads it on its way, with something of the satisfaction with which he mails a letter, or flushes a toilet, or puts in another week at Unitek Electronics. Catty-corner across the awkward intersection (Wharf Street swerves south and meets Reservoir Road and Prudence Avenue at acute, half-blind angles), Mr Latroy, a milkman who is home from noon on, and who is also an auxiliary policeman, directs automobiles uncertain if, to reach the famous old textile mill in Lacetown, they should bear left around the traffic island or go straight up the hill. There is nothing on the corner to hold cars here except the small variety store run by an old Dutch couple, the Van Der Bijns. Its modest size and dim, rusted advertisements are geared to foot traffic. Children going to school stop here for candy, and townspeople after work stop for cigarettes and bread, but for long tracts of the day there is little for Mr Van Der Bijn to do but sit behind his display windows and grieve that the cars passing through take the corner too fast.

There have been accidents. Eight years ago, around eleven o'clock of a muggy July morning, when Susan Craven had been standing on her sidewalk wondering whether she should go to the playground or give Linda Latroy's back yard one more try, a clam truck speedily rounding the corner snapped a kingbolt, went right up over the banking, swung – while the driver wildly twisted the slack steering wheel – within a foot of unblinking, preoccupied Susan, bounced back down the banking, straight across Prudence Street, and smack, in a shower of shingles, into the house then owned by Miss Beulah Cogswell. She has since died, after living for years on her telling of the accident: '*Well*, I was in the kitchen making my morning *tea* and naturally thought it was just *another* of those dreadful sonic booms. But, *when* I go with my cup and saucer into the front parlour here *right* where my television set had been was this dirty windshield with a man's absolutely *white* face, mouthing like a fish, the carpet *drenched* with shingles and plaster and the corner cupboard three feet into the room and not one, would you *believe* it, not a single piece of bone china so much as *cracked*!' Now her house is occupied by a young couple with a baby that cries all night. The Cravens have moved to Falmouth, selling their house to the Blandys. And the Latroy girls have heard that Susan is married, to an Air Force man from Otis Base; it's hard to believe. It seems just yesterday she was brushed by death, a rude little girl with fat legs.

Long before this, so long ago only the Van Der Bijns and Mrs Billy Hannaford witnessed the wreckage, a drunken driver took the corner too fast in the opposite direction from the truck and skidded up over the kerb into the left-hand display window of the variety store. No one was hurt; the Van Der Bijns were asleep upstairs and the drunk, well known locally, remained relaxed and amused. But the accident left a delicate scar on the corner, in the perceptible disparity between the two large plate-glass panes: the left one is less wavery and golden in tint than the right, and its frame is of newer moulding, which does not perfectly match.

Somewhere between these two accidents there is an old man down from New Hampshire, lost, blinded, he said, by blazing headlights, who drove right over the traffic island, straddling it in his high 1939 Buick, shearing off the Stop sign and eviscerating his muffler on the stump. And lost in the snowy mists of time is the child who sledded down Reservoir Road and was crushed beneath a Studebaker, in the days before cars could be counted on to be everywhere. It is strange that more accidents do not occur. Everyone ignores the rusty Stop sign. Teen-agers begin drag races down by the wharf and use the traffic island as a finish post. Friday and Saturday nights, there is screeching and roaring until two and three in the morning. Trucks heave and shift gears, turning north. Summer weekends see a parade of motorboats on trailers. The housing development, Marshview, on the east end of town, adds dozens of cars to the daily traffic. The corner has already been widened – the Van Der Bijns' house once had a front yard. Old photographs exist, on sepia cardboard; that show fewer wires on the poles, a great beech where none now stands, a front yard at the house that was not then a store, the dark house painted white, no porch at the Blandys', no traffic island, and a soft, trodden, lanelike look to the surface of the street. When the Van Der Bijns move or die (the same thing to the Town Clerk), their house will be taken by eminent domain and the corner widened still further, enabling the cars to go still faster. Engineers' drawings are already on file at Town Hall.

Yet, though the inhabitants strain their ears at night waiting for the squeal of tyres to mushroom into the crash of metal and the splintering of glass, nothing usually happens. The corner is one of those places where nothing much happens except traffic and weather. Even death, when it came for Miss Cogswell, came as a form of traffic, as an ambulance in the driveway, and a cluster of curious neighbourhood children.

The weather happens mostly in the elm, a vast elm not yet felled by the blight. Its branches overarch the corner. Its drooping twigs brush the roofs of the dark house, the young couple's house, and the Latroys'. Shaped like a river system, meandering tributaries thickening and flowing into the trunk, but three-dimensional, a solid set of streets where pigeons strut, meet, and mate, the tree's pattern of limbs fills the Blandys' bedroom windows and their eyes on awaking in all weathers: glistening and sullen in November rain, so one feels the awful weight the tree upholds, like a cast-iron cloud; airy tracery after a snow, or in the froth of bloom; in summer a curtain of green, with a lemon-yellow leaf, turned early, here and there like a random stitch. Lying bedridden in fever or in despair, each of the Blandys has concluded, separately, that though there was nothing to life but lying here looking at the elm for ever, it would suffice – it would be, though just barely, enough.

The elm's leaves in autumn blow by the bushel down Prudence Avenue into the Van Der Bijns' side yard, confirming the old man's contention that the weather is always outrageous. He came to this country before the war, foreseeing it, and still finds the intemperances of the American climate remarkable. The faithful grey damp of Holland is in his bones. For months ahead of time he foresees the troublesome wonder of snow, and gloats over his bizarre fate of having to shovel it. Though weak from his long days of sitting, he shovels compulsively, even during a blizzard trying to keep his forty feet of sidewalk as clean as swept tiles. Some ironical gallantry seems intended – a humorous grateful willingness to have the land that gave him refuge take his life with its barbaric weather. Our summer's extremes also astonish him. Four sunny days become a drought in his eyes, which are delft blue and perpetually wide open, within deep, skeletal sockets. Each growing season, as he observes its effects on Mrs Hannaford's bushes and lawn, seems in some way abnormal, unprecedented, weird. 'Naaow, da forsydia last yaar wasn't aaout yet vor two weeks!' 'Naaow, I'fe nefer once zeen her grass zo zoon brown!'

And Mrs Hannaford, whose house of all the houses on the corner is most distant from the elm, sees this tree as a benign veil drawn across the tar-shingled roofs and ungainly dormers of the neighbourhood, as a sea fan superimposed on a cockleshell sunset, as a living entity that had doubled its size since as a girl she studied it from the same windows she now sleeps behind, and thought she saw the robed shadow of Jesus moving in its branches, and prayed that the end of the world be not yet come.

The people on the corner do not know each other very well. It is the houses who know each other, whose windows watch. Mrs Billy Hannaford goes to the Episcopal church whenever Communion is offered; she dresses in purple and walks with a cane, her cheeks painted salmon, her hair rinsed blue. Some weekend nights, cars belonging to the Blandys' friends are parked in front of their house until hours after midnight. The young couple's baby cries. The man who lives in the dark house is off in his car from seven to seven, and his wife is indistinguishable among the two or three ginger-haired women who come and go. The Latroys have beautiful blonde daughters, and much of the hot-rodding on the corner is for their benefit. This is what the houses know of each other's inner lives, what their windows can verify.

Rain made Ray Blandy romantic and he had hoped to make love, but his wife had fallen asleep in the middle of an embrace, and he had risen from the bed in anger. It was Saturday midnight. He stood by the window, wanting to be loved by the rain. There was a nearing roar of motors and a braking slither, and he saw (this is what he thought he saw) a speeding VW bus pursued by a black sedan. The bus disappeared behind the edge of the dark house. The sedan skidded on the smooth patch where just that April some frost-heaves had been re-tarred. The sedan's weight swung from side to side, like an accelerated dance step. Out of control, the car went up with one pair of tyres on to the sidewalk, and also disappeared. Then, there was a thump, not deafening but definite, and deeply satisfying; and a silence. Then the high-pitched gear whine of a prolonged backing-up. The VW bus appeared, backward, from behind the dark house. Shouting voices dropped to a mutter. Mr Latroy, wearing his auxiliary policeman's badge, appeared in front of his house. The Van Der Bijns' lights went on.

June Blandy sat up in bed. 'What was that?'

'You mean you weren't asleep, you were just faking?'

'I was sound asleep, but something thumped.'

'Sonic boom,' he told her. She missed the allusion. He told her, 'A car lost control going around the corner and hit something up the street. I can't see what.'

'Why are you just standing there! Let's *go*.' Last year, when a dog had been hit on the corner and their neighbours from the kerb idly watched it yelp and writhe, she had spontaneously run into the street and taken the broken animal into her arms. Now she put on her bathrobe and was past him, and down the stairs, and out of the door. He looked in two closets for a bathrobe or a raincoat and finally, afraid of missing everything, followed her into the drizzle in his pyjamas.

The corner had cracked open like a piñata, spilling absurdly dressed people. Mr Van Der Bijn wore a long nightcap, with a tassel – who would have imagined it? Mrs, her daytime braids undone, had grey hair down to her waist. The young mother, baby on hip, wore bell-bottom pants of crimson crushed velvet: her normal at-home costume? Why were so many people up and dressed after midnight? Did Mr Latroy never sleep? His milk route began at four. From the dark house emerged two middle-aged women, ginger-haired and flirtatious, in house slippers. 'That's a cute costume,' one of them said to Ray. A tense, slight man with a rash of pimples on his forehead, he looked down and adjusted his pyjama fly.

His wife told him, 'About six people got out of the car into the bus and drove away. Shouldn't somebody have stopped them, or done *some*thing?' She had turned from him to address a larger audience, her voice lifted operatically.

The mother in red pants said, 'One of them came into the house to call the police and another one came after her and said not to bother, they'd drive to the station, it'd be faster.' She had a narrow, impoverished face but an exotic broad accent, Midwestern or Western. As she spoke, she kept bouncing the baby on her hip.

A ginger-haired lady said, 'One of them said it was all right, she was the wife of a fireman.'

'Uh-ohh,' the other said. 'He's been going to too many fires.' There was general laughter.

The drizzle was lifting, but they drew snugly closer beneath the sheltering elm, as if to consolidate their sudden conquest of the distance the houses had always imposed between them. 'Naaow, isn't dis wedder somezing,' Mr Van Der Bijn said, and again they all laughed, having heard him say it so often before. The driver of the disabled car glanced towards them enviously. His sedan was up the street, sideways against a telephone pole; it had spun almost totally around. His gaze inhibited the carnival crowd on the corner. He smelled of recent danger, and was dangerous. The man who lived in the dark house emerged in pants and rumpled shirt and spectacles; his eyes looked rubbed, as after sleep or a long bout of television. His ladies grew animated; the more flirtatious one told Ray her version of the accident. The VW was coming down Prudence Street, and didn't stop at the Stop sign, they never do, and the black sedan, to avoid hitting it, swerved to the left, into the pole. Ray told her, No, he had happened to be at his window, and the VW was being chased by the other – a drag race, obviously. June asked, 'Hasn't *any*body called the police?'

Mrs Van Der Bijn said, 'Mr Latroy has.' But by this she meant, probably, that in a sense he *was* police; for he had not moved from the sidewalk. He stood there serenely, his face tilted upward, as if basking on a sunny day. The window above him lit up, and two of his beautiful daughters were framed in it, their blonde hair incandescent. A carload of male teenagers swung around the corner, abruptly braked, and eased by. The two daughters waved. Another car stopped, and asked the way to East Mather. Three voices at once – Ray, Mr Latroy, and a ginger-haired lady – chorused the directions.

June was conferring with the girl in velvet pants. The girl agreed to go inside and call the police. Her husband was asleep. He was a very sound sleeper. 'I can never get the lunk up, to take care of the brat. Every night it's the same story.'

'She has fear,' Mrs Van Der Bijn announced. 'You must sing her to sleep.'

The girl studied Mrs Van Der Bijn and handed her the baby and went into her house. The baby began its feeble, well-practised whimper, paced to last for hours. Mrs Van Der Bijn began to sing, in a distant lost language, low in her throat.

The driver of the sedan came closer. He swaggered like a man with something to sell, his hands in his pockets. He was a young stocky man, with hair combed wet, so the tooth furrows showed. 'It's all right,' he told them, 'I got everybody's number. Nothing to worry about,' he said, and told them his story. There was a third car. A yellow convertible, a crazy man. Down by the wharf, it had cut right in front of him, right through that metal rail there, and tried to run him off the road. He had given chase, lost control at the corner, and had this accident. There was a VW bus right behind him. It had stopped, and the people in it had said they knew the driver of the convertible, and would catch him and bring him back. As some kind of insurance, the sedan's passengers had crowded into the bus, and off they had all gone. They should be back any minute. At any rate, it didn't matter, because he had the numbers.

It was a strange story, but he pulled from a pocket the little pad upon which he had firmly written down two long numbers. Ray wondered how the man had focused his eyes on those speeding, shuttling vehicles, and why in his own memory the bus had been ahead of the sedan, and why he had not seen the third car, the convertible. The rest of the corner, too, distrusted the driver's story, and, amid polite comments and expressions of interest, slowly closed against him, isolating him again. Undiscouraged, like an encyclopaedia salesman turned from the door, the driver walked briskly away, towards his crippled car and, farther down the street, an approaching blue twinkle.

The police car pulled up. They all knew the cops that emerged; one was a wife-beater, and the other had been a high-school football star. The baby's mother came out of her house and stood so close that Ray, looking down, saw beside his own knobby bare feet cerise satin slippers, with bunny-tail pompons. It was as when bombs fall, baring swaths of wall-paper, tasselled pull-cords, unexpected bathroom tiles, broken diagrams. The two policemen softly interviewed the driver, the people at the corner watched from a safe distance and kept their versions to themselves, the gentle event of the rain ceased, the law closed its notebook, the elm sighed, the little crowd reluctantly broke up and returned to their houses. Later, some heard, but only the street lamp saw, the tow truck come and take the sedan away. Overhead, the clouds, paled and pulled apart, revealing stars.

The driver's story had been strange, but no stranger, to the people who live here, than the truth that the corner is one among many on the map of the town, and the town is a dot on the map of the state, and the state a mere patch on the globe, and the globe insignificant from any of the stars overhead.

Acknowledgements

Of these forty stories thirty-eight were originally published in the *New Yorker*. 'Under the Microscope' and 'During the Jurassic' were originally published in the *Transatlantic Review*.

'The Alligators', 'Friends from Philadelphia', 'The Happiest I've Been', 'Ace in the Hole', 'Dentistry and Doubt', 'Who Made Yellow Roses Yellow?', 'Toward Evening', 'Sunday Teasing', 'Incest' and 'A Gift from the City' first appeared in book form in *The Same Door*, Knopf, 1959.

'You'll Never Know, Dear, How Much I Love You,' 'Pigeon Feathers', 'Flight', 'A Sense of Shelter', 'The Persistence of Desire', 'The Blessed Man of Boston, My Grandmother's Thimble, and Fanning Island', 'Packed Dirt, Churchgoing, a Dying Cat, a Traded Car', 'Still Life', 'A & P' and 'Lifeguard' first appeared in book form in *Pigeon Feathers & Other Stories*, Knopf, 1962.

'In Football Season', 'The Christian Roommates', 'A Madman', 'The Stare', 'The Family Meadow', 'At a Bar in Charlotte Amalie', 'The Indian', 'The Music School', 'Leaves' and 'Four Sides of One Story' first appeared in book form in *The Music School*, Knopf, 1966.

'The Orphaned Swimming Pool', 'The Witnesses', 'The Day of the Dying Rabbit', 'Under the Microscope', 'During the Jurassic', 'The Hillies', 'The Deacon', 'The Carol Sing', 'I Will Not Let Thee Go, Except Thou Bless Me' and 'The Corner' first appeared in book form in *Museums and Women*, Knopf, 1972.

Illustration credits

p. 292: Cyclops from 'Some Pond Creatures and Their Sizes', sheet printed by the Massachusetts Audubon Society, Lincoln, Mass.

p. 292: Daphnia, *ibid*.

p. 292: Water-mite (*Hydrachna geographica*), from *Field Book of Ponds and Streams*, by Ann Haven Morgan, New York: G. P. Putnam's Sons; 1930.

p. 293: Fairy shrimp, *ibid*.

p. 293: Diatoms (*Meridion, Tabellaria*), *ibid*.

p. 293: Volvox, *ibid*.

p. 293: Anatomy of a rotifer (after F. J. Myers), *ibid*.

p. 293: Stentor, *ibid.*

p. 293: Spirostumum, *ibid.*

p. 294: Brown hydra (*Hydra oligactis*), *ibid.*

p. 294: *Hydra oligactis* after eating, *ibid.*

p. 296: Jurassic high life (left to right, Plateosaurus, Polacanthus, and Rhamphohynchus), from *Le Monde après la création de l'homme*, by Louis Fingier, 1870. Artist: Antoine Jobin. Engraver: Vermoreken.

p. 297: Skull of *Stegosaurus Stenops* from 'Osteology of the Armored Dinosauria in the United States National Museum, with Special Reference to the Genus Stegosaurus', by Charles Whitney Gilmore, Washington, D.C.: Govt. Printing Office; 1914.

p. 298: Skeleton of Brontosaurus from Webster's New International Dictionary; Second Edition, © 1959 by G. & C. Merriam Co., publishers of the Merriam–Webster Dictionaries.

p. 299: Skeleton of *Iguanodon bernissartensis* (after Dollo) from Encyclopaedia Britannica, Eleventh Edition, article on 'Iguanodon'.